ON THE PLACE OF REFERENCE

The Great War has left England scarred and in a frenzy to forget. Escape lies in the heady excitement of the new. Dizzy flappers, wild parties and movie madness invade 165 Eton Place, shaking a world of time-honored tradition to its very roots.

ENDINGS AND BEGINNINGS

The era of gracious nobility is over. The doors of the grand old houses close and generations of servants who knew the protection of a master's roof must emerge from belowstairs to manage on their own, to face the unknown burdens and opportunities of a rapidly changing world.

UPSTAIRS, DOWNSTAIRS

These two exciting novels in a single volume bring to dramatic climax and conclusion the fascinating story of the Bellamys, the unforgettable English family that has made America's heart its home.

On with the Dance / Endings and Beginnings

Michael Hardwick

A DELL BOOK

Published by
Dell Publishing Co., Inc.
1 Dag Hammarskjold Plaza
New York, New York 10017

On with the Dance and *Endings and Beginnings*
were originally published in two volumes
by Sphere Books Ltd., London.

Dell ® TM 681510, Dell Publishing Co., Inc.

ISBN: 0-440-16599-7

Printed in the United States of America
First U.S.A. printing—January 1980

On with the Dance

CHAPTER ONE

EIGHT months before, the guns which had deafened Europe had been silenced, and the joyful hysteria of Armistice Day had subsided. But in July, 1919, the rejoicing still went on. In the kitchen of 165 Eaton Place the servants listened intently to the strains of the military band which accompanied the Victory March as it passed through Belgravia on its way to Buckingham Palace: right on time, twenty minutes to eleven, Mr. Hudson noted by the timetable in the newspaper. There would be soldiers, sailors, V.A.Ds., and among them their Miss Georgina in her trim uniform.

'Couldn't we slip down the end of Eaton Place and see 'em go by?' Rose ventured. 'We might just catch a glimpse of her.'

Lily, the new maid who had taken Daisy's place, backed up the head house-parlourmaid. The pleading expression on her pretty face did something to soften Mr. Hudson's heart. She had the complexion of a diarymaid, smooth shining fair hair gathered into a commendably neat knot on her slender neck, and she needed few reproofs. Mr. Hudson felt that she made an agreeable change from Daisy, who had been getting distinctly above herself since her marriage; very uppity and inclined to answer back. And Frederick, the new footman, Edward's replacement, was also a change for the better. In army life he had been Trooper Norton, Major Bellamy's soldier servant; he brought an upright demeanour, a military precision and readiness to obey orders and even anticipate them, to his job, not to mention a handsome Greek-profiled face which charmed the women.

'Be a sport, Mr. Hudson,' Rose urged, seeing the butler weakening. Mr. Hudson put up a token resistance.

'We can't have all the servants scampering out of the house at once.'

7

'But Miss Georgina won't be back for ages, not if she's got to march all the way down through the East End and fetch up again at Hyde Park Corner this afternoon.'

'What if the Major comes in?' said Mrs. Bridges, the cook. 'He won't be back till after twelve o'clock at least.'

'How do you know?'

'The Major,' said Mr. Hudson with pride, 'is on duty at the Saluting Base opposite Buckingham Palace, escorting important personages to their seats.'

'Well, then,' Mrs. Bridges pleaded, 'let 'em go out and see what they can. It's not every day we have a procession come by here.'

Mr. Hudson gave in. 'Oh, very well, just down to the corner of Belgrave Street and no further, mind. And behave yourselves. No pushing or shouting on the pavement.'

He watched them go; the sedate Rose, the eager Lily, Ruby with flour on her hands and her hair on end. Then, armed with his father's old deer-stalking telescope, he led Mrs. Bridges upstairs to the drawing-room balcony, from which they could see clearly the marching figures, the stiff-backed generals on their horses, the glitter of bayonets and swords in the July sun, the Naval Detachment immaculately shipshape and Bristol-fashion, the red, white and blue of the nurses.

Standing there, the music, cheering and tramping in their ears, both felt thankful for a lively interlude in a world which had become strangely drab. Hazel Bellamy was dead, a victim of the terrible influenza which had swept the country last year. The Major had taken his wife's death badly: but then he took everything badly. Lonely, neurotic, inward-turned, he spent most of his time shut up in his room, where he could be heard playing noisy ragtime music on his gramophone. Sometimes Miss Georgina would sit with him, but more often she was out at parties and dances. Mr. Hudson shook his head at the thought. Once the staff had suspected that there was 'something between' the Major and Miss Georgina. After all, they were suited in age, and there was no actual relationship. But since the excitement of the war had died down, whatever spark they had lit in each other had died down with it. No. 165 had become a sad, dust-sheeted house.

Lord Bellamy had made a wonderful new start, of course, with his marriage to the pretty, sparkling widow who had been Virginia Hamilton. Curious to think of him and her and her two children in a house of their own, which they were hoping to buy when they returned from Paris. Mr. Hudson felt they would leave a gap in his life.

It was late afternoon when Georgina and James returned. Georgina collapsed on the stairs and dragged off her shoes. 'Thank God *that's* over,' she said. 'My feet are bloody well killing me.'

'Georgina!' James was shocked. Even now that women were emancipated and their skirts were getting shorter and shorter, it seemed strange and wrong to hear them swear.

'Well, they are. One of the Queen Alexandras behind us said she'd read in the paper it was over five miles.'

'Good for you. Keep you slim.'

'It's all very well for you, sitting down in a covered stand all the time.'

'I didn't sit down all day. Had to keep giving out free souvenir programmes to all the high-ups, including an Indian Prince who handed me five pounds.'

She laughed. 'Did you give it back?'

'Had to, unfortunately.'

Mr. Hudson appeared, genie-like, to express his approbation. 'Mrs. Bridges and I managed to see something of the procession from the drawing-room balcony, and I understand Rose and the others caught a wee glimpse of you in the V.A.D.'s column. They were very proud and excited, Miss.'

'There you are,' James said. 'Wasn't it worth sore feet?'

Mr. Hudson watched them go upstairs together, the tall slender uniformed man, with the limp which would never leave him, and the pretty girl in her trim uniform. His face was sad and brooding as he went downstairs to the servants' hall.

'Tea's ready, Mr. Hudson,' Rose announced. 'And you'll never guess who's come to see us.'

'I've no idea.'

'You go in and see for yourself.'

What Mr. Hudson saw for himself, seated at the tea-table with Mrs. Bridges pouring tea for them, was Edward and Daisy. It was hard to believe they had ever been part of the household. Edward's civilian suit fitted him considerably worse than his footman's uniform had done. His military moustache had gone, leaving a look of bareness behind it, and his hair shone with violet-scented brilliantine. Daisy wore a large, ostentatious hat, and her unbecoming high-waisted dress emphasised the fact that she was some months pregnant.

Mrs. Bridges beamed. 'They come in for a cup of tea and to see how we all was.'

'That's right,' said Edward. Daisy bestowed on Mr. Hudson a superior smile.

'You haven't changed a scrap, Mr. Hudson. Has he, Eddie?'

'No, but I have.' Edward sleeked down his hair. 'I'm a civvy, now, you see. What they call a door-to-door salesman.'

'He goes round from house to house,' Rose explained, 'ringing the bell and selling people hairbrushes, bootlaces and combs and that, out of a suitcase.'

'I see.' Mr. Hudson did not appear impressed.

'Only temporary, mind,' Daisy put in hastily, seeing his expression. 'He's . . . he's thinking of chucking it in and getting a more permanent situation as storeman in a furniture place out Romford way.'

'So we can settle down in a nice house, out of London,' Edward amplified. 'And Daisy can have the baby, where there's a bit of garden.'

'Daisy's expecting Christmas time,' Mrs. Bridges explained.

'So I observe,' Mr. Hudson said coldly. 'Congratulations, both of you.'

Daisy bridled proudly. She was thoroughly enjoying herself, the only married woman present, a Little Stranger on the way, a husband who was no longer the slave of Mr. Hudson or anybody else; only nobody seemed as impressed as she had hoped they'd be. Lily entered, and Daisy looked without pleasure on the girl who had taken her place, and who was undoubtedly as pretty as a picture. Edward was equally daunted by the handsome appearance and soldierly carriage of Frederick, when his successor joined them for tea. Somehow, they'd both thought they were irreplaceable; but nobody seemed to feel the draught.

Cheekily, Edward asked, 'Well, how's the nobs, then – all flourishing?'

'The nobs?' Mr. Hudson repeated the term in a voice of awful chill.

'I think Edward's referring to the Family upstairs,' Rose explained unnecessarily.

'Then he should say so,' returned Mr. Hudson, and went on, fixing Edward with a steely eye. 'For your information, Edward, the Major and Miss Georgina are in residence here and both "flourishing", as you put it. His Lordship and Lady Bellamy went over to Versailles for the signing of the Peace Treaty and remained in Paris for their honeymoon.'

Edward stared. 'What, all you lot to wait on the Major and Miss Georgina?'

'I shouldn't fancy you've got enough to do, have you?' Daisy added.

This was so painfully true that Mr. Hudson was goaded into rising abruptly.

'Frederick,' he said. 'If you can spare a moment.'

Frederick had only just started his tea, but obedience was second nature to him. 'Yes, Mr. Hudson,' he said, swallowing his first mouthful of bread and butter.

'I should like to go through the cellar book with you and check the port wine. There are a number of bottles to be earmarked for His Lordship. If you would kindly come with me to the pantry . . .'

'Certainly, Mr. Hudson.'

'I shall be making you responsible from now on for checking and ordering the spirits and minerals,' Mr. Hudson told him as they vanished cellarwards, making Edward feel smaller than ever, for he had never been awarded such a responsibility. Rose, Lily and Ruby gazed fondly after Frederick's straight back. 'Lily and me think he's quite good-looking, don't we, Lil?' Rose said.

Daisy was furious. It was all a plot to disparage Eddie and herself. Edward covertly glanced at her flushed face.

'Well,' he said brightly, 'me and Dais mustn't stop too long. We're thinking of taking a walk through Hyde Park, see all the dancing and singing, and there's fireworks later.'

'You people going out to see the fireworks?' Daisy enquired patronisingly.

'Not tonight,' said Rose.

'And we're not "people" neither, Daisy.' Mrs. Bridges' voice and look were enough to cool the well-cosied teapot. Silently, Edward and Daisy prepared for departure. They were not wanted any more.

Taking a tray of whisky and soda into James's room that evening, Frederick thought that peace seemed to be doing the Major no good. Slumped in a chair, a pipe in his mouth, he looked the picture of bored melancholy. Georgina, lying on a sofa in a Japanese-patterned teagown, flipping through the *Tatler* magazine, gave Frederick a pretty smile. Once it would have been thrilling for her to be alone with James like this. Now, somehow, the excitement had gone out of it. At least the ex-Trooper Norton was someone to flirt with.

'Little did I realise,' said James, taking the glass Frederick had poured for him, 'when you used to bring me that revolting stew in a mess-tin down in the dugout with the shells bursting outside, that one day you'd be handing me a whisky and soda in my own house. I'll bet you never did, either.'

'It did ocour to me as a possibility, sir,' Frederick replied, gazing straight before him as a footman should. 'When I came here with your kit, sir, after you were posted missing.'

James stared. 'How could it? Everyone thought I was dead.'

'I didn't, sir.'

'He had faith – didn't you, Frederick?' Georgina said.

As Frederick began to agree a sudden burst of sound shocked James almost out of his chair. 'What the devil's that row?'

'That'll be the fireworks in Hyde Park, sir.'

Georgina ran to the window and opened it, staring with wide wondering eyes at the flashes of gold and green, the showers of glittering sparks, the tails of white fire bursting in the air with resounding bangs. 'Oh, look! There! Oh, how lovely, all red and orange!'

The bangs and cracks were going through James's head. 'Thank you, Frederick,' he said, 'that's all,' anxious to get the footman out of the room before he began to shake visibly. But Georgina was still intent on the fiery spectacle.

'Do come and look, Jumbo. Such marvellous colours, and you can see everything . . .'

James had his hands over his ears. 'Close the window, Georgina.'

She turned, surprised. 'Why?'

'Because . . .' he looked round the room for inspiration, 'because I want you to hear a new record I bought at Selfridge's. It's the latest jazz-band – playing rather a jolly tune.' He was putting on the record, winding the handle, anything to stop himself wincing and shuddering at the explosions. Only when the saxophones of 'The Darktown Strutters' Ball' almost drowned them did Georgina turn away from the window and see his distress. She shut the window and came over to him, taking him in her arms.

'There, Jumbo, it's all right. It's all right.'

Mrs. Bridges and Mr. Hudson were at a loose end. It was only mid-morning, yet the housework was done, finished by Lily and Rose in a quarter of the time it would once have taken. Frederick, having completed his duties, had been given an hour off, and Ruby dispatched to the butcher's. Both the older servants were thinking of the same thing.

'Of course,' said Mrs. Bridges, 'she'll have to have a proper staff, wherever it is they're going to live. I mean, His Lordship's been accustomed to having servants wait on him, ever since he married Lady Marjorie. He wouldn't like having to fend for himself.'

Mr. Hudson sighed. 'It's a question of money, Mrs. Bridges. Wages are a good deal higher nowadays, and Her Ladyship's not wealthy. And it'll be a smaller house than this one – with a modest household.'

Mrs. Bridges looked shocked. 'You mean, just a cook-general and one girl to do all the rest, like the middle-class families have out in the suburbs?'

'I wouldn't be surprised.'

It was her turn to sigh. 'Well, I don't know, I'm sure. Perhaps it's time you and me give up service and retired.'

'The thought has crossed my mind more than once since the end of the war,' he said.

'I mean, from what you say, they're not likely to take us on in their new house, any of us. The Major and Miss Georgina can look after themselves now. And I'm not staring work in a new place at my age . . .'

The shrilling of the telephone in the passage interrupted their gloomy reflections. Mr. Hudson's face brightened as he answered it and heard Richard Bellamy's voice at the other end. After a short conversation he returned to report to Mrs. Bridges.

'They're back from Paris, safe and sound.'

'Staying at the Hyde Park hotel again?'

'Aye, but his lordship wants two or three of his suits, his cigar-case, and a few other items he left behind here. He's coming over to fetch them at tea-time.'

'I see. How did he sound?'

'Remarkably cheerful. And who's to blame him?'

Later that afternoon James rose from his armchair to greet his father. Richard waved him down.

'Don't get up, old boy.' He bestowed an affectionate pat on the shoulder as James subsided again, and took another chair himself. James could sense a new briskness and relaxation in his father's manner. Richard gave him his characteristically tentative smile, using only one side of his mouth. The greyness which had conquered the dark of his hair enhanced his good looks, and, with his slim figure, belied his age, rather than accentuating it.

'Everything all right?'

'I suppose so.' The smile faded at James's morose tone. If, in his new contentment, Richard had hoped to find a corresponding change in his son, he was disappointed.

'Did you enjoy Paris?' James made the effort to ask.

'Fascinating. Versailles was like one great international garden party . . .'

He would have gone on, but it was patently obvious that James had enquired merely as a rudimentary courtesy. Richard finished lamely, 'I just came round to fetch a few things. Hudson's packing a valise for me. With . . . your permission, I trust?'

'*My* permission?'

'He's your butler, James.'

'And yours, Father.'

Richard shook his head. 'I no longer live here.'

An awkward silence fell between them, broken at length by Richard.

'Do you prefer to sit up here – in your room? I mean, the life of this house has always centred on the morning-room.'

'The morning-room depresses me. Besides, I prefer my own company to other people's these days. I'm happy enough up here, with my books and things.'

Richard frowned his concern. 'I should have thought it more depressing to shut yourself up. You know, you must try to cheer up, old boy.'

'It's not easy, Father.'

'I know.'

15

'The house is so quiet. Even the servants haven't enough to do. But I can't give them notice, after all these years, or I'd seriously think of selling the house. Then, where would Georgina go? She has no other home, until she marries. Besides, I want to live here. It's my home.'

Richard nodded, infected now by his son's depression. James said, 'You and Virginia – have you found a place yet?'

'A house?' Richard attempted nonchalance, but failed. 'Oh, Virginia's seen one or two she likes, but nothing's settled. It takes time, you know.'

The intensity of passion with which James responded startled Richard.

'Live here, Father. Please! This house can be yours again, from top to bottom. Just leave me my two rooms and Georgina hers. I can't run it alone, and it'd save you having to get something else. Please, Father.'

Richard felt his growing gloom replaced by pity for his son, a victim, it seemed to him, of life and circumstances and of something unenviable in his very genes; almost, it occurred to him, that same black vein of self-destruction that had made his own brother, Arthur Bellamy, his own worst enemy and blighted his life and others' in their turn.

He said, 'It's a very kind offer, old boy, and I'm very touched. I'm sure Virginia would be too. Only . . .'

'What?'

'It would have to be her decision. She is my wife and will be mistress of whatever house we choose to live in. As you know, she's pretty sure of what she wants in life – not someone to be easily talked out of anything, once her mind's made up.'

'But if you haven't actually bought a house yet, surely . . .'

'Yes, yes. I'll speak to her about it, of course. This evening. But don't hang too much hope on it, James. You must remember that recently married people . . . well, usually prefer some degree of privacy.'

His new sympathy for his son decreased abruptly when he heard the bitter retort, 'Privacy? With two noisy

16

children shouting all over the house! Look, Father, don't even bother to ask her. 'You're not in favour of it yourself, I can see, so just let's forget it.'

Restraining himself from replying in kind, Richard said, mixing firmness with genuine sympathy: 'I don't know what's the matter with you, James. I do know – we all know – that you've had a rotten deal, with the war and then losing Hazel. But one has to go forward in life, build something new, find something worthwhile to do. You're alive, you've got enough money to live on in sufficient comfort.' He got up. 'Don't give up, old boy. I shall speak to Virginia tonight. I promise.'

James roused himself to nod his thanks.

'Do your best, Father.'

Richard nodded, all too aware what Virginia's likeliest answer would be.

'I will. Now I'd better see if Hudson's got my case ready. Give our love to Georgina, will you? – Virginia's and mine.'

'Yes. She'll be in . . . sometime, I suppose.'

He lapsed into his increasing habit of staring unseeing into space. After a moment's hesitation Richard left the room. James did not hear him go.

Mr. Hudson was in the hall, trying to appear busy, when Richard came down. Richard's packed case stood near the front door.

'May I call you a taxi, m'lord?' the butler asked.

'Thank you, Hudson.'

'Er, will you be sending over for the remainder of your belongings? I can instruct Frederick to have them packed and ready.'

Richard considered. 'I think . . . until her ladyship settles on a house my things might as well stay here.'

It was not the decisive reply, one way or another, that Mr. Hudson had been seeking, but it would have to suffice.

'I shall go and sit in the morning-room while you telephone for the taxi,' Richard told him.

'I, er, am not sure whether Rose has raised the blinds yet

or aired the room, m'lord. I'm afraid since the Major comes downstairs so rarely these days, and Miss Georgina . . . is so often out . . .' He ventured a desperate try. 'No doubt the Major will be closing down the house altogether in due course . . . er . . . er . . .' He wanted to add 'and dispensing with a staff', but couldn't bring himself to ask so direct a question of the former master whom he had served for so many years.

Aware of the anxiety, which it occurred to him for the first time must be prevalent below stairs, Richard could only answer, 'Things are far from settled, I'm afraid, Hudson. Don't ask me what the future holds.'

He let himself into the morning-room. The confident briskness with which he had come to his old home that afternoon was altogether gone now.

When he returned to No. 165 two days later he had Virginia on his arm. She appeared, to Mr. Hudson, opening the door to them, younger than before. He had always thought her too apparently young to have lost a son in action; now it seemed even less credible. In her ivory-coloured dress and matching light coat and her fetching 'Merry Widow' hat she gave an impression of light, immediately dispelling the gloom of the silent house. Hudson's spirits rose a little. If only . . .

'Welcome home, my lady,' he beamed. 'The Major had to go out briefly, my lord. He gave orders for you to be shown into the drawing-room until lunchtime. Rose has opened up one end, and I have put a decanter of sherry in there.'

'I've never seen your drawing-room,' Virginia reminded Richard as they went upstairs.

'James's,' he corrected her.

The drawing-room was for the most part dust-sheeted, a repository for scarcely identifiable lumpy shapes, with the pictures covered and most of the blinds drawn. Richard wrinkled his nose at the mustiness as he went to raise another blind, admitting more of the cheering sunshine.

'Like a furniture store,' he grumbled.

'It's beautiful,' Virginia said.

'Well, it's seen some interesting gatherings in its time.'

'I'm sure the whole house is full of memories for you, darling. I think that's partly why I'm so anxious for us to have our own place.'

Richard went to pour sherry from the decanter on the closed grand piano, thinking unhappily of the forthcoming interview with James. She went on, 'That little house in Clarendon Street would be perfect for us. I could make it so comfortable and charming.'

He said diffidently, 'There's room for all of us here,' and added quickly, 'for the time being'; but she was shaking her head emphatically.

'No, Richard. I know we've been asked here to lunch because James wants to persuade me, and hopes you'll support him. It puts me in a very awkward postion. What am I to say to him? You know I don't want to come and live here. It's not my home, and it's not yours any more. So please . . .'

She was interrupted by James's entrance. Richard could see immediately that he was on his best behaviour, smiling and businesslike as he limped energetically down the big room to them.

'I'm awfully sorry. Good morning, Virginia. 'Morning, Father. I had to go out to the bank.'

'I was just admiring your lovely drawing-room,' Virginia smiled. 'Such elegance. And that ceiling !'

'Yes. Splendid, isn't it ? I thought we'd use it, for a change. Sort of celebrate your return. Ah, I see Hudson's used his initiative.'

'We helped ourselves,' Richard said, handing his son a filled glass.

'Good. Well, then . . . here's to your return . . . to Eaton Place.'

A silence continued after they had drunk, until Richard said, 'Virginia and I have seen a rather fine little house just north of Hyde Park.'

'In Clarendon Street,' Virginia added. 'Just about perfect for us, and a price we can afford.'

James looked into his glass. 'Did you happen to mention to Virginia what I said the other day, Father?'

Before his father could reply, Virginia had said, in a tone so gentle that she might have been addressing one of her own children, rather than a man a year or two her senior, 'James, come and sit beside me and let me try to explain.'

And as petulantly as a child he answered, 'There's no point.' But he obeyed, and they took places side by side on the settee. Richard joined them.

'I do understand how you feel,' she told James earnestly. 'I know it's very sad and quiet for you, all alone in this house. Perhaps you'll want to sell it eventually and find some comfortable rooms somewhere.'

James stirred restlessly. 'Where would Georgina go? This is her home, as well as mine. And the responsibility for her is mine now, no longer my father's.'

'I understand that, too.'

'And the servants? If I leave here they'll all have to be given notice. All of them. It's unthinkable.'

'I know, James, I know.' Virginia was fighting herself now, as well as him; trying not to weaken. 'You must see this from my point of view, too. I've married your father, whom I dearly love, and we're looking forward to a fresh start, away from our own sad memories. I have my two children to consider. I want them to grow up in a home that's theirs, not someone else's. You and your father have been through so much in this house, James; sad times and happy times as well. I think those memories, and the house itself, will belong to you both for ever, but in the past. The war's over now, and I think we all hope you can find a new life and a new kind of happiness. So, please allow your father to find his new happiness and his new life, too.'

James did not need to exaggerate, even unconsciously, the depth of his self-pity.

'I can't argue with what you say. The idea that you

should come and live here was just a thought – a silly thought. My greatest wish is for you and Father to be happy. I'm sure that before too long Georgina will marry and have a home of her own. Meanwhile, it's just that . . . well, six people to wait on . . . one tiresome, bad-tempered widower . . .'

He bit off the rest of his sentence as one of those six people entered the room. 'Luncheon is served, sir,' Mr. Hudson told him.

James heaved himself to his feet and straightened his back. 'Come along, Virginia,' he said, offering his arm. 'I want to hear all about Versailles and your stay in Paris.'

As they filed past him, Hudson, beside the door, searched each profile, but still nothing gave him the answer he and his fellow servants awaited.

It came a few days later. At James's order, Mr. Hudson had mustered the staff into a line in the servants' hall. James came limping down the stairs, his great height causing him to stoop to safeguard his head. He nodded to them. 'Do sit down, Mrs. Bridges, please.' She thanked him and resumed the chair from which she had risen. James cleared his throat and addressed them in tones he had often used at the Front, a blend of decision and compassionate understanding.

'I expect you can all guess why I've asked you to see me this morning. I'm afraid this is a very sad occasion for me, because, as you may have heard, my father and stepmother are going to live in a house of their own and . . . and since Mrs. Bellamy's death I haven't felt able to justify living by myself in so large a house as this with . . . with a full staff, you see . . .' He swallowed and plunged on, less confidently now. 'So I'm afraid the . . . the sad moment has come for me to say thanks to you all for the years of devoted service – well, anyway, those of you who've been with us since before the war – and ask you to consider yourselves under a month's notice . . . I mean, to have time to find positions in other households. I'm really and truly sorry that such a time has come, but I must now think of selling the house and moving into rooms, so in any case I can't possibly keep a staff on any longer. I can only repeat my grateful thanks to you all.'

He had never felt so wretched, even about sending men over the top in hopeless circumstances. The faces in front of him showed, in varying degrees, regret, unhappiness, apprehension, and even fear of the unknown future. The example of Edward and Daisy had not been overlooked.

Mr. Hudson spoke up in the way it had been agreed he should if ever this present situation were to come about.

'If I might be permitted, sir, to speak on behalf of us all, we had anticipated such an eventuality as this, and please be assured that we understand your difficult position. Sir, I am authorised to say that all of us below stairs are willing to continue in your service for reduced wages, if that could in any way influence you to change your mind.'

James answered, 'It's very good of you Hudson – of all of you – and naturally I'm very touched by your offer. But it's not really a question of wages. It's just that this house is too big for me alone, and Miss Georgina and I . . . well, I'm afraid we've reached the end of a chapter. That . . . that's all I can say. Thank you.'

He almost fled back up the stairs, leaving them motionless, stunned by the shock that was none the less for having been half expected. Mr. Hudson rallied them in the best way he knew. 'Very well. About your duties now, all of you.'

Mrs. Bridges got to her feet. 'Come along, Ruby, and help me with the vegetables.'

Rose moved out of the line-up like an automaton. 'After all them years !' she said to the air.

'You'll find another place easy enough, Rose,' Mrs. Bridges assured her. 'You're young enough and healthy. And so will Lily and Frederick. I'm not so sure about you, Ruby,' she added, meaning it as a heavy joke rather than an unkindness, which the girl was too unsubtle to recognise. She retorted, 'I'll get work in a hotel, easy. I've seen advertisements in t'newspapers for kitchen staff for hotels and boarding houses. And they pay good money, nowadays.'

Mrs. Bridges snorted and they went off into the kitchen together. Lily and Frederick had gone. Only Mr. Hudson and Rose remained. He seated himself dejectedly at the plain table and she went to take a chair opposite him.

'I expect you'll be thinking of retirement now, Mr. Hudson. That is, if you've got enough saved.'

He shook his head, but there was little determination in his eyes.

'I hadn't anticipated giving up service yet awhile, Rose.'

'No, but if it's a question of finding a little house somewhere and putting some money down, I mean, there's always what my Gregory left me in the bank. I could . . . let you have some of that, if it would help.'

Only later did he see the irony in this gesture from the spinster who, on several dramatic occasions, had accused him of blighting her hopes, conniving with Fate to keep her unmarried and in service, of having a perpetual 'down' on her. He patted her hand and smiled wearily. 'It's a very kind thought, Rose, and much appreciated. But you'll need all your savings for yourself. In old age a woman can become needy sooner than a man. As long as I am blessed with good health I shall continue in service as a butler, provided a suitable place can be found. Otherwise, perhaps, as porter at a club or one of those new apartment houses.'

She was not really listening. 'All good things have to come to an end, don't they? We've had a good run.'

'Aye. The very words Mrs. Bridges used the other day.'

Rose got up with a sigh. 'Well, there's still the laundry to be sorted out.'

She went, leaving him sitting, unable to issue himself with any orders which would occupy his hands or his mind.

James told Georgina what had happened when she came in from having a lesson in dancing the Fox-Trot and the Black Bottom. She took the implications for her own future with the easygoing indifference of the well-attached Society girl, but worried about James, depressed and haunted by the expressions he had seen on those faces in the servants' hall. He told her about the ordeal of breaking the news.

'Oh, how awfully weepy!' she exclaimed, sincere despite the slang. 'I wish you hadn't told me that. Anyway, I think they've been happy here. It's been like home to them for such a long time, hasn't it?'

'That makes it worse,' James said grimly.

'I'm sorry, Jumbo. Try not to think about it. Tell me some news. I haven't seen you since Wednesday.'

'There isn't much. I had a letter from Father. They're bringing the children to London on Friday for a few days. William's got the dentist and Alice needs some new clothes.'

'I'm longing to see the children. Why not invite them to tea?'

'Are you suggesting I entertain a couple of brats while Father and Virginia go off shopping?'

'Yes, I am – only I'd be here to help you. I adore children.'

'Oh, well, if you're going to take part . . . Only, mind you do.'

And she did, as did every member of the staff, save only Mr. Hudson, whose role was confined to hovering uncertainly, apprehensive for the sound of something fragile being shattered or the report of one of their small guests having been sick on an immaculate carpet. Neither fear was realised. Georgina and the servants liked Alice and William on sight, and, after a brief period of natural awe on the part of children unused to so grand a house or so many servants, found themselves evidently liked in return. As the pretty Alice and the lively William gained confidence, the pace of their exploration quickened, and so did their consumption of food and drink. After they had demolished a quantity of paste sandwiches, jelly, specially baked cake and lemonade which Mrs. Bridges had envisaged having to be finished off for them by the servants that evening, there was no hesitation about the way in which they answered Georgina's inquiry whether

24

they had had enough, and Lily had to be despatched to the kitchen for more supplies.

'Poor mites!' Mrs. Bridges declared. 'That's what comes of living in hotels. Ruby, fetch out the shrimp paste again and cut some more bread.'

Mr. Hudson winced as the whistle of the speaking tube sounded shrilly outside. He had answered it three times already, and each time heard only childish giggles at the other end.

'Little devils,' said Mrs. Bridges, smiling when Mr. Hudson returned to report that this time someone had blown down into his ear. 'What time are his lordship and her ladyship fetching them, Mr. Hudson?'

'About half-past six.' He smiled rather forcedly: he would not have smiled at all if he had known that it was Rose upstairs who had shown Master William how the tube worked and urged him to try it in the first place.

'Would you listen to the wee rascals?' he exclaimed as the sound of heavy pounding of piano keys reached their ears.

'Bless my soul!' Mrs. Bridges beamed. 'That piano hasn't been played for donkey's years. Not since Miss Lizzie left home.'

The 'tune' was 'Chopsticks', and this time Georgina was the instigator, playing the treble to Alice's obedient bass. When William heard them he ran to the drawing-room and, of course, demanded to join in, so a third pair of hands was added to the performance, and a third voice pealing with delighted laughter.

James, who had done his best to look and sound benevolent, but had been relieved to leave Georgina, Rose and Frederick to participate most actively in the afternoon's entertaining, warily entered the drawing-room to show willing.

'Sorry, James,' Georgina shouted above the din. 'Is it too much for you? We'll stop, if you like.'

'It's all right,' he bellowed back, though his head was beginning to hammer slightly. Then inspiration came to him. He called, 'I wondered whether William would care to come up and see my train?'

The playing halted. Georgina asked the flushed little boy, 'Would you, William?'

'A train! Oh, yes please!'

'Come along, then,' James said, and tentatively took the child's hand to lead him away. Georgina, Alice and Rose followed.

When Mr. Hudson let Richard and Virginia in, Richard enquired uncertainly, 'Everything all right, Hudson?'

'Oh, yes, my lord,' the butler was able to say truthfully. If he had had his own reservations at first, none of the others had; and the sound of sustained gaiety in the house which had for so long been shadowed by doleful quiet had quite lifted his spirits.

'Yes, m'lord,' he said again. 'Things have been quite lively in the house.'

'I'm so glad,' Virginia said. 'But I must round them up and take them away before they wreck the house.'

'Let's go up,' Richard grinned, 'and assess the damage.'

When they reached the open nursery door they paused at the threshold and stared. On the floor knelt James, in the act of restoring a toppled clockwork locomotive to its track for William to start off again. Behind them, Rose had the front of the dolls' house open and was showing Alice items from the miniature tea-set. Nearby, Georgina was squatting on the floor, trying to dress a doll.

As Richard and Virginia looked at one another James glanced up and saw them.

'Hello, Virginia – Father,' he said, in a tone more cheerful than they had heard for they didn't know how long. 'I say, these wretched points are sticking. Need a drop of oil.'

Feeling as if she were including him in the order, Virginia said, 'Come along now, children. I'm afraid it's time to go.'

The children protested in unison, but their mother shook her head. 'It's gone half-past six. Come along downstairs and get your coats on.' But Rose was already going. 'I'll fetch them, m'lady.'

Georgina struggled to her feet. 'Alice and I have been playing the piano together, haven't we? Rather well, we thought.'

'And blowing through the whistle,' Alice added excitedly. 'Oh, Mummy, it's a such a lovely house. You can talk through the whistle to someone in the basement all the way from upstairs.'

William put in, 'And there's lots of rooms to hide in, and cupboards for hide and seek.'

'Yes, I . . . I'm sure there are,' Virginia faltered. 'But you must say goodbye now and come downstairs. We mustn't outstay our welcome.'

James, standing beside her now, murmured, 'That would be quite impossible, Virginia, and you know it.'

'Couldn't they stay for just another half hour?' Georgina pleaded, a child again herself. 'Please, Virginia.'

Cornered and out-gunned, Virginia heard Richard say, 'Why not let them, darling? If they're having fun.'

All eyes were on her face. Everyone was hanging on her decision. She had no option left.

'Very well. But just for half an hour.'

James was already discussing the sticking points with William and Georgina had sunk down to take up the doll again as Richard and Virginia turned away towards the stairs.

When the half hour, and a little more, was up, James and Georgina dutifully came into the drawing-room, where Virginia had been playing the piano to Richard a good deal more softly and expertly than it had been played earlier.

'Rose is getting their coats on,' Georgina said. 'Hudson's calling a taxi.'

Rose appeared at the door at that moment, the children behind her. 'Beg pardon, m'lady, but we're just going down to say thank you to Mrs. Bridges for our tea.'

Virginia stepped forward. 'I'd like to take them down to the kitchen myself. May I?' she asked James.

'Of course.'

Mrs. Bridges looked up with surprise from her mixing bowl and hastily wiped her floury fingers on her apron.

'The children just wanted to come down and say goodbye, and thank you for their tea,' Virginia told her.

'Oh, it was a pleasure, my lady, I'm sure.'

'This is William – and Alice.'

'How do you do, my dears? Did you have enough to eat?'

'Oh, yes, thank you. It was a lovely tea.'

'Especially the jelly.'

Mrs. Bridges beamed. 'Well, next time Mummy brings you here to tea I'll make some nice strawberry tarts, eh? How about that?' Impulsively, she seized the children in turn and gave them a great hug. Virginia felt tears start behind her eyes. With further thanks to Mrs. Bridges she hustled them back up to the hall, where Mr. Hudson hovered as usual.

'His lordship is up in the drawing-room, m'lady. Your taxi should be here in two or three minutes.'

She thanked him and took the children up to the drawing-room, where she found Richard wih James and Georgina. The gravity of her husband's expression surprised and alarmed her, and she was glad that the children ran down the big room out of immediate earshot.

'What's the matter?' she asked, low.

'D'you know what James has just told me?' Richard said. 'All the servants are under month's notice.'

James appealed to her. 'What else could I do? I can't go on living here.'

Virginia did not respond at once, but then said slowly, almost to herself, 'Rose seems to have a wonderful way with children. Better than my old nanny.'

'She'd make a marvellous children's maid,' Georgina agreed.

'Who'd do the housework?' Virginia speculated.

'Lily. We only need one housemaid now, don't we, James?'

Hardly daring to, James muttered agreement. Georgina said, 'Frederick would valet Uncle Richard, as well as you, James. And Lily's such a good housemaid that Rose would have time to be Virginia's lady's maid as well . . . That is . . . I mean, if . . .'

Georgina checked herself, embarrassed.

'Does there really have to be an "if"?' James asked huskily.

He could have cursed Hudson for choosing that moment to enter and announce, 'The taxi is here, m'lady.'

'Thank you, Hudson,' Virginia said serenely, summoning the children with a wave. 'And thank you, Georgina and James, for looking after these two for me. They've had a lovely time and you've really spoiled them.'

'That's all right,' Georgina answered, subdued now.

Virginia smiled at Richard. 'I think we'd better telephone the agents tomorrow morning and withdraw our offer for the house in Clarendon Street. Don't you?'

He floundered: 'You don't mean . . . Are you sure, Virginia? I mean . . . Please . . . !'

Her smile embraced them all. 'Yes, I do mean. I may be a pretty stubborn and obstinate person, Richard, but I know when I'm beaten. Come along, children.'

And without a backward look she shooed children and husband away before her.

CHAPTER TWO

WITHIN minutes of Virginia's decision the news of their reprieve had been given to the staff. James delivered it himself, feeling it the least he could do after having pronounced sentence in the first place. Only subconsciously was he prompted by the certainty that a *fait accompli* in this quarter would disarm his stepmother of any possibility of changing her mind.

Richard and Virginia's move into his former home was managed, with almost imperceptible smoothness, by an eager and now happy Mr. Hudson. Apart from new faces above and below stairs, and some modernisation of the decor of certain parts of the house, the only substantial difference lay in the exuberant presence of two young children. Long years before, of course there had been a boy child and a girl – James and Elizabeth – compared with whom William and Alice seemed to Hudson to be allowed a wee bit too much licence to come and go as they pleased. But if this were to be all the change that had to be borne, it was small indeed alongside the post-war upheaval Mr. Hudson had foreseen, and he was content to bear with it.

Barely had she heard with equal relief that she was to be kept on than Rose received a letter from Southwold, where she had been born the daughter of the gatekeeper to the estate of the late Earl of Southwold, Richard Bellamy's father-in-law. It was to tell her that her aunt there had died and to ask her to attend the funeral and help sort out some neglected and complicated affairs. She was reluctant to ask for extended leave at such a moment, but Virginia insisted on her staying for quite as long as might prove necessary.

'I won't say you're not indispensable here, Rose,' she smiled, 'but I'm sure we'll manage while you're away.'

Only Lily grumbled about the extra burden of work

she would have to carry, but found the taste of brief superiority to her liking. In the way that upset or gloom upstairs had always had its way of depressing the spirits of those below, a general air of contentment about the household as a whole subtly touched everyone alike. Even James, at this time, cast aside his lethargy and infectious gloom. His personal future was still so vague as to seem non-existent; but his immediate dilemma had been solved in the way he had wanted it to be, and even he had grace enough to show his thanks through the nearest he could rise to cheerfulness.

He roused himself into going about more, becoming an almost daily visitor to his club, the Guards'. It was there one morning that he heard something from a fellow-member which, though he would at one time probably have brushed it aside with some cynical comment, caused him to sit down and dash off a letter, which he sent out immediately to the post. He re-read it the following morning, in print, in *The Times*. Mr. Hudson read it, too, aloud and with pride to the servants. Richard Bellamy read it, and so did many others. Its burden was this:

'I have recently heard of a story which fills me with horror, dismay and shame. It is the case of a former sergeant of the King's Royal Rifle Corps, unable to find employment, who has been reduced to living for the past nine months, with his wife and four children, in a patch-work shack made up of tarpaulins and old army ground-sheets. The total space in which the family must live, eat and sleep is ten feet by six.

'Nor is this an isolated incident. I am informed that there are thousands of ex-Servicemen of all ranks in a similar plight all over the country: men who fought so gallantly and endured horrors and deprivations in the worst war mankind has ever known; men whose welfare should be the first consideration of any Government. But what is this Government doing? The pledges given at the last Election to re-house and re-employ returning soldiers are already shown to have been pitifully inadequate. Can we truly claim to be building a land fit for heroes to live in?'

One who inevitably read it was Sir Geoffrey Dillon, the Bellamy family's solicitor, a man of inscrutable temperament and many associations in influential places. The following evening he made one of his rare visits to No. 165 Eaton Place and took his sherry with Richard and Virginia in the morning-room. What he had to propose, in his usual circumlocutory way, provoked Richard into a sharp response.

'Out of the question, Geoffrey. Not even worth discussing.'

'I'm not to take it, am I, that you disapprove of the letter?' Sir Geoffrey's voice had about it its usual oiled-silk smoothness.

'Of course not. I'm simply saying that one letter from a gallant ex-officer doesn't turn him overnight into a peace-time politician.'

He gave Dillon a sharply suspicious glance.

'Look here, Geoffrey – have Central Office sent you here?'

'Good heavens, no. I've no . . . official connection with Central Office. But certain people have let it be known they're interested in James. I'm surprised if no one has spoken to you about it.'

'Well, there have been congratulations, of course, and the subject has been . . . mentioned, here and there. But I dismissed it right away.'

'Wasn't that being a little hasty?' Virginia asked.

'No, my darling, it is not being hasty. I know what's behind this as well as Geoffrey does. The boy is intelligent, he's won an M.C. That carries its own aura. The Conservative Party simply want to use him to enhance their own prestige. But what happens when he gets in? He has no experience of government affairs. He won't know how to make a speech. He'd never survive.'

'He's survived worse.'

'I tell you, he's an amateur. He has no training for the life.'

'Don't you really mean that he's your son, and you're afraid of what people might say about favours?'

'Nonsense, darling. If I really believed he had something to offer, I'd back him to the hilt.'

Dillon intervened, 'I understand your feelings, Richard. But don't you think the Party and the country need new blood?'

Virginia agreed warmly, 'I quite agree with Sir Geoffrey. Anyway, James has lived in an atmosphere of politics in this house all his life. Isn't that sufficient training for the life?'

Before Richard could defend his attitude the door opened and James came in, as briskly as his limp would permit. Sir Geoffrey rose automatically to the master of the house.

'Hello!' James said cheerfully. 'What's this? Not financial trouble, I hope?'

'No, James. I just called in to congratulate you on your letter, and . . .' He hesitated and turned to Richard. 'May I tell him?'

'If you must,' Richard scowled. 'I can't stop you.'

'Tell me what, Sir Geoffrey?'

'Have you ever seriously thought about going into politics?'

James laughed incredulously. 'Me? Good lord, no!' He went to pour himself a drink. Richard ranged his glance from Virginia to Dillon. 'There you are, see?' he said quietly.

Over his shoulder James asked, 'What's all this about, anyway?' His father answered, 'Geoffrey has what amounts to a proposition from Conservative Central Office.'

Dillon was about to protest, but James had turned with his filled glass. 'What? On the strength of one letter? Scribbled in haste? They must be hard up for candidates.'

'They are,' Dillon agreed. 'Of the right sort.'

Virginia said, 'Young men who fought. Who can truly represent the interests of ex-Servicemen and their families.'

'But my letter was supposed to be attacking the Government.'

'The Coalition Government,' Dillon reminded him. 'Not the Conservative Party. The Coalition won't last for ever.'

'I should hope not. Well! I must say, it's an intriguing idea. Would I be tied to the Party line, or could I speak my mind?'

'I think you'd be free to say whatever you liked – assuming you'd support the Party's basic principles.'

'The principles, yes. But not always the way they go about things.'

James sat, as his father rose to pour himself a further drink.

'What do you say, Father? I've been looking for something to do with my idle life.'

Richard paused. 'I'm strongly against the idea, James, as I've made quite clear to Virginia and Geoffrey. When you speak of filling your idle life, I'm delighted you should feel well enough to be ready to do something. Politics is a serious business, not to be entered into light-heartedly . . .'

'Am I giving that impression? Father, I do believe you're jealous.'

Dillon saw his chance. 'Of course, if the life turns out to be not to your taste . . .'

'Or if I fail to get in,' James corrected.

Now Richard turned on Dillon. 'Of course he'll get in. That's not in doubt. The question is, what does he do afterwards? He'll find himself in an entirely false position, handling constituency problems, making speeches. It's a job for professionals.'

James said seriously, 'With all respect, Father, you weren't a professional at the start.'

Richard had to admit to himself the truth of this. His mind flew back swiftly over his own youthful uncertainty and lack of purpose; of the chance way in which he had come to the attention of Benjamin Disraeli, who had instilled into his mind the idea of a political career, and, with the aid of Lord Southwold – and, not least, Lord Southwold's daughter Marjorie, Richard's first love and first wife – had shaped his future for him. He had been so

34

long in politics now that he had forgotten ever having been a novice at it. He considered James unfitted; but how fitted had he himself once been?

James was continuing, without rancour. 'I do take your point, Father. But if I have an opportunity I must be allowed to decide for myself.' He turned to Dillon. 'If I agree, how would I go about it?'

Sir Geoffrey permitted himself a faint smirk. 'There's to be a by-election soon. Old Harry Weatherall, who contested the seat unsuccessfully for years, died last month at seventy-three. It's Barking East.'

'Barking! That's dockland, isn't it?'

'Yes it is,' Richard snapped impatiently. 'A cast-iron Labour seat. Really, Geoffrey, he'd stand no chance there at all. If he really wants to get in, let's for Heaven's sake find him somewhere safe.'

'No, Father,' James said, quite sharply. 'I wouldn't want that.'

Dillon let the objection hang on the air for a moment before putting in, 'Plenty of ex-Servicemen, homeless, unemployed, in Barking, I should imagine. Interesting to see what impression could be made.'

'Very little, I should think,' Richard growled. James turned to his stepmother to ask, 'Virginia, you've been very quiet. What do you think about it all?'

She looked from him to Richard, then back again. 'Well . . . for what my opinion's worth, I think you should do it, if you want to. Richard, I don't want to seem disloyal to you, but quite frankly I find your objections impossible to fathom. There's no great mystique to politics. It's not some exclusive club. If a man, from any walk of life, has an honest and sincere wish to serve his fellow men, then we should encourage him as much as we can.'

'There are other ways,' Richard said flatly, anticipating the usual defeat. James told him earnestly, 'Father, I promise you I'm not going to take this lightly. But I believe I've started something with this demand letter which I have an obligation to see through. Politics is the way you

35

chose, so why shouldn't I? It's in my blood, both sides of the family. I feel fit now – energetic. Perhaps I've just been waiting for the right moment.'

Pausing first to see whether Richard would reply, Sir Geoffrey Dillon asked James, 'May I tell them you're interested? The local association are vetting the applicants this week.'

'You can do more than that. Tell them, if they want me, I'm game.'

Sir Geoffrey positively beamed, like a gratified cat. 'Splendid! Well, I really must go. You know, I think I detect a new influence in this house. Yes – this room's been redecorated, for a start.'

Virginia smiled. 'I hope you approve, Sir Geoffrey.'

He could not suppress a non-committal little sniff. 'We must all move with the times, I suppose.'

'I should hope so,' Virginia said, moving to the door with him.

A few days later, James came in out of the rain, one dark late afternoon, to announce that he had been adopted as prospective Tory Member of Parliament for Barking East. At Virginia's prompting, Richard sent down for champagne.

Two visitors were below stairs when the news of the Major's adoption was received. They were, again, Edward and Daisy, bedraggled with walking through the downpour and distinctly more subdued in manner than when they had last called. Mrs Bridges, as welcoming as ever, placed them before the fire and ordered Ruby to make tea. Mr. Hudson's greeting when he came downstairs and found them was enough to counteract the welcome warmth.

'What are you both doing here?' he asked unsmilingly.

'Just . . . just passin', Mr. Hudson,' Daisy said tensely.

'Yeh,' Edward supported her. 'Thought we'd look in. See how you all was.'

Mr. Hudson could see all too plainly that it was not only damp that had made their clothes so unkempt-looking. Edward's suit was frayed and almost threadbare in places, and Daisy's shoes were not only sodden, but cracked open. She saw his gaze on them.

'Actually, it was Rose we really come to see. Wasn't it, Eddy?'

'Yeh. Dais thinks she left a . . . a pair of winter shoes here, and we thought if Rose's kept them we'd pick 'em up.' He forced a laugh. 'No point in spending on a new pair.'

'No, indeed,' Hudson replied, and told them curtly of the circumstances of Rose's absence. 'But Lily can find the shoes for you,' he concluded.

Daisy said hastily, 'No, no, don't worry, Lily. They're . . . probably lost, after all this time.'

Edward said heavily, 'Well, we'd better be getting back to Camberwell . . .'

'No you won't,' Mrs. Bridges ordered, bustling about. 'They're staying for supper – aren't they, Mr. Hudson?' Giving him no chance to reply, one way or the other, she ordered, 'Lily, lay two places extra.'

Edward and Daisy looked unhappily at one another, but were glad to obey.

'Anything come of that furniture job out Romford way?' Frederick asked Edward a little later, his voice betraying something of his resentment over Edward's earlier boasting about having cut himself free of the bonds of 'service'.

'Oh, that! No, I didn't get that, actually. Fell through, you know.'

'Still selling brushes, then?'

'That's it.'

'Going all right, is it?'

'Up and down. Bad weather doesn't help.'

His embarrassment was obvious, even though he tried to cover it with a feebly humorous anecdote about one of his door-to-door calls. The eternally tactless Ruby had a more hurtful, though innocently meant, question to ask Daisy.

'Whatever happened about your baby, Daisy?'

'Quiet, Ruby,' hissed Mrs. Bridges, who had wondered the same thing as soon as she had seen Daisy's slimmer

37

figure, but had drawn her own conclusions and kept her mouth shut. Daisy said, trying to sound casual, 'Oh, it's all right. You have to know some time. I lost it. Miscarriage. Six months.'

Mrs. Bridges paused to give the thin, damp shoulder a little pat. 'I'm very sorry, Daisy. Truly.'

'Yes,' they heard Mr. Hudson say. 'So am I, Daisy. A great shame.'

'Well, it was disappointing – 'specially for Eddie. But the doctor says I'd be able to have another one. Plenty of time.'

'Course there is,' Mrs. Bridges agreed, but she secretly wiped the corner of each eye as she went to fetch the supper.

The arrival of rabbit pie – 'Just like old times, Mrs. B.!' Edward cried – improved the atmosphere somewhat. Mr. Hudson noted how ravenously he ate.

With genuine curiosity Lily asked Daisy, who was also eating eagerly, 'You got any regrets, leavin' service, Daisy?'

Edward had to answer for his wife, whose mouth was full. 'No regrets, Lily. Just . . . happy memories.'

Daisy managed to mutter, 'Yes. We live on 'em.'

'What do you mean, Daisy?' Mr. Hudson was unable to prevent himself asking.

'Nothing, Mr. Hudson . . .' Edward began, but Daisy threw down her knife and fork and said, near to tears, 'Why keep pretending, Eddie? They aren't fooled.'

Hudson said gently, 'I think we have guessed the truth haven't we, Edward?'

Edward looked at his wife, but she didn't raise her head, only said, 'Tell 'em. For pity's sake.' He looked round the table, then put his own knife and fork on his plate and explained haltingly: 'I think . . . what Dais wants me to say is . . . brush selling didn't work out. I'm out of a job . . . at the moment. But I'll get something else. Can't keep us down for long, can they, Dais . . .? Oh, Dais . . . don't . . . please!'

She was crying openly, fiercely. 'I'm sorry . . . but they're so cruel to people like my Eddie, and I get so angry. Stupid hoity-toity women and butlers shoutin' rude things, slammin' the door in his face. Don't they know what he did for 'em out there? What he went through?'

'Shut up, Dais,' Edward ordered pleadingly. 'They don't want to hear about that.'

'Well, they should hear about it. They're our friends. They're the only friends we got!'

The following pause, broken only by her weeping, was broken by Mr. Hudson, blundering in with, 'We do sympathise, Edward. It's a strange and cruel world. But you did make your own bed, the pair of you . . .'

Edward's restraint went. 'Yes. I remember what you said to us when we was leaving. You wanted us to stop here, rest of our lives, like Rose. Well, me and Dais wanted something better. I reckoned we'd earned it. Only, Dais is right. You don't know what it's like out there in the rotten world, because you never tried it. And until you do, you got no right accusing us . . .'

'Eddie, don't . . . ! Daisy tried, but he went on: 'He hasn't, Dais. He wants to try looking for work, and supporting a wife in a miserable little room with the rain coming in. That's why she lost her baby,' he told them all. 'Because it wasn't possible, the way we was living.' He rounded on Mr. Hudson again, though still speaking to the rest of them. 'He's just a smug, self-satisfied old man, who didn't do nothing in the war except serve bleedin' sherry!"

He threw back his chair and stumbled from the table to where their coats hung. Daisy, with a fearful glance at the ashen-faced Hudson, joined him, and together they went quickly out by the back door, slamming it behind them, leaving only an intense silence over which the hiss and drip of the rain could be heard from the area.

The rain relented next morning, but it was again a dank, drab day to herald James's first appeal to his potential constituents.

The place chosen for him by his agent, Arthur Knowles, an experienced campaigner in his mid-forties, was a street corner close to a dockyard entrance. Tenement buildings overshadowed the site. Occasionally a women came to one or another of the windows to shake out a rug, look down with mild curiosity at the setting up of the flimsy platform and the banners exhorting them to VOTE TORY, or VOTE BELLAMY, or even to MAKE BRITAIN A LAND FIT FOR HEROES, before disappearing again and slamming the windows firmly against the clammy air.

The 'crowd' so far consisted of two dejected-looking women, an old soldier on a crutch, some ragged children, and a dog whose expression displayed, if anything, more interest than any of the humans.

'You sure this is a good spot?' James asked, surveying his audience.

Knowles grinned knowingly and gestured towards the dockyard. 'They'll come through those gates in a minute for their dinner hour. The pensions office is just round the corner, so we should draw the Servicemen. And the women will come out of the buildings.''

James sighed. 'Am I preaching to the employed or the unemployed, then?'

'Preaching?'

'It feels rather like a revivalist meeting.'

Knowles produced a small brandy flash from his coat pocket. 'Here, Major, have a drop of this. Mr. Weatherall always used to loosen his tongue before he spoke.'

James sipped gratefully and felt marginally more assured. He handed back the flask and accepted a tin megaphone.

'I'd start now,' Knowles advised. 'Good luck.'

James nodded and raised the megaphone with his right hand, finding to his consternation that it meant his squinting over to the left to see his notes, and wondering how he would manage to turn the sheets with one hand.

'Good morning!' he cried, putting practised heartiness into it, and startled himself by the noise his amplified voice made and the echo it produced off the grey walls. 'Good morning. I am ... I am your Conservative Party candidate, James Bellamy. I'm asking for your support at this coming by-election, but first I want to introduce myself to you and explain my reasons for standing here today.'

His audience at this point increased dramatically – virtually doubled itself, in fact – as two men, obviously ex-Servicemen, rounded the corner and paused to listen, and another woman who had chanced to open her window did not immediately withdraw, but stayed leaning on the sill.

Directing his megaphone at the men, James went on.

'Most of my life I have been a professional soldier. Now, it's sometimes said that soldiers should stick to what they know and shouldn't meddle with politics. I believed that once. But these times we're living through – the aftermath of this terrible war in which we've all suffered – they've caused me to change my mind. The gallant working men of this country, with whom I fought in the trenches and whom I gained an undying respect for, I believe they deserved a better deal than they're getting at the moment. Decent housing, proper employment, higher wages ...'

A drift of men came from the dock gates, but did little more than pause to look James up and down before moving on, their waiting dinners of more interest to them than yet another ration of political hot air. The woman at the open window withdrew her head. The listening ex-Servicemen trudged away. Only the children and the dog remained; but James ploughed on.

'Central Office are rather concerned about him,' Sir Geoffrey Dillon reported to Richard and Virginia one evening later in the week. 'Or rather, the local association, mainly. They've passed on some criticisms.'

'And you've been sent here to pass them on to us,' Richard said. 'Well, come on, Geoffrey, be specific.'

'One example – he's taken rather an unorthodox line on housing. He wants cheap, jerry-built houses by the thousands, it seems, and he doesn't care who pays for them. When it's pointed out that he'd merely be creating the slums of the future he says the future must take care of itself.'

'Can't it?' Virginia demanded.

'No, I take Geoffrey's point,' Richard nodded. 'The Coalition Government's housing policy is the same as the Conservative Party's. By coming out with this stuff he alienates his supporters and puts himself at his opponents' mercy.'

Dillon told her, 'There were even cries of "Communist" at one of his Tory Club meetings. Ironic, I know. But I'm afraid the feeling is growing that he's out of his depth.'

Richard raised his shoulders and let them drop meaningfully. 'It was you who pushed him into the deep end, Geoffrey. You can't blame the boy now.'

'Good heavens, no. I'm merely suggesting he needs a little advice. That's why I've spoken to you, rather than to James.'

'We'll see what we can do,' Richard promised; 'but I rather think I'm the last person he'll listen to.'

Before Sir Geoffrey could speak again James had come briskly into the room. The lawyer muttered something about urgent business, greeted James briefly, and saw himself out. James poured himself a large whisky and sipped thankfully, looking at Richard and Virginia over the rim of his glass.

'What did the old fox want?'

'Just to see how you were getting on,' Virginia answered.

'He could have asked me.'

'You weren't here.'

'So, what did you tell him?'

'Only what you've told us. How did it go today?'

James answered confidently, 'Not badly. Beginning to break through the barriers of apathy. Oh, and I caught sight of my Labour opponent, Harry Shadbolt. No charm at all, as far as I could see. I discovered he didn't fight – lung trouble or something. That's a help.'

Virginia and Richard exchanged glances as he passed them, to sit on the settee. James added, 'We're holding a big open meeting on the day before the poll, in a Seaman's Mission Hall. A final rallying call.'

'Wednesday?' Virginia said. 'May we come?'

Richard said quickly, 'If you felt it would help, I'm prepared to speak . . .'

As if he had anticipated the offer — which he had — James replied promptly, 'Thank you, Father, but I don't want to draw any more attention to my background than the Press are doing already. It doesn't help much, I'm afraid.'

'Then we can easily get someone else . . .'

'I want to do this on my own.'

'My dear boy, no one has ever fought a campaign entirely on his own.'

'Please, Father, I don't want to sound churlish, but I can't think of anyone in the Party who'd be much use to me. Not down there.'

'That's nonsense. There's Austen Chamberlain, Stanley Baldwin . . .'

James got to his feet in a way that left no doubt about his wish to end the discussion. 'Look, I've had a very exhausting day. I'm whacked, and I've got a lot of work to do yet.'

Accepting the dismissal, Richard turned to the door. 'Yes. Well . . . Virginia and I are going to the theatre. Are you coming to change, my dear?'

'Yes, darling. In a moment.'

Richard nodded and went out. James tossed back the last of his drink and went to pour another.

'Can't he realise?' he said. 'They're all the same old men hanging on to pre-war notions. Can't they see the gulf there is now?'

'Yes, of course they can — and they have all their wisdom and experience to bridge it. No, I'm sorry, James, you can't expect me to side with you against Richard all the time. I know what his feelings were to begin with, but since your nomination he's done all he can to support you.'

'Huh! He offers me the kind of advice that would be very useful if I were fighting some safe seat in Gloucestershire.'

43

His stepmother's eyes flashed, and her Scottish accent seemed suddenly more pronounced as she retorted, 'You don't know that, because you haven't listened to him. He's been here every night, with a lifetime's experience behind him, longing for you to discuss your problems. Only, you shut him out, and then have the gall to accuse him of being a meddling old man. Quite apart from the hurt you're causing, I think you're being thoroughly pig-headed.'

James, who had physically recoiled before this tirade, stared silently for a moment before saying, 'I admire your loyalty, Virginia. I understand how things may seem to you. But you don't know everything that's been going on. I have to fight the local Conservative association, my own damn people, day after day.'

'We do know that, James,' she said quietly, and touched his arm in a peacemaking gesture. 'We hear things, and it seems to me you need friends. Well, your father is the best friend you've got. So just think about it, will you?'

Without waiting for an answer she went off to go upstairs and change.

On the Tuesday evening Edward and Daisy paid a further visit to the house. Their manner was distinctly subdued and embarrassed.

The day following the earlier contretemps, Frederick had called at their lodgings, bringing a note from Mrs. Bridges and pair of worn but sound winter shoes. Defiant to Edward's protests that they weren't reduced to accepting charity, Daisy had insisted on trying on the shoes. They fitted perfectly. Near to hysteria, Edward had threatened to leave her if she wouldn't give them back. She had refused, and her husband had had to relieve his feelings by almost throwing Frederick out through the door, which he had then slammed and leant against, weeping.

It had been a further note from Mrs. Bridges that had brought them round now, for tea. Her sleep had been troubled at the thought of their plight and on receipt of a polite note of thanks from Daisy for the shoes she had impulsively invited them, though not without asking the approval of Mr. Hudson, who had answered stiffly that she was, of course, free to invite any guests of her own she might choose. He would have preferred not to have been present himself, but his duties prevented his going out. He and Edward greeted one another formally and warily, and when Edward tried to put together an apology for his behaviour the butler silenced him with the opinion that the subject was best left alone. At least, Daisy was now comfortably dry-shod.

They sat uneasily at the table in the servants' hall, waiting for tea, Mr. Hudson self-consciously and unnecessarily polishing his spectacles, Edward and Daisy exchanging halting conversation with Mrs. Bridges and Lily, while Ruby made the tea in the kitchen. Frederick came in, in his green uniform. Addressing Mr. Hudson, he announced, 'Her ladyship would like to see Edward and Daisy before they go.'

'Us!' Edward exclaimed. 'What for?'

Hudson looked up. 'I suggest you go up now, before tea, rather than keep her ladyship waiting.'

Apprehensively, they obeyed, and some moments later were standing side by side, like a pair of errant children, as Virginia came across the morning-room towards them.

'It must be over a year since you left here, isn't it?' she said, in a tone calculated to allay whatever fears they might be feeling.

Daisy answered, 'Fourteen months, my lady.'

'So long? Where are you living now?'

'Small room in Camberwell, m'lady,' Edward said.

'Well it occurred to me . . . the flat above the garage is empty. It hasn't been occupied since Mr. and Mrs. Watkins left, before the war. You remember them?'

'I do, m'lady,' Edward said, suddenly dry-mouthed. 'Daisy wasn't here then.'

'I see. Well, it seems ideal for a married couple, and such a waste. Also, we need a chauffeur. Can you drive, Edward?'

He could scarcely manage to reply, 'Yes, m'lady. I learnt in the war.'

'Good.' She turned to the wide-eyed Daisy. 'We also need another housemaid, especially at the moment with Rose away. And when she comes back she'll be my personal maid, so that wouldn't affect you.' Quite matter-of-factly she added, 'Lily would be under you.'

Permitted a natural instinct, Edward and Daisy would have fallen into one another's arms; but Daisy just said, 'Thank you ever so much, my lady.'

As though uninterrupted, Virginia went on, 'Frederick will continue as footman and will also valet his lordship. But the Major needs a valet, so it would be helpful if you could combine your duties, Edward.'

As he mumbled his thanks she was already moving to ring the bell. Daisy could hold back tears no longer. 'We're so grateful, m'lady. We . . . we'll work ever so hard. Really . . .'

They heard the door open behind them. 'Hudson,' Lady Bellamy was saying, 'Edward and Daisy are willing to come back into service. It was a good idea of yours, thank you.'

'Thank *you*, my lady,' the astonished young couple heard the butler reply; but as they turned to go they could read nothing in his features nor in the eyes which did not seem to notice them as they passed.

'Yes, Hudson told me,' James said to his father next day, when Richard mentioned, for want of a conversational opening, that Edward and Daisy would be rejoining the staff. 'I'm very pleased.'

James was dressed in a quiet, perfectly-cut city suit, with a blue and white rosette in one lapel and an unostentatious buttonhole in the other. He had been making the last revisions to his notes for the open meeting. His father, all uncertainty, turned to leave the room again, but James said, almost blurting it out, 'Father, I'm sorry if I've seemed . . . high-handed, these past weeks. It wasn't really

46

meant or . . . directed against you personally. I somehow, quite wrongly, lumped you with certain Party attitudes, and . . .'

'You don't need to apologise, James.'

'I had to prove myself, you see.'

'I understand.'

'Do you . . . would you come to the meeting today?'

Richard hesitated. 'Virginia and I had planned to go to the Leicester Galleries to see the Epstein sculptures.'

'I'd like you to come,' James said, quietly, looking down at his notes.

'Both of us?'

'Both of you.'

Richard smiled at last. 'It'll be a pleasure.'

'I wouldn't count on it. I'm having trouble with this damned speech. Would you . . . look at it . . . please?'

Still smiling, Richard took it without a word and sank into the settee, fishing with his free hand for his spectacles and already frowning with the effort to read before he had got them on.

'. . . During the two weeks I've been among you . . .'

Whistles and boos. '*Two weeks!*'

'. . . I've been impressed by many things. By the industry and dedication of the dock workers . . .'

'*Hurray!*'

'. . . striving to get this country back on to its feet . . .'

'Wot – wiv the bleedin' Tories!'

'. . . and the fortitude . . .'

'The Tories are the enemies of the working classes!' That damned woman again, tall and sharp-faced, her hair scraped back, her accent anything but working-class. James waited patiently for the cheers and boos which her every intervention – and they were constant – provoked in this almost packed hall. He went on. 'Yes, the fortitude of those of you who are unemployed – many of you ex-Servicemen – in what must be the most disheartening circumstances . . .'

47

An eruption of catcalls and suggestions greeted this. Seated at the back of the hall, unobtrusively dressed, Richard and Virginia held hands tightly. Edward, who had chauffered them all there, stood nearby, feeling the sweat running into the collar of the smart uniform which, he was all too conscious, had attracted suspicious looks from several of the heavily-built dockers around him.

James was forging on gallantly, and not without support. But it was apparent that the general mood of the meeting was against him and the cause for which he stood, not least because of the well-rehearsed interventions of the woman heckler. Unbeknown to him, she had been one of the earliest to arrive at the Seaman's Mission, with the purpose of securing the position which she knew from long practice would give her more command of the meeting than any platform speaker.

When James produced a copy of his pamphlet, which hopeful supporters had proffered at the hall door and earned more coarse jibes than thanks as a result, the conduct of the meeting seemed to become reversed, with the woman making the speech and James endeavouring to intervene.

'Upper class propaganda!' she yelled.

'In this pamphlet, I repeat, I have tried to lay down . . .'

'Down with the class system! The workers are the wage slaves of their employers. We want common ownership. Abolish the social classes!'

'Madam . . .' James shouted over the mixture of cheers and boos, '. . . the spirit of co-operation and fellowship between all classes which was built up in the war has to be maintained if we . . .'

This time the professional agitator's work was done for her by a spontaneous mixture of male and female cries from all parts of the hall.

'We don't want to hear about the war!'

'Enough of the bloody war!'

'Blame the war for everything!'

One voice amongst them all brought a deep flush to

James's face: 'Where'd you get your bleedin' medal? Sittin' in some chateau behind the lines?' Richard's grip tightened on Virginia as he felt her move to get up. James was telling the heckler, clearly furious but not without control on his temper: 'I risked my life for you to say that! You can't ignore the war as if it never happened . . .'

'Don't you accuse us!' a woman cried shrilly, to sympathetic cries. 'I 'ad two sons and a 'usband die for this rotten country.'

'Yer!' a gigantic man standing almost next to Edward bellowed. 'You're not one of us.'

Stung, James called back, 'No man under my command in the trenches ever said that!'

This was adjudged highly hilarious, with questions to him as to whether he thought he was 'Douglas-bloody Haig' or which other war leader. In one part of the hall a slight scuffle broke out but was quickly quelled by one of the few policemen present. James tried to salvage the situation.

'To move on to one of the most important issues – housing . . .'

It was like lighting the fuse of a firework, or pulling the pin of a grenade.

'You gotter nice 'ouse, 'ave yer?'

'"ow many bleedin' rooms?'

'"ow many bloody servants?'

'I want more houses for the *people*,' James insisted, before being howled down again.

'Please, ladies and gentlemen,' cried Arthur Knowles, whose expression in the last moments had been growing increasingly dismayed. 'Please let your candidate speak.'

The militant young woman, who had been studiedly conserving her energies while others were unwittingly serving her cause, now returned in full voice.

'He's got nothing to say. There's only one way to save this country, and that is by revolution!' Undeterred by the rising tide of booing this alien sentiment provoked, she continued, 'Follow the lead of Russia! Smash the greedy

Capitalists! Send them back to the barbaric ages where they belong!'

Amidst the uproar another female voice was heard now. Seated beside its owner, Richard Bellamy felt himself almost numbed to realise that it was Virginia's. She was on her feet, waving one arm, commanding, through sheer surprise and urgency, the attention of the people who had turned astonished faces in wonder at these cultivated Scots tones.

'You don't want Communism,' she was yelling at them. 'You've had enough of fighting. And that's what a Bolshevik revolution would mean. Now's the time for unity, for working together. Not disruption, not strikes. Ignore the hotheads, the enemies of this country. Vote for peace and prosperity. *Vote for Bellamy!*'

Richard, almost succumbing to the temptation to bury his face in his hands, couldn't help recalling a political clamour about his own ears, long ago, touched off by a woman who had loved him. But this was very different. After a second or two of hesitation, and a few cries of support for Virginia and for the staring candidate on the platform, the rehearsed rioting began; the specially-gathered tomatoes from the gutters of the street market-places were produced and hurled platform-wards; the crowds began to surge, and the police moved forward.

Edward, heavily jostled, interpreted Richard's signal and slipped out to where the car was waiting. Richard flung an arm round his wife and edged her towards the door. What seemed to be a menacing wall of gigantic dockers almost surrounded them; but their emotions were directed at more distant objectives, and, with the aid of a bearded police constable who seemed possessed of the strength of ten, the couple escaped into the night, to reach the car at the same moment as an infuriated James and his shaken agent. They could hear the racket in the hall until they had driven the length of the street in which it stood.

At his end of the long servants' table Mr. Hudson cleared

his throat for silence. A newspaper, just put into his hand by Frederick, was folded to an item prominent on the front page. Frederick resumed his seat beside Lily. Mrs. Bridges, Edward, Daisy and Ruby watched, awed, as Mr. Hudson began to declaim in the portentous tones of any Returning Officer, the result of the by-election:

'Bellamy, Conservative, seven thousand three hundred and sixty-nine votes.' (Gasps of approval.) 'Macneill, Socialist Labour Party, one thousand and forty-three votes' (a quickly-silenced cry of 'He's won!' from Lily), 'Shadbolt, Labour – eighteen thousand nine hundred and twenty-eight votes.' Mr. Hudson nearly added, 'And I declare the said . . .', but quickly changed it to, 'Mr. Shadbolt is duly elected to Parliament.'

Before lunch, Richard, Virginia and Sir Geoffrey Dillon drank sherry and tried in vain to persuade James that he had fought courageously and with dignity, had not disappointed his predecessor's staunch supporters, and – Richard's sentiments – gained invaluable experience and proved to him and to others that the necessary qualities were there for some other occasion. James merely shook his head, his cloak of despondency donned once more, almost welcomingly.

'I didn't do well at all. I failed. But it's not the result that upsets me. It's what I saw with my own eyes – what I heard. I believed there was one spark of hope – just one – that came from the hideous waste of that war. That was the courage, the fellowship, the sheer bloody good sense that officers like me saw for the first time in the working man. I believed if we could just hold that common ground, keep trusting each other, we could build something in peacetime. But what happens? We become two nations again. Back to the old entrenched positions.'

He got up from the chair in which he had been slumped and went to stand facing his father.

'What did we have to offer them, Father – *our* Party? What a pathetic lot we are, skulking behind Lloyd George's Coalition, complacently biding our time . . . Well, if ever that time comes, I can tell you there won't be a country left worth governing. All decency, all traditional values gone – vanished without trace.'

He turned to Dillon.

'You can tell Central Office, Sir Geoffrey, I won't be standing again. And now if you'll excuse me, Father, Virginia, I really don't think I can face lunch. If anyone wants me I'll be at the Guards' Club.'

Before anyone could say anything he was across the room and at the door, reaching it just as Hudson entered.

'I shan't be lunching in today, Hudson,' James said. 'I'm going to my club.'

'Very good, sir. May I, er, on behalf of the staff, sir, offer our sincere congratulations on your reducing the Labour majority . . .'

James halted, turned, and stared.

'Did I?'

'Yes indeed, sir. By six hundred or so votes from the last General Election. It was a notable achievement, sir.'

For the first time that day, James smiled.

'Thank you, Hudson.'

Without a look at the others he strode out. Hudson turned towards Virginia.

'Luncheon is served, m'lady.'

CHAPTER THREE

EDWARD and Daisy had been lucky; many more were not. The search for work, for decent homes, for bare subsistence, even, remained the only full-time occupation of tens of thousands of disenchanted men and women who had played their part in winning the 'war to end all wars'.

The hardship was by no means confined to those on humbler social levels. In some ways, these were less hard hit than their former 'betters'; having never had much in life, they had less to feel deprived of and found it easier to make the best of meagre allowances and assistance. Worst afflicted of all, perhaps, were the middle-class and self-made men who had worn officers' uniform. Their brief authority and privilege at an end, they had to try to merge into the surroundings from which they had originally come, but for many it was no easy thing to do. Either they could not swallow their acquired dignity and return to humdrum tasks, often under the orders of men who had held common rank, or no rank at all; or they found their jobs usurped by others, or simply vanished; or their own natures, made restless by their years out of context, would not let them settled down, but kept them moving from one thing to another, always searching for they knew not what, and never finding it.

One of the latter was a friend of Georgina's, Robin Eliot, a well-built, fair-haired youth a year or two younger than she, of unfailingly good-humoured disposition. To anyone who passed him in the street, or saw him roar by on his indispensable motor-bike, he gave the impression of being one of the war's luckier survivors. His daytime suits were immaculately pressed and groomed, and almost every night saw him in full evening dress, as often as not dancing with Georgina and a varying party of her friends at the Berkeley or some other fashionable rendezvous. His father was known to have an estate in Wiltshire, and Robin himself had all the appearances of a carefree ex-captain with a full wallet and a rewarding future that merely awaited his making the effort to catch up with it.

The truth was very different. Although it was by now the autumn of 1921 and he had got his discharge almost a year before, he had been able to find no work anything like commensurate with his standing as a minor gentleman. He was qualified for nothing; he possessed neither outstanding intelligence nor the quick-wittedness which can be even more valuable, when it comes to making opportunities against the odds; and the father who would gladly have helped him was himself on the verge of bankruptcy and about to sell his estate for less than it needed to pay all his debts.

What Robin would not do, though, was to give up his social life. Increasingly, it seemed to him to be the one thing left to cling on to before circumstances washed him away; and increasingly, too, he saw Georgina as his personal last refuge. While he could still dance at the Berkeley – where, given the right clothes and company, one could do so for very little actual expenditure – he was all right. He knew that once he had to start making excuses for not joining in, he would never be able to face them or her again.

He swallowed his pride and took what jobs he could get, and made no effort to conceal them from his fashionable friends, playing instead the role of a jokey adventurer who didn't care what he did during the day because he only lived for the evenings. They laughed hugely with him when he told them he was selling brushes – the very trade at which Edward had failed utterly – and shared his merriment when, within a few weeks, he recounted, with a wealth of anecdote, the downward course of his own failure at it, mentioning no word of the many humiliations he had experienced. They were positively convulsed by his story, a week or two later, of an even more diastrous door-to-door round, trying to sell haircurlers on behalf of a wartime profiteer who had become a British national only just before the war.

Still the evenings at the Berkeley continued; and several times Robin asked Georgina to marry him. She took it as just another facet of his joking and refused to answer anything but flippantly. To her surprise, at a fancy dress party, he got her alone and asked her again, obviously earnestly this time. When she refused, he let his guise slip for the first and only time, and almost pleaded that everyone needed someone to hang on to.

'I don't want to have anyone to hang on to,' Georgina said unsympathetically. 'I'm awfully fond of you, Robin, but I don't want to spend the rest of my life with you and nobody else.'

She didn't notice how pale he was as he said, deliberately, 'I love you Georgina. I can't live without you.'

'Oh, it's too sick-making to hear boring and stupid things like that!' she exclaimed, and flounced away.

Ten minutes later he shot himself dead in a cupboard.

A note in his hand was addressed to her as 'Dearest Georgina'. Fortunately for her, the person who reached him first concealed and then destroyed it, and her name was not mentioned in the newspapers. She made a determined attempt to act as if the incident had not affected her at all; but James, who had often talked with Robin when he had come to collect Georgina at Eaton Place, saw through her pretence and persuaded her to take up a long-standing invitation to visit his sister Elizabeth and her American husband in that country.

James's personal brand of restlessness was of longer standing. It was part – a major part – of his very personality. It had to a large extent blighted his life, and in varying degrees the lives of almost everyone with whom he had any sort of intimate association. It had brought his father and his late mother much sadness, and his late wife heartbreak. But he remained his own principal victim, and the wartime return to soldiering, which had seemed to come as a blessed release from the boredom of commercial life, had only brought him new bitterness, not to mention physical and mental scars. The unsuccessful flirtation with politics had inevitably added to his disillusionment.

In a way, it was a pity that he was well enough placed financially not to have to take on some humble occupation, which would at least have kept him busy and perhaps done his soul some much-needed good. He spent most of his time prowling restlessly about the house, or listening to his gramophone, or, more rarely, reading the newspapers at his club. He had no long-term ambition, nor even any short-term object: a dangerous state for a man of his temperament.

Richard, entering the morning-room one evening, resplendent in white tie and tails and wearing the orders of a Privy Councillor and the Grand Cross of the Order of St. Michael & St. George, was surprised and at once pleased to see the cheerful expression on his son's face, and the brisk way in which he moved unbidden to pour him a whisky.

'Hello, Father! Where are you off to, all got up like that?'

'A banquet at the Guildhall,' Richard said, accepting the glass. 'If Virginia doesn't make us late, that is.' He glanced at his watch, frowned, and then said, 'Well, what have you been up to today? Looking for a job?'

'No. As I told you, I'm pursuing various lines. I'll tell you when there's any news.'

Richard frowned again. 'I just hope you're not squandering the money Great Aunt Kate left you.'

At most times James would have seized upon this mild caution as an excuse for a petulant outburst. Now, he merely smiled and answered, 'As a matter of fact, I've just spent – *not* squandered – some of that money on something you may regard as an extravagance, but I see as an investment.'

Richard looked at him almost suspiciously. James went on.

'You know I've been having flying lessons at Brooklands.'

'Of course. And got your "A" Certificate.'

'Well, I'm really rather keen on this whole aviation business and its commercial future and . . .'

Richard glanced at the door, wishing Virginia would hurry.

'What are you trying to tell me?'

Sounding like a guilty schoolboy who has spent the change from his shopping errand on sweets, James said, 'I've bought an aeroplane.'

'You've *what*?'

It was easier, now that it was out. 'It's an old two-seater reconnaissance machine, from the Aircraft Disposal Company. An Avro 504. A bit primitive, of course, but absolutely airworthy, and only cost me £275. I took her up today for the first time.'

Richard suppressed a sigh. 'Did you? Well, I suppose you know what you're doing.'

'Of course I do, Father. She handles beautifully – like a thoroughbred hunter with a soft mouth . . .'

Virginia's arrival at that moment cut short the conversation; but the simile between the aircraft and a horse was repeated next morning after breakfast when James came briskly into the morning-room, handsome in jodhpurs, hacking jacket and polo neck jersey, and found his father and stepmother there with the newspapers. Richard had mentioned the aeroplane to Virginia on their way to the Guildhall, and now she questioned James about it, with, he noted, an interest and enthusiasm his father had not displayed.

'Funny thing about riding and flying,' James remarked, having told her all. 'They're really quite alike. My instructor says if you're a good horseman – good hands and a sense of balance – you should make a good pilot.'

'And you're a good horseman,' Virginia said, 'so you must be a good pilot.'

'Well, I don't want to boast, but I *am* pretty good. Got through the course without a mishap and passed my navigation test first time. D'you know, two chaps landed in the sewage farm last week. It's a regular hazard down there – that and the motor-racing track.'

Virginia laughed. 'How fast does your aeroplane go?'

'Oh, 80–90 miles an hour.'

Richard, behind his *Times*, heard James stop suddenly, then say, 'Virginia, I've had a capital idea. It's such a glorious autumn day. Why don't you come down with me and see the old crate? I'll take you up in her, if you like.'

Without hesitation she replied, 'Oh, yes please! I've always wanted to fly.'

They both turned with surprise at the sharpness with which Richard said, 'I don't wish to dampen your enthusiasm, James, but Virginia knows quite well that I'm opening an important debate on Foreign Affairs in the Lords this afternoon.' His annoyed gaze moved to Virginia. 'We arranged last night, you'll recall, that you'd sit with Lady Morling in the Strangers' Gallery and we'd all have tea after the debate.'

Virginia did recall. 'Yes, we did. How depressing.'

James put in, 'Oh, come on, you don't have to, do you? Send word you've got a cold, or something, and come with me.'

His stepmother's answer was a glance at his father, now standing grim-faced.

'Father,' James urged, 'I'm sure Lady Morling won't die of a broken heart if Virginia isn't in the Lords today. It's not always perfect flying weather like this, and she can hear you make a speech any time.'

For one brief instant Richard wondered whether he wasn't being selfish in insisting on his wife's duty to himself. It *was* a beautiful day, and he hated to feel himself the cause of the change of expression on her face from happy excitement to glum acceptance. But his real reason for objecting asserted itself at once: he knew his James and the seeming inevitability with which every point at which he touched life was left bruised. That the boy – the man, nearing middle age, Good Heavens! – was a competent pilot, he didn't doubt, and he expected the machine was sound enough. It was simply that, shameful though it was to admit it, he would trust his wife's safety into many people's hands, but not in those of his own son.

He would never permit himself to put such a hurtful thought into words, however. Instead, he said coldly, 'Virginia is perfectly entitled to choose how she wishes to spend her afternoon. Excuses can be made to the Morlings, if necessary. I merely suggest that it might be more fitting for her to be seen in the Gallery of the House of Lords, when her husband is opening a debate for the Government, than to be seen going up in an aeroplane with her stepson.'

'That's unfair!' Virginia protested, annoyed by the way the pronouncement had sounded, as though she were not even in the room to be consulted.

'What is?'

'To put it all on to me. You know it isn't my decision at all.'

'Do you want me to forbid you to go flying with James – like some stern Victorian husband?'

'I'd almost rather you did. Of course I'd sooner go up in James's machine than sit in the Lords all afternoon. It would be something new. Something to do with the future, not the past.'

A painful silence descended like a fog blanket and hung between them all, until Richard said, 'If you're coming with me to the House, Virginia, we must lunch at one sharp and leave by two-fifteen. I shall be in my study, if you want me.'

He went out, closing the door behind him. Wide-eyed at the schoolmasterly admonition, Virginia turned slowly to James, who said quietly, 'And if you want to come for a joy-ride in my aeroplane, we could leave here at twelve, lunch at Brooklands, and be up in the clear blue sky by two-fifteen. It's for you to say, Virginia. It's your life – not Father's.'

She wandered away to the window, to gaze up at the tempting shimmering blue.

It had not been one of the easiest afternoons below stairs, on account of one new arrival in the household and one relative newcomer.

The latter was Frederick. Startled no less than the female servants by an almighty crash which seemed to come from the butler's pantry, he had rushed to see what was the matter and found Mr. Hudson staring at the dropped tray and scatter of dining-room cutlery at his feet.

'You all right, Mr. Hudson?' Fred asked, genuinely alarmed.

'I ... the tray fell, that is all.'

'I'll see to it,' Frederick offered, squatting to start picking things up, just as Ruby's vacant face peered round the door.

'What's happened?' she asked.

Hudson twitched angrily. 'Nothing has happened. The tray is too wide for the door, that is all. Go back to the kitchen, girl.'

She went, her parting stare irritating him further.

'You should've let me carry it,' Fred said, well-meaningly. 'It's heavy.'

'Frederick, I have been carrying the butler's tray in and out of this pantry since before you were born.'

'Then it's time you stopped, Mr. Hudson. Let a younger man do the heavy work. You've only to call me when there's something you can't manage ...'

Hudson erupted. 'Now, you listen to me, Frederick! If you're going to continue as footman here you'll kindly carry out my orders to you and refrain from making suggestions of that nature. In a residence of this size the butler is responsible at all times for the smooth running of the household ...'

'I was only trying to help, Mr. Hudson. Rose said you wasn't getting any younger, and I was to help you as much as possible.'

'Rose had no business to say that!' Hudson retorted, and Fred retreated, crushed. But he had spoilt Hudson's day.

The other ruffler of domestic tranquillity was Miss Treadwell, the newly-appointed governess to Virginia's children. She had not been encountered in advance by anyone at No. 165, so there had been no chance for report and assessment. Virginia had met her when she had been staying at Harborough Castle, where Miss Treadwell was then in charge of the Honourable Charles Tatham. That young man had now gone away to school, and Virginia had invited the governess to come to London and take charge of Alice and William, over-riding their protests that they were happy enough with things as they were.

Miss Treadwell had not been in the house long before she had made it quite clear what status she proposed to assume. She was in her mid-thirties and not unpleasant to look at, though a prim severity in her face matched her manner. She had been engaged to an officer who had been killed in the war, and since then had worked in aristocratic surroundings. Neither of these was conducive to rapport with ordinary servants. She announced that she would be taking her meals in her room upstairs, or with the children in the dining-room.

'Who's she think she is?' demanded Edward, who had brought her from the station in the car. 'Insisted on sitting behind, 'stead of up front with me.'

'And what's she have to have a tray for?' Ruby asked, laying tea things on it. 'Why can't she eat down here? We could lay a corner of the table.'

'That is out of the question,' Mr. Hudson told her. 'As governess, Miss Treadwell is entitled to her meals in her room, except when she eats with the family.'

'Well, don't expect me to take them up,' Rose snapped, bustling about other duties. 'Daisy can see to all that.'

'I'm not carrying trays up to no governess!' Daisy retorted. 'It's Frederick's place.'

'Don't think I'm the nursery footman!' Fred cautioned them, and received another of Mr. Hudson's reproofs for his pains.

'Now, that's quite enough for one day, Frederick. And all of you, listen to me. I shall assign your duties in consultation with her ladyship and you will carry them out. This is not the kind of household in which we indulge in petty arguments about who is to carry a tray.'

Fred turned away with a wry smile as he recalled the passage of arms about another tray. As he did so he chanced to look out of the window.

'Here!' he exclaimed. 'What's that? Fog?'

'Never!' said Mrs. Bridges, hurrying to peer out into the area. 'It's as bright as . . . Why, I never! You're right, Fred. Must have come down sudden.'

'Cor!' said Edward. 'Can't hardly see the railings.'

Mrs. Bridges turned away with an exasperated click of her teeth.

'Now what's it going to be about dinner? What with his lordship at the House of Lords, and her ladyship and the Major motoring in the country . . .'

'Her ladyship told Miss Treadwell she'd be back by five,' Rose said. 'Because of the children.'

Mr. Hudson looked at his watch. 'Well, it's gone that now. It depends how widespread the fog may be. Best allow for some delay, Mrs. Bridges. If his lordship returns first I will take his instructions.'

Richard did return first. It was after seven, and he told Hudson that his taxi cab had positively crawled the short distance from Westminster. He showed surprise and then annoyance when he was told that no telephone call had been received from the Major and somewhat brusquely told Hudson to find out the number of Brooklands Flying Club and ask for the secretary there.

When Hudson had made the connection and put it through to the morning-room extension he could not restrain himself from listening in. None of the staff had been told the purpose of the motoring expedition and Hudson's expression changed from surprise to incredulity and finally to grave concern as he heard the secretary report to Lord Bellamy that his son had taken off that afternoon in perfectly clear weather, with his stepmother as his passenger, and had not been heard of since.

'Heading for *where*? This line's terrible.'

'South West. Wiltshire. Major Bellamy said he intended showing his stepmother his ancestral home.'

'Southwold! All that way! Would he have enough petrol?'

'Oh, yes. When we hadn't heard anything by six we telephoned to Southwold. A servant answered and said that a plane flew over at about half-past four. That'd be about right.'

'It didn't land?'

'No. Just circled once or twice, then disappeared into cloud.'

'Is this fog down that way, too?'

'I'm afraid so, Lord Bellamy. Naturally, we've put in calls to all the likely aerodromes, civil and military. I'm afraid there's been no news yet.'

'But surely they must be down somewhere by now.'

'Possibly in a field – anywhere. Major Bellamy's been taught how to pick a safe spot for an emergency landing. He wouldn't stay up after dark, for sure.'

'Well . . . thank you, then. You'll telephone me here the very moment you have any news?'

'Of course, Lord Bellamy. I shouldn't worry, if I were you. Your son has all the resource it needs, judging by the way he swam through his training.'

Hudson waited for the click of the morning-room receiver going down before he replaced the earpiece of the wall telephone below stairs. Then, as was his custom, he made a point of immediately visiting the morning-room on some errand and was rewarded by hearing an account of the conversation from Lord Bellamy himself, thus enabling him to report it to the other servants without having to admit to having eavesdropped.

Lily, whom only that morning Rose had taken it into her head to caution about the Major's old propensity for making advances towards female servants, burst into tears as soon as she heard the news. James had never, in fact, given her so much as an appraising look, but Rose's warning had thrilled her and left her speculating how she really

63

would respond if he ever did make approaches to her. She had started to feel almost proprietorial towards him, as the only female in the house likely to attract his interest if he should start feeling 'that way' inclined; and now it seemed as if he had been taken away from her personally.

'Supposing they're crashed and dead!' she wept.

Hudson, harbouring the same fear, tried to reassure himself as well as comfort her.

'It is all in the hands of the Good Lord, Lily. You must not give way to ungrounded fears. Try to have faith and patience.'

'I am, Mr. Hudson. It's just that I couldn't bear to think of the Major . . . and her ladyship . . . I mean, they're both good, kind souls . . .'

'That is indeed so, Lily. On the other hand, we must all spare a thought for his lordship in his anxiety, while we keep in mind the old saying that no news is good news. Now, dry your eyes, girl, and run along with you.'

Upstairs, Richard paced the morning-room, his feelings a bitter mixture of anxiety that some accident had occurred, irritation that, if none had, neither James nor Virginia had seen fit to telephone to reassure him, and the resentment which had been growing in him ever since he had learned finally that Virginia had decided to break her promise to attend the debate and go chasing off with James.

Fortunately for him, a chance caller was the old family friend Lady Prudence Fairfax, cynical looker-on at so many Society dramas and scandals in her time. She was just the sounding-board he needed for the outpouring of the full range of his feelings.

'That bloody fool of a boy! Irresponsible ass. I blame Virginia, too. She ought to have known better.'

'Richard, dear, you must keep calm,' crooned Lady Prue, giving unspoken thanks that she had chanced to become embroiled in something which might be the talk of every-one's table for the next few days at least.

Her soothing only provoked him into deeper unreason.

'They both know perfectly well we dine at eight o'clock

in this house. It's five to eight now. I detest unpunctuality
... keeping the servants hanging about.'

Lady Prue had known him for too many years to rebuke
him. Instead, she calmly suggested that they sit down to
dinner together, and afterwards insisted upon staying with
him as long as might be necessary, even if it meant sleeping
on the settee. When a late hour had been reached with still
no word, Richard tried to make her go home or at least
take one of the bedrooms, but she told him to send the
servants to bed and go up and try to sleep himself. The
telephone should be left connected through to the morning-
room and she would take any call there might come.

Gratefully obedient, for the events of the day on top of the
strain of the debate had produced a fatigue that no amount
of worry could dispel, Richard left her there by the fire,
alone with her thoughts of what might have been, if only
he had needed her after Marjorie's death nearly ten years
ago...

The sound of horse's hooves and the cheery cry of
'Milko!' woke Rose. She raised her eyes blearily, surprised
to find that she had spent the night at the table in the
servants' hall, her head resting on her arms. She shivered
and got up stiffly, noticing simultaneously that it was just
seven o'clock and that Mr. Hudson was asleep in his chair,
his glasses still on his nose and his open book on his knees.

She tiptoed up the stairs, on her way to her first duty,
which was to wake the children. In the hall she met his
lordship coming down, looking rumpled and unshaven.

'Is ... was there any news, my lord?' she asked. He shook
his head.

'Evidently not. Rose, I'm glad to have caught you. You
haven't woken the children yet?'

'No, my lord.'

'Good. Tell Miss Treadwell first that they're not to be
told anything yet. I don't want them upset.'

'Yes, m'lord.'

As Rose went away upstairs the telephone in the morning-room began to ring. Richard hastened in, aware of Prue stirring on the settee. She watched him as he took the call, eagerly at first and then with growing disappointment. His face was set as he put down the instrument at last and turned to her.

'Brooklands. They've had a message from the Coastguard people at Padstow on the North Cornish coast. The lighthouse on Trevose Head reported seeing a small biplane flying low over the sea at about seven o'clock yesterday evening. They couldn't see it clearly for the fog and low cloud, so they weren't sure which direction it was going in. That's all.'

'It can't have been James,' Prue said, sitting up and straightening her hair.

'He could have been off his course.'

'Well, I still think it was some other aeroplane.'

Hudson, who had been awakened by the ringing bell, appeared in the doorway, his face full of frank curiosity.

'Hudson, you'd better tell them downstairs that there's still no news,' Richard said heavily. 'I'd like you all to carry on with your duties as best you can. I shall go up to my dressing-room and shave. Perhaps you'd tell Rose to go up and open the curtains in her ladyship's room. Lady Prudence will need to tidy up in there.'

'Very good, m'lord.'

'We'll breakfast in the dining-room at nine o'clock.'

Breakfast-time came and went with still no news. Twice the telephone rang, and twice it proved to be some call unconnected with the crisis. The third time it started to shrill, Hudson wearily asked Frederick to go and answer it. He had earlier squashed another well-meant effort of the footman's to do one of his tasks for him – Hudson was feeling as tired and drawn as he looked – but now he no longer cared about putting his dignity second. He listened dully as Frederick, unused to telephoning, struggled to hear and shouted back seemingly unnecessarily.

'Pardon? I can't hear you very well. No, the footman speaking. A what? A trunk call? Where from...?'

66

His tiredness forgotten, Hudson sprang to take the receiver, almost wresting it from Frederick's hand and pushing him aside.

'This is Lord Bellamy's butler speaking . . .'

The call was swiftly transferred to the morning-room. From the heightened pitch of Richard's voice and the rapidity of his speech, Prudence could tell that the news was good, though his expression remained grim.

'What time into Paddington? One-seventeen. I understand. Yes, yes, I'll have the train met. I'm most grateful for your help and for letting me know. Goodbye.'

He put down the receiver and turned to Prue, his expression still unchanged.

'They're safe.'

'Thank God. Where?'

'In a train, on their way back from North Cornwall. Newquay, of all places. That was the police. Apparently James lost his bearings in the fog over the West Country. They flew North West from Southwold instead of due East and didn't break through the cloud base until Padstow. The plane ran short of fuel and he had to land it on a deserted beach. They spent the night in it, and this morning James walked four miles to a farm, where there was no telephone. Someone took him into Newquay by pony trap.'

Prudence sighed. 'I'm so very glad it's turned out all right, Richard. I thought it would, but one worries, all the same.'

'Prudence, my dear, you've been a wonderful help. Must you go, though?'

'You've got them back, so I'll retire from the scene. You know you can call on me at any time.'

She kissed him on the cheek and turned towards the door.

'Anyway, I've got my Unmarried Mothers' Committee, so I couldn't have stayed, anyway. Just give them my love.'

'I will.'

'But tell James that if he insists on flying his wretched machine he should fly it round and round the aerodrome by himself. Some of us are getting too old for scares like that.'

She let herself out. A few moments later Hudson entered, to be told the good news by a surprisingly grim-faced Lord Bellamy.

'How dare you do this to me? Damn you! Both of you!'

Richard's face was more than grim as he addressed his damp and dishevelled wife and son, who had, on his orders, been directed into the morning-room immediately on arrival, without being given time to wash or change.

'It was unforgivable,' he went on. 'The entire household has been worrying over you.'

They stood side by side in front of him like an errant brother and sister being chided by their father for some more than trivial offence. James licked his lips, and said, 'I'm sorry, Father. It was all my fault. I shouldn't have attempted Southwold when the cloud started. Then the fog came down so suddenly, and my compass let me down, too. I'm sorry.'

Richard had made no move to kiss or comfort Virginia when they had come in. His rage had to be vented first. Now, though, she ran to him, and he was holding her tight and saying, 'Oh, my darling, I'm sorry. I shouldn't have shouted at you. You're not hurt, are you – either of you?'

She lifted her tear-stained face.

'No, we're not hurt. But you are, and I need your forgiveness. I did a childish, impetuous thing, trying to show my independence, I suppose. I'm deeply sorry, Richard, for all the fuss and worry I've caused you and the servants.'

'You must blame me, Father,' James intervened. 'I egged her on to come. She got caught up in my enthusiasm, that's all.'

Richard at last gave his little smile with one corner of his mouth.

'Well, these things happen, don't they? I suggest we forget the whole thing and thank God you're back. Suppose you

68

go and get cleaned up and changed. I've ordered luncheon at two.'

James nodded and turned away. 'By the way, my aeroplane's only slightly damaged,' he said. 'It will fly again.'

Richard forebore to comment as James went out. Virginia remained in his arms.

'Promise you're not angry any more,' she pleaded up into his eyes.

'My anger was born of sheer blinding fear, my dear,' he said. 'Ever seen a mother thrash her child for running into the road? All that matters now is that I've got you both back – the two people who matter most to me in all the world.'

His smile broadened and he added softly, 'Damn you!'

She nestled her head against him and he stroked her hair.

CHAPTER FOUR

THE younger female servants, except Lily, who was away on her holidays, were frowning over close-work in the servants' hall. The table was a jumble of items of small boy's clothing.

Daisy was sewing Cash's name tapes on to the soft garments. Ruby, her concentration – for want of a better word – fully engaged, painfully lettered the name WILLIAM HAMILTON and the number 48 on the insides of canvas shoes. The tongue which protruded between her lips was empurpled from licking the point of the indelible pencil.

'Fancy,' she said, withdrawing the tongue and grimacing at the taste: 'Master William having a school number. It's like going to prison.'

'And all these labels,' Daisily grumbled.

Mrs. Bridges sat apart in state. She glanced up from her magazine.

'You're lucky. Aren't they, Rose? Remember when the Major went away to his school? No fancy shop-made labels in them days.'

'Yeh,' Rose agreed. 'Every blessed initial to be sewn by hand. I was kept at it for weeks, even with that woman who came in special to help.'

Daisy sighed. 'One day, Ed and I'll have a nice little boy like William.'

Mr. Hudson had entered in time to overhear this hopeful utterance.

'Time enough for that when you get a bit more put away, Daisy. After what occurred last time.'

Daisy protested, 'We're putting something away in the Post Office Savings every week. 'Sides, it wasn't our fault last time. I mean, it was everyone the same. Government said it was a country fit for heroes, and then wouldn't give us no work . . .'

No one answered. It had become a familiar refrain from Daisy since her return to security.

Ruby sighed gustily. 'I wish I could have a little kiddy to send to school.'

Mrs. Bridges and Hudson exchanged a quick and meaningful glance.

'You're well off where you are, Ruby,' Mrs. Bridges told her. 'Remember what happened when *you* went off last time. You got blown up.'

'And you're not even married yet,' Daisy couldn't forbear to add.

Ruby grimaced. 'And it says in t' papers there's a shortage of men . . .'

The tongue emerged again, moistened the purple pencil tip, and she bent to the task of etching an unsymmetrical M.

That evening, James's old school trunk and tuck box, both re-lettered WILLIAM HAMILTON, had been packed, with every last item carefully placed by Rose, assisted, as tally clerk, by Alice. Then Rose withdrew, leaving the children washed and bedded and reading their books, until Virginia came in, dressed for dinner, to kiss them goodnight. The usual requests for time to read 'just one more page' having been turned down, she reminded them of their prayers. Both dutifully got out of bed and knelt. Alice, as always, prayed silently; William, out loud.

'God bless Mummy and Alice . . . and Uncle Richard, and . . . and Aunt Georgina, and Uncle James . . . and Rose and Mrs. Bridges and Mr. Hudson and . . . and everyone else downstairs . . .' He made his usual pause before adding, 'And Daddy and Michael, in Heaven.'

He was getting up, when Virginia reminded him, ' "And Miss Treadwell".'

'Oh, lor',' he groaned, subsiding briefly. 'And Miss Treadwell.' He scrambled up and into bed. Virginia sat on the coverlet.

'Darling, you must promise to go on saying your prayers every night at school.'

'Yes, Mummy. Can I say them in bed?'

'Unless the other boys kneel. Do what they do.'

She picked up the Teddy Bear nestling beside him and regarded its worn countenance, so long taken for granted, with new awareness.

'Perhaps . . . it would be best not to take Edward to school.'

It was the end of something in the lives of mother, child and toy bear.

'Yes, Mummy,' William said. 'I suppose it would.'

'He'll be all right here – waiting for you when you come home.'

There was a knock at the door.

'Yes, Rose,' Virginia called. 'All right.'

Both children stared as Rose entered, wondering how their mother had known it was she who had knocked. Rose was smirking.

'Rose has a surprise for you both,' their mother said. 'Are you ready, Rose?'

'Yes, m'lady. If the children will put on their dressing-gowns and slippers . . .'

It was no sooner requested than done. Rose led all three to her own room. She pushed open the door and stood aside for them to go in.

Blinking in the electric light was a small, brown, long-haired dog, sitting up on its forelegs in a wicker basket.

The children gaped vocally.

'It's to keep Miss Alice company while you're away, Master William,' Rose explained in a rush. 'Of course, it's yours too, though. You remember that day when we was in the park, and you said you wished you could have a dog . . .'

They ran to pet the little animal, which writhed and rolled appreciatively.

'Oh, darling doggie!' Alice exclaimed. 'But aren't you thin! Lots of lovely dinners . . .'

'Thanks so much, Rose,' William said, going to give her a kiss. 'Mummy, can we show him to Treadie, please?'

Virginia nodded. 'I have to go down, darlings. Rose will see you to bed again. Not too long, now.'

They kissed her and she went away, her long dress caught up in one hand. Alice scooped up the dog before William could beat her to it. 'You can carry the basket,' she condescended.

Miss Treadwell was reading in the schoolroom. She looked up, frowning, when the door burst open without a knock and the voices of her two charges cried, excitedly and simultaneously, 'Look what Rose has given us, Miss Treadwell!'

'A dog,' William added superfluously.

The governess stood up, wrinkling her nose. 'I can see that, without having it thrust in my face.'

Rose came forward from the landing. 'Her ladyship said it would be all right, seeing as Master William was going to school.'

'Did she? Is it house-trained?'

'Oh, yes. It said on the notice I saw in a shop in Pont Street. "A well trained dog, ten months, wanting a nice home," 'cos the people was going to Canada.'

'What shall we call it, Rose?' Alice asked.

'Oh, he's got a name already, Miss Alice. He's Thimble.'

'Thimble! Darling Thimble! Oh, what a perfect, divine name!'

Rose looked from the children to Miss Treadwell: clearly, she was not amused.

The painful moment of William's departure had come and gone. He had gone bravely, smart in his new grey flannel suit, in a trouser pocket of which reposed a half-guinea piece, slipped to him by Richard at the last moment: it was the most valuable coin the child had ever possessed. Grave handshakes for all the staff ('Proper little gentleman; he really is,' Daisy had declared afterwards); but for Rose, a fierce hug and a warm kiss, which had made the watching Miss Treadwell's lips tighten. Then Edward had driven the car away, and in a moment it was out of sight.

Hudson closed the front door, and a pall of anti-climax fe
upon upstairs and downstairs, as everyone resumed his
her activity, a little sadder and quieter than before.

The ex-diplomatist in Richard had ensured that I
should have a plan ready by which to divert his wife
thoughts. Meeting him in the hall a few days previously
he returned from the House of Lords, she had looked wi
concern at the lines of tiredness in his face and begged hi
to take things more easily. He shook his head.

'I went to see Dr. Foley only this morning. Everythin
fine. Just getting old, that's all.'

She led him by the arm into the morning-room a
poured him a whisky and soda.

'Mind you,' he confessed, 'would you forgive me if
didn't change for dinner?'

She was already changed, but she shook her head e
phatically.

'Of course I wouldn't. It's almost ready, anyway, a
there's a cheese *soufflé* first. If you were late it could tu
out a disaster and I'd have Mrs. Bridges to reckon with.'

'I might have Hudson to reckon with if I don't chang
he answered with his wry smile. 'Ten years ago I would
even have dreamed of it. He'll think I'm getting sla
and slovenly.'

'You're just tired, and he can think what he likes. Darli
I really do think you ought to get out of this French tri

'Oh, not possible. The King and Queen are going, a
I'm on the War Graves Committee.'

His cue had come to enact his plan, and he took it.

'I've just had a splendid idea, though. I'm going to t:
you with me.'

'Oh, darling!'

'Yes. And afterwards we'll go on to Baden Baden fo
week's rest, and then to the Martels, near Aix. They
absolute old darlings, and they never stop asking us.'

'Well, I suppose with William gone it would be a go
idea to be out of the house to let the servants do the spr
cleaning. What about poor Alice, though?'

'Oh, Miss Treadwell and the others will look after her. They'll all spoil her like anything, you'll see.'

The door opened and Hudson entered. He viewed Richard with open surprise, though it was Virginia he addressed.

'Er, pardon me, m'lady . . . are you and his lordship ready for dinner?'

'Quite ready, thank you, Hudson,' Virginia said, amused by the unspoken criticism, but not showing it.

'In er, that case, m'lady . . . dinner is served.'

And so, William having departed, the eve of Richard and Virginia's own going had been reached. In the schoolroom, Virginia conducted her final interview with Miss Treadwell; or rather, Miss Treadwell conducted the final interview with her.

'The novelty of it is quite exciting at first,' she remarked of the brave face William had worn on leaving home. 'I usually find the second term is the worst, especially for boys.'

Dampened, Virginia said, 'I hope Alice will be all right.'

'I am sure she will. Alice is by no means a stupid girl, but she finds it difficult to concentrate. I think it will be easier for her with William away. We can do proper school hours and evening homework.'

Virginia made the best of things.

'Miss Treadwell, it is such a relief for my husband and myself to be able to go away leaving Alice – indeed, the whole household – in such capable hands.'

'Thank you, Lady Bellamy.' Miss Treadwell gave one of her rare, thin smiles. 'I hope it will be understood by everyone in the house, including the butler, that I am responsible in your absence.'

'Oh yes. I shall make that quite clear.'

'Thank you. I only hope the dog will not prove another, er, disruptive influence.'

'I'm sure not. Rose is willing to look after him during school hours.'

Miss Treadwell made no reply. After a few more words on practical matters Virginia left her, to go downstairs. As she was about to pass William's bedroom she paused, opened the door, and switched on the light. It looked neat, so tidy, so . . . empty. She went in. Edward Bear w sitting on the chest of drawers, his glass eyes unusual devoid of their make-believe life. Impulsively, Virgin picked him up and took him to the bed. She turned it dov and tucked him in.

A shadow fell across her from the doorway. She turne to see Richard, in evening dress. He came to her and kiss her tenderly on the cheek. She brushed away a tear.

'It didn't seem so bad when Michael went away Osborne. But William . . . he seems so small, and defend less.'

'He'll be all right. He's got good manners and he kno how to get on with people and when to keep his mou shut. It's the bumptious ones who get into trouble.'

'I know. But . . . why? I mean, the French don't . . .'

Richard seated himself beside her on the bed, his ar around her.

'I don't know why,' he said, 'but we're the only nation the world that tears the male patrician child from the boso of his family, to be subjected to cold baths, football a Latin infinitives, at the tender age of eight years.'

He felt Virginia shudder slightly.

'What is it?''

'Just suddenly, I wish we weren't going away.'

'I think it's a jolly good thing we are. Make a change ! you. Miss Treadwell's perfectly competent, isn't she?'

'Yes. I think so. I don't like her much.'

'Governesses aren't supposed to be liked, are the At least she seems a stayer, and that's a rarity in my perience. I can't tell you what a time we had with Elizabe Her governess came and went like clockwork mice. course, it was mostly Elizabeth's fault. She was a little dev There was one rather pretty, shy French woman . Elizabeth found out that she had a silly crush on me a forced the poor creature to race her down the back sta on a tin tray and give her free sweets, or she'd give her aw to Marjorie.'

76

Virginia smiled at last.

'Girls are much nastier than boys, Richard. They've much more imagination – but I can't see Alice getting Miss Treadwell racing downstairs on a tin tray. Still, you're right. It's probably quite a good thing we're going away.'

That wasn't how the servants saw it, however.

'Schoolroom, Frederick,' Daisy said, as the bell rang, yet again. It was two days after Lord and Lady Bellamy had left. To those below stairs, it seemed as if their considerate master and mistress had been replaced by some sort of Corporation For The Full-Time Employment Of Servants.

Frederick put aside his pipe and newspaper and went out without a word.

'Whatever can she want now?' Rose speculated, holding wool for Daisy to wind. 'They've had their tea.'

Mrs. Bridges looked up from her magazine.

'Marvellous, the way that boy never complains. The way he has him going up and down them stairs, like an Egyptian slave. If it's been once, it's been twenty times today . . .'

'Now, Mrs. Bridges,' said Mr. Hudson, coming into the servants' hall from his pantry. 'If the governness wants something, that is what the footman is here for. With *Them* all away, there's very little else to occupy him – or any of you, come to that.'

He said it unconvincingly, and made no attempt to rebuke Rose when she threw the wool down on to the table and stalked out.

'She can't keep still, that girl,' Mrs. Bridges said uneasily. 'Fidgety.'

Up in the schoolroom, Miss Treadwell was saying to Alice, who had just kissed Thimble and been licked in return: 'Alice, you must not put your face near that dog. Dogs are dirty. Think of the places they go. And I said that dog was not to be brought into the schoolroom during study hours.'

There was a knock at the door and Frederick came in, his handsome face impassive. He did not speak.

77

'Frederick,' Miss Treadwell commanded, 'you will take the dog to Rose's room, please.'

'Yes, Miss Treadwell.'

He went to take the animal from Alice. It seemed that she might turn her back on him, holding Thimble tighter in her arms. His expression gave her no hint about what he might do if she did. She thought it prudent to surrender.

The spring cleaning began next day. In all the reception rooms sheets were spread over the furniture and the net curtains taken down for washing. On a trestle table in the morning-room, basins of hot and cold water stood on a sheet, upon which were also strewn the hundreds of crystal drops which had formed one of the chandeliers. As Daisy washed each one in the warm water and then rinsed it in the cold, Rose took it over to give it a first polish and then a little wiping with powder-blue, to give it an extra sparkle after the final brisk rub.

Both heads turned and both pairs of eyes stared astonishedly as the double doors opened and Miss Treadwell entered, followed by an expressionless Frederick carrying a coffee tray. He moved ahead of her and whisked back the dustsheet from a fireside chair. Miss Treadwell seated herself stiffly. Frederick set down the tray and began to pour.

Though each felt her indignation matching the other's, Rose and Daisy remained faithful to their training. They laid down their work and quietly they quitted the room.

'Well! Who's she think she is?' The explosion came outside, in the hall, from Daisy. Rose remained silent, white-faced and tight-lipped, until Frederick emerged, closing the doors behind him. Their challenge needed no words to convey it. He shrugged, and told them, 'It's not my place to disobey orders.'

Mr. Hudson supported him, in the servants' hall, a few angry moments later.

'She asked Frederick to serve her coffee in the morning room, and Frederick consulted me. I could see no reasonable grounds for refusing her request. Miss Treadwell is the governess in this house, and before she left the mistress asked me to do my best to see that she was comfortable.'

'All right for her to be comfortable!' Rose flared. 'Whoever heard of a governess being served coffee in the morning-room? Anyway, couldn't the little cow see we was working in there?'

'Rose!' Mr. Hudson admonished, though with less than complete conviction. 'I am sure Miss Treadwell has two eyes in her head, the same as everyone else. Could . . . you not find some other occupation in the meantime?'

'I tell you, Mr. Hudson,' Rose threatened between her teeth; 'if her ladyship was here . . .'

He could only reply lamely, 'Her ladyship is not here. So let us please be sensible.' He gesticulated with unhappy authority. 'All of you . . . Mrs. Bridges, Ruby . . . you too, please. I want you to listen. The governess, Miss Treadwell, does not wish Miss Alice to visit the servants' quarters in future.'

He raised his hand to quell a murmur of disapproval; both children had always been welcome below stairs, and only that morning Mrs. Bridges had been teaching Alice to bake tartlets and make Genoese paste.

'In future, when you come upon Miss Alice in the normal course of your duties you will treat her with polite formality, just as you would any other member of the family.'

Rose demanded, 'What's all this in aid of, Mr. Hudson? That's what I'd like to know.'

'And so would I,' Mrs. Bridges pouted.

Before this firing-squad of females, with no hope of rescue by the silent Frederick, Mr. Hudson floundered on, 'It, ah, it appears that Miss Alice has been somewhat backward and inattentive with her work lately. The governess believes that fraternising with the servants has not been, ah, beneficial to her concentration.'

'Piffle!' Rose told him. ' "Fraternising with the servants", indeed! I'm going to treat Miss Alice just like I've always treated her – so there!'

'Oh dear, oh dear,' said Mr. Hudson's oldest and staunchest ally, Mrs. Bridges, when the hostile meeting had dispersed. 'How long's this going on for, Mr. Hudson?'

He shook his head. 'I don't know, Mrs. Bridges. I really don't know.'

They had not long to wait for the next crisis. Alice had arranged to collect the little dog from Rose's room next morning at eleven, to take him into the park. When that hour came, Miss Treadwell was just ordering her pupil to write out Coleridge's poem *Kubla Khan* four times.

'But it's nearly eleven, Miss Treadwell. I'm to take Thimble to the park.'

'Well, we are not now going to the park, so let this be a lesson to us not to be inattentive.'

'But Miss Treadwell . . . !'

'*And* argumentative!'

Rose was busy and had expected Alice to fetch the dog. Since neither went for him, the result, by the time both did, meeting in the doorway, was that the poor little thing had long since been unable to contain himself. He watched contritely as both mopped away with cloths at the surprisingly large pool, for so small a dog, which he had reluctantly created.

'He must have been bursting,' Rose said pityingly, though with something of a giggle.

'I'm sorry, Rose. Miss Treadwell just wouldn't let me go.'

'Alice!' snapped that lady's voice from behind them. 'Go to the schoolroom at once. At once, please.'

Rose glared malevolently at the figure in the doorway as the child slid past.

'I thought that dog was supposed to be house-trained,' Miss Treadwell said, as she turned and went. Rose made a gesture she would not have resorted to had the child still knelt beside her.

'Bread and water!' Mrs. Bridges exploded when the governess's latest edict reached her as she was finishing preparing that evening's meal. 'I never heard nothing like it. It's like putting the poor child to medieval torture. And

80

I suppose *she* expects a slap-up dinner in the dining-room.'

Mr. Hudson did his unenthusiastic best to defend the rule of law.

'Miss Treadwell's orders are to be obeyed, Mrs. Bridges. And we do know that Miss Alice can be very wilful and obstinate on occasion.'

'Stuff and nonsense! She's as sweet as a lamb, that child. And clever. It's the way people are treated that counts. Why, she's only a little girl still.'

'When I was her age,' Ruby offered, 'I'd run away from t'mill into service.'

Mrs. Bridges flourished a saucepan under her nose.

'Yes. And from the state of this, it's a pity you didn't stay in the mill.'

'Dried up old bitch!'

They all looked up in astonishment, to see Rose in the doorway, the dog in her arms. Her usually pale cheeks were scarlet and her fine eyes were like polished minerals, flashing with her reflected hate.

'Really, Rose . . .' Mr. Hudson began, but she ignored him.

'I don't care what anyone says. She *is* one – and a witch, too, if you ask me. I love Miss Alice. She's a real darling, and that dried up stick of a woman hates her. She shouldn't be allowed near her, let alone in charge.'

'What is it, Rose?' Mrs. Bridges asked. Even Rose's fury had not burned up her sense of propriety: she put the animal down in the servants' hall, rather than commit the gross sin of bringing him into Mrs. Bridges' kitchen. Then she herself came in and told them of the latest outrage.

'Miss Alice had Thimble in her room for a bit . . . Well, I know she wasn't supposed, but I thought it would calm her after that telling-off. She heard that woman coming and hid him in a cupboard, but she found him. She was going to thrash the poor little animal with a slipper, only Miss Alice pulled her away. Then Miss Treadwell slapped her, and Miss Alice hit her back and scratched her.'

81

'That was a terrible thing for a child to do to her governess,' Hudson said, genuinely horrified.

Mrs. Bridges added thoughtfully, 'Master William seemed very fond of her. She can't be all that bad . . .'

At that moment, Frederick came in from the servants' hall, to ask, 'Schoolroom supper ready, Mrs. Bridges?'

Mrs. Bridges seemed to make up her mind.

'Yes, it is,' she said firmly. 'Two trays tonight. Bread and water for Miss Alice.' She gestured towards a tray Ruby had already prepared. 'And for Miss Treadwell . . .' Mrs. Bridges picked up a saucepan from the side of the cooker and poured its contents unceremoniously on to a cold plate: '. . . some nice congealed stew.'

They all watched intently as the glutinous mess spread and settled in its own fat. Even the impassive Frederick gulped.

'She won't like it.'

The cook demolished him with a glare. 'You just take it up, and stop answering back.'

'Yes, Mrs. Bridges.'

Miss Treadwell did not like it, and presently summoned Mr. Hudson to the morning-room, where he found her grimacing over a cup of tepid and gritty coffee.

'You wished to see me . . . ?' He managed to avoid saying 'Miss' or 'Miss Treadwell'.

'Yes, Hudson, I did. Firstly, it was to ask you to tell Mrs. Bridges that my supper was quite inedible. One would have expected, in a house like this, that something might be properly cooked, even if simple.'

'I will speak to her . . .'

'Now, about the dog. I'm sorry to say I find its presence in this house a distruptive and disturbing influence which cannot go on. I have decided to take it to a veterinary surgeon, to be disposed of in a humane manner.'

For once in his life, Hudson almost stammered.

'I . . . I am sure that Rose could . . . could keep the dog in some safe place . . .'

'On the contrary, I find that Rose has signally failed to look after it, as I was promised she would.'

'I see. But, er, have you mentioned this to Miss Alice . . . ?'

'I think that is hardly your concern, Hudson,' Miss Treadwell said, rejecting the coffee finally. 'Please see that the animal is put into a basket or other receptacle and brought to the hall at ten o'clock tomorrow morning. I shall require a taxicab and the services of the footman to carry the animal. That is all, thank you.'

Shattered, Hudson picked up the coffee tray and went in silence. When he told his news in the kitchen the servants' brief feeling of triumph won for them by Mrs. Bridges was swept away by a flood-tide of dismay, anger, and then rebellion.

At ten o'clock precisely next morning Mr. Hudson entered the hall from the pass door, to find Miss Treadwell standing there, thin and erect in her severe outdoor clothes.

'Well?' she demanded without preamble. 'Where is the dog?'

'I, er, I'm sorry, Miss Treadwell. It appears it has been, er, mislaid.'

She had been half-expecting this. Her look blended anger and disdain.

'You mean it has been deliberately mislaid. Hidden, no doubt.'

'Er, Rose reported to me that . . .'

'Where is Rose?'

'In the servants' hall . . . Miss.'

Without hesitation, Miss Treadwell swept past him and through the pass door, down into the hall. The servants were grouped together, apprehensive but defiantly silent as her gaze raked them.

'Hudson, will you please ask the staff the whereabouts of Miss Alice's dog?'

Her eyes had come to rest on Rose. Before Hudson could obey or answer, Rose was saying, 'If you 're asking me . . .'

'Yes, I am asking you, Rose.'

'Very well, *Miss* Treadwell. In the first place, my name isn't Rose. It's *Miss* Buck, so please don't forget it. I'm Lady Bellamy's maid and I don't take orders from nobody else in this household – certainly no governess. And secondly, that dog don't belong to you or me or to anyone else except Miss Alice, and she loves it.'

'Where *is* it?'

'I dunno; and if I did I wouldn't tell you. You're the last person in the world I would tell, because you can't stand seeing people fond of each other, like Miss Alice is fond of Thimble, and I'm fond of her, and she's fond of me. It drives you mad with jealousy, doesn't it?'

'Rose!' Mr. Hudson interjected weakly, but she ignored him, thrusting her face towards Miss Treadwell, as if to give more velocity to her words.

'Poor thing! What hope for you is there in this world?'

The contempt, put in this form, hurt Miss Treadwell, war-widow, keenly; but Miss Treadwell, governess, managed to conceal it. She turned her look upon each servant in turn. They stared her out blankly – all except Ruby, who lacked the resources to do so.

'It . . .' she blurted. 'It run away.'

In the moment of silence which followed there was almost an air of apprehension that Rose would fling herself on Ruby to silence her physically. But there was no need; Miss Treadwell was turning contemptuously away.

'So this is a conspiracy of silence. I hope you are aware of what you are doing, that's all I can say. Lord and Lady Bellamy are returning tomorrow – and then, God help you all.'

They watched silently as she stalked away up the stairs and let the door at their top thud behind her. There was no jubilation at her rout. Mutiny by servants against their officially designated superior was almost as serious a matter as its equivalent on the high seas; and if the penalty were not quite so drastic, the thought of possible dismissal with a bad reference, or no reference at all, was a sobering one.

Even the considerate nature of Lord and Lady Bellamy couldn't be taken for granted.

They went about their duties quietly. Only Frederick, the war survivor who had come unscathed through too much to care overly about the possible outcome of a domestic fracas, moved close to Daisy and whispered, 'After all that, where is it?'

She couldn't help giving a little smirk as she replied, 'In Eddie's and my room, over the garage.'

Later, when they could bring themselves to discuss it, the servants debated whether or not Miss Alice should be told of Thimble's whereabouts. Rose, who had heard the child sobbing, was all for writing a reassuring note and pushing it under the child's door. Mr. Hudson, whom the conspiracy had regarded as merely a watcher-on so far, hastened to deter her.

'I think you would be most unwise, Rose. A child in Miss Alice's state should not be entrusted with secrets. She'll blurt it out and then that . . . that woman will have the dog along at the vet's first thing.'

Rose regarded Hudson with new respect, but said, 'You mean we've got to leave her in ignorance all this time? Thinking maybe he's run away, or something?'

'I tell you, it's the only way, Rose. In fact, if Miss Alice does question you – any of you – you'd better say her dog is missing. The police have been informed and are confident of finding him. Remind her that he has his name and this address on his collar.'

The night held many anxious minutes for most of them, on several accounts. They were not to be kept long in suspense next morning, however, for their master and mistress were due at an early hour off the boat train. Edward drove off to meet them and the bustle of getting the house into final immaculacy made the time go swiftly. At length, the car was at the front door, Frederick was bringing in the many pieces of baggage, and Mr. Hudson and Rose were helping their employers off with their coats. The holiday had clearly done them both good. Lord

85

Bellamy looked relaxed and younger. Her ladyship, in a Paris-tailored outfit in mauve, with a hat to match, was smiling and positively lovely.

'I trust you had a good trip, m'lord?' Hudson enquired.

'Excellent, thank you,' Richard smiled, allowing himself to give his stomach a meaningful little pat. 'Wonderful food . . . Oh, don't tell Mrs. Bridges I said that!'

Hudson smiled and asked, 'M'lady, will you be requiring breakfast?'

'No thank you. We had it on the boat train. Some coffee would be nice, though, wouldn't it, Richard?'

He had barely had time to nod when a little thunderbolt in white hurtled down the main stairs and into Virginia's arms.

'Oh, Mummy, Mummy!' Alice sobbed.

Surprised at the emotional greeting, Virginia asked, 'Darling? How are you?'

'Terrible! Everything's awful. Come in here.'

She dragged her mother into the morning-room. Richard paused for a questioning glance at Hudson and Rose before going quickly in. The two servants exchanged a look of their own, before Hudson jerked his head and they went below stairs to order the coffee.

Richard Bellamy had never been a man eager to come to grips with the crises of domestic life. When Marjorie had been alive she had been so adept at handling any situation, whether it stemmed from above stairs or below, or both, that he had acquired the habit of leaving her to deal with it, while he shut himself away with his letters, or, in more extreme circumstances, hurried off to his club or suddenly remembered some business needing urgent attention at his office.

Now, he found himself thinking, he had only to step happily back into the house after only a fortnight away, to find himself beset by turmoil at once. Instinctively, he took out his watch, but put it away at once. No possible excuse would do this time. Besides, he was genuinely concerned to know what had upset his stepdaughter to make her cry so bitterly.

After some moments her mother succeeded in calming her and persuading her to tell what was the matter.

'Poor . . . poor Thimble's lost and Miss Treadwell's been dreadfully horrid. Rose thinks she's a bit cuckoo, and so do I. And,' the child added, more urgently, to her astonished mother, 'whatever she says, don't believe a word.'

The warning was delivered only just in time, for Hudson had entered. He paused respectfully to gain Virginia's attention before saying, 'The governess would like a word with you, m'lady.'

Richard protested, 'But we've only just come off the train . . .'

But Miss Treadwell was pushing past the butler and into the room. Her thin face was paler than ever and her lips were trembling with agitation as she said, 'This matter is extremely urgent, Lady Bellamy. If you please . . .'

Virginia looked at Richard. He could only shrug.

'All right,' she agreed. 'Alice, darling, you go and help Rose unpack our things.'

'Yes, Mummy,' Alice said, casting a meaningful glance behind her as she went to the door, where Hudson gently ushered her out and followed.

Virginia sat down and gave Miss Treadwell a smile.

'We were so sorry to hear about the dog,' she told the governess, who still stood unsmiling.

Miss Treadwell came close to snorting.

'If you ask me, the servants are hiding it. It's not lost. Not lost at all. It's all part of their plot.'

'Plot?' Richard and Virginia exchanged glances again. Miss Treadwell saw them.

'Oh, I expect Hudson's been telling you a pack of lies about me.'

Richard could be firm when provoked. 'Miss Treadwell, I have known Hudson half my life, and I can assure you he is one of the most honest men I've ever come across.'

Virginia said, more gently, 'What has been the trouble?'

With a rush, the governess let off all the steam which had been building up inside her.

'Every single person in this household has conspired to subvert my authority, Lady Bellamy. The lady's maid has been impertinent and has insulted me to my face in front of the others. The butler has disobeyed my orders and lied to me. The cook has tried to poison me. The footman laughs at me behind my back. In all my experience, I have never known such a disobedient, mutinous pack of servants. No wonder your daughter is such a tiresome, wilful girl when she is allowed to mix with them. She actually struck me, that child. She needs a good beating. And as for that dog . . .'

Her near-hysterical tirade was cut off, not by any reprimand from her amazed employers, but by the sound of the door opening behind her. She stopped and turned to see Frederick carrying the silver tray with the coffee things. Mr. Hudson entered the room with him and deftly helped him set out the pieces.

'There is good news about the dog, m'lady,' Hudson said blandly, as though unaware of the tension in the air. 'It has been found in the mews.'

His smile took in Miss Treadwell as he turned to follow Frederick out of the room. The governess was beside herself.

'There! What did I tell you, Lady Bellamy? The second you get back, the dog is miraculously found. And the sooner it is got rid of and put to sleep, the better . . .'

'Put to sleep!'

'It is a dirty, destructive animal. Half the trouble in this place has been caused by that dog. As I said at the time . . .'

Virginia's expression was anything but smiling now as she cut in briskly, 'Miss Treadwell, it sounds to me that you would be happier away from here.'

'I can assure you, I wouldn't have stayed another minute in this miserable house but for a sense of loyalty to you and Lord Bellamy.'

'That is very loyal of you. Well, we are back now, so you

needn't worry any further. May I suggest two weeks' wages in lieu of notice?'

A flush which had risen to Miss Treadwell's cheeks with her outburst deepened swiftly.

'So I'm to be thrown out, like a . . . a . . .'

Richard reminded her, 'But you yourself suggested . . .'

She interrupted rudely, 'I suggest you get rid of Rose and that . . . that butler, and then perhaps you might get some control over your own daughter.'

'I think that's up to us to decide,' Virginia snapped back.

'Oh, yes! I knew you wouldn't listen to me. You never do, you sort of people. No wonder your servants run riot the moment your back is . . .'

'Miss Treadwell!' Richard stopped her. Even in her rage she knew better than to go on.

'Very well. I know when I'm not wanted. I'll go with pleasure. *Four* weeks' *salary* it should be, if you look at the usual terms of employment as laid down by the agencies.'

She turned swiftly and went. When the door had shut Richard groaned aloud and began to pour the coffee.

Virginia said, 'Oh dear! I really think she is rather mad. I do hate rows. I wonder if I've enough money to pay her, without going to the bank.'

He got out his wallet and peered in.

'How much a week?'

'One pound ten.'

Richard fingered notes. 'Yes, I can manage.'

He sighed inwardly. In the absence of the complete freedom of being away on holiday, the hurly-burly of politics and his clubs seemed so inviting, compared with domesticity. It was a pity. He'd known so much happiness in this home. A good deal of sorrow and strife, too, but happy memories predominated. It was the niggling, tiresome little incidents such as this which seemed to drain one so.

He wondered passingly what it would be like to live without servants. Simply exchanging one lot of problems for another, he was sure. In any case, such a notion was as unthinkable as another world war.

Virginia felt suddenly deflated, too. After drinking the coffee and glancing through a few letters she went slowly up to her room, where she found Rose and Alice putting her things into piles for washing, sending to the laundry, and other purposes. The smiles with which both greeted her lifted her spirits a little.

Rose managed to whisper, briefly out of the child's earshot, 'I hope you don't think I deliberately disobeyed Miss Treadwell, m'lady.'

Virginia shook her head. 'Of course not, Rose.'

'If I did, it was for Miss Alice's sake – and for poor Thimble.'

Alice came and clung to her mother.

'Mummy, when Miss Treadwell's gone, need I have another governess?'

'I don't think so, dear. Uncle Richard and I have just had a word or two about it. He thinks it would be best if you went to a day school.'

'Oh, yes please, Mummy! Horrible old . . .'

Virginia stopped her firmly.

'That's enough, now.' She changed her tone deliberately. 'I've had a letter from William. Here you are.'

Alice took it eagerly. 'Listen, Rose,' she commanded, and read out carefully: 'Dear Mummy, I hope you are well. I am very well. We had a lecher – he means lecture, silly – about lifeboats it was very good. I am in dorm. B. Must stop now. Lots of love to everyone including Treadie and Thimble.'

She handed the letter back with a smile.

'Well, William loved her, anyway. I suppose that's something.'

CHAPTER FIVE

MR. HUDSON, Mrs. Bridges and Daisy watched, with varying expressions of curiosity and trepidation, as Edward gestured to Lily, positioning her exactly where he wanted her a few feet away from the servants' hall table, round which the others were gathered. In her hand she held a short, wand-like piece of metal, connected by a wire to the box of gadgetry on the table.

'Just there, Lily. Now, hold perfectly still.'

'That looks very dangerous, Edward,' Mr. Hudson said. 'Are you sure you know what you're doing?'

Edward nodded, intent upon connecting two more wires from the box to the lower end of a metal horn, fluted at its mouth like an open flower and clearly descended in design from the long-familiar gramophone horn.

'It's all right, Mr. Hudson. It's just an aerial. There's no electricity going through it. Now, all we have to do is connect the terminals to the battery . . . Now, to switch on . . .'

He turned one of the knobs protruding from the side of the box. There was no explosion, no movement, no sound – nothing at all.

Mrs. Bridges snorted. 'Just as I thought.'

'It's got to warm up,' Edward told her. 'Just wait and see.'

And in a few moments a pink glow was appearing in each of the two valves on the box's top. Faintly, then louder, there came from the horn the moans and crackles of 'atmosphere', to give way at last to the tinny sound of a soprano voice warbling an operatic aria to piano accompaniment.

Edward looked round the others proudly.

'There you are – Station 2LO of the British Broadcasting

Company, Savoy Hill. Been broadcasting every day since last November.'

'Isn't it beautiful music?' Daisy said, wide-eyed.

'More like a parrot squawking, if you ask me,' Mrs. Bridges said. 'Where's it coming from, anyway? Them bulbs?'

'Valves, Mrs. B,' Edward corrected. 'It's coming through the air, in waves.'

'Through the air? If you expect me to believe that that voice is coming here from Savoy Hill, all through the traffic and the houses and that . . . *And* with the window closed! How can waves of air get through solid glass? Answer me that one.'

Lily tried, 'Perhaps they're getting through that crack under the back door.'

The song ended and a male announcer's voice was heard.

'And now to the Sporting News. The Football Association Cup Final this year will be held at the new Wembley Stadium and will be between Bolton Wanderers and West Ham United . . .'

'Switch off the apparatus, please, Edward,' Mr. Hudson requested. 'West Ham should never have reached Wembley.'

'Oh, no, Mr. Hudson!' Daisy was protesting, but it was not objection to the content of the news that had motivated him. He alone had heard a taxicab stopping outside the house and anticipated the ringing of the front door bell, which now occurred.

'That will be the Major returning. Now, do as I say, please.'

Edward obeyed, and Mr. Hudson went away up the stairs.

'Out again, was he?' Mrs. Bridges said, shaking her head. 'Poor lonely soul. I wonder what he does?'

'Goes to his club, I reckon,' Daisy answered. 'Or one of them. He belongs to dozens.'

Edward corrected his wife. 'Most likely the Hot Cat Club in Gerrard Street, these nights. His evening things don't half stink of scent.'

It had, indeed, been the Hot Cat Club; as it was again the following evening. James's restlessness was increasing. As each new attempt at diminishing it failed, it was as if it fed upon that failure, and grew. His foray into politics had got him nowhere. The sudden preoccupation with flying had only forced-landed him into trouble. Now, feeling himself virtually incapable of positive effort, he had taken to mooning about the house or his gentlemen's clubs for most of the day, then a taxi to the Hot Cat in the evenings, there to dance and drink with any girl who would share his table and his bottle and his dance-floor embrace for the going rate of payment.

Now, on this spring evening of 1923, he was dancing again with a girl who had partnered him several times before – a respectable young war orphan who had taken the job at a friend's urging in order to escape the tumult of the apartment she shared with two other girls from the wholesale clothing store in which she worked by day. They had little to say to one another: the tired girl going through the paid motions, the listless James unsuccessfully seeking however little of that increasingly elusive quality, pleasure.

On one or two of their encounters he had wondered whether it would be worth asking the girl to go to bed with him. She didn't seem the promiscuous type, but perhaps she would agree. He could no doubt persuade her to accept some sort of present which would not leave her feeling she had prostituted herself.

He was thinking such a thought again this evening. But, as always, the problems seemed insuperable. He couldn't ask her to take him back to her small shared room. He couldn't take her to Eaton Place. There were no rooms on the premises of the Hot Cat Club. The only remaining alternative was to hire a short-time room in some back-street hotel, a notion which filled James with revulsion as he pictured the receptionist's studied nonchalance, to be followed by a leer at the girl when James's back was turned.

Yet again, he abandoned the idea, and wondered, as the

dance ended, whether to retain the girl. As he hesitated, and she waited to see whether he would lead her to a table, he heard laughter and saw a party of young people, dressed in evening clothes, coming down the stairs. He recognised them, and saw amongst them the kittenishly beautiful Diana Newbury, the young wife of his friend, the Marquis, who, he noticed with interest, was not one of the party.

James turned to his partner and gave her a quick, friendly smile.

'Make yourself scarce, there's a good girl, eh?' he asked. She recognised the situation, smiled back, and went away without rancour.

She had barely left his side when Diana came skipping across. She was dressed in up-to-the-minute butterfly-wing colours, her brown hair modishly fringed and bobbed, her huge eyes glittering with vivacity.

'James! How marvellous! I'm not interrupting anything, am I?'

'Lord, no. I'm here by myself,' he only half-lied. 'How splendid to see you, Diana. I say, do sit down.'

'No. You come over and join us. You know them all – Christabel, Mouse, Davina . . .'

He shook his head. 'I don't think I will, if you don't mind. Diana, do have a drink with me. Please.'

Puzzled, she nodded and joined him at a small table, waving to the others to carry on without her. James was lucky to catch a passing waiter. He ordered two Sidecars.

'What are you doing here, all alone?' she asked.

'Well, something to do, you know. Father and Virginia and the children are still up in Scotland. Georgina's visiting Elizabeth and her husband in America. The house is so damned quiet. Anyway, I like the pianist here. Have you heard him?'

'Not yet. That's why Davina suggested we come tonight. Do join us, James. You shouldn't be alone.'

The drinks came. They touched glasses and sipped the cocktail. James left her invitation unanswered and made no move to get up.

'Had a good season?' he asked.

She shrugged and pouted. 'I suppose so. I'm rather bored with hunting, and the country. Everyone endlessly moaning about the miseries of farming.'

'Where are you going to live in London? I see Bunny's selling Newbury House.'

'Thank heavens. It's a dreadful old barrack, really. They're going to pull it down and build a big block of luxury flats. We're supposed to have the best one, at the top overlooking Hyde Park. As a matter of fact, I'm meant to be looking after moving everything out, but I'm staying at the Ritz and just buying new clothes. It's a lovely change.'

She gave the brilliant smile in which every part of her features played its share. James said, 'Where is Bunny?'

'Somewhere in the wilds of Wales. Fishing.' She grimaced. 'He never comes to London, unless it's for a meeting or a dinner. But then, you never come to see us in the country these days.'

'That's true.'

'Not for want of asking, you know.'

'No.'

'No Hazel to hold you back any more.'

'No. Poor Hazel.'

'Does she haunt you from the grave?' she asked mercilessly, despite the smile. She had never hidden her contempt for his seemingly joyless wife and her suburban background.

'Not at all,' he said without resentment. 'My memories of her are happy ones. Happier than when she was alive, I'm afraid.'

Diana said suddenly, 'What are you doing this weekend?'

'Going down to Sandwich for a week or so, to play some golf. The Danbys have lent me their cottage.'

'Who with?'

'By myself.'

'Can I come, too?'

It was said with a casual directness that was entirely typical of Diana. She always said what came into her mind,

95

and anything she impulsively wanted she asked for, without qualification.

For the first time for days James felt a little leap of excitement inside him. She was adding, 'That's if you'd like me to.'

He said carefully, 'It would be ... rather risky.'

'Why? My maid's absolutely all right.'

He considered. 'So's my man, I suppose.'

'Good, then.'

And that was that. Diana informed him that she would make her own way down, with her maid, by train and go straight to the cottage, which she knew. She finished her drink; leaned over and kissed him; and went gaily away to rejoin her friends. James paid his bill and went straight home.

Two days later found him in the Danbys' cottage in the delightful, half-timbered little Kentish town. Gothic windows looked on to a small, well kept lawn and walled flower garden. The interior furnishings were simple but had cost money.

James heard Edward, who had driven him down, tinkering with something in the small kitchen. He went through and found him priming an oil lamp.

'Just testing it, sir,' Edward explained. 'In case the electricity goes, like last time.'

'Just like the war,' James said. He could hear an edge of nervousness on his voice which reminded him of some wartime moments. 'Er, Edward ... you know I mentioned the possibility of ... of a visitor ...'

'Yes, sir. I've made up the spare bed.'

'Oh, good. There may also be a servant. A maid.'

'There isn't any other room, sir. I could try in the town for her ...'

'No, no.'

'Well ... I could make a bed up for myself on the settee in the lounge, if you don't mind. Then she can have my room.'

'Good idea. Thanks. Er, it may not be necessary, but ...

Anyway, I'm sure the maid will be a help . . . give you a hand.'

'Yes, sir.'

James said deliberately, 'I know I can rely on your discretion, Edward.'

His servant's expression didn't change.

'Yes, sir.'

James relaxed. 'Splendid. They should be here any time now.'

As if on cue, they did arrive, before Edward could offer to take the car and meet them at the station, which would have been unnecessary, anyway, for it was only two minutes' walk away. He answered the doorbell and recognised Lady Newbury at once, and thought how smashing she looked in her checked coat with leopard-skin trimmings.

'Oh, good afternoon, m'lady. Major Bellamy is in here.'

He gestured across the short passage to the open living-room door. There was no space to move to announce her. She gave him a radiant smile and went in.

Edward turned to see the maid waiting just inside the cottage door. A smart piece, too, he noticed approvingly: young, nice figure, bright blonde hair, nicely made-up.

'Hullo,' he grinned. 'My name's Barnes – like the bridge.'

'Mine's Marshall. How d'ye do?'

'Here, let me.' He took the suitcases and went first with them up the narrow stairs.

In the living-room, James and Diana stood back from their kiss and she wandered over to the smouldering fire in the ample grate.

'Some sherry?' he suggested.

'What I'd really like is some gin. Gin and water.'

He poured. 'I thought we might go out to lunch. There are several quite respectable pubs.'

'I've brought some cold food. It would be rather more sensible to eat here, wouldn't it?'

James took her meaning. 'I suppose it would.' He passed over her glass. 'Sorry the fire's rather smoky. Wet wood, I expect.'

They saluted one another silently and drank.

'Well,' James said, 'you're here.'

She wandered over to the sofa and sat. 'Didn't you think I'd come?'

'Well . . .'

'I always do what I say I'll do – you should know that. Aren't you going to say you're glad to see me?'

He quickly went to bend over and kiss her again before joining her on the sofa, leaving a respectable little space between them.

'Of course I am. Tremendously glad. Diana, it's just . . .'

'Just what?'

'Well, Bunny.'

She looked cross suddenly. 'Look, if you've suddenly developed a conscience, why the hell didn't you tell me not to come?'

'I haven't.'

'Right. So let's get it quite clear – no more Bunny.' The smile returned. 'And I've just realised I'm starving.'

James went to the bell. Edward, who had just regained the kitchen, hurried in to answer it, instinctively pausing to knock first.

'Oh, er, Edward,' James said, 'do you think you could rustle up a spot of lunch? Lady Newbury's brought some things. On a tray will do.'

'And a bottle of Burgundy,' Diana put in.

'Yes, sir, m'lady.'

When Edward had gone, Diana said, 'What a nice, willing boy.'

'Yes,' James agreed. 'He's a jolly good fellow.'

'My girl's a bolshie little stuck-up bitch,' she went on. 'The way she behaves, you'd think she was the Queen of Sheba.'

'Why d'you keep her?'

'Oh, she can sew. She's brilliant with hair. And she makes me laugh. You know, your Edward would make someone a very good butler.'

'Diana, you're scheming.'

98

'Me? Never.'

'You are. Behind that pretty, innocent little face of yours there's a cunning, devious brain.'

Without tilting her head she glanced upwards and at him and smiled enigmatically. He found all thoughts of Bunny receding fast.

In the kitchen, Edward and the 'bolshie little stuck-up bitch' worked side by side to prepare the luncheon of Harrods' comestibles, fresh that morning.

'Lucky we brought our own food,' she said. 'To judge by the look of the larder.'

'The Major usually eats out,' Edward defended.

'I wasn't thinking of them. Poky little place, isn't it?'

'Quite cosy, really. I mean, it's not what we're used to . . .'

'It's not what *we're* used to either, I can assure you, Mr. Barnes. Still, in the circumstances . . .'

'Yeh. You know, you could have knocked me down with a feather when I saw who it was. I mean, I've known Lady Newbury for years. I've been up at Somerby with the Major for the hunting. That was before your time, of course, Miss Marshall. Yeh, you could've knocked me down with a feather.'

'Men are all the same, Mr. Barnes.'

'But I . . . I always understood the Marquis was one of the Major's best friends.'

'What's that got to do with it?'

He jerked his head towards the living-room. 'Well, you know.'

'I think you sound old fashioned, Mr. Barnes . . . Or is it that you've led a sheltered life?'

'No I haven't, not really. I'm married – to Daisy, our head housemaid. And I've been all through the war.'

'I'm glad.'

'About the war?'

'No, the other. I much prefer valets who know what's what. As we seem to have to keep each other company quite a bit, you may call me Violet.'

'Ta. I'm Edward.'

'Edward. That's quite nice. Ready?'

They carried a tray each into the living-room. Once again, Edward paused to knock and waited to be called.

Early that afternoon he put aside the washing-up things and went to answer the living-room bell. This time he went straight in.

'Edward,' said Violet Marshall from the sofa in a languid tone, 'you may pour me a glass of Crème de Menthe.'

'Yes, m'lady,' he said, playing up to her.

'Go on, boy, hurry,' she ordered, and got up to go to the gramophone.

'Here, you're going it a bit, aren't you?' Edward said, as the quick strains of 'I'm Just Wild About Harry' burst out and Violet launched into an abandoned dance.

'They're playing golf,' she said, dancing on. 'Won't be back for hours.'

'Here,' he said with genuine admiration, 'you can't half dance.'

'That's what Noël said to me, dahling,' she replied, and after a few more steps flung herself back on to the sofa. Edward sat nearby.

'Where did you learn?'

The mimicking voice continued: 'I picked up that step at Deauville, last season, dahling. A fancy dress ball at the Casino. Everybody was there – the Aga Khan, Gaby Deslys, the Prince of Wales, wrapped round Mrs. Dudley Ward, of course. The King of Sweden winked at me. Elsa Maxwell asked me to one of her parties. A baron asked me to marry him. It was all so terribly gay and boring.'

She dropped the accent and said, not quite in her own voice, 'I think I'll have a bath. Run up and turn it on for me, there's a pet.'

'Here, who d'you think I am?'

'You are quite a dear boy, that's what I think you are. At home I have a footman who is madly in love with me enough to obey my slightest whim. Here, I've only got you.'

Edward got up, grinning. 'Oh, all right.'

'Oh, and Edward . . . don't forget a hot water bottle for my bed. It's bound to be damp.'

She winked and popped into her mouth a chocolate from an open box on the low table beside her. Edward went off, telling himself he might have to watch that one, before the week was out.

'Why did you come down here, Diana?' James asked, two evenings later.

He had been nerving himself to ask it for hours, but had been more than half-afraid to hear what her answer would be. Now he had to.

The fire, unextinguished since it had first been lit, was now well established in a steady, soothing glow. The curtains were drawn against the world; a single electric table lamp gave light but no glare, and the shadows softened the planes and angles of the walls.

James sat on the sofa, looking down at Diana who was on the floor, leaning against his legs. Warmth, comfort and relaxation after a good meal made the asking of a frank question a safer proposition than at some other times.

'Not for a naughty weekend,' she answered. She turned her head to look up at him. 'You silly old thing, it's because I love you.'

She smiled to see his eyebrows go up, but went on, half-flippantly, 'I've loved you ever since an awful dance at Crewe House. I mean awful, because I was thirteen and had spots and was the scourge of many governesses, and you were still at Eton, tall and slim and beautiful. And because our parents knew each other, you actually danced with me, out of duty, because you were properly brought up.'

James smiled. 'Did I?'

She went on, the flippancy left behind. 'And I fell in love with you. And when I found myself in your arms all last night and the night before, I was feeling that same pang. And now that you haven't a wife any more . . . well, I'm yours, if you'll have me.'

'Well . . .' he hesitated, wondering how to answer.

'Well?' she challenged.

He took the risk he had to take. 'Why did you marry Bunny?'

There was no flare-up this time.

'You should know very well, I agreed to marry him in a fit of pique. Old Lady Newbury asked me to stay at Somerby because she thought I would make a more suitable marchioness than the chorus girls Bunny was running after at the time. I really went there because I knew you were going to be there. And when you didn't pop the question, I just said "yes" to poor old Bunny, who'd been asking me dutifully twice daily after meals. Of course, I didn't know then about Hazel and her bewitching middle-class magic. It's taken me a long time to run you to ground, James.'

'I'm sure Bunny's always been kind to you.'

'Of course he has. Always considerate and thoughtful, even when I've been at my most bloody. Life at Somerby is so dull and organised and . . . and *decent*. There's no spice in it; no adventure; no risk. I'm just part of the furniture, beautifully looked after, polished daily. And Bunny's so . . . wet.'

'He did jolly well in the war.'

'He was an A.D.C. most of the time.'

'Only the last year, when most of the heirs of the nobility had been killed and the King wanted to be sure there would still be a House of Lords in the future.'

She frowned. 'Anyway, why are we talking about Bunny again?'

'Well, he is rather germane to the issue, as they say. He is your husband and one of my oldest friends. Don't you think he'd be terribly upset if you just left him for me?'

'I don't think he'll mind, once he's got over the first shock. In fact, I should say he'll be secretly rather relieved. And his family will be delighted that he'll be free to marry again and find a girl who can produce an heir.'

James got up uneasily, walked ruminatively about, then stooped from his great height to kiss her, before moving away to lean against the mantelpiece and gaze into the fire.

'I wish I could see into the future,' he confessed. 'Diana the enchantress. How I chose Hazel, when I could have had you ... You know, we'd be outcasts. Bunny has thousands of friends and they'll most of them be bound to side with him.'

'Nice to know who one's own friends really are.'

'And you might be in for rather a shock. I know divorce is becoming a commonplace sort of thing nowadays ... but not among marquises. The King and Queen won't like it a bit.'

'Trying to frighten me?'

'Yes.'

'You've picked the wrong girl.'

He sighed expressively. 'What do you want to do?'

'Go and live abroad. We've both got a bit of money. Let's spend it. We could live in Paris, hunt with Bendor Westminster's hounds at Pau ... Brioni for the polo ... and we could rent a villa with a wild romantic old garden at Fiesole. There'd be parties all the time – skiing parties in the Alps, yachting parties in Greece, mad gondolier parties in Venice, bathing parties at Monte. We'll go everywhere and do everything. There's nothing we couldn't do together.'

The infection of her enthusiasm had found a susceptible subject. Pushing his misgivings firmly to the back of his mind, James raised her to her feet, and, his arm round her, led her away up the stairs.

They heard little of the rain which started soon afterwards and continued through most of the night. But in the morning the lowering wet sky, the soaked garden, and the dank smell of renewed dampness throughout the cottage did nothing for their spirits. Mah Jong, which James persuaded Diana to try, was soon pronounced boring, complicated and silly. Bezique was rejected as being fit only for dowagers. Rain sputtered down the old chimney on to the fire, making it black and smoky.

'Darling, please don't light another of those cigars,' Diana said irritably. 'The whole place stinks of them already.'

He put it back in the box. 'All right, darling. What about a walk? Bit of exercise, fresh air . . .'

'In this weather?'

There was no pleasing her. He went to the window, to peer out at the downpour and wonder what to suggest next. The initiative came from her.

'James, darling . . .'

'Mm?'

'Why don't we go and look for the sun?'

He turned, surprised. 'Now? Where?'

'France. We've got your car. I've got plenty of money on me. There's the ferry from Dover. We could just nip across.'

'Well . . . it's a bit . . . sudden, isn't it? We can't just up sticks and . . .'

She came over to stand in front of him, looking directly into his eyes, her own flashing an unmistakable challenge.

'Why not, James?'

He couldn't answer.

She smiled. 'I think we should pack.'

Mrs. Bridges' eyes widened at what she had just read in the Sunday newspaper.

'Daisy! Just listen to this. "Another nasty murder in Pimlico. Woman found with all four limbs dismembered . . ."'

'Ooh, don't Mrs. Bridges!' Daisy pleaded. 'It's bad enough all on my own over the mews. Every creak sounding like a footstep . . .'

'Yes,' Mrs. Bridges said, not listening: 'and it says here the maniac murderer is on the rampage, seeking his next victim, "like a wild animal that has tasted blood and will not be denied".'

'Oh, please! Oh, why does Eddie have to be away so long?'

'He has his duty to do, same as all of us,' Mrs. Bridges answered matter-of-factly; but even she gave a start and glanced round alarmedly when they heard a noise outside he servants' hall door. The door opened and no one more sinister came through it than Mr. Hudson in his reet clothes, followed by Lily in hers. Each carried a rayer book. They were very wet.

'We had a sermon about Noah and the Ark,' Lily couldn't ait to say. 'Mr. Hudson said it was very appropriate.'

'Never mind jokes, Lily,' Mrs. Bridges said. 'Mr. Hudson, is lordship's back suddenly from Scotland, by himself. Ie wants to see you.'

Hudson bustled out of his wet things and put on his black cket.

'Yes,' Daisy said to Lily, 'and there's his room to be aired nd dinner laid, so you get changed quick.'

The girl and Mr. Hudson left the room. Daisy started to ove about her own duties, but paused to ask, wide-eyed: Mrs. Bridges – did they find the *head*?'

'Oh, yes. See here . . . "The severed head was found . . ."'

In Richard's study, Mr. Hudson lost no time in establishg the reason for his lordship's unexpected return.

'I trust you and her ladyship are enjoying your stay in cotland, m'lord?'

'Very much, thank you, Hudson.'

'I, er, was distressed to read in the newspaper of the rime Minister's illness and resignation.'

'Yes, it's a sad business. That's why I've come up to ondon. We have to choose a successor. Not too easy.'

'I'm sure, m'lord.'

'Hudson, who would you choose – in confidence? Mr. aldwin or Lord Curzon?'

The butler pursed his lips judicially, but it was a matter which he had already given thought and resolved unesitatingly.

'Lord Curzon would be my choice.'

'Oh? Why?'

'Well, m'lord, Lord Curzon is more . . . is very much of a entleman . . .'

Richard gave him a quizzical look, but forebore to pursue ie topic.

'I believe the Major's out of town just now,' he said instead.

'That is so, m'lord. He's down in Kent for a few days golfing.'

'Oh yes, he did say something . . . And by the way Hudson, I'm expecting Lord Newbury round to see me any time now. He telephoned.'

'Very good, m'lord.'

The front door bell sounded.

'Ah, that will be his lordship now, no doubt. Shall I fetch some sherry?'

'Yes please, Hudson.'

The butler went out momentarily and returned briefly to usher Lord Newbury in.

Bunny was, like James, in early middle age now but he was one of those beings, lucky in some respects if not in others, who seem ageless, stuck in some limbo of their mid-thirties. His hair remained dark and full, his face schoolboyish, his expensive brown Harris Tweed suit baggy and outsized, as if it had been a hand-down from some older brother. In fact, he had been Marquis of Newbury for many years, and, like James again, had soldiered throughout the whole, and the worst, of the war.

'Hullo, Bunny,' Richard greeted him, shaking his hand. 'How very nice to see you.'

Bunny gave him his shy smile, blinked a few times, and asked, 'Er, how are you?'

'We're all fine. How's your lovely Diana?'

'Well, quite honestly, I . . . I haven't the least idea. That's why I've come to see you.'

'Do sit down.'

'Thanks. I've been away, fishing on the Usk. No water so I came up last night, meaning to pick Diana up at the Ritz and take her back to Somerby. But . . . she's not there. This, er, note was waiting for me at the club.'

He got out the paper from his inside pocket and handed it to Richard, whose expression changed as he read it from curiosity to horror.

'Good Lord! I honestly don't believe it.'

'Well, neither did . . . I mean . . . Well, where *is* James?'

Richard thought quickly and replied, 'I'm not at all sure. I'm only just back from Scotland myself, and the servants don't seem too sure . . .'

Mr. Hudson had entered with the sherry tray just in time to hear this. He felt Lord Newbury's gaze on him and held his enigmatic expression.

'Extraordinary!' Lord Newbury was saying, to which Lord Bellamy responded, 'Look, Bunny, I'll find out what I can and let you know right away.'

Lord Newbury declined the drink and took his leave, saying, 'Thank you. I'll see myself out. I've a taxi waiting.'

'Don't, er . . . don't do anything rash . . . you know,' were Lord Bellamy's parting words.

The younger man shrugged. 'What can I do – on a Sunday?'

He went. Mr. Hudson concentrated on placing the tray symmetrically in the centre of a low table.

'Hudson,' he heard. 'Do you know the Major's telephone number in Kent?'

'Yes, m'lord. It's Deal two . . .'

'Just get it for me, please. At once.'

'Very good, m'lord.'

Mr. Hudson knew better than to pause to offer sherry. There was something in his lordship's tone that made him think better, also, of listening in on the main receiver after the call had been successfully put through.

'James,' Richard said without ado. 'Is Diana Newbury down there with you?'

'Father! What an extraordinary question.'

'Look, James. I've just had Bunny here with a note he's had from Diana, saying she's run off with you.'

Diana, at James's elbow, was hissing, 'Who the hell's that?' 'My father,' he said out of the corner of his mouth. 'Yes,' he said into the mouthpiece. 'She's here.'

'For heaven's sake, James!' Richard raved. 'Have you gone quite mad?'

'Why on earth did you tell him?' Diana whispered angrily. James ignored her, listening to his father.

'I'm deadly serious, James. Come back to London straight away.'

'Yes. All right, Father. Goodbye.'

James hung up and turned away, his mouth twitching.

'*Why?*' she demanded. He rounded on her.

'Bunny's been round brandishing a note from you saying you've run off with me. How dare you?'

She stood her ground. 'It's no use shilly-shallying. I mean once you said I could come down here with you, I made up my mind, and I knew you'd agree.'

'Oh, did you!'

'Yes. Anyway, I didn't expect Bunny back till Wednesday. Listen, darling, let's just go as we planned. Let's leave now. It's all perfectly simple ...'

'No. We can't go now. It'd be running away. We must go back and clear it up.'

'No!'

'*Yes!*'

'The whole thing sounds to me like an absolute farce,' an angry Richard said that evening.

'Yes, Father,' James agreed, calmly enough. 'It certainly contained some farcical elements.'

'But the consequences aren't likely to be funny. I must say, I do find your behaviour quite extraordinary. I know that morals are pretty loose these days, and having a mistress is quite the usual thing ...'

'Diana Newbury isn't my mistress ...'

'You know perfectly well what I mean. Good heavens, aren't there enough stray women about without you having to pick on the wife of one of your best friends – a man in your own regiment, and, what's worse than anything, a peer of the realm?'

James smiled grimly. 'If anyone did the picking, it was Diana.'

'That's a very gallant remark, I must say. It will sound

ery well in court and in the gutter Press. For God's sake,
an't you think of the family? I do have a certain position,
ou know.'

Never having cared to be put on the defensive, James
ounter-attacked with his usual weapon, sarcasm.

'I doubt if anything even your wicked, evil son can do
ould shake the rock-like foundations of your shining
eputation.'

The telephone rang at his elbow. He answered it, then
overed the mouthpiece, turning to his father with a
urprised look.

'It's Bunny!'

Richard moved urgently. 'For heaven's sake, don't
peak to him.'

It was too late; James had taken his own decision.

'Yes. Hullo, Bunny. Yes, I see. Fair enough. Well, we
an't very well meet at the club. Why don't you come here?
ight? Good. Goodbye.'

He hung up and rang the bell, his father watching
ghast.

'You must be quite mad,' Richard said. 'Don't you under-
and, you must not talk with Bunny Newbury until you've
een your lawyer?'

'Why not? As you said, he is, or was, an old friend. I
on't see why we can't talk this whole thing over in a
ivilised manner.'

'Use your brains, boy. If he wants to ruin you over
his . . .'

'Father!' James snapped, moving on to the offensive
roper. 'Thank you for all your advice, even if I didn't
sk for it. I hate to say this, but while I'm delighted that
ou and Virginia and the children should live here, this
oes happen to be my house, and who I ask to come here
s my business and no one else's . . . And, just this one
vening, I'd be very glad if you would leave me alone.'

Pale with anger and hurt, Richard turned on his heel
nd strode from the room, oblivious of the presence of
Iudson, who had entered in time to hear the last words.

The butler's face registered shock and disapproval. James either did not notice, or ignored it.

'Hudson, his lordship will be out to dinner, and I would like some sandwiches in here right away.'

'Yes, sir.'

'And plenty of them. I'm very hungry.'

'*Sandwiches!*' Mrs. Bridges echoed as she hurried to prepare them. 'Like it was a railway train! I don't know . . . First voices raised, and his lordship slamming out of the house, and now sandwiches!'

She turned on Edward.

'What is it, Edward? That's what I'd like to know.'

He swallowed, but succeeded in standing on his dignity. 'I'm sorry, Mrs. B. I'm not in a position to divulge . . .'

' "Divulge"! "Di-vulge"! Wherever did you learn such words? You are in a position to, but you won't, and that's the plain truth. We all know you was down at that cottage in Kent . . .'

'Well, if you all know, why ask?'

She flourished the bread-knife at him. 'Don't you be cheeky, Edward. What I always say is that secrets don't do nobody any good. They fester inside, and cause trouble. I shall have to talk to Mr. Hudson about you, I really will. After all these years . . .'

'Sorry, Mrs. Bridges,' he said humbly, glad to escape from her kitchen. In the servants' hall his wife caught up with him.

'What is happening, then?' Daisy asked.

He looked round. 'Come over here, Dais. You won't believe me, but . . .'

As he whispered in her ear her eyes grew bigger and rounder.

'Oooh, Eddie!'

'Yeah. In the same bed – and not a very big one, at that. I mean, I had to take their breakfast up to them. It was . . . embarrassing.'

'Well, I never did! It's like a . . . a . . . What's going to happen next?'

'They'll get married. I mean, they'll have to, won't they?'

'And then they'll come and live here and kick the others out.'

'No. They won't live here, because of the disgrace, you see. Violet – I mean, Lady Newbury's maid – said she heard they was talking of going to the Continent.'

'P'raps they'll take us, Eddy? Oh, no. She's got a maid.'

'Yeh.'

'What's she like?'

'Lady Newbury?'

'No, the maid.'

'Oh, Miss Marshall. She's . . .'

'You called her Violet.'

'Oh, yeh. Well, I mean, as there was only the two of us . . .'

Daisy regarded him, smiling but watchful.

'Just Violet and Eddie, eh? All alone in a tiny cottage.'

He blushed violently, annoyed to have to defend an innocence that was genuine.

'Look, there was nothing went on between us. Honest! Anyway, she's an ugly old cow, with buck teeth like a rabbit.'

He put his arms round her.

'Here, Dais . . . I missed you ever so much. I really did.'

'Beg pardon, I'm sure,' said Lily, sweeping past close to them. 'Lord Newbury's back upstairs.'

'What, again?' Daisy exclaimed.

'That's what Mr. Hudson said.'

It was indeed the Marquis of Newbury whom Mr. Hudson had shown into the Major's presence in the study, a few seconds after delivering a generous plateful of sandwiches there. He paused briefly outside the door, listening, but heard only the low murmur of voices, and went back downstairs.

Anything less like the avenging lion than Bunny Newbury could not have been imagined.

'I know this isn't the way I should be behaving,' he told James apologetically, fidgeting with his feet and not knowing what to do with his hands. 'I ought to be threatening to knock you down, and beating Diana, and sending all over the place for lawyers . . . That sort of thing.'

James, seated in his armchair, seemed very much in command of the situation. He gestured towards the settee.

'I'm very glad you've come,' he said. 'Have a sandwich.'

Happy to have found some positive activity, Bunny took one, thanked him, and sat down. He took a small bite, then said, 'I've thought an awful lot about this, James, and I realise that it isn't entirely your fault . . . or Diana's, come to that. You knew her before I did and I've always known how fond she was of you. I probably shouldn't have married her in the first place, but Mother was very keen. In those days I was very inexperienced in the ways of the world.'

'You were, rather, I remember,' James smiled.

'I was desperately shy, that was one of my troubles. I haven't been a very good husband, I suppose.'

'A lot better than most.'

'Well . . . nice of you to say so. I admit I've rather taken Diana for granted.'

'Do you . . . do you love her still?'

'It's such a . . . funny word. Yes, I think I do. There's never been anyone else. I'm going to miss her most awfully. But what I really came here to say, James, was that I'm not going to divorce Diana under any circumstances. If you tell me that she truly loves you, and that you love her and will . . . you know, look after her and all that, then I'll give her grounds to divorce me.'

'That's very decent of you, Bunny,' James said steadily.

'Well, I was brought up to believe that no man should divorce a woman. It may sound a bit old-fashioned, but I think it's right.'

'Yes.'

Bunny got up, putting his unfinished sandwich down in an ashtray.

'So, I'd be very grateful if you could talk to Diana about it, James. I don't think I could face her, just at present.'

James got up, too.

'Yes, yes. I'll have to do a bit of thinking and then I will. I'll let you know. Goodbye, Bunny.'

'Goodbye, James.'

And they parted company as though they had been bidding one another goodnight on the club doorstep.

'I wish he wasn't being so nice about it,' Diana complained to James next day. 'It makes it all so difficult. Perhaps it was being nice made him such a dud as a lover, and me such a dud at being loved.'

'You're not a dud at being loved,' James protested. He paused, then added, 'It seems I should ask you to marry me.'

'How d'you mean "it seems"?'

'Well, isn't that the next move in the game?'

'Why don't you make it, then?'

'Diana, darling, before I do, I think we must be very honest with each other . . .'

She gave a little puff of exasperation. 'Must we? That sounds terribly boring. And it hurts so – being honest.'

'Bunny wants me to promise him that if I marry you I will make you happy.'

'How can anyone promise that? Anyway, you do.'

'No. I don't even think I do. I don't think I can.'

'Why?'

'I mean, even in those few days we had rows.'

'That was just because we were so cooped up.'

'If you're married, you have to survive being cooped up.'

Diana sighed heavily and let her shoulders sag. For once, the light of excitement and quick thought went from her eyes.

'Oh, dear. It's all my fault. I always think I'm right. James, darling, I wasn't all selfish when I saw you in that dive with that woman – yes, I spotted her. You were all alone, really, and you looked so . . . so lost and lonely. I just wanted to wrap a warm mantle of . . . of feeling wanted round you. To make you feel that someone loved you and needed you. I thought there was still a spark and that I could blow it back into flame.'

James could feel his temporary good spirits draining away. The familiar old leaden weight was beginning to settle itself on him once more. He said morosely, 'The spark was snuffed out five years ago, in the mud of Passchendaele Ridge. I'm a fraud, Diana. I'm not the James Bellamy you once fell in love with. I'm counterfeit.'

'That's nonsense. You can't blame everything on the war. You've got to pull yourself together and get on with life again.'

He was already too far gone for a pep talk to help him.

'I've tried, honestly I have. It hasn't worked. I mean, I'm not particularly unhappy. Things just don't seem worth doing. I'm quite content just sitting comfortably, watching the world go by . . . success . . . love . . . Yes, I'll marry you, Diana, but you must know the terms.'

'I don't want you to marry me out of decency. James, what are we to do?'

He shook his head slowly as her eyes searched his glum face in vain.

'I don't know,' he said. 'I haven't got as far as that yet.'

Two mornings later he had still not thought it out. Once more he had retired to the seclusion of his own room, and so did not see the large motor car which stopped outside the house, nor see the woman who got out of it and went down the area steps. He would have recognised her; but Daisy didn't when she opened the door to her.

'I wish to see Mr. Barnes,' the woman said, in a superior tone.

'I'm sorry,' Daisy said, polite but curious; 'Mr. Barnes is not available. I'm Mrs. Barnes, if I can help you.'

'Oh,' said the visitor, 'so you're Daisy. Well, I am Miss Marshall, Lady Newbury's maid.'

'Pleased to meet you, I'm sure.'

'I've got a note from Lady Newbury to Major Bellamy. I wanted Edward to deliver it personally.'

'If you'll leave it with me, Miss Marshall, I will see that it's delivered personally.'

'That's frightfully good of you, Daisy,' Violet said, handing over the envelope. 'Now I must rush. I've got to pick up Lady Newbury. Lord Newbury's taking us on a cruise, so there's so much to organise.'

'Oh!'

'Give Edward my kind regards, and tell him from me that I think he's very lucky to have such a pretty little wife.'

Restraining herself, Daisy replied, 'I'm sure my husband will be desolated that he missed you, Miss Marshall.'

Violet took a grand departure, leaving Daisy seething. As soon as Edward came in, minutes later, she sniffed ostentatiously and wafted the air with her hand.

'What's all that for?' Edward asked.

'Can't you smell the sweet perfume that fills the air?'

'Eh? Come on, Dais.'

'An old friend of yours called while you were out.'

'Who?'

' "An ugly old cow with buck teeth" according to you.'

'Not Vi . . . Miss Marshall?'

'She sent her kind regards, but couldn't wait as she was going on a cruise. Don't you wish you was going, too?'

'Don't be daft, Dais. But are *they* going – the Newburys?'

'Seems like it.'

'Then it's all come out right. I'm glad.'

'There's a note from *her* to the Major. You're to deliver it personal.'

He did. James read it when he was alone and then took it with him, in search of his father. He found him in the study.

'I gather Bunny's talked to you again – or rather, you've talked to him.'

'He wanted my advice.'

'He seems to have taken it. Thanks, Father.'

Richard smiled at last. 'Well, I've had quite a lot of experience, one way and another. You know, James, I seem to have been getting you out of scrapes since you first went to school.'

'Yes. I'm sorry. And I'm sorry I was rude to you the other evening. It was inexcusable. I wasn't quite myself, I'm afraid.'

Richard went to him and put his arm round him.

'Look – now Baldwin's settled in I'm lunching at No. 10, then going back to Scotland tonight. Why don't you come with me?'

James shook his head. 'Thanks all the same. I'll be all right.'

His father hesitated, then said, 'For all our sakes, James – do try and be more sensible.'

James nodded and went away to his room. The sound of his gramophone was shortly heard throughout the house. Downstairs, the concensus of opinion was that the Major was 'himself' again.

CHAPTER SIX

GEORGINA, back from America, was enthusing to Richard and Virginia about the experience.

'And when we docked this morning there were thousands of people on the quay, cheering and screaming for Douglas Fairbanks and Mary Pickford. I thought we'd never get down the gangway.'

'Did you see them close-to?' Virginia asked, quite agog.

'Oh, yes. They walked round the Promenade Deck every morning, however rough it was.'

'Well,' Richard smiled, 'you seem to have enjoyed the voyage. How was New York?'

'Oh, so thrilling. I wish you could see Elizabeth's apartment. It's on the 14th floor, overlooking the Hudson River. Hudson! That's appropriate, isn't it? You know, she's longing for James to go over and stay with them. I've got all sorts of messages for him. He is a bore, going off to France like that when he knew I was due.'

Richard said wistfully, 'He wanted to tour the battle-fields and visit the graves of some of his friends. I sometimes feel the poor chap has more affinity with them than with the living.'

'Well... Anyway, Virginia, how are the children?'

'They're at the sea for Easter. William's loving Summer Fields. He got quite a good report. Alice is at day school now – Miss Faunce's.'

Mr. Hudson entered and announced luncheon.

'You must be ravenous after all that sea air,' Richard said to his niece as he took her in. 'I expect Virginia told you we're due at the opening of the Wembley Exhibition this afternoon. Sorry to desert you so soon, but it's an official invitation just for the two of us.'

'Oh, I'll go some other time,' Georgina replied. 'It'll take me the whole afternoon unpacking.'

'Ruby,' Daisy said one afternoon. 'You seen Lily?'

'Not since lunch.'

Daisy scowled. 'She's supposed to be upstairs, helping me. I've whistled for her twice and nobody answered, so I've had to come all the way down.'

'I heard Mr. Hudson telling her she could go round to the shops sometime to buy her mother's birthday present.'

'Oh, he did, did he? Well, that does it!'

She stamped through to the butler's pantry and entered uninvited. Mr. Hudson took off his round steel spectacles and frowned up at her from his seat at his table.

'Knock when you come into the pantry, Daisy,' he reminded her.

'I forgot.' He could not mistake the defiance in her tone. 'I want to know where Lily is.'

'She is out, posting a letter for me.'

'That's not what Ruby says.'

'Never mind what Ruby says.'

'Now, look here, Mr. Hudson, Lily's supposed to be my under-housemaid. There's work to be done upstairs and she's never here when I want her these days.'

'I am in charge of the staff, Daisy, not you.'

'I know you are. But that doesn't explain why Ruby tells me one thing and you say something else. Lily's been allowed to go out shopping and everything's left to me. Does she get special favours or something in this house?'

'Hold your tongue, girl,' Hudson snapped. 'And get out of my pantry.'

'With pleasure. I just hope the work gets done proper, that's all, because I'm not doing it on my own.'

She shut the door behind her with unnecessary firmness and marched past Ruby into the kitchen, where Mrs. Bridges was working at the table.

'Blinking butler's pet!' Daisy stormed.

'What's all that?' Mrs. Bridges demanded.

'I'm looking for Lily. She's not here to help me, because Mr. Hudson's let her go out. Does what she likes these days, if you ask me. Or what *he* likes.'

' "*He!*" Daisy, how dare you say such things? You're not to speak like that.'

'Butler's pet!' Daisy repeated, as Rose came through from the servants' hall.

'What's all the squabbling?' she asked.

'Nothing.'

'Didn't sound like nothing. Where's Lily?'

'Don't ask me.'

'I just did. I've got some mending for her.'

'Well, I've got some work for her. As for where she is, try asking *him*.'

She jerked her head pantry-wards, glared at Mrs. Bridges, and stalked away.

That evening Georgina went into Virginia's boudoir, to find Rose assisting her with her evening dress.

'Just in time, darling,' Virginia smiled. 'You can tell me whether to wear my pearls or these beads. We're dining with the Fitzaland-Howards and there's going to be a bishop there.'

'Should you wear jewellery at all for a bishop?'

'I'm not sure. It's a Roman Catholic bishop.'

'Then wear the beads – like a Rosary.'

Rose joined in their giggles.

'Your bag and gloves are on the bed, m'lady,' she said.

'Thank you, Rose. There isn't anything else.'

Rose left. Virginia adjusted the beads and said to herself in the mirror, 'I suppose beads aren't quite as voluptuous as pearls.' She addressed Georgina's reflection. 'What did you think of Wembley?'

'Oh, marvellous. Only, Virginia . . . I'm not sure whether I ought to mention something to you, but it seemed a bit odd . . .'

Virginia turned. 'What did?'

'Well, in one of the African pavilions, where some Gold Coast natives were weaving mats, I suddenly saw Hudson – just a glimpse of him through the crowd.'

'It was his afternoon off. Everyone's going to Wembley.'

'You may well say that. He had Lily with him.'

'Lily? Our Lily?'

'Yes. They didn't see me, of course.'

'Well, I suppose he wanted to show her the exhibition. You know what he's like – rather schoolmasterly, I've always thought.'

'Are schoolmasters supposed to hold their pupils' hands?'

'Georgina! You don't mean to say . . . !'

'Absolutely certain. You don't blame me for mentioning it?'

'I think it's probably as well you did. I thought Lily was such a quiet, respectable girl. As to Hudson . . . ! I suppose there must be some innocent explanation, but I'll really have to make some tactful enquiries.'

She naturally turned to Rose when next they found themselves alone.

'Rose, you're the one who knows most about the others downstairs. I've noticed lately that Lily seems a little . . . quiet, subdued. Is she all right?'

'Far as I know, m'lady.'

'You don't get the impression that she's unsettled, or worried about anything?'

'Not to my knowledge.'

'Do you happen, by any chance, to know if she has a young man? Someone she meets on her days off?'

'I couldn't say, m'lady,' Rose said, her face expressionless. But she knew very well what her ladyship was hinting, and as soon as she could get Lily alone she intended to drag it into the open.

Her chance came quickly; the next evening, in fact. Lily had been taking her twice-weekly bath and was sitting on her bed in her cheap, flowered dressing gown, combing her hair. Rose knocked and entered.

'Hullo, Lily,' she smiled. 'Nice bath?'

'Yes, thanks.'

'Water still warm enough?'

'Oh, yes.'

'That's good.' Rose paused, then went on: 'I wanted a word, private like.'

'What about?'

'I thought you ought to know her ladyship asked me this morning if I thought you had a young man.'

'What did you say?'

'I didn't know.'

Lily nodded dumbly, volunteering nothing more.

Rose added, 'There is someone, though – isn't there?'

'I . . . I'd rather not say, Rose.'

'Look, I know there's someone. Everybody downstairs does.'

Lily looked startled. 'They don't!'

Rose nodded. 'Most of us have been living amongst each other too long not to notice when there's . . . there's any change. Lily, it's best to be truthful, and I promise I won't tell. It's . . . Mr. Hudson – isn't it?'

Lily looked down miserably, and barely audibly said, 'If her ladyship knew I'd get notice, wouldn't I?'

'He would, more likely.'

'Oh, not Mr. Hudson!'

'It is him, then?'

Lily could only nod again. Then she said animatedly, 'He's done nothing wrong, Rose. He's been ever so good and kind to me, telling me all sorts of interesting things about foreign parts and all that, and he takes me to museums. One night he took me to a real music concert at the Albert Hall. It was beautiful music, Rose. Only, it's just that . . .'

'What, Lily?'

'Oh, nothing.'

'What happens after these concerts and museums and things?'

'We have some tea sometimes – in a teashop.'

'And then?'

'We talk for a bit. Or rather, he does – all serious about people needing happiness and . . . love . . . and things. He's a very clever man, Rose. He can't half use words. But after a while he stops himself and we come home. He waits about round the corner while I go in first, so's not to come in together.'

Rose pursed her lips. 'I bet he does.'

'Please, Rose – you won't tell anyone.'

'I've promised not to, haven't I?'

But, as she had told the unhappy girl, others had been putting two and two together. Nothing had been discussed, though, and in fact the unavoidable crisis was precipitated by silence – Rose's silence that same evening when Mr. Hudson asked her if her ladyship was in her room upstairs.

'I asked you a question, Rose,' he said sharply. She still didn't answer, and walked pointedly up the stairs and out through the pass door, never moving her head when he called her name.

He turned to Mrs. Bridges, with whom he was left alone. 'That was insubordinate and quite uncalled for!' he fumed. 'I shall take the girl to task in front of her ladyship, if necessary.'

Mrs. Bridges raised a sorrowful eyebrow.

'I can only suppose she feels strongly about . . . well, you know what, Mr. Hudson.'

'I don't know . . .'

'Oh yes, you do, Angus. We all do.'

He opened his mouth to retort, but no words came. He stared at her for some moments, then lowered his gaze and said, 'What am I to do, Kate?'

'You must do what you feel is right, Angus. I can't advise you. It's not for me to tell you how to live your life.'

'I can hardly expect you to understand,' he muttered. 'You of all people.'

'If you've decided you're . . . in love with her, or something, well, that's nobody's business except yours and hers. She's a nice enough girl – modest and clean and decent. But have you thought about your position here? I mean, it's not exactly usual. Butlers in good houses don't go out with young housemaids. It's going against all you've stood for over the years, Angus. All what's proper and respectable.'

Mr. Hudson bridled. 'There is nothing that is not respectable in my situation, Mrs. Bridges. And nothing unusual, other than Lily's extreme youth.'

'That's what I mean. If it was some woman more your own age . . .'

He was stammering, 'I . . . I believe it is her youth that inspires me, more than anything else. She makes me feel that my . . . my future is . . . worthwhile.'

Mrs. Bridges made no answer. Thoughts and memories chased one another in her mind, and unhappiness welled. The silence between them was a long one. Then, at last, he said, 'I'm going up now to see if her ladyship is alone. If so, I must consult her.'

'Yes, Angus,' she said, her voice more than usually husky. 'I think you should.'

She watched him go sorrowfully.

Virginia was by herself in the morning room, writing a letter at the desk. As soon as she saw the expression on Hudson's face she knew what it was that he was requesting to discuss with her. She got up and stood facing him. He swallowed and commenced.

'I feel it my duty, m'lady, in all honesty, to inform you that I have become extremely attached in a personal way to . . . to Lily, the under-housemaid.'

Virginia regarded him steadily, showing neither surprise nor curiosity. He was obliged to plough on.

'I have to confess that over recent weeks I have developed very deep feelings towards the girl, young though she may be. I have been attempting to instruct her in many things. To open her eyes to the world outside. To teach her to better herself, and so forth, with a view to eventual marriage.'

Virginia had to react now.

'Are you telling me that you wish to marry Lily?'

'I have come to respect, love and cherish the young person, m'lady. I trust your ladyship will not doubt my sincerity.'

'But Hudson, Lily is only just twenty-two.'

He ignored the point. 'We have been sharing our time off for some little while, visiting museums together, picture galleries, places of historic interest . . . delighting in each other's company.'

'But are you quite sure that Lily's feelings aren't simply those of a young girl who's flattered by the attentions of an older man? It's possible that she sees you more as a father or a kindly uncle than as . . . as a man she might wish to marry!'

'She has brought a new meaning to my life, m'lady.'

'Yes, but has she actually told you she is in love with you?'

'She has indicated her gratitude for my attentions, m'lady. She has allowed me to . . . express my . . . my affection for her . . . without, of course, in any way . . .'

He tailed off unhappily. At that moment the door opened and Richard came in. Virginia lost no time in apprising him of the situation. His mind reeled.

'What . . . what do you propose to do, Hudson?' he asked weakly.

'In the circumstances, m'lord, it would of course be quite unsuitable for me to continue as butler here. So I must ask you to accept one month's notice, if that will be convenient.'

'It's hardly convenient at all, Hudson,' Richard snapped, and turned away to where the whisky waited. Virginia nodded an indication that the interview was at an end and the butler withdrew.

'It's beyond belief!' Richard raged as soon as the door closed. 'That a man of his character should be willing to abdicate – that's the only word for it – to abdicate entirely his authority and position in this house; to throw up all he's achieved and built up over the years for the sake of some ignorant chit of a girl, less than half his age . . .'

He swallowed whisky recklessly. Virginia said, 'It's not entirely unknown, Richard. Perhaps he's reaching out, as men sometimes do at his time of life, to grasp at something he's always dreamed of but never achieved.'

'Huh! What?'

'Some sort of ideal vision of love and marriage, before it's too late.'

Richard snorted again, tossed off the contents of his glass, refilled it, then voiced what was concerning him most.

'We'll never find another butler like Hudson.'

Virginia smiled, causing him to scowl even more. She took his arm.

'Darling, no one's indispensable. You're the one who's always said that. Frederick can perfectly well announce dinner and clean the silver and open the door to visitors. It's not the end of the world.'

But he would not be mollified. 'It would never be the same, Virginia. Never. Damn the man!'

Below stairs, the object of his disgruntlement sat brooding at the table in his pantry. He lifted his head at a tap on the door and heard Lily asking if she might come in.

'You said it was all right to come to the pantry and talk to you if I was ever worried,' she explained when he had closed the door behind her. She went to stand at the other side of the table from him.

'That's quite all right, Lily. What is it?'

'They all know about us. Don't they? Everyone in this house.'

He had to nod.

'What are they saying, Mr. Hudson? What do they think of us?'

'What they say or think should not concern you, my dear. The important thing is that our feelings for one another are now generally known. Our friendship is out in the open at last. There will be no further need for our small untruths and deceptions.'

'I see,' she faltered. 'That's . . . all right, then.'

He could tell that she was seeking words to say something more, but discretion led him to go to the door.

'You must return to your room before anyone hears you,'

he told her. 'Try not to be anxious. We have nothing shameful to hide.'

'No, Mr. Hudson,' she said in a tone devoid of conviction. 'I'm sorry I disturbed you.'

'Run along, then, my dear,' he smiled and ushered her out without touching her.

Frederick said to her next morning, 'He must be proper gone on you to give in his notice. I mean, he's got a good job here.'

'I know he has,' Lily answered unhappily. Her gloom was apparent to all except Mr. Hudson, who bore the air of a man under hypnosis.

She went on, 'I've told him I'm not sure about marrying or anything like that. It frightens me. If only he could . . . well, find someone else to love. Some nice woman. I mean, I like him. He's always been nice to me. So I just can't bring myself to . . . to tell him I don't fancy him. I couldn't stand to hurt him that much.'

'You can't go on dangling him on a string.'

'I don't know what to do, Fred. He wants to go to my home at Banbury and see my mother. I don't want him going there, but he wants to go on Sunday and take me with him.'

'You'll have to say something to him soon, then, else you'll wake up one day and find yourself at the altar.'

That was a growing fear which Lily took to bed with her at nights and found awaiting her again each morning.

'Get me out a plain scarf, will you, Rose?' Virginia requested later that morning. They were in Virginia's boudoir. She was dressing to go to a meeting of the committee of the Naval Education Fund, the body in whose cause she had first come to this house during the war and had so irritated the man who was to come to love and marry her.

That same man came in now, clearly irritated once again.

'Hudson's just been up to see me,' he growled. 'No, don't go, Rose. You might as well hear this too. He's going to see Lily's mother at Banbury.'

'Whatever for?' Virginia asked, wide-eyed.

'To ask for her consent to the marriage.'

Rose's mouth fell open.

'He means it,' Richard said. 'He says he's given the matter careful thought and he intends, with our permission, to go there with Lily on Sunday. I just thought you'd like to know.'

He stalked out again.

Rose told Virginia, 'I would like to say, m'lady, that I'm very sorry this has happened. You and his lordship have my deepest sympathy.'

'You mustn't worry on our behalf, Rose. We'll survive. Ask Edward to have the car ready for eleven o'clock, please. Oh, and better ask Mrs. Bridges to step up about the meals.'

That good lady made her way upstairs with her pencil and pad. Virginia, however, could see that she was upset and in no state to discuss culinary matters.

'We're all upset downstairs, my lady,' Mrs. Bridges answered her solicitous inquiry.

Her lower lip trembled.

'I just can't understand it. You see, years ago, m'lady, when I was in a bit of trouble with the police, Hudson helped me and stood by me. He spoke up for me in court, and, like, gave me to understand that if ever he thought of getting married one day it'd be me he'd ask to be his partner in life. And I told him I would always be . . . like, holding myself in reservation for him. But now . . . but now . . . I don't know what's come over him, m'lady. I really don't.'

'I know how worrying it must be for you especially, Mrs. Bridges,' said Virginia, who knew all about the one indiscretion in her cook's past. 'Perhaps we'd better postpone doing the meals until I get back. Come up at tea-time, will you?'

As she watched Mrs. Bridges go, her thought was 'Hudson! Hudson! What are you doing to us all?'

Georgina asked that question out loud that evening. At least, she did so metaphorically, and it was Lily whom she addressed as the girl was closing the morning-room curtains.

'You do know, don't you, Lily, that Hudson's leaving us because of you?'

Lily turned to face her, but found it hard to meet the gaze of those beautiful eyes.

'Yes, I do, miss.'

'And you'll be leaving as well, I imagine, so that you can both get married.'

'Well, Miss Georgina, I . . . I don't know. It's all muddled.'

'Does Hudson think you're willing to marry him?'

'I think he does, Miss.'

'And you? Or don't you want to talk about it? You don't have to.'

'Oh, no, miss, I don't mind talking about it to you.'

'Then what's the matter, Lily? Are you worried about Hudson's age? Or is it that you're frightened to tell him how you really feel?'

Lily burst out urgently, 'Miss, I've got to speak to him. Before tomorrow, 'cos he's taking me on the train to Banbury to see my mother, and I don't know what to do.'

'Tell me everything, Lily,' Georgina said gently. 'Perhaps I can help in some way, if you'd like me to.'

The girl poured out her feelings, growing in articulation as her mind unburdened. Georgina prompted her with questions. She was no intellectual, but she was a beautiful young woman who had seen a good deal of life, and in these circumstances that was more important.

And next morning, when Mr. Hudson, wearing his best suit with a yellow rose in his buttonhole and carrying a bunch of tulips and a small cake in a presentation box, came looking for Lily, she bit her lip and said, 'I'm sorry, Mr. Hudson, but I'm not going with you to see my mother. There's no point.'

'But there's every point, my dear,' he said. 'I would never dream of embarking on marriage without at least visiting the parent of . . .'

'I'm not going to marry you, Mr. Hudson. You haven't asked me to, anyway.'

'Lily, it has been understood ever since . . .'

'I never, never said I'd marry you.'

'You have never denied your feelings for me. Have I not been entitled to assume your consent?'

'No, you haven't. I don't wish to marry you, Mr. Hudson, because you're not a romantic person for a young girl.'

'But you've said over and over again how much you've enjoyed learning, accompanying me to interesting places . . . You're tired and strained, child. Try . . .'

'I'm not tired or strained, thank you. I just don't love you. When I marry I want to marry a young man who's strong and good-looking and romantic. Someone who can take me in his arms and make love to me and give me babies.'

'Lily . . . !'

'Yes, and laugh with me and make jokes. I don't want to spend my whole life in and out of museums and getting lectured about art and all that. Do you call that loving someone?'

Hudson found himself pleading.

'I have given in my notice here, Lily. I have thrown away my whole career as a gesture of my love for you. Why have you not spoken like this before?'

'Because I've always been afraid of you . . . What you'd say. I went out with you when you asked me because it was something to do on my days off. But I don't fancy you. I want a young man to marry me, not some old schoolteacher who talks Scotch and all about history and God and things and never touches me but holds my hand on a park bench or on top of a bus when it's dark and no one can see. That's not love. No, I wouldn't marry you, Mr. Hudson, not if there was nobody else left in the world. No, please go away and leave me alone.'

Hudson, pale-faced from the harsh and breathless attack, managed to say, through half-frozen lips, 'It seems . . . I have made quite a wee fool of myself. I must apologise to you, Lily. I ought to have known better. I'll go and change out of these things.'

He went away. Lily realised that she was trembling. She marvelled that she had found the courage to speak out in the way that Miss Georgina had urged she should. But she was profoundly relieved that she had.

An air of tension seemed to hang over the whole house that day. As it was Sunday, the staff were in contact with one another less than on other days. Hudson remained for most of the time in his pantry; Lily stayed in her room. Their recent custom of disappearing one after the other on a Sunday afternoon for what was meant to be taken for separate walks was not followed. The other servants looked at one another and wondered, but none ventured to question either of them.

The following morning Hudson stood once more before Lord and Lady Bellamy in the morning-room.

'What is it, Hudson?' Richard asked without attempting to soften his tone or offer the understanding of a smile.

'I merely wished to say, m'lord, that Lily has evidently left the house.'

'Left?' Virginia echoed.

'Early this morning, m'lady, without giving notice. Ruby saw her getting dressed and then she was gone. Her cupboard is empty.'

He turned his gaze to Richard.

'It would seem, m'lord, that my affections for the girl were misplaced. I had misjudged her character. From a conversation with her yesterday, it became clear to me that hers is in reality an ungenerous, cruel and somewhat malicious nature. I . . . realise I was wrong in my estimation of her.'

'I see. Er, what do you wish to do then, Hudson?'

'In view of the circumstances, m'lord, I wonder if you would require me to continue in your service.'

'Of course we would,' Virginia intervened before Richard could reply. He had been about to say the same thing, though more reservedly.

'I very much regret the incident, m'lady,' Hudson said.

'That's quite all right, Hudson. I think the sooner it is all forgotten, the better. I can't vouch for the others downstairs, but so far as his lordship and I are concerned the matter need never be mentioned again in this house.'

'Very good, m'lady. Thank you, m'lord.'

Hudson bowed and left the room. He went straight to his pantry, ignoring the other servants' questioning looks. Then he took out the letter that had been found by Ruby in Lily's room.

As he was ripping open the envelope there came a tentative tapping on the door. He paused and called, and Mrs. Bridges came in.

'I'll not stop long,' she said. 'Just to say, well, I'm sorry ... but I'm glad.'

'Yes, Kate.'

'Is that Lily's letter?'

He nodded and drew it from the envelope. He glanced over it swiftly, then read aloud, with unaccustomed emotion in his voice.

' "Dear Mr. Hudson,

I'm sorry I said all the nasty things I said, because I didn't mean it. I only wanted you to give up caring for me and make you think I was not a nice person. I really think you are a kind man and the times we had together were very happy times I shall always remember.

I'll look for another place now. One last favour, will you be so kind as ask her ladyship to forward a reference to above address which is my home you never come to in the end.

Your affectionate
Lily".'

Mrs. Bridges said huskily, 'I'm just going up to her ladyship now. I'll ask about the reference, if you like. She's sure to give it.'

Hudson nodded, unable to speak.

Mrs. Bridges touched his shoulder before turning to go. 'I'll not be long, Angus. You stop here, and when I come back I'll make you a nice cup of tea.'

CHAPTER SEVEN

Perhaps romance is contagious in a close community. Or perhaps Fate, having contributed an absurd situation to amuse itself with, finds the act agreeable and wants to do it again before moving on to other business. In seeking an even more bizarre subject for its attentions than Mr. Hudson, Fate could not have chosen better than Ruby.

That awkward, fumbling semi-literate stood in the servants' hall one morning clutching the bundle of envelopes which an astonished Hudson had just handed to her. She was smirking in a fashion that was almost repellent in its sickliness.

'Whatever is she doing with all them letters?' Mrs. Bridges demanded of Hudson, as though Ruby were not standing within four feet of her.

'Ah, now, Mrs. Bridges,' Hudson said, 'I think that Ruby, like the rest of us, is entitled to her privacy.'

'Thank you, Mr. Hudson,' the girl simpered, and went away to deal with her correspondence.

'I know what it is!' Rose declared when Ruby reappeared with the opened letters in her hand. 'You answered that advertisement for a pen-pal.'

'No, I didn't.'

Something fluttered to the floor from her grasp. Frederick moved quicker than she did and had a good glance at it before handing it back.

'Really!' Mrs. Bridges ejaculated. 'Bringing all those letters into the house from perfect strangers. You throw them on the fire this minute. Why, you don't know where they've been.'

'I won't.'

'Ruby!'

The girl turned to Hudson.

'I don't have to, Mr. Hudson, do I?'

'Well, I really . . . You can hardly write to them all.'

'Oh, no. I'll only write to one.'

'How are you going to choose?' Rose wanted to know.

'I already have.'

'Is it the fellow in the photograph?' asked the knowing Frederick. 'Come on. Read us his letter.'

'Yeh. Go on, Ruby,' Rose urged.

Ruby blushed coyly, but unfolded one of the sheets of paper.

' "Dear Madam",' she began.

'Madam, indeed!' from Mrs. Bridges. Ruby ignored her.

' "I should very much like to engage in correspondence with you. I am thirty-five years old, a bachelor, of a quiet dispos . . . dispos . . ." '

' "Disposition," I imagine,' Hudson offered.

'Oh, go on, Ruby,' Mrs. Bridges snorted impatiently. 'Let Mr. Hudson read it out. Or Rose.'

'I will,' Rose volunteered and took the letter before Ruby could protest. She launched straight into it.

> ' "Dear Madam,
>   I should very much like to engage in correspondence with you. I am thirty-five years old, a bachelor, of a quiet disposition. I live at home with my invalid parents, and am employed as a clerk in the Post Office. I like Hugh Walpole . . ."

'Who's Hugh Walpole, Mr. Hudson?'

'A novelist, Rose. A popular novelist.'

'Oh.'

> ' "I like Hugh Walpole and H. G. Wells. I am fond of good music, and listen to it on the wireless, though I do sometimes go to the Queen's Hall. I hope that, if your tastes are similar, you will send me your name and address, with a view to further correspondence and possibly acquaintanceship.
>   Yours truly,
>   Herbert Turner." '

'Similar tastes!' Mrs. Bridges declared. '*Ruby?*'

'You want to be careful,' Rose warned as she handed the letter back. 'He might be Jack the Ripper.'

Frederick asked, 'If he doesn't know your name and address, how has he written to you?'

'The newspaper sent all the letters on. I just had to fill in a form – not more than twenty words – and they printed it. I put "Genteel young lady wishes to correspond with eligible young man".'

Mrs. Bridges rolled her eyes ceiling-ward.

Ruby asked, 'I can write to him, can't I, Mr. Hudson?'

'I, er, suppose so, Ruby. It's not what I would recommend, corresponding with a stranger.'

Ruby produced the photograph Fred had picked up for her.

'He looks just like Rudolph Valentino,' she cooed wetly.

Rose took the picture from her and examined it, passing it on to the others. Not her idea of Valentino, exactly. More like a Post Office clerk. Still, she thought, the poor chap had yet to see Ruby.

In the morning-room, Richard said with an unusually diffident air, 'Virginia, I wonder if you would do something for me?'

She raised her eyebrows. 'You sound very doubtful. I'm just trying to think what you could possibly ask me to do that I wouldn't be prepared to.'

'Nothing very desperate. I wondered if you would invite Guy Paynter to lunch?'

'Why, of course. Whom would you like me to ask with him? Mrs. Merivale, I suppose, if she's still his current . . . hostess.'

'That sounds like an echo of one of Prue's cattier comments.'

'It was. She told me that Sir Guy Paynter has paid attention at different times, to three widows and two divorcees, and married none of them, so she wondered how long Polly Merivale would last.'

'Darling, Paynter, like any other rich bachelor, needs a hostess – a pretty, charming, unattached woman to preside over his dinner-table and help him with his house-parties. They understand the situation perfectly, and so does everyone else. I assure you, he's not the kind of man you need hesitate to have inside your home.'

Virginia laughed out. 'Richard, how absurd you are! Of course he shall come. I merely want to know who else. We owe Lady Bush, and the Bannisters . . .'

'I thought, er, something rather more intimate. Just ourselves, Prudence, and perhaps James.'

'I thought he always had such big, lavish parties.'

'I think I'd better tell you the truth. The fact is that Guy Paynter is very influential and he uses his influence politically. He's a friend of Baldwin's and of Beaverbrook's. He quite often goes to Max's little "cabinet meetings" at Fulham.'

'And you want him to persuade Lord Beaverbrook to give more support to the United Nations in his papers.'

'No, no. I've, er, heard . . . well, Winston told me, that the Under Secretary for Foreign Affairs is resigning on his doctor's orders.'

'And you'll be offered the post?'

'I'd like it very much, but I don't think I'll be offered it. I've been out of the Government so long that they all think of me as an Elder Statesman.'

'Nonsense!'

'Exactly. I know that we were told we'd made such a mess of things with the war, and that afterwards we must leave it to the younger men. But the young men are either dead or cynical. I feel I've still an active part to play. I've a lot of experience to put to use.'

'Of course you have,' Virginia agreed readily, but she frowned a little. 'But surely the Government are all friends of yours? Winston, Austen Chamberlain, Mr. Baldwin . . . Surely you could just . . .'

'I can't very well go and say "I know you think I'm too old, but I'm not".'

'Not in those words. But . . .'

'I wouldn't dream of embarrassing myself, or them. But if someone like Guy Paynter casually mentioned my name in connection with the post . . . Said that I'd been very active with the League and working on the Treaty . . . He is very influential, you know.'

No more fervent champion of Richard Bellamy's qualities than Virginia existed. She felt unease and vague distaste that he should have to resort to such tactics to gain a preferment which, in her view, he was entitled to ask for straight out. But she had seen enough evidence of his life-long unwillingness to be seen to be pushing himself.

'Money talks,' she said cynically. 'Well, of course I'll gladly invite him. But you know I'm hopeless at politics.'

Richard gave her his little crooked smile.

'My dear, just be your own charming self and you'll captivate him without even trying.'

And that was what she did; though it was not her charm that made the deepest impression on him.

They had finished the meal and were taking coffee in the morning-room. Sir Guy Paynter, middle-aged but youthful in appearance, with fair hair and a chubby, slightly florid face, had begun the evening a trifle warily, as if surprised to have been invited and wondering what could be behind it. But Polly Merivale, whom Virginia had decided to ask after all, knew his conversational foibles and drew him out skilfully. Mrs. Bridges' excellent cooking obviously came as a surprise and a pleasure to him, and by the time coffee was reached he had put all his reservations aside.

'I have always believed,' he declared as he took cream and sugar from Frederick, 'that the less politicians do, the better. That's why I moved heaven and earth to make Baldwin Prime Minister instead of Curzon.'

'I didn't realise you were responsible,' James said, disliking the brash claim.

'I played my part among others. I approve of Baldwin because he never does anything at all if he can possibly

137

help it. Things always sort themselves out, left to their own devices. It's the violent action taken by politicians which turns an unfortunate situation into a disaster.'

Glancing at Richard, Virginia perceived that he was not too happy. Such sentiments scarcely coincided with his hopes.

Polly went on encouraging Paynter to talk.

'What do you think the ideal Member of Parliament should do, then?'

'What he always does, fortunately – spend all his time arguing about things which don't matter in the very least. Look at Parliament's present exploit – debating the abolition of the death penalty for cowardice in the field.'

Both Richard and James looked sharply at Virginia and saw that her expression had frozen. They would have been too late to head Paynter off, though.

'We fight a war in which millions of men are killed,' he was saying. 'What can it matter to some poor boob who runs away whether he's shot at by a firing squad or whether he's shoved back in the line to be shot at by the enemy?'

He looked round his listeners and was surprised to find his half-flippant remark not taken up in similar vein. Everyone suddenly looked grim – even the butler and footman, standing side by side against the wall, not listening but unable not to hear.

Then Virginia said quietly, 'My son was Court Martialled for cowardice in the field, and found guilty. At his own request he was sent back into action and was killed. I'm sure it mattered a great deal to him how he was killed. It did to me.'

The silence after she had spoken hung in the air for almost a minute. Sir Guy Paynter's face registered horror but his feeling was one of annoyance. A man who took supercilious delight from other people's *gaffes*, he prided himself on never making one. Before accepting the hospitality of comparative strangers he made a point of reading them up in the appropriate social registers and inquiring about them of his friends. He had been able to find out little about Virginia Bellamy, because of her undistinguished provincial background, and it had never occurred to Polly Merivale to tell him of the wartime tragedy. In fact, he realised as he glanced at Polly now, she was rather enjoying his discomfiture over it.

He got to his feet and said quietly to Virginia, 'I am so sorry. Of course, I had no idea that you were personally involved in the question.'

She was too deeply hurt to return a conventional acceptance of the apology.

'Even if I weren't,' she snapped, 'I hope I would have the sensitivity to feel for those who were.'

He bowed slightly.

'I stand corrected. I'd better be off before I disgrace myself completely. Polly, can I give you a lift, or are you going to stay and have your character improved?'

'Oh, you know my character is beyond praying for, let alone improving.'

She rose as he bowed again to Virginia, thanked her for a most delicious luncheon, and bade farewell to everyone in turn. Then he ushered Polly to the door, opened by Hudson, and followed her out.

Later, when Lady Prue had gone and James had retired to his room to play his gramophone, Virginia told Richard, 'I'm awfully sorry about what happened.'

'I can quite understand your being upset, my dear. It's just a pity you couldn't have accepted his apology when he made it.'

'I didn't believe he really meant it. Besides, it annoyed me that he obviously thinks he's so rich he can say anything he likes and people will put up with it. I hate to think of a man like that having influence.'

'You mean, you hate to think that I'm prepared to make use of it.' Well, I can assure you, Virginia, things are always done this way – a word here, a word there, a little discreet string-pulling. They have always been done that way in politics of all parties, and I'm sure they always will be.'

'Then I think it's a great pity.'

Her stubborn refusal to appreciate the situation irritated him suddenly. He said sourly, 'Anyway, the whole thing was my fault for asking you to give the luncheon in the first place. I know you don't want to be a political hostess.'

'Like Marjorie,' she couldn't prevent herself flashing back.

The sharp little tiff was interrupted by the entry of Hudson, bearing a wrapped bunch of roses.

'For you, m'lady. Delivered by hand just now.'

He handed them to Virginia and retired. She fished out the accompanying card.

' "Please forgive me. I am proud to believe that my own mother would defend her son as you defended yours. Guy Paynter." '

'They're beautiful,' she had to admit, burying her nose in one of the rich blooms.

Richard was smiling when she looked up.

Virginia was able to thank the sender personally next morning. Just as she was writing a note to him he was announced by Hudson.

'I really came,' he said, after thanks and mutual apologies had been expressed, 'to see whether by any extraordinary chance you were free to come and have lunch at the Ritz. Arnold Bennett is coming.'

'Oh, I've always wanted to meet him!'

'And Freddie Birkenhead. And a rather interesting young musician. Malcolm Sargent.'

It was irresistible and she was free. It was her ideal chance to make it up to Richard, to Paynter, and to herself.

'What time were you ...?'

'We've arranged to meet in the Long Bar of the Trocadero first for a cocktail. So if you really would do us the honour of joining us, we could go there in my car now.'

'Oh, I'd have to change.'

He smiled. 'Naturally. By "now" I meant in the hour or so that any woman takes to change from one frock into another and to comb her hair.'

Virginia laughed. 'I'm glad you understand these things. But what will you do while I'm gone?'

'Stay here and make myself at home. There's a lot to be learned from someone's room.'

'And what do you learn from this one so far?'

He glanced round it.

'That you have good taste without ostentation. Family affection without being a *hausfrau*. Elegance without snobbery.'

'I'm sure that's flattery – but I must admit I enjoy it.'

'Now, why are pleasant things always called flattery and ugly things called the truth? Dear Lady Bellamy – Virginia, if I may? – do let us admit the truth to each other, however pleasant it may be.'

They exchanged warm smiles and Virginia went away to change, leaving her intriguing flatterer to wander round the room, peering at every picture and ornament with a discerning eye. She was back with him in under half the hour.

'I don't like it,' Mrs. Bridges was saying. 'In my young days we went out with the milkman or the postman or the butcher's boy . . .' Or a policeman, she recalled with momentary wistfulness from the depths of personal memory, but did not say it. 'Anyway, someone respectable,' she concluded instead.

'He may be respectable, Mrs. Bridges,' Daisy said.

'A man that answers advertisements? I'd never trust a man like that.'

'I really think you should have stopped her, Rose,' Mr. Hudson said. 'To engage in correspondence might have improved even Ruby's mind. But to allow her to go and meet a man who is, in effect, a total stranger . . .'

For Ruby was the one person absent from the servants' hall that evening. In her best hat and coat, and a deal too much powder and lipstick, she had gone to her first encounter with the quietly disposed Mr. Herbert Turner. It was ten o'clock now, and she had not returned.

'I couldn't stop her,' Rose protested.

'She's over twenty-one,' Edward pointed out.

Daisy giggled. 'You don't think he wants her for the white slave trade, Mr. Hudson?'

The others' expression registered the unlikelihood of the proposition. Only Mr. Hudson still showed genuine concern.

'She is not . . . well, versed in the ways of the world,' he answered gravely.

At that moment the area door was heard to open and shut. Frederick looked at his watch as relief showed all round. A moment later, Ruby appeared in the doorway, beaming idiotically.

'Ruby, you are late.'

'Sorry, Mr. Hudson.'

Mrs. Bridges snorted. 'How dare you go out and meet someone without telling me?'

'Yes, Mrs. Bridges.'

Ruby turned to depart, thereby disappointing them all. Daisy asked quickly, on the general behalf: 'What was he like, Ruby?'

The girl turned back again.

'Oh, he was ever so nice.'

'Stood you a bit of supper after the pictures, did he?' Frederick deduced.

'Oh, yes. I had tomato fish-cakes and bread and butter, and an ice cream and a nice pot of tea.'

She yawned suddenly.

'I must go to bed now. Goodnight, Mrs. Bridges. Goodnight, Mr. Hudson.'

Daisy and Edward went off to their own apartment over the garage and Frederick to his room. The butler and the cook sat on, silent and ruminative, for some minutes.

'We cannot stop the girl going out,' Hudson said at length. 'She has the right to meet whom she pleases, so long as she does not bring him back here.'

Mrs. Bridges' eyes gleamed with sudden inspiration.

'That's just what I want her to do, Mr. Hudson. Bring him back here. I feel responsible for that girl, and I reckon it's my duty at least to find out what sort of man he is. Yes, that's what we'll do, if you agree, Angus – have him to Sunday tea, and take a good look at him.'

Hudson, who preferred life to remain above all things orderly and free from nagging little irritations and worries, supported the idea readily, and the following morning, when the breakfast bustle was over, Ruby received her orders.

Three days later, in the afternoon, the denizens of Downstairs awaited Herbert Turner's coming with mixed expectations. Despite her reservations, Mrs. Bridges had given him the benefit of the doubt by changing out of her working clothes into one of her best dresses and had chivvied the others into laying the servants' hall table with tea things as correctly as if the guest they were about to receive for scrutiny was worthy of established respect. And, indeed, they were agreeably relieved when at last there came the knock at the door and Ruby, wearing her best green dress and, with her hair carefully done and not wearing her spectacles, looking passably attractive for once in her life, went out and in a few moments returned with a neatly dressed man with short-back-and-sides haircut and small round spectacles. He paused to stand self-consciously just inside the room.

Blushing faintly through the thickness of face powder, Ruby announced, 'This is Mr. Herbert Turner. Mrs. Bridges, Mr. Hudson, Miss Buck, Mrs. Barnes, Mr. Norton, Mr. Barnes.'

'Very pleased to make your acquaintance,' Mr. Turner said as his first utterance, bobbing his head in a little gesture of respect. His speech was precise and 'clerkly'. 'It's very kind of you to invite me here, I'm sure.'

'A pleasure, Mr. Turner,' Mrs. Bridges beamed; and Mr. Hudson hastened to indicate a chair at the table and say, 'Won't you sit down here, Mr. Turner? I imagine tea is ready, Mrs. Bridges?'

'Quite ready, Mr. Hudson. Ruby, you sit down, too. Daisy, perhaps you'd be so kind as to fetch the tea?'

Daisy had not foreseen this development and wasn't too sure that she approved of it; but there was no refusing, so she went off into the kitchen with her nose a little higher in the air than usual.

'You live in Balham, I believe, Mr. Turner?' Mrs. Bridges was saying.

'Yes. My parents and I have a house there.'

'A very pleasant area,' Mr. Hudson said.

'Oh, yes. Unfortunately, my mother is a martyr to rheumatism and my father's health has not been good since he was gassed in the war.'

'In the trenches, was he?' Edward asked, more interested now.

'Yes, Mr. Barnes. He was one of the Old Contemptibles.'

'Was you in the army, then?' asked the other ex-Serviceman, Frederick.

Their guest shook his head and glanced around them uncertainly.

'I'm afraid not. I always feel very awkward about it because, well, I was kept out by . . . by flat feet, of all things. Of course, being in the Post Office I was considered to be in a reserved occupation, but naturally I volunteered, and that was the answer I got.'

'Well,' Mr. Hudson said, trying to spare the man's feelings, ' "They also serve who only stand and wait".'

'Even with flat feet?' responded their guest, and got a general laugh which eased the tension immediately.

Indeed, as tea progressed Mr. Turner revealed himself to be the possessor of quite a pawky vein of humour and a lively interest in everyday matters which coincided to an agreeable extent with that of his hosts. The chance mention of the latest murder sensation in Sussex provoked an animated discussion in which he argued freely with Edward and Frederick until, upon the introduction of some of the more gruesome particulars, Mrs. Bridges called for an end to the subject.

'My fault entirely, Mrs. Bridges,' Mr. Turner apologised. 'I mentioned it first. I'm sure I did.'

'Are you interested in crime?' Hudson asked, trying to restore the guest's ease.

'Well, I think we all are a bit, Mr. Hudson, don't you? It's the drama of it, I always think. But I prefer what one might call a better class of murder. The classic cases, you know.'

'Fancy that!' Mrs. Bridges declared, admiring a scholar, and pressed Mr. Turner to another generous slice of her specially baked cake. Without perhaps realising it, they were all beginning to feel he was one of them already.

Carrying crockery into the kitchen together when the meal was over, Edward murmured to his wife, 'What d'you think?'

Daisy answered, 'I don't know what he sees in *her*.'

Overhearing, Frederick said, 'Ruby hasn't hardly said a word since he's been here. You know what I think? I reckon he's grateful to have a found a good listener.'

Ruby had gone up to her room to apply yet more powder and get into her outdoor clothes. With the other servants busy, Mr. Hudson and Mrs. Bridges were left alone with Herbert Turner for a few minutes. They proceeded to interrogate him in a way more suited to Ruby's parents than to her superiors in service.

'How old are you, Mr. Turner, if I might ask?'

'Thirty-five, Mr. Hudson, And done nothing, as you might say. I've lived a very quiet life, what with the war and my parents being invalids. Too quiet, really. I read the novels of H. G. Wells, and about those people he writes about who just . . . well, just exist. And I think, well, that's me.'

Mrs. Bridges asked carefully, 'Haven't you thought of getting married ever?'

'Well, I have, Mrs. Bridges, but I'm afraid money's always been a bit tight. Until my recent promotion, that is.'

He glanced from one to the other, swallowed visibly,

and added, 'I . . . I suppose I may as well admit that's why I answered that advertisement.'

Mr. Hudson was on the point of eliciting further details of Mr. Turner's hopes and intentions, but Ruby robbed him of the chance by entering in coat and hat. Mr. Turner rose with the alacrity of relief.

'Ah, there she is. Well, we'll be off, if you'll excuse us. I thought we might go back for a bite of supper with my parents a bit later.'

Mrs. Bridges stood up. 'Well, all right, Mr. Turner. But I don't want her home late, if you please.'

'Oh, no, Mrs. Bridges, I wouldn't do that. She's a bit too . . . precious for that.'

The simper on Ruby's vivid scarlet mouth was almost nauseating.

'All right, Ruby?' he asked, offering his arm.

'Yes . . . Herbert.'

The farewells to Mr. Hudson, Mrs. Bridges and the rest were mutually warm. Mr. Herbert Turner had been tested and approved.

'Well, Mrs. Bridges,' Hudson said, 'I think you can start looking for a new kitchen-maid.'

When Daisy opined that anyone who would want to go out with Ruby must be 'a proper Charlie', both rebuked her.

Virginia had completely forgiven Guy Paynter's indiscretion to the extent of having forgotten that he had ever uttered it. She had enjoyed the luncheon at the Ritz immensely. As the only woman present, she had been the centre of attention from the susceptible Arnold Bennett, who had stammered compliments. The ebullient Lord Birkenhead had coruscated especially for her with the witty erudition which few men of the time could match. Young Malcolm Sargent had proved intelligent and gallant in a way which Virginia sensed would be difficult for any woman to resist in years to come. Guy had been amusing, scandalously gossipy, and most assiduously attentive to her. The food and wines he had chosen quite outdid anything she was accustomed to.

'Why not?' Richard said later. He and James had been listening to her account of the occasion and he had raised his eyebrows and smiled when she added, a little diffidently, that Guy had invited her to lend him her support a fortnight hence at his country house, Shelbourne, where he was giving one of his celebrated 'political weekends'.

'You don't mind, then?'

'My dear, I'm only too delighted. I'd hate you to miss such a chance.'

'Won't it look rather strange, though – if I'm there without you?'

'Just because I have to go to Paris to meet the French Foreign Minister is no reason for your refusing a pleasant invitation while I'm away. People understand these things nowadays.'

'I suppose so. He sent me this round.'

She held up a small book.

'What is it?'

'Browning's poems. An autographed first edition.'

James whistled. 'That must be worth a pretty penny.'

'I know. We were talking about first editions, and which ones we'd particularly like to possess. I said I'd like to have a favourite book of poems, so that every time I read it I could pretend it was sent to me personally by the author. Perhaps I should take it back when I go to Shelbourne.'

She went out. The note which had accompanied the gift lay on the table beside James. Without stooping he could read the flamboyant scrawl: 'Just to thank you for being such a perfect hostess.'

'Father,' he said, 'do you think it's a good thing, Virginia seeing so much of Paynter?'

Richard regarded his son for a few moments before replying, 'She's perfectly safe with him.'

'Why do you say that?'

'For a reason I could not possibly mention to her.'

'You don't mean he's married?'

'No. He is . . . not the marrying sort.'

Understanding dawned on James's face. Richard continued, 'He's devoted to his mother. Innumerable ladies have acted as hostess at his table, and I dare say at least half of them expected to marry him. I'm sure nothing would horrify him more than to have a woman permanently in his house – or even temporarily in his bed.'

'Well, I'm damned!'

'Fortunately, Virginia is much too innocent to understand these things. I'm only too happy for her to enjoy herself with what one might reasonably describe as a safe man. She'll have a wonderful weekend.'

She did, too. With Rose to attend her whenever she needed a change, a bath, or a refurbishment of her make-up, and to supply a familiar presence in unfamiliar surroundings, Virginia revelled in meeting the distinguished, the ultra-fashionable, above all the scintillating, men and women whom Guy Paynter habitually selected as his guests. Her quiet intelligence and unostentatious beauty charmed them in turn, and the regretful farewells when the last taxi-load departed on the Sunday evening were as sincere as they were prolonged.

Guy led Virginia back into the drawing-room of his superbly furnished manor house, with its quiet lighting, *trompe l'oeuil* impression of classical columns and arches and paved pathway, and steadily burning open fire in a large hearth.

'Why do one's guests always have to take forty minutes to say goodbye?' he groaned, stretching. 'Parsons, we'll have a bottle of champagne, please. And some caviare. Not that horrid black stuff. Haven't we some of the amber?'

'Yes, sir,' his butler said, and went out.

'I'm sure they'll miss the train and all arrive back here insisting on staying the night,' Guy continued to Virginia, leaning in mock dejection against the mantelpiece. 'I must say I hope they don't, especially Margot. One never knows the meaning of a long weekend until one has Margot to stay.'

Virginia laughed. 'You know you enjoyed every minute of it.'

'No. I did *not* enjoy Winston's rendering of "My Old Dutch". As for Lloyd George's Welsh hymns, I've never admired them as much as many people pretend to.'

'But *they* enjoyed it. That was the important thing. The whole weekend has been a great success.'

He straightened up and went to kiss her gently on the cheek.

'Thanks to you. You are a splendid hostess.'

'No, I just like people.'

'And they like you. Now then, I thought you might like to see Charlie Chaplin's new film. I managed to get hold of a copy.'

'*The Gold Rush!* You . . . don't mean to say you have a private cinema here?'

'I don't usually tell people, or they want to spend the entire weekend watching Felix the Cat or Harold Lloyd when I want to play bridge. But as it's just the two of us I thought it might amuse you.'

'Yes.' Virginia hesitated. 'I didn't realise we were . . . going to be alone here tonight.'

'Does it embarrass you?'

'It does, rather.'

He laughed out loud.

'The thing I love about you is your delicious honesty. My mother would adore you. I say, would you come to a little dinner at her house? Tuesday?'

'I'd love to meet her, but Richard gets back tomorrow and I'm not sure what he's doing.'

'Not Richard. D'you mind? Just you. She's a little bit of an invalid and doesn't go about much. But a quiet dinner party, with just one person . . .'

Virginia was regarding him calculatingly as he gazed seemingly pleadingly into her eyes. The return of the butler interrupted what he was saying. Champagne in an ice bucket, an opened pot of caviare, biscuits and the appropriate impedimenta were set down.

'All right, Parsons,' Guy said. 'I'll deal with it.'

The man bowed and went out. Paynter went to draw the champagne cork.

'I wonder how Richard's getting on?' Virginia said deliberately. 'It's a very important meeting. He does care so much. I . . . I wish he could get a post in the Government again – where he could put his talents to better use.'

Guy's back was half to her as he worked gently at the cork. He was smiling to himself.

'Yes. Of course, it's not so easy, now he's in the Lords.'

Virginia faltered on, 'I believe there's. . . . a post of . . . of Under-Secretary of State for Foreign Affairs which is going to be vacant. It would be rather nice if . . .'

The cork came out of the bottle with a cultured sigh. Guy poured two glasses and brought her one.

'You know,' he said, 'I would do anything to please you. If I happen to have any influence in that direction I will certainly use it.'

They raised their glasses to touch gently and sipped a little. Then he wandered away to cover some of the biscuits with caviare. Virginia watched him uneasily, wishing she hadn't spoken. It was too late.

'You know,' he was saying over his shoulder, 'I thought of taking my yacht on a long cruise this summer. I was talking to the Prince of Wales last week. I think he'll probably come, and Freddie Birkenhead and one or two others. It just occurs to me . . . I wonder if you'd like to come. Richard could join us, whenever his duties allow.'

He returned with the plate of generously covered biscuits, and a napkin, which he set on a small table beside the settee.

'Well, Virginia? What do you say?'

She found herself looking up at him, wondering, unable to answer. Suddenly, she wished she was back in Eaton Place – or even upstairs, in some small room where the familiar, dependable Rose was probably reading her magazine tales of romantic make-believe.

'You know, Daisy,' said Rose next evening, 'I never saw such luxury in my life. They even had champagne in the servants' hall.'

She dumped Virginia's empty luggage on the table.

'Sounds a bit of all right to me,' Edward said, as he examined them. 'I'll give these a bit of a rub up before they're put away.'

'Ta, Eddie. Mind, it wasn't as good the last night, after all the others had gone.'

'All gone, Rose?' The inquiry came from Mr. Hudson, who had emerged from his pantry just in time to overhear. 'You mean, her ladyship stayed on alone last evening?'

Rose stared back at him, her mind working upon implications which had not so far occurred to her. The others watched her silently. After some moments, Ruby, who had been fidgeting in the background, spoke up.

'Mrs. Bridges, can I have tonight off, instead of next week? Herbert can't get off next week. It's his turn to be on duty in the evenings.'

'Oh, very well,' Mrs. Bridges snapped, her mind concerned with greater issues. 'Only, don't make a habit of it. Now, come on, Rose. Lunch is waiting. It'll all get cold.'

The servants sat down to table in preoccupied mood, though none more so than Rose.

'Well?' Polly Merivale asked James. 'Did your stepmother enjoy her weekend at Shelbourne?'

'Very much, I believe. Weren't you there?'

'Oh, no. "The Queen is dead; long live the Queen".'

He scowled. 'I don't think that's very funny.'

'Nor do I.' She wandered away to the morning-room mirror, to adjust her hat. 'Do you know where she's going tonight?'

'No.'

'She is going to dine with Guy's mother. I wonder if your father knows?'

'I imagine so,' James said, controlling his temper with no little difficulty.

Mrs. Merivale turned and came back to him.

'I wonder if he really *knows*?' she said, and he frowned less with anger than with curiosity. 'I nearly got invited there, James. Just before I came here to lunch with Guy that day. I knew at once what it meant. It meant that, after years of fending off every woman in sight like a demented old ocean-going tug, his dear mama had said "Guy, dear, you must get married. You know you'll need someone to look after you when I'm gone".'

James grinned at last. This woman really was a bitch.

'Sit down and stop talking rubbish, Polly,' he ordered. 'Look, I'm sorry if you're upset because your friendship with Guy has broken up, but that's no reason to . . .'

'You know why it did?' she interrupted, smiling in return. 'I cared too much. Oh, not for Guy. I don't like charm and ruthlessness in men. One or the other, but not both together.'

'Then, if you felt like that . . .'

'All that money, James. It's so beastly being poor. Harry left a mass of debts, and all I have is my widow's pension and a pittance his parents give me. Then along comes Guy, and suddenly I've only to mention something and have it. To say "I'd like to go to New York", and you're there. "Wouldn't it be pleasant to cruise round the Mediterranean" – and it happened. It's irresistible – or almost. I'm sure Lady Bellamy will find it so.'

She flashed him her brightest smile and went swiftly, leaving him staring.

'Father,' he said late that evening.

'Mm?'

Richard had not long returned from the Lords. Virginia had been out since before lunch and had still not come in.

'Has . . . Virginia said anything about . . . about Paynter lately?'

Richard looked surprised. 'Of course, from time to time. She's out with him and some others today. Brighton or somewhere. He has a new Lagonda he wanted to show off.'

'I . . . see.'

'As a matter of fact, he's invited her on his yacht in the summer. I shall join them, as and when.'

'Oh, no!'

'What on earth does that mean?'

'Father, you must forbid her to see him.'

'Forbid!' To James's irritation his father was actually smiling. 'I hardly think I can do that. And I'm very sure Virginia wouldn't obey me if I did. Besides . . .' He hesitated momentarily, 'If you must know, it was I who first asked her to cultivate his acquaintance. I wanted him to use his influence to get me a post.'

'Oh, for God's sake, Father! Do you mean to say that some post means more to you than Virginia does?'

Richard suddenly raged back, 'How dare you say that? Of course it doesn't! I've already told you, haven't I, that Virginia's perfectly safe with Guy Paynter? As safe as that Polly Merivale or any of the others have been. She's enjoying his company, and I'm glad for her, and that's all there is to it. Really, James, I do wish you would stop your eternal interfering in other people's happiness.'

James's face muscles twitched.

'There is such a thing as respect,' he retorted. 'Does anyone respect Polly Merivale and the others? Will they respect Virginia – or you, when it gets about that you bought some job or other with her reputation? Don't you understand that, Father? Or don't you care?'

He crashed out of the room, leaving Richard to sink into a fireside chair and stare into the glowing coals, suddenly horrified by the images he could picture there.

He was sitting there when Virginia came in. She wore a loose pink coat over a white dress and carried a white hat in one hand, her handbag and gloves in the other. A single strand of pearls was about her throat.

'Still up, Richard?' she said. 'I'm sorry I'm so late. We had dinner at Brighton.'

'You and Guy?' he asked, still picturing things in the fire.

'And the rest. Is . . . anything wrong?'

He got up stiffly and faced her.

'Virginia, I want to ask you something. You remember I asked you a favour a short time ago. I want to ask you a much greater one now. I want to ask you not to see so much of Guy Paynter.'

'You mean, you've got the Under-Secretaryship now?' she said it without sarcasm.

'No. That's nothing to do with it. You know, I've been made to feel my age quite often, lately . . . but I find suddenly that I'm still young enough to be jealous.'

The merest fraction of time elapsed before she flung her arms round his neck and pressed her cheek against his.

'Oh, Richard! I'm so glad!'

At that very moment, Ruby was facing an outraged Mrs. Bridges in the servants' hall. Mr. Hudson and Rose looked on.

'I've told you twice already, my girl, I will not have you stopping out this late, Herbert Turner or no Herbert Turner. I spoke to him when he first came here, and he agreed. I'm as disappointed in him as in you.'

'Yes, Mrs. Bridges.'

'It's not respectable in a young girl. Besides, you're only half awake in the mornings as it is, without late gallivanting.'

'It won't happen again, Mrs. Bridges.'

'It certainly won't. I'll see to that. You'll fetch that Herbert Turner round here and I'll have a few words to say to him, too.'

Rose ventured to ask kindly, 'Did you have a nice evening, Ruby?'

'Oh, yes.'

'I mean, did he . . . have anything special to say, like?'

'Oh, yes. He asked me to marry him.'

'Marry!' Mrs. Bridges almost shrieked. 'Well, why didn't you say, girl?'

'Because I said I wasn't interested, Mrs. Bridges.'

'You said *what*?'

'I thanked him very much for the honour, but I wasn't interested.'

Three stunned expressions faced her. She explained patiently, 'He was all right, but he hadn't got much go in him, really. Besides, he would never give up his father and 'specially his mother, and I didn't want to spend my days as nursemaid to invalids while he'd be out to his work.'

'*And*,' she closed the subject, once and for all, 'he didn't look nothing like his photograph. He wasn't a bit like Rudolph Valentino.'

Next afternoon, Sir Guy Paynter was shown into the morning-room, where Virginia and James sat. He was, as always, immaculately dressed, with a fresh buttonhole. The bland smile was on his lips as he nodded a silent greeting to James.

'Thank you for your note,' he said to Virginia. 'It was kind of you to send it round by hand, so that I should receive it as soon as possible.'

Virginia moistened her lips and explained to James, 'I had to refuse Guy's kind invitation to go on his yacht this summer. Richard and I are going to Austria.'

Guy said, 'Actually, I really just came round to pick up the book I lent you.'

'Book?'

'Browning's poems.' He glanced at the desk on which the little volume lay.

'Ah, of course,' Virginia smiled, and brought it to him. 'Thank you for lending it to me.'

'Not at all. Goodbye, Virginia. Goodbye, Major Bellamy.'

Still smiling, he bowed and showed himself out of the room.

'Well!' James exclaimed. 'Pretty cheap of him to take the book back.'

'Yes, I thought so. But effeminate men often are rather petty.'

'Effem . . . ! Does . . . does Father know you know?'

'Oh, no. He'd be terribly embarrassed. James, please – I'd rather he didn't.'

James gave her a reassuring grin, but said nothing.

They were still together when Richard came in a quarter of an hour later.

'Well?' Virginia asked. 'What did Mr. Baldwin want?'

'He sent for me to offer me the post of Under-Secretary of State for Foreign Affairs.'

James moved quickly to this father and shook his hand.

'Well done, Father. I hoped you'd get it.'

Virginia was looking puzzled.

'You don't mean . . . that Guy . . . ?'

'Sir Guy Paynter had been round and left a note at Downing Street earlier this morning. For some reason it had occurred to him suddenly to advise the Prime Minister that I was much too old to return to the Government.'

Virginia's hands flew to her mouth, but Richard was going on, smiling into her widened eyes.

'Baldwin said that that had made up his mind. He said he'd always considered giving the post to me, but he didn't want to have someone who appeared to be in Guy Paynter's pocket.'

He and Virginia regarded one another solemnly for some seconds. Then she was in his arms again and James was making a quiet exit, to go up to his room and put on his gramophone a record which caused the servants who heard it to raise their heads in surprise at its unusual cheerfulness.

Endings and Beginnings

CHAPTER ONE

'Not a penny off the pay; not a second on the day.'

It was the response of the militant new leader of the miners of South Wales to the report, published in March 1926, by Sir Herbert Samuel on the declining state of their industry. Like many official reports before and since, it proposed wide-scale reorganisation and improvements of structure, administration and working methods, but as long-term measures. The only short-term one in this case was for a cut of nearly one eighth of every miner's pay.

A. J. Cook responded characteristically. Discussion continued between the Trade Union Council and the uneasy government. A compromise seemed to be coming closer. Then, adamant in their refusal to accept wage cuts, more than a million miners were 'locked out' by the pit owners, and the incensed T.U.C. threatened a sympathy strike by more than two million workers in other industries.

The possibility of a general strike, an expedient first mooted by William Benbow in the 1820s, seemed, a century later, imminent.

'Rain and a sharp north-easterly wind, sir. Quite abnormal for the first day of May. Shall I put more coal on the fire, sir?'

Hudson hovered near the coal scuttle beside the grate in James Bellamy's sitting room. He had just drawn the curtains against the bleak dusk outside in Eaton Place.

James nodded. 'Coal fires in May! Miners out on strike and the rest of the country all jumping on the bandwagon. What a mess.'

'I gather there's still hope of a settlement, sir,' the butler said, shovelling coal. 'The Trade Union leaders are at Downing Street at this very moment, according to the wireless.'

'It shouldn't have been allowed to get this far, Hudson. A

general strike is a direct affront to the government. It should be forbidden by law.'

'I agree with you, sir. I feel ashamed of my fellow working man.'

'Not your fault, Hudson. It's men like Cook, and J. H. Thomas, and Ernest Bevin. So-called leaders with the nerve to hold the country to ransom and threaten the liberty of ordinary decent people like you.'

Hudson replaced the small shovel and straightened up.

'I understand the government have been laying in stocks of food and essential supplies for some months.'

'Oh, yes, we'll win all right. But what will it cost us? The whole world's gone stark, staring mad.'

James relapsed into dark brooding. He was only subconsciously aware of his butler's withdrawal with the announcement, 'Dinner will be at eight o'clock, sir.'

Hudson returned to the servants' hall to find his subordinates in anxious discussion.

'All army leave's been cancelled,' Edward was saying. 'There's troops roaming about all over the country.'

'Yeh, and two battleships sitting in the Mersey,' added Frederick, who had been down at the pub with Edward, listening to a Sergeant of Marines who had not needed to pay for a single drink for himself all day on the strength of his self-professed knowledge. 'They're probably going to call up the reservists.'

'Well, you're not going, Eddy,' Daisy flashed at her husband. 'You're not fighting again.'

'Who's fighting who?' asked Ruby, wide-eyed.

'Yes,' Rose challenged the handsomely impassive Frederick, 'who are you going to fight? The miners? The bus drivers?'

'Anyone who goes on strike,' he responded, unperturbed. 'Just doing our duty for the country again. Eh, Edward?'

Mr Hudson stepped in at last, as Edward opened his mouth to agree.

'That's enough of that, both of you. How many times have I told you not to be influenced by pub talk? There are decisions

8

being made, even now, by responsible people in calm debate. I'm still hopeful that common sense will prevail.'

'With respect, Mr Hudson,' Frederick said, 'it was you told us yesterday all miners was Reds.'

'They aren't!' Ruby protested, flushing. 'My Uncle Len's a miner, and he's not a Red. He *isn't*, Mr Hudson.'

Hudson, as so often when challenged, fell back upon Higher Authority.

'I gained the information in good faith from Mr Winston Churchill . . . That is to say, quoted in yesterday's newspaper.'

'Peace on earth comes to men of good will,' the actual voice of Higher Authority told them over the crackling wireless waves shortly afterwards, when the phlegmatic Prime Minister, Stanley Baldwin, gave his public reassurance that all would be well. Not much later, the General Strike had begun, and neither peace nor goodwill reigned in Great Britain.

'It really is dreadfully inconsiderate,' Lady Prudence Fairfax pouted. 'I'm giving a dinner party on Wednesday, and they say there'll be no deliveries. And on Saturday I'm going to Wales.'

'There's no chance of that, my dear,' Richard Bellamy told her. 'From midnight tonight trains, buses, all public services come to a grinding halt.'

'Not if we can help it,' Georgina retorted from the morning-room settee, where she sat alongside James. 'We'll drive the trains ourselves. Archie Dunlop's dying to drive a train. He'll take you to Wales, Prue.'

'Does he know the way?'

'Oh, you just point the thing and follow the rails, don't you?'

Lady Prudence shuddered elaborately. 'The thought of any of my friends manning the railways fills me with absolute terror.'

'What happened to the talks last night?' a serious James asked his father above the chatter.

'They ended in confusion. Apparently some *Daily Mail* printers refused to print an article condemning the strike. Baldwin got to hear about it and sent Thomas and company packing. Far too hasty, in my opinion. They were looking to

9

Baldwin to help them save face. Nobody wants this wretched strike.'

'Well, it's been coming since the end of the war, only people have shut their eyes to it,' James replied morosely. 'What happened in Russia's going to happen here.'

'No one tells me who the fight's between,' Lady Prudence complained. 'The strikers say they're not against the government, but against the mine-owners.'

Richard said, 'It's rather more complicated than that. I don't go so far as James, but there's certainly a strong feeling of solidarity in the working classes – rather like the early days of the war.'

James was on his feet now, the old restlessness re-emerging and causing him to prowl like a pent-up beast.

'Then, we must meet it, Father. We've got law and order on our side. It's intolerable we should be threatened like this.'

His father nodded, though without assurance. 'That's the line Winston's taking. Trade Unions have thrown down the gauntlet. They must suffer the consequences.'

He got up, too.

'Well, I've got to get to the House and see what I can contribute. Ah, Hudson, tell Edward to bring the car round, will you?'

'Yes, my lord,' said the butler, who had just entered. 'I was, er, wondering about her ladyship, my lord. She was to have returned from Inverness tomorrow, but in view of the uncertainty of the trains . . .'

'Good lord, yes! I'll telephone her tonight.'

'Very good. Er, one other thing, my lord . . .'

'Yes?'

'They've been calling on the wireless for volunteers for special constabulary duties. I wondered if I might have your lordship's permission to re-enlist?'

'Of couse, Hudson. Very good idea.'

They left the room together. Georgina turned to James, smiling.

'Will you be volunteering, Jumbo?'

'For what?'

'Anything. I'm going to. Dally says she's going to be a post-man. After all, if they won't do the jobs, we've got to do them instead. Then they'll have to give in.'

'Huh! You think they'll just stand by and watch you? You're breaking a strike. Blood will be spilt.'

'In England! What do you suggest we do, then? Drive round in armoured cars?'

Her flippancy was unmatched by James's grim frown and the twitching of his jaw.

'Listen to me, Georgina. A small group of people are quite deliberately trying to cripple our economy. They've forced us to mass our defences, and they might just be misguided enough to fight us all the way. And all you and your friends can do is treat it as some huge lark, to fill the boredom of your empty lives.'

He stamped out of the room from which his so easily exasperated nature had often caused him to stamp.

'Pompous ass!' Georgina said quietly after him.

Virginia was not the only member of the household stranded away from home. Mrs Bridges was at Yarmouth, visiting her sister. She took the momentous step of telephoning Eaton Place to advise the stocking up of food against the shortages she believed to be imminent.

'You seen Eddie?' Daisy asked Frederick, while Mr Hudson and Rose were taking it in turns to try to reassure the absent cook that mass-starvation had not yet manifested itself. 'He's bin gone ages for the milk.'

'Probably having to queue,' Frederick said.

Edward had gone in the car to the emergency centre in Hyde Park. At that moment he came in by the area door, his face red and his nose even more so. Daisy flew to him.

'Eddie! What's happened? You had an accident?'

'All right, Dais, all right. Don't fuss. It's nothing serious.'

'There's blood!' she wailed, and Hudson called, 'Ruby, get some water, quickly!'

Edward sank down at the table, thrusting an already bloodied handkerchief to his nose.

'It was all quite peaceful,' he explained in muffled tones. 'Crowds of people, but I'd just got the milk and back into the car . . . Oh, thanks, Rose.'

After brief ministering he continued.

'I had my sign up in the window, like his lordship told me, saying "Signal for Lift", and this great big bloke comes up, about eight foot tall. He looks in the window, calls me "scab", and then gets hold of my nose and twists it half off my face.'

'He's torn some of the skin off,' said Daisy, peering.

'It's bloody painful, I can tell you. Why pick on me, though?'

Rose explained the obvious. 'You was wearing a chauffeur's uniform and driving a posh car. He thought you should've been striking, too.'

'That's daft,' Frederick interjected. 'I mean, we got no grievances. Have we?'

'No, Frederick, you have not,' Mr Hudson told him firmly. 'And now, I must be off and report for duty.'

He thrust his constable's truncheon into his coat pocket.

'If any hooligan attempts to twist my nose, God help him!'

It was so rarely that Mr Hudson had ever been heard to invoke his Maker that even Edward forgot his distress and watched with as much awe as the rest as the master of their downstairs domain took his leave.

Four days later the nose was still tender, but in the meantime Edward's social conscience had become even more tender.

'You know, Dais,' he ruminated, 'I know it bloody well hurt at the time, but driving round since then, and seeing all those blokes just standing about in groups – bus drivers, engine drivers, and all that, out of work because they're sticking up for the miners – well, it's made me think a bit. I mean, they're only asking for a decent wage.'

'Don't agree with you,' said Frederick, who by this time had been enrolled as a probationary Special and assigned the duty of escort to an omnibus driven by Volunteer Driver Major James Bellamy and conducted by a young Oxford scholar, by name Andrew Bouverie. 'They're disrupting the country,' Frederick went on. 'You can't do that and get away with it.'

As always, Daisy rounded on anyone who did not side with her husband.

'Eddie and me know what it's like to go without a decent wage. There's nothing you can do if nobody'll listen to you.'

Rose asked, 'How do you know they don't listen? You think people like his lordship don't listen?'

'If he listens, why don't he give 'em what they're asking for?'

Frederick said patiently. 'It's not up to him. There's not enough to go round, anyway.'

'Yeh,' Rose agreed. 'And it's not right for you to be talking that way, Daisy. Didn't his lordship come down here yesterday, explaining how all our loyalties was needed not only to this house but to the country? Well, that's a fine way to repay him!'

'Eddie and me's not disloyal!'

'Then show it and shut up, both of you. Every day there's people telling us the strike's all wrong – cleverer people than Edward and you. On the wireless – saying it's wicked and causing misery, and you come out with this drivel! All I can say is, don't let Mr Hudson catch you.'

The bell from the morning-room, where James and his conductor had been refreshing themselves with a drink while their omnibus stood parked incongruously outside in the fashionable thoroughfare, summoned Frederick back to duty. Edward wandered over to his wireless set and switched it on. After the long moments of its warming up they heard the precise tones of an announcer in mid-bulletin.

'. . . that there have been no formal moves towards resumption of negotiations. Mr Baldwin's declaration still stands that the general strike order must be withdrawn before there can be any discussion of peace. To this, so far, the answer of the T.U.C. has been an uncompromising refusal. The Cabinet declares firmly that it cannot discuss terms while any question of intimidation remains.'

'There, see?' Rose said. ' "Intimidation".'

'Meanwhile, it is reported that London has solved most of its traffic problem . . .'

Daisy glanced out of the window. 'There's two people coming down.'

'. . . Omnibus services have steadily increased. Yesterday several hundreds were available, many of them running normal services at a few minutes' interval.'

There was a knocking at the area door. Daisy got up to answer it.

'Cricket,' the announcer was continuing. 'Against Surrey at the Oval the Australians have scored 246 for 6. Taylor made 76 and Woodfull is 60 not out.'

Edward switched off and they heard a man's voice heavily-accented saying to Daisy, 'Be a good lass and tell her her Uncle Len's here, with Mr Thompson from Barnsley.'

Instead, Daisy ushered them in, two stocky, middle-aged men with pale, lean faces under flat caps, which they removed as they entered the servants' hall. Their suits were drab and of rough shoddy cloth.

'Uncle Len!' Ruby exclaimed.

'Hello, Ruby,' one of the men said, smiling with his lips, though not with his tired eyes. 'Just thowt we'd drop in to see thee. Have a piece of cake and a cup o' tea, if there's one going'.'

Introductions were made and tea made and served at the long table. The visitors ate and drank eagerly.

'Come all the way from Yorkshire, have you?' Edward asked.

'That's right, lad,' said Uncle Len. 'Mr Thompson and me's pit delegates for t'Mineworkers' Federation, up for t'big meeting tonight.'

'What are things like in Barnsley?' Rose asked.

'Are you winning?' Edward added.

'Oh, we'll win, right enough. We're fighting for bread, not t'moon. Nobbut a simple living wage.'

'Church says we're right,' Mr Thompson put it. 'Archbishop of Canterbury hisself – only t'wireless won't let 'im broadcast because government says they're not to. Call this a Christian country!'

'Aye,' Uncle Len agreed, 'When they let Winston Churchill

go clattering on about revolution and civil war. It's nobbut a stunt to panic folk.'

'My Eddie got attacked,' Daisy said. Edward fingered his healed but still tender nose.

'Aye, well, a few maybe,' Uncle Len had to admit. 'But most of us, we're peaceful, law-abiding folk.'

Mr Thompson pulled out the newspaper they had seen sticking from his jacket pocket and tossed it on to the table.

'If tha wants truthful picture, take a look at our paper. Most folk don't know nowt about a miner's life. Every five hours a man or boy killed. Nine hundred maimed every day, some for life. You still find skeletons of little lads and lasses down there.'

The servants were staring at the grey men opposite them with incredulity and growing horror.

'And all for what?' Uncle Len took over. 'Fifty-six shillings a week. And now t'owners want to drop it to seven-and-six a shift. Work that out over a five and a half day week. Forty-one shilling, to keep a wife and bairns.'

Edward swallowed. 'We . . . never knew it was like that.'

Uncle Len shrugged. 'We're not asking you to fight our battles.'

'No,' said Mr Thompson, whose voice was harsher and sharpened to a more bitter edge, 'but millions are. Most working folk know we've got a cause.'

The area door opened and closed again with a firmness which the servants knew to be Mr Hudson's particular touch. He entered and surveyed the visitors with surprise. He was less than his immaculate self.

'You bin in a fight, Mr Hudson?' Edward asked.

'A wee scuffle. Two youths, writing seditious slogans on the pavement. I managed to apprehend them both. They won't trouble us again for a while, I fancy.'

'Get Mr Hudson a cup of tea, Ruby,' Rose ordered, then proceeded to introduce their guests. 'They've come up for a miners' delegates' meeting,' she explained finally.

Hudson regarded them with unconcealed distaste.

'I'd have thought the only thing to meet about was to call off

15

this wicked strike,' he said. 'You've gained nothing from it. The country is still on its feet, in spite of your efforts.'

Uncle Len said quietly, 'We've no wish to wreck this country, Mr Hudson.'

'No,' Mr Thompson said less moderately. 'You're the ones wrecking it. Blackleg labour and special constables. Putting young strikers behind bars.'

'It is the duty of every loyal subject to do what he can against the forces of evil who are out to destroy our liberty.'

'Liberty! Oh, you can talk about liberty, living comfortable down here . . .'

'We know what he means,' Uncle Len interrupted his colleague. 'Come on, Arnold. We've out-stayed our welcome. Goodbye, Mr Hudson. It's been instructive meeting you. So long, Ruby, lass. Your Mum'll be glad we dropped by.'

He nodded once in farewell to the rest of them and went out, followed by Thomson, who made no gesture. Mr Hudson sat down to the table, to the tea Ruby had just brought him. He saw the newspaper lying there. Recognition of its title caused him to put down his cup before he had even sipped from it.

'Do you know what that rag is?' he raged. 'It is a seditious propaganda sheet, put out by communists.'

'It isn't, Mr Hudson,' Ruby retorted. 'My uncle Len brought it.'

'You be quiet, girl. I tell you it's printed by traitors, and I forbid a copy of it in this house. Take it out and burn it at once. Rose, I want to talk to you.'

He got to his feet, leaving the tea untouched, and went into his pantry. Rose followed and closed the door. He turned angrily on her.

'You know perfectly well that you are responsible here when I am absent. I can see it isn't safe to leave this house for a moment, though.'

'What d'you mean, Mr Hudson?'

'Those two miners you saw fit to entertain are the very sort of people we're fighting . . .'

'It's Ruby's uncle! I couldn't turn him away.'

16

'You could, and should have, as a duty to this household. Have you no intelligence, girl. This is the house of a prominent member of the government. Things are spoken here and written down that could be of immense value to the wrong people.'

'They're not spies, Mr Hudson.'

'They're enemies and traitors.'

'They're not! They're Englishmen, same as us. They're not enjoying the strike any more'n we are. At least we can treat 'em with a bit of civility.'

'Calm down, Rose, calm down. All I'm trying to point out to you is that feelings on both sides are running high at the moment. It's up to the saner ones amongst us to cut out any loose talk that could unbalance people like Edward and Daisy and Ruby. It's up to us to set an example of responsibility and loyalty. Do you understand, Rose?'

Less than convinced, she could only nod.

'Very well, Rose. We'll say no more about it.'

He ushered her out and followed her, to return to his teacup.

Mr Hudson was not the only man in Britain who feared the direct consequences his country might suffer from the General Strike. Many who had sympathised with the miners on sheer humanitarian grounds had begun to grow alarmed by reports – both true and false – of rabble-rousing, damage and personal violence. A High Court judge upheld Sir John Simon's denunciation of the strike as illegal, causing law-respecting Unionists to re-examine their views and bringing nearer the likelihood of widespread arrests and active intervention by the armed forces, who so far had been used principally only for escorting convoys of vital supplies and protecting volunteers in the public services from attack.

No lives had been lost through direct violence, but there had been many scuffles, injuries and arrests. The derailment of the Flying Scotsman express train by strikers near Newcastle shocked and outraged the nation.

In the Trades Union Congress headquarters in Eccleston Square, moderate leaders grew increasingly alarmed at evidence of foreign moves to manipulate the striking workers into violent confrontation with the forces of law and order and to accomplish a political revolution. It began to appear to some onlookers that the T.U.C. were doing more than the government to bring the strike to an end.

'Over a week now!' Richard Bellamy exclaimed to James as they sat over evening brandies in the morning-room. 'Baldwin claims to be the man of peace and sits back doing nothing.'

'What can he do, Father? The strike notices are still up.'

'There are plenty of things he can do. He can bring people together in private – mine-owners, Union leaders, and anyone else with something to offer. He can listen to them, discuss with them; listen to members of his own party. Men with vision and vast experience. Last night I was with Reading and Wimbourne, two ex-viceroys, and a few others. We sat up half the night, drafted several schemes, presented them to Baldwin this morning – and he hasn't even acknowledged them. I'm not saying we have the answer, but at least we're trying every way to find it.'

'But why compromise at all? We're winning. We're proving that, the longer it goes on.'

'The longer it goes on, James, the worse will be the consequences. The war of attrition will be absolutely disastrous.'

James shook his head emphatically. 'We've got them on the run. Why let them escape?'

Georgina had come into the room in time to hear him.

'They're beaten already,' she said. 'They're saying the country has let them down.'

'They can't blame the country,' James persisted. 'It's their own leaders they should blame. Defy them and get back to work.'

Richard disagreed, 'If they defy their leadership, it's the end of the Trade Unions. The country must have Trade Unions.'

'Not with leaders who've been discredited. They've committed a criminal act and they must be punished.'

Georgina, weary from a trip to Manchester and back that day in the care of a young man-about-town, delivering a consignment of the government published newspaper, the *British Gazette*, flared up at this.

'Why do you always have to talk like that, James? Always about punishment . . . and war. People don't want to hear about it any more. They just want to be left in peace, with enough to eat, to enjoy themselves.'

She turned back to the door.

'I'm exhausted. I'm going to bed. Goodnight, Uncle Richard.'

But even as this brief clash took place, talks were going on elsewhere which would bring the strike to its end. Sir Herbert Samuel, who had been away in Italy had returned – driven from Dover to London by the racing motorist Sir Henry Seagrave as if to symbolise the urgency of his return – and plunged at once into secret negotiations with the T.U.C. The miners' leaders were carefully not consulted.

At No. 165 Eaton Place next day, Richard spoke into the morning-room telephone, watched by his son.

'Yes, yes. It's splendid news. Thank you for telephoning. Goodbye.'

He replaced the receiver and turned to James.

'The end's in sight. The T.U.C. leaders are at Downing Street now. They've agreed to call off the strike so that negotiations with the miners can begin. It should be over within the hour.'

'J. H. Thomas has accepted Samuel's formula?'

'That's it.'

'Well, he may have done, but what about the miners?'

'They must accept, too. They've no choice left. You don't look particularly pleased, James.'

'Yes, I'm pleased, Father. Just wondering what happens when we've all finished congratulating ourselves.'

Richard regarded him with little surprise. Little ever seemed to gratify James. Nothing did wholly.

'There'll be no vindictiveness from this government,' Richard answered. 'Baldwin has given his word on that. The industry will be reorganised. All strikers will be reinstated without penalty. Don't you see, James, we've kept our civil liberty. Our greatest asset.'

James nodded, but said morosely, 'A campaign fought with a mass of guns – against a pathetic, futile enemy.'

Richard raised his shoulders and let them sag as he expelled his breath in a sigh.

'Ah, well . . . If you won't join me in a drink to victory, at least take one to avoidance of defeat.'

He went to ring for Hudson and champagne.

'Going to miss your constable duties, Mr Hudson?' Frederick asked some time later.

'Not a bit, Frederick. It gives me no pleasure chasing hooligans at my age, I can assure you.'

Edward said, 'Bit of a let-down, now it's all over. No more bloody battles in the street.'

'No more getting your nose tweaked,' Daisy reminded him, tapping it lightly, causing him to wince away.

Rose was over by the wireless set, trying to tune it finely, frowning as she concentrated against the background conversation. Ruby stood puckering her brow, fiddling doubtfully with the hem of her apron.

'Will they get more money?' she asked suddenly. Everyone except Rose looked at her inquiringly. 'Miners,' she explained. 'Will they get more?'

'Course they will,' Edward assured her. 'Your Uncle Len and all of 'em. Won't they, Mr Hudson?'

'I, er . . . From what I can gather they'll get . . . the same, at any rate, Ruby.

'Listen!' Rose exclaimed from across the room. The final bars of the National Anthem crackled over the ether.

They listened in silence until it ended. Hudson looked at his watch.

'Right,' he addressed them all briskly. 'Now back to your duties, everybody. We have allowed things to become very slipshod in this household, these past nine days. It behoves us to follow the example of the nation as a whole and return to our work with a will.'

He strode pantry-wards. Exchanging a variety of glances, the rest obediently began to move their separate ways.

CHAPTER TWO

As he came down the stairs into the hall of No. 165, carrying a breakfast tray, Mr Hudson suddenly grimaced. He paused on his way towards the kitchen stairs and laid the tray on a side table, to free himself to massage his left arm with his right. The pain he had just felt there had been sudden and intense.

As he continued to rub the still throbbing arm he heard the morning-room bell ringing distantly. Hudson would never have allowed personal discomfort to come before duty. He adjusted his cuffs, straightened his back, and went in. He found Lord Bellamy, the Major and Miss Georgina, evidently comparing diaries.

'Ah, Hudson. The French Ambassador's coming to dinner. Monsieur Fleuriau. Friday the sixteenth.'

'Very good, my lord.'

Hudson could feel the onset of new pain, but he stood impassively, hearing James say, 'Sorry, Father, can't manage. Playing polo. Shan't be in any sort of form for ambassadors after six chukkers at Cowdray.'

Georgina said, 'And I've been invited sailing at Bembridge that weekend.'

'But I was counting on you both!' Lord Bellamy protested.

Hudson ventured, 'Will her ladyship not have returned from Scotland, my lord?'

'Yes, she returns on Monday. She'll be here.'

'There you are, then,' James said. 'You don't need us.'

'But I do. I want Georgina to bring her own special charm to the occasion . . .'

'Thank you, Uncle Richard.'

'. . . and you to take care of the Fleuriau daughter.'

'How old?'

'Well, er, about sixteen.'

'Steady on, Father!'

21

They laughed. Hudson felt himself beginning to perspire.

'Well,' James said, shutting his little diary with a snap, 'it shouldn't be too hard to think of someone. I'm sorry, Father, but . . .'

Mr Hudson suddenly knew he had to get out of the room quickly. For once in his life he interrupted.

'Will it be eight for dinner, my lord?'

Three surprised faces looked at him.

'Yes, Hudson, eight,' Lord Bellamy said. 'You can tell Mrs Bridges to start thinking it over before her ladyship returns.'

'Yes, my lord.'

'You . . . all right, Hudson?'

'Quite all right, thank you, my lord.'

All the same, he was glad to get beyond the door and even allowed himself to sit on a hall chair for some moments before taking up the tray again and going slowly down the kitchen stairs.

He felt normal again by supper time, but he merely picked at the food on his plate.

'You going to give them your French cuisine, Mrs Bridges?' Daisy asked.

'I don't know yet. Depends on her ladyship.' An afterthought struck her. 'I never given French cuisine to a Frenchman before.'

'Expect they'd like something simple for a change,' Frederick said. 'Good old Yorkshire pud.'

'Yeh, and Ruby's apple dumplings,' Edward supported him. 'I bet your dumplings is famous at the French Embassy, Ruby.'

'Why ever should they?'

'Mr Hudson knows the butler there, don't you, Mr Hudson? Bound to've told him.'

'Ed's only teasing,' Daisy said. 'You know him, Ruby.'

But the exchange had drawn Mrs Bridges' attention to Mr Hudson's neglect of his plate. She frowned and became the second person that day to ask if he was feeling all right. He murmured an untrue apology about having had two large slices of bread and jam at teatime and lost his appetite. He gave them all a reassuring smile; but he was feeling vaguely uncomfortable about the arm and chest. He retired to bed before any of the others, and was thankful to do so.

'What's that you're reading?' Daisy asked Frederick.

'A book.'

'I can see it's a book. What about?'

'Not for little girls.'

Rose leaned over the back of his chair and grabbed it playfully.

'It's about wine,' she announced, surprised.

'That's right. Mr Hudson lent it me.'

'What do you want to know about wine for?'

'I'm interested, that's why.' He seized the book back. 'It's a footman's duty to know about things.'

'Not wine,' Rose argued. 'That's a butler's duty.'

'Yeah, well . . . I'm not going to be a footman all my life, am I?'

Edward came in. Daisy told him, 'Fred's learning up about wine.'

Edward shrugged. 'I know about wine. Give us a question, Fred.'

Without consulting the book, and wearing the look of supercilious amusement which Ruby secretly thought highly romantic, Frederick complied.

'Where are the Saint-Emilion wines grown?'

'Not that kind of question,' Edward said. 'You don't have to know where they're grown.'

Frederick's dark humour increased.

'Right,' he accepted. 'Give us the names of four different clarets.'

'Clarets? Er . . . Chauteau, er . . . Chateau, er . . .'

'Latour, Lafite, Margaux, Haut-Brion . . . Got a long way to go to catch me up,' Frederick said smugly, getting to his feet and stretching. 'So long.' He went off to bed, leaving Edward and Daisy affronted and the others impressed.

A small crisis hit the household a few mornings later. It came

23

in the form of a telephone call from Virginia, to say that an outbreak of mumps had occurred in the Scottish village she was visiting. She herself was feverish and had been ordered to bed by the doctor. He was unsure whether she had caught the complaint, but was being adamant that she must not travel to London in time for the dinner party.

'Postpone it,' Georgina told Richard. He shook his head. She knew enough of the niceties of diplomatic relations to be aware that one didn't disrupt an ambassador's forward planning, but adopted emergency measures to ensure that those plans went smoothly and agreeably.

'Ah, well,' she said. 'To avoid a diplomatic incident I'll cancel Bembridge. I'm not awfully fond of sailing, anyway.'

Richard thanked her warmly. His look of relief made up her mind for her, and she sought out James to tell him it was his duty to help in the backing-up operation. At length he raised his hands in a mock gesture of surrender and they summoned Mrs Bridges to the morning-room.

'The most important thing,' James prepared his cousin as they awaited her coming, 'is not to let her bully you. Ah, Mrs Bridges, do come in. We thought we should discuss this menu.'

'Yes, sir,' their small but formidable cook replied. 'I was thinking of a saddle of lamb.'

'Oh, ah, you were? Well, all right. Plenty of garlic . . .'

'Not too much, sir. And my onion sauce, if you think that's suitable.'

'Oh, yes. Fine. Now, the soup. Mulligatawny?'

'Mock turtle, sir. Followed by fillet of sole à la Colbert and my vol-au-vents of oysters.'

James opened his mouth to attempt some slight modification, but Mrs Bridges sailed on.

'After the lamb, partridge.'

'Oh!' James managed. 'Had my fill of partridge lately. Can' it be grouse?'

Mrs Bridges crushed him with a firm shake of her grey head

'The partridges from Southwold are just about ready, sir With one of my salads, of course. Then sorbets. Meringue o

Peach Melba to follow, and perhaps an apricot soufflé.'

James turned to Georgina, annoyed to find her smirking at him.

'How does that sound to you?' he asked, hoping she would over-rule some detail, but was annoyed to hear her say, 'Lovely!'

James accepted defeat with abrupt courtesy to the cook, who left them, quite under the impression that she had just received orders for the dinner party from the master of the house.

As ill luck would have it, Mr Hudson felt, the evening of the dinner coincided with a harsh return of the symptoms he had been feeling from time to time recently. In pain and perspiring copiously, he found it impossible to move briskly about his duties. His distress was exacerbated by what he took for nagging on the part of the other male servants.

'Haven't you opened the wine yet, Mr Hudson? I'll do it for you, if you like.'

'Cocktails are all ready in the drawing-room, Mr Hudson. The fire's made up.'

'His lordship's clothes is all laid out. Just waiting for the Major to call me.'

'Frederick!' he exploded. 'Your shoes are squeaking. Take them off and soften them up.'

'But I bought them special, Mr Hudson.'

'There is nothing more intolerable at a dinner party than a footman with squeaking shoes. Go on, now. No, wait. Is the drawing-room ready?'

'I just told you.'

Rose bustled in with a necklace in her hands.

'An enormous great bunch of flowers has just come from her ladyship to wish Miss Georgina luck,' she reported excitedly. 'Mr Hudson, can you get this necklace of Miss Georgina's unfastened? I can't.'

Hudson made no answer, but turned away, his head reeling. Frederick took the necklace from Rose and began to fiddle with its clasp himself.

In his pantry, Hudson mopped his brow yet again and slowly went about the suddenly laborious business of changing into his evening dress and white tie.

'Mr Hudson's in a funny mood,' Rose remarked to Mrs Bridges. 'Looks all hot and bothered.'

'Yes, well I'm all hot and bothered, with the help I'm getting. Oh, Ruby, where's the stewpan got to now?'

'Just behind you, Mrs Bridges.'

'Well, give it here, then.'

And so it continued for half an hour longer, until it occurred to Rose that she had better give Mr Hudson a knock and remind him that it was approaching seven-thirty. He had not emerged from his pantry, and both Edward and Frederick had kept glancing uneasily at the six unopened bottles of Chateau Latour 1906, waiting for him to reappear and draw the corks.

He answered her knock with the impatient reply that he would be out in a minute. Rose was just turning to go when there came a crash from within the pantry which reached the ears of the others in the hall. As they moved towards her, their expressions registering puzzlement and alarm, Rose knocked harder on the door and called Mr Hudson's name. This time there was no response.

Rose jerked open the door and went in. Hudson was lying almost at her feet, his body jerking in pain, one hand clutching his chest, his lips drawn back as he gasped fiercely for breath.

'Mrs Bridges!' Rose cried. 'Fetch Mrs Bridges somebody.'

But Mrs Bridges was already approaching, wiping her hands on her apron. She took one look and ordered, 'Rose – telephone for the doctor. Quick!'

Rose hurried to obey. Frederick asked, 'What about the dinner?'

'Never mind the dinner,' the cook replied, getting down on her knees beside the prone man. 'Go and tell 'em upstairs there may be a bit of delay.'

She lowered her mouth close to Hudson's ear. He was making little moaning sounds, trying to speak.

'It's all right, Angus,' she told him. 'It's Kate here. You had a fall, that's all. It's all right, dear.'

Edward, Daisy and Ruby watched petrified as she cradled him, stroking his hair like a child's. He was silent now, his eyes closed, and he lay inertly against her. He looked as if he were dead.

Dr Foley was round within minutes. While he examined Hudson in the privacy of the butler's pantry, the rest tried to concentrate on preparations for the dinner party. It was not easy.

'Sauce is ready, Mrs Bridges,' Ruby reported.

'I can't think about sauces!'

'You must,' Rose intervened. 'Now come on, taste it and see if Ruby's done it right.'

She thrust a spoonful at Mrs Bridges as though force-feeding a child. The cook admitted it to her mouth then spluttered dramatically. 'Garlic! Full of garlic.'

Tears started to Ruby's eyes as she protested, 'I only rubbed the bowl with it, Mrs Bridges – like you told me.'

'It's ruined.'

Rose had tasted it meanwhile. 'No it isn't. It's just right, Ruby. Frenchmen like garlic, anyway. Now is the soup coming on all right?'

'Is it his heart, d'you think?' Mrs Bridges was asking. 'Pray God it isn't his heart. Oh, dear, I'll have to sit down a minute.'

Rose guided her onto a chair and fetched a glassful of the cooking brandy. 'Just you drink that,' she half-ordered. 'It'll buck you up. And don't you stare, Ruby. Get stirring that soup. Mr Hudson wouldn't want the dinner spoiled because of him.'

Through in the servants' hall a debate was taking place. The participants were Frederick, Edward and Daisy. There was an abrasive edge to the voice of each.

'Who's it goin' to be, then?' Frederick had asked, jerking his head meaningfully towards the pantry.

'My Eddie, of course,' Daisy said at once. 'He was footman here long before you was.'

'I'm footman now. Edward's chauffeur. Footman's next in line, strictly speaking.'

'Don't let's argue about it,' Edward pleaded. 'Let his lordship decide.'

'No, Eddie, you stand up for your rights. They'll be here in twenty minutes, an' you've got to be ready to do butler duties by then. Never mind what he says . . .'

The argument was cut short by the emergence of the elderly, balding Dr Foley from the pantry. He closed the door behind him. His expression was inscrutable.

'It's important he stays resting and has no excitement,' was all the information he gave them. 'This dinner party is rather on his mind, but I insist no one must disturb him. Is that quite clear? I'm going up to see Lord Bellamy now.'

He went away up the stairs, neither Edward nor Frederick thinking to hurry ahead to show him to his lordship's presence. They merely went mechanically about their preparations, glancing frequently at the closed pantry door and wondering what the situation was behind it.

'It's rather serious, Lord Bellamy,' Foley said, his glance embracing James and Georgina, too. All were in evening dress in the drawing-room. The grandfather clock showed a mere twenty minutes to go before the guests were due.

'It is a heart attack. Quite mild, but there's always the danger of a second one following. I don't want to move him tonight. My concern is that he's worrying about his duties.'

'Uncle Richard, we must cancel,' Georgina urged. 'If you telephone there's just time.'

The doctor saved Richard from reminding her that such a move could not be countenanced. 'In some ways,' he pointed out, 'it might be better to carry on as normally as possible, o he'll feel he's let the side down and worry more.'

'I agree,' James said, with a promptness that almost shocke Georgina. She turned to her uncle, but recognised his familia look of relief whenever spared having to make the vital deci sion in a crisis.

Dr Foley said, 'There's nothing more I can do just now. I'll b round first thing in the morning – unless there's any change, o course, in which case, please call me at once.'

He went out. The three looked at one another.

'Well,' James said. 'All we can do is depute Edward or Frederick to buttle, and hope for the best.' He pressed the bell. 'Which of them do we choose?'

'Eddie!' Daisy alerted her husband when the bell sounded in the servants' hall. But Frederick was already at the foot of the stairs. 'I'll go,' he said, and did.

Daisy gave Edward an exasperated shake.

'What's the matter with you? I'll tell you this. If they decide on Frederick, they can say goodbye to me in this house. You, too, if you've got any pride. They're not goin' to trample over us.'

But when Frederick returned, very shortly afterwards, he wore a grim look and announced, 'It's you they want.'

Edward's eyes widened with apprehension. Daisy gave him a little shove. 'Think so, as well. Go on, Eddie.'

Edward obediently went up the stairs, watched sardonically by Frederick.

'Don't push him too hard, Dais,' he advised. 'He might fall over one day.'

In the morning-room, Edward received his instructions from Lord Bellamy, conscious of the watchful attention of the Major and Miss Georgina.

'When you bring them into the drawing-room you'll announce them as His Excellency the French Ambassador, Madame Fleuriau and Mademoiselle Fleuriau. Have you got that?'

Edward tried the name and was relieved to get it right.

'Good. And our other two guests are Lord and Lady Swanbourne. You must announce them as the Earl and Countess of Swanbourne.'

'Yes, my lord.'

'Wine's the most important thing,' the Major said. 'Does he know what we're having?'

Richard shot his son a glance of disapproval for having spoken in this third-person way, as if Edward were not even in the room. In the brief discussion over the choice of Hudson's understudy, James had favoured Frederick, but had been out-voted. He could see that the servant was having to rack his memory. He explained carefully, 'We're having Amontillado with the turtle soup. Then champagne to follow – the Moët and Chandon Dry Imperial.'

'That's all ready, my lord,' Edward said thankfully.

'Good. And the claret is the Chateau Latour '06.'

James put in, 'And a Trocken Beeren Auslese with the sorbet.'

Edward had not been told about this last. He committed it to memory without having to admit the deficiency.

'The carving, Edward,' Georgina said, smiling encouragingly. 'You can manage saddle of lamb, I'm sure.'

'Oh, yes, miss. I've carved several times when Hudson's . . . been away.'

'You'll manage splendidly,' Richard smiled. It was James again who, characteristically, struck a chord of uncertainty.

'Will he fit into Hudson's black coat?'

'His black coat, sir?' Edward queried, bringing himself into direct communication.

'Well, you can hardly buttle in chauffeur's uniform, can you?' Richard said firmly, 'I think you're roughly Hudson's height and build, aren't you?'

'Just about, m'lord.'

'Well, you'd better go and get ready. We haven't much time.'

'Very good, my lord.'

Georgina asked, 'How's Mrs Bridges?'

'Well . . . rather upset, miss.'

'I'm sure. One of us would have come down, only we don't want to get in the way just now.'

'Yes, miss. She's carrying on all right – with Ruby's help, and Rose's.'

'Wish her luck,' Richard told him. 'And good luck to you, Edward.'

'Thank you, m'lord – Miss Georgina.'

He felt no temptation to thank the Major, as well.

'You didn't exactly give him confidence,' Georgina snapped at James, when the servant had gone.

'Now, now,' Richard ruled. 'No arguments, please. I've no fears at all. Some of Hudson's influence must have rubbed off on him in all this time. I'm sure he'll come through with flying colours.'

James's lack of encouragement above stairs was matched by Frederick's below.

'Bit of a loose fit, eh?' he commented, watching Daisy tightening the strap of Hudson's waistcoat to its utmost to make the garment fit her husband more snugly.

'Looks better than it would on you,' she retorted. 'Great beanpole!'

Unabashed, Frederick said casually, ''Bout time you un-corked the wine, isn't it, Edward? Want to get some air at it. I'll do it.'

'No, I'll do the wine,' Edward said, with rare determination.

'Yes. He'll do it,' Daisy echoed, still struggling with the waitscoat. 'Oh, Eddie, do stand still.'

But he almost jumped in the air as the front door bell sounded.

'Cor! They're here, and I'm not ready yet.'

Rose came through from the kitchen, hissing, 'Shush! Keep your voices down. He's only next door, remember.'

They all glanced at the pantry door. Behind it, Hudson, conscious of the agitated murmurs, stirred anxiously.

With the authority of her longer service, Rose ordered, 'You go up, Frederick. You go with him, Dais. I'll finish helping Eddie. Go *on*!'

The two went obediently. Edward wailed, 'He won't know the right announcin', Rose. Oh, blimey! An' the blinkin' wine's not opened yet, and I'll have to be in the drawing-room serving cocktails. Oh . . . !'

'Stand still and let me do your tie. Fred'll do the cocktails, and there's half an hour before dinner. Plenty of time for the wine to air. There. You look fine.'

As it transpired, the arrivals had been Lord and Lady Swan-bourne. By the time the doorbell rang again, Edward was ready to open it to the Ambassadorial family.

'Good evening, your Excellency,' he said, with a bow.

The Ambassador was middle-aged, small and elegantly slim. His eyes twinkled good-humouredly and he replied in excellent English.

'Good evening. Am I right? Is it Hudson?'

'No, your Excellency.'

'No? But my own butler told me I was meeting the famous Hudson this evening.'

'Hudson is . . . indisposed, your Excellency. I . . . I'm Barnes.'

If Fleuriau was disappointed he was too good a diplomat to show it. When Frederick and Daisy had taken their coats, Edward led the guests up to the drawing-room and made the introductions with accuracy and aplomb.

Back in the lower regions, Frederick soon deflated his self-satisfaction. He indicated the bottles of claret, now uncorked.

'You do know that's best claret, Edward?'

'So what?'

'I mean, you wasn't going to serve it like that, surely?'

'It's having enough time to breathe. Air temperature.'

Frederick said pityingly, 'Best Chateau Latour – from the bottle! It wants decanting.'

'Decanting? His lordship didn't say nothing about decanting.'

'Expected you'd know, that's why. Daisy, fetch some decanters, quick.'

She gave him a glare, but obeyed. She offered a decanter to Edward on her return, but Frederick took it.

'I'll do it. Needs a steady hand, or the deposit'll be disturbed. You go up and pour the champagne.'

Edward hesitated. Daisy opened her mouth to protest, but managed to restrain her anger when she saw the concentration Frederick was already applying to the delicate task. Edward had no alternative but to obey the order from his temporary underling.

Despite the disruption of the ordered way of things; despite the rivalry, the jealousy and the sporadic outbursts of bickering; despite Mrs Bridges' distraction; despite even a dramatic appearance by Hudson, ghost-like in pyjamas, who had to be hustled back to bed and reassured that they were coping all right; despite all these difficulties, the evening seemed to have been a success. The plates came down cleared, the bottles and decanters all but emptied. Nothing spilt, nor overlooked, nor wrongly timed.

When the guests had at last departed, Georgina came to the kitchen, where washing up and putting away were interrupted for her to address them all.

'I just want to thank you for the wonderful job you did tonight. I was nervous. It was the first time I'd been hostess for such a distinguished dinner, but I needn't have worried, it seems. The Ambassador was delighted. He complimented every course, Mrs Bridges.'

'Very kind of you to tell me, miss. Rose and Ruby was a great help.'

'I'm sure they were. Thank you both, too. And Edward, I know his lordship was as pleased as I was at the way you handled everything.'

'Thank you, miss.'

'Frederick and Daisy . . . all of you, you did Hudson proud. Thank you most sincerely. Goodnight.'

They chorused their thanks. Awake in his bed, Hudson heard the sound and identified it. He knew that all had gone well, after all. It did not bring him full relief, though. He felt suddenly that, in his absence, things had no business to go without a hitch. He felt out of it and forgotten already.

'Six months' complete rest at least,' was Dr Foley's verdict to Richard and Georgina after he had seen his patient again next morning. 'I don't want to move him for a week or so, but I think it's important he should go away from here.'

Richard asked, 'Frankly, what are his chances of recovery?'

'Oh, there's no reason why he shouldn't get over it.'

'And return to his duties?'

'In time. But he must change his ways. Take proper rests in

the afternoon. No heavy lifting. Delegate some of his responsibilities.'

'He'll hate that,' Georgina said.

'I gather he's a stubborn fellow, but he must learn to live with it or risk the consequences. He'll be his own worst enemy unless he has the firmest handling.'

'Come in, Mrs Bridges,' Richard called, as there came a knock at the morning-room door. As Hudson's most senior colleague and known friend, the cook had been summoned to represent downstairs in the appraisal of the situation. Her eyes widened with alarm when Richard told her the doctor's pronouncement.

'No, not for ever,' he hastened to reassure her. 'Just a few months, for a complete rest. Now, have you any ideas where he might go? I was wondering about his sister in Hastings.'

'Well, my lord, I do know she suffers dreadful with arthritis these days. Finds it hard to manage her guest home.'

Dr Foley shook his head. 'He's going to need some careful nursing.'

Mrs Bridges' eyes lit up. 'There's his old friends down at Southwold, my Lord. Mr and Mrs Trantor. She's the village postmistress and I think she did a bit of nursing in the war.'

'He'll be an invalid for some time,' the doctor said. 'It would be quite an undertaking for them. Do you think they could manage?'

'Oh, I'm sure they could. They're kind souls and have been very fond of Hudson since he was a young footman at the House. I know they've kept up regular correspondence, my lord.'

I seem to remember them. They sound ideal. I'll write to them. Thank you, Mrs Bridges.'

She hesitated 'He . . . will get better, my lord, won't he? I couldn't bear to think . . .'

Dr Foley took her gently by the arm and led her to the door.

'He was one of the lucky ones, Mrs Bridges,' he told her. 'He'll be all right.'

She went downstairs much relieved and dispensed the news

to the others. After the initial reaction of relief, it provoked almost predictable events.

A little later that morning, Frederick was glad to find the excuse he had been seeking to have a word alone with his former officer. James had sent him out for some tobacco. He delivered it to James in his own room, then lingered.

'Anything else, sir?'

'Not at the moment.'

Frederick still waited.

'How are things downstairs?'

'Bit unsettled really, sir. We just heard Hudson's going to be away quite a while.'

'So I gather. You'll manage, won't you? The dinner seemed to go off all right.'

'Thank you, sir. Apart from the mix-up about the claret . . .'

'What was that? I didn't notice anything.'

'We, er, managed to cover it up, fortunately.'

'What happened?'

'Well, it's all over now, sir . . .'

'No, come on. Tell me.'

'It was just . . . I noticed Edward about to serve the claret straight from the bottle. Luckily, I . . .'

There came a knock at the door and Daisy entered, carrying bed-linen. James waved her through to his bedroom. As she went she heard him say, 'Not decanted, eh?'

'Well, it was in the end, sir. Luckily I noticed in time. He had a lot of things on his mind, after all, sir.'

'Very sharp of you, Frederick. Terrible blunder to have served our best claret straight from the bottle.'

Daisy glanced back through the open door, seething inwardly at Frederick's smug smirk as he replied, 'Specially to a Frenchman, sir.'

'To anyone,' she heard the Major say. 'You an expert on these matters, Frederick?'

'Wouldn't say an expert . . .'

'Don't be modest. Very useful knowledge for someone in your position who wants to make his way in the world. Ever feel you're dragging your heels a bit, do you? Been here – what? – seven years. Want to move on?'

Frederick answered carefully, 'I'd be very sad to leave your employment, sir. I've always been very happy here . . . and there was the war.'

'Mm. But you don't want to go to waste, do you? Got resource, ambition.'

'I look at the future sometimes, sir.'

'And wonder what it holds for you, eh?'

'Yes, sir.'

James had finished filling his pipe. He gave Frederick a thoughtful glance, before saying dismissively, 'All right, *Trooper* Norton.' Frederick's purpose had not escaped him.

Daisy had never made a bed so savagely in her life.

'Don't you try denyin' it,' she accused Frederick as soon as she could get down to the servants' hall to confront him. 'You brought it up deliberate, just to make Eddie look stupid. I know your game.'

'Leave it, Dais,' her husband requested mildly.

'That's right, Ed,' said Frederick. 'You want to stop your wife puffing and blowing, or she's going to get me angry.'

This was too much even for Edward.

'Now just a minute. She's entitled to speak her mind. Strikes me what you did was pretty underhand. I wouldn't've done it to you, so don't you start on her. You tell me if you got anything to say.'

'I got nothing to say to you. I got no grudge – but she keeps on at me.'

'No grudge?' Daisy flamed. 'No grudge, when you go suckin' up to the Major, tellin' tales . . .'

'Shut up, you silly cow!' he yelled back, causing her to catch her breath and fall silent. 'Sorry, Eddie,' he said quickly, 'but I did warn you.' But Daisy was too far gone in fury to heed him.

'Yeh – and you bin suckin' up to Mr Hudson these past weeks, too. Don't think I haven't noticed, with your fancy wine book.'

'Oh, yeh. I knew he was going to have a heart attack, so I

36

started telling nasty tales about Edward.'

Edward pleaded with them both. 'Shut up, will you? For pity's sake. Look, I know my worth in this household. It's up to them upstairs to decide anything.'

Daisy turned on him. 'Someone's got to do your talkin', Eddie. You'll never do it yourself. You're older, you've been here longer, and you was a corporal in the war and he was only a trooper. You know you're the better man.'

'But I saw the war out, didn't I?' Frederick demanded viciously. '*And* I was here when they took you back on sufferance.'

'You – dirty – pig!' Daisy breathed, half stunned. 'If I was a man, I'd box your head in for that. Eddie, you're lettin' him walk all over you and doin' nothin' . . .'

Rose stormed in. 'What's all this shouting? You're making enough noise to waken the . . . What's going on?'

'Just a private discussion,' Frederick said impassively.

'About who's takin' over – my Eddie or . . .'

'Nobody's takin' over anything,' Rose told Daisy angrily. 'You give me the pip, you lot do. There's poor Mr Hudson lying there fighting for his life, and you lot got him buried already. It's disgustin'. I'm disgusted with the lot of you!'

She swept out again, leaving them quelled and uneasy.

All the same, Daisy, in her turn, took her chance when it came later that morning.

'Can you take this to the post, Daisy?' Georgina asked, and licked the gum of the envelope she had just addressed at the morning-room desk. 'It's to thank her ladyship for sending the flowers.'

'Yes, miss. How is her ladyship, miss?'

'Oh, much better. It wasn't mumps at all, apparently. Just a bad cold. I'll be very relieved when she gets back.'

'Well, it'll be easier for us all when . . .'

'When she gets back? Don't say you think I'm not coping, Daisy.'

'Oh, no, miss. I meant . . . well, when Hudson's successor's been announced.'

37

'But Edward's managing, isn't he?'

'Yes, miss. Only, I think he'd just like to know for certain if . . . if the job's his. I mean, on a temporary basis, of course.'

'I assumed it was.'

'He hasn't been told anything definite, and Frederick seems to think he's got rights to it. It's led to a bit of bad feeling.'

Rose entered the room, carrying a coat of Georgina's on to which she had re-sewn a button and was just in time to hear Daisy conclude. 'Not that I've got anything against Frederick, miss . . .'

Rose withered Daisy with a look. Georgina saw it and said, 'Rose, Daisy was just saying . . .'

'I know what she was saying, miss' Rose said between her teeth. 'And I wouldn't listen to a word of it, if I was you.'

'But is there really bad feelings downstairs?'

'Yes, there is, miss. They're like jackels, Frederick and Edward, both of them. I know it's none of my business, but I don't think either of them deserve the job. We should get in a proper temporary butler while Hudson's away, and teach 'em both a lesson. When I think of all he's done for them over the years it makes my blood boil.'

Georgina stared at this vehemence. Daisy was glad to slip quietly from the room.

While this unrest seethed about him, Mr Hudson lay still, as he had been instructed by Dr Foley, and contemplated his future. He did not like what he saw. For so many years he had been the upholder of the *status quo* in that household, his name known in all the grand homes of Belgravia and well beyond as synonymous with the old standards; the days when servants were servants and masters were masters, and the demarcation lines between them were as clearly drawn as they were between the different degrees of society above stairs and of status below them.

For years – through war, national upheaval, domestic crisis – he had, he fancied not incorrectly, been the principal stabilising influence on those closest to him, and not a little upon those whom he served. And now, ironically, he suddenly found

38

himself helpless, impotent, aware from what he had overheard through his door that his very elimination had brought about a breach in relationships which might never be healed and which might preface the end of the story of the Bellamy household.

He unburdened himself miserably to his one regular visitor, Kate Bridges, as she sat at his bedside and held his hand.

'I feel so lost, Kate. All these years, and to finish up like this.'

'It's *not* finished, Angus. Dr Foley said you were one of the lucky ones, so long as you're careful and take things easy.'

'Lucky? Kate . . . if anything should . . . happen . . .'

'Oh, don't say that!'

'No, no. One must face these things. I just want to tell you that some time ago I arranged to leave all my possessions, such as they are, to you.'

She only just managed not to cry. She had cried so often lately.

'Thank you, Angus. I appreciate that. I've . . . done the same for you.'

He seemed surprised. 'Oh! Thank you. Well . . . there's a little money, and some gold cufflinks his lordship gave me after twenty-five years' service. You can sell them.'

'I couldn't. Never!'

'If times ever get hard . . .'

'I could never sell anything of yours, Angus.'

'Don't cry,' he pleaded. 'Is . . . everything going all right? Without me?'

'No,' she admitted wretchedly. 'It's all topsy-turvy.'

'But Rose told me what a success the dinner was.'

Mrs Bridges remembered that he was not to be worried. All she could find to say was, 'They seem pleased upstairs. You have a nap now. I'll come and see you again this evening.'

She went out and left him staring at the ceiling; ill and concerned.

Upstairs, his office, if not himself, was the subject of further argument.

Richard was saying, 'We mustn't judge Edward simply on the matter of the claret.'

'No,' James conceded. 'But you must agree that a butler's principal function is knowledge of the cellar; and Frederick clearly has the edge in that department.'

Georgina said, 'Rose thinks a temporary butler would be best.'

'Yes, well I've spoken to Virginia on the telephone,' her uncle said. 'She favours Edward, and of the two of them so do you, don't you, my dear?'

She nodded. He said, 'Sorry, James. You're outvoted.'

'I always am. But what's wrong with Frederick? He's got spirit. He's a young man who knows where he's going. Edward's a nice fellow, but soft where it matters. Not his fault. The war's probably to blame for that. But he did go off to make his way in the world, and failed.'

'That wasn't his fault,' Georgina objected. 'Thousands of people . . .'

'All right, maybe that was harsh. But what about Daisy? From what I've seen, she's the drive behind Edward. Do we really want a butler who sits in the housemaid's pocket?'

'Daisy isn't like that. Don't be silly.'

'Well, from what Frederick says . . .'

Richard intervened. 'Look, we can put Edward above Frederick after Edward's performance the other night. I'll discuss it with Hudson. Unless he has any strong objections we must give the boy a chance.'

Hudson had no strong objections, though the very discussion of a candidate to stand in for him proved painful when Lord Bellamy raised it the next day. At least he had been able to diminish the ordeal by bringing with him to Hudson's bedside the reply from Mr and Mrs Trantor, just received, to say how delighted they would be to care for their old friend for as long as might be necessary. Dr Foley had been consulted by telephone and had confirmed that, subject to a final examination later that day, Hudson could be permitted to make the journey within twenty-four hours.

'We'll arrange for an ambulance to take you down, of course,' Lord Bellamy said. 'I'm sure Rose or Mrs Bridges will do your packing for you.'

'I'm very grateful for all the trouble you've taken, my lord.' Hudson was sitting up, looking more relaxed and cheerful.

'The least we could do, after all you've done for us. You've carried a great deal of responsibility. I don't know what we shall do without you these next months . . .'

Richard realised he should not have said that. He went on hastily, '. . . but you mustn't rush things. Take as long as you like.'

'There's just the matter of my successor, my lord. I am sure that, as you suggest, Edward can manage. However, if you feel, for the benefit of the household, that it would be desirable to appoint a new butler – a permanent man – then I have no wish to be a burden . . .'

'There's no question of that. This post is yours, as long as you want it. When the time does come for you to retire, you'll be the best judge. Now, is that understood, once for all?'

Hudson nodded and replied huskily, 'I'm very grateful to your lordship.'

Then, left alone, he lay back and actually began to look forward a little to a break in the country, telling himself that it would, in fact, be no time at all before he was back in harness.

The following lunchtime Edward stood before him. They were alone in the pantry, the young man nervously at attention, the older seated in a wheelchair, with rugs about his legs. Two large, packed suitcases stood nearby.

'The keys to the silver cupboard,' Hudson intoned solemnly, handing them over. 'The keys to the cellar. The cellar book. Remember to record every single bottle that's drunk. And those are the household accounts. Reckon them up once a week, on Saturday mornings. And never drop behind with settling the bills. This house has a most valued reputation with the local tradesfolk.'

'Yes, Mr Hudson.'

'Lastly, here's my pantry book of useful advice I've recorded over the years, privately, for whoever should need it some day. You may borrow it, for the time being.'

Edward took the scrapbook reverentially.

'Remember,' Hudson was concluding, 'to be butler in this household is a sacred trust. Absolute loyalty and devotion to duty are what is asked of you.'

There was a knock at the door. Frederick was admitted, to announce that the ambulance was at the door. He gave Edward an old-fashioned look as he took up the suitcases and went out. Rose entered to push Mr Hudson out in his chair.

'Remember, Edward,' he said at the door, 'if there's ever any advice you need, don't hesitate to write to me, care of Mr and Mrs Trantor, the Post Office, Southwold.'

'Thank you, Mr Hudson.'

'Off we go, then, Rose.'

He held out his hand to Edward.

'Good luck, my boy.'

Edward watched him go. Then, left alone, turned around to survey his new surroundings with awe.

When the ambulance had gone, they all settled down to cold luncheon at the long table in the servants' hall. For a moment, Edward hovered beside Mr Hudson's accustomed place, uncertain whether to put out his hand for the chair. He caught Mrs Bridges' eye. An almost imperceptible shake of her head made him move along to his own usual seat.

There was an uncomfortable silence, in which no one moved. He felt Daisy nudge him.

'What?' he said aloud.

Frederick grinned.

Rose stepped into the breach: 'For what we are about to receive . . .'

CHAPTER THREE

A strange air of depletion hung over No. 165 Eaton Place.

The continued absence of Mr Hudson, by now well on the mend but facing a lengthy recuperative period, was a major absence from the downstairs 'family'. Being Ascot week, Edward, too, was away, his permanent duty as chauffeur having to take precedence over his temporary one as butler at the order of James, who had wished to be driven to the house of friends near the racecourse and valeted there. James could perfectly well have gone by train, taking Frederick with him as valet. His friends would have transported him locally during his stay. But he had ordered Edward to go, as a little act of getting his own back on the man whose choice as stand-in butler he had opposed. His own favourite, Frederick, was thus left as sole male servant at Eaton Place.

His duties were minimal, however. Upstairs was even more depleted than down. Lord and Lady Bellamy were in Germany, attending an international function and residing in the splendour of a castle whose owner, possessor of the blood royal, had insisted that they would be waited on hand and foot by his own staff and need not bring personal servants.

It left only Miss Georgina Worsley to be cared for; and that beautiful and wilful young lady was preoccupied with exciting new plans.

From the morning-room she rang for Frederick and ordered cocktail ingredients to be fetched. When he had put the tray down on the sideboard she opened the cupboard door and surveyed the bottles of variegated shapes, sizes and colours.

'I think I'll make a Sidecar,' she pronounced.

'Yes, miss. That's two parts brandy, one part Cointreau, the juice of a quarter of a lemon, crushed ice, and shake it well.'

'Thank you, Frederick. Are you sure that'll be strong enough,

43

though? Lady Dorothy likes her cocktails with a terrific kick in them.'

'I think you'll find that quite satisfactory, miss,' Frederick said, and excused himself to answer the front door. A moment later he was back to announce 'Lady Dorothy Hale, miss.'

'Sorry I'm late, darling,' gushed Lady Dorothy as she almost ran into the room. She was in her late twenties, petite, with cropped auburn hair and an intriguingly snub nose. Bit of all right, Fred thought, not failing to note that she had given him a lightning appraisal in return.

'Paul's not with me,' he heard her telling her hostess. 'He's coming on, though. He telephoned at the last minute to say he was delayed at the studios. Oh, cocktails! Marvellous!'

'Frederick's just been reminding me how to mix a Sidecar. Would you like one?'

'Yes, please.'

Georgina set confidently about the task, saying, 'Thank you, Frederick, I'll ring if we need any more ice.'

'Very good, miss.' He bowed and went.

'I say!' Lady Dolly murmured after he had closed the door. 'What a divine-looking young man!'

Georgina was surprised. 'Frederick? I suppose he is, rather. But tell me about Paul Marvin.'

'Well, he's said to be Rumanian, but you never quite know with these film people. He's distinctly oily and full of artificial charm. Frankly, I'm rather bored with him but I thought you ought to meet him. Flatter him for a week or two, at least till you see whether you can wangle a job in one of his films.'

Georgina popped cherries on sticks into both their glasses and they went over to the settee. Dolly sipped.

'Ooh, what a divine cocktail!' She sipped again. 'Heavenly.'

Georgina need have had no doubts about the strength of her mixture. 'Gosh!' she said, after tasting it. 'I'll be tight by the time Mr Mervin gets here.'

'Nonsense.'

'Anyway, supposing he doesn't think I'm pretty enough for the films?'

'Of course he will. It's great fun, darling. You get ten shillings a day, just to sit in front of the camera and look alluring. Patsy Cremorne did it a few weeks ago, out at Islington or somewhere in the wilds. They all had to be in bathing costumes round a pool with no water in it.'

'Sounds chilly.'

'Apparently the arc lamps kept them all warm. They have these very strong lamps everywhere. I say, where's your tall, dark, handsome cousin?'

'James? Staying down at Ascot.'

Dolly pouted excessively and drained her glass. 'What a bore. I was hoping he'd be here. I adore him. Didn't you know?'

Georgina was amused. 'You? Seriously?'

'Of course I do. But it isn't recipro . . . gosh! . . . recip . . . ro . . . cated. He doesn't adore me.'

They heard the front door bell.

'That'll be Paul.'

'Oh, dear!' Georgina said, getting up and walking about. 'I'm nervous now.'

'Well, don't be. Look poised and cool and disdainful. Like Gloria Swanson. Take your cocktail in one hand, cigarette holder in the other, and lower your eyelids and sort of . . . smoulder.'

Georgina giggled. 'I'll try. I've never smouldered before.'

She had just time to strike a half-hearted attitude which she imagined might be appropriate before Frederick showed Paul Marvin in.

Dolly's description, though sketchy, had been accurate, Georgina thought. Charm emanated from the dapper man as obviously as an expensive but ostentatious perfume. He was middle aged, his hair engagingly greying, a monocle screwed into one bright eye. His clothing was tasteful and beautifully cut. A fresh carnation adorned his lapel and there were uncreased spats over his brilliantly-shone shoes.

He advanced straight to Georgina and bowed over her hand, just brushing the back of it with his lips.

'Miss Worsley. How delightful! And my Lady Dolly!' He

seemed to notice her for the first time, but merely nodded in her direction before turning back to Georgina. 'I am so sorry if I'm a little late. My star ripped a Paquin dress into a thousand pieces and stood on the set in her chemise until they carried her screaming to her dressing-room and gave her smelling salts. So we shoot no more today.'

From behind him, Dolly gave Georgina a look which could only signify 'He's making it all up, to impress you.'

'How fascinating,' Georgina told him. 'I mean, how awful. Poor dress. Poor you.'

'Ah, we are used to such scenes in the film studios, Miss Worsley.'

She seated him and poured him a cocktail, replenishing Dolly's glass and topping up her own. It was established that he had expected her to call him Paul, since everyone else did, though she didn't in turn offer him the use of her christian name.

'What actually is the film you're making?' she asked.

'*Paris by Night*. I have Carl Brisson, Anny Ondra, Max Reiler and Zita Young. My director is Miles Mander, who is a master.'

'It all sounds very thrilling.'

'It will be a superb moving picture.'

Dolly, who had demolished most of her cocktail already, put down the glass over-carefully and began to fish around a trifle hazily for her bag and gloves.

'Georgina, darling, I've simply got to fly,' she said. From the way she stood up it seemed that any immediate flight would be of less than stable nature, but she appeared resolved. Georgina pressed the bell. Dolly explained, 'Dear Robert's taking me to the Cochran revue. I'll give you a ring in the morning. 'Bye, Paul.'

He half-rose, then subsided. Georgina followed her to the door.

'The footman will get you a taxi, Dolly, she said.

At the recollection of Frederick's Roman features, Dolly paused distinctly and said, 'Oh! That would be nice.'

Frederick appeared at the door, his usual impassive self.

'A taxi for Lady Dorothy, please,' Georgina said.

'Very good, miss.'

'Look, Georgina, you stay and talk to Paul. I'll get my coat and things and just go. Go on . . .' Dolly insisted; and Georgina obeyed, shutting herself in the morning-room with Paul, who had risen to greet her return.

Frederick held Dolly's coat for her.

'Won't take a minute to get a cab, m'lady,' he told her. 'Plenty past here – though I can ring the rank if you wish.'

'Never mind, Frederick,' she said. 'It *is* Frederick, isn't it?'

'That's right, m'lady.'

'Yes. I remember you from when I came to a fancy dress party here some time ago.'

'That's right, m'lady. I remember you.'

'You do?'

'You was dressed as a nymph, m'lady.'

'So I was. How clever of you to remember.'

'I noticed you special, m'lady.'

She studied him for a moment. His expression told her nothing. The dark eyes were inscrutable.

'I'll see you out and get you a taxi, m'lady,' he said, and touched her elbow ever so slightly as he ushered her to the door.

However much she was aware of the superficiality of Paul Marvin's charm – and she believed Dolly had been a good deal less than fair to him, no doubt because he had clearly lost interest in her – Georgina found herself chatting unreservedly with him. He fascinated her with tales of the romantic world of the film studios, amused her with his semi-scandalous anecdotes of the private lives of the stars, and flattered her in an acceptable way. She was sorry when, at half-past seven, he regretted that he must take his leave, to be in time for a dinner appointment with some moving picture financiers from the U.S.A. But by then the suggestion which she had half hoped for, yet half feared, had been made and hesitantly agreed to.

'Then, that's settled, my dear. I will have the studio people telephone you next week for a costume fitting.'

'Yes, I see,' Georgina said, beginning to thrill as the idea sank in. 'Oh, Paul, I've always longed to be in a film. Oh, you dear, kind man!'

She kissed him impulsively, to his pleased surprise. He took the opportunity of asking, 'Maybe we can lunch together one day soon, yes?'

'If you like,' she agreed readily. 'I'll ring for the footman.'

'Please don't trouble. My flat is quite close to Sloane Square, so I shall walk. My dear Miss Worsley, I am so pleased that we are to be associated. My compliments, please, to Lord and Lady Bellamy.'

He bowed elaborately and kissed her hand again, then confidently let himself out of the room and the house. Georgina swallowed the rest of her neglected cocktail, whirled round the room in a solo waltz, and finished up before a mirror, striking a dramatic pose, head held high and eyelids provocatively lowered.

A few evenings later, Rose, sitting alone in the servants' hall, looked up from her sewing as a man came in from the area entrance. It took her more than a second to recognize Frederick. He wore a brown teddy bear overcoat she had never seen on him before and was just taking off a wide-brimmed fedora hat, such as she had seen American film stars wearing on the screen.

'You still up?' he said, cheerfully and superflously.

She looked at the wall clock. It showed eleven.

'Just finishing off some sewing. Look at you! Nice coat.'

He took it off. 'Yeh.'

'Want some cocoa?'

'No, ta. Just smoke a cigarette before I turn in, if you don't object.'

'Course not.'

She noted that the cigarette came from a slim silver case and that its aroma, when he lit it, was strangely pungent.

'What's that?' she asked.

'Balkan Sobranie. Turkish.'

'Bit dear, aren't they?'

'A bit. I prefer 'em.'

'You come into money, or something?' He followed her pointed glance at his coat, draped over a chair.

'Me? No. I reckon to put my wages by for a rainy day. Got to have a new coat sometime.'

He smiled patronisingly at the puzzlement on her face and proffered the open cigarette case. Rose hesitated, then took one. She didn't exactly like the unaccustomed taste; but there was something expensively exotic about it that made it pleasing, just the same.

When James got back from Ascot and heard Georgina's excited outpouring of her news his reaction was deflating, if characteristic.

'The wretched man doesn't have to go to the fitting with you, hang it!'

'He's the producer, darling. He's got to be there to approve that it fits me.'

'Oh, I'll bet he does!'

'Look, James, Paul Marvin's a well-known film producer. He's not likely to throw me on a couch at a costumier's shop in the Strand at ten-thirty in the morning and ravish me.'

'You don't know film producers.'

'How many do you know? I know this one, and he's not like that. At least, I don't think he is. Anyway, I met him through Dolly.'

'Huh! Dolly Hale's friends are a rotten, third-rate lot. And I have heard a lot about film people. They're all greedy, immoral and unreliable. I strongly object to you getting mixed up with them.'

Her beautiful eyes flashed up at him.

'Well, I *am* mixed up with them. So that's it, isn't it?'

He was compelled to retreat to a secondary position.

'Well, if you must have this dago at your costume fitting, I suppose you must. But I beg you, Georgina, please don't be seen lunching with him at the Savoy afterwards.'

'I told you it's arranged. It's the least I can do to thank him for giving me a part in his film.'

James's fragile temper broke. 'Now you're really talking like a prostitute!'

'As I'm appearing in a film as one, I might as well get in some practice.'

'Oh, God!'

As always, she hated upsetting him, knowing that his rudeness stemmed from his own basic discontentment and from a genuine concern for her well-being. She swallowed her resentment and tried conciliation.

'Listen, Jumbo, if you're worried about my undressing in front of Paul – and I don't for a moment believe it'll be necessary – I'll ask Dolly to come as my chaperone. Paul won't like the implication, but at least he'll have me alone for lunch afterwards.'

Her fair compromise came too late. Muttering that he didn't care what she did, he strode out of the room, with his familiar, childish slam of the door. Georgina sighed and tried to return to the state of euphoria in which she had been luxuriating earlier. It wouldn't come, however. By the evening, she knew that she must make some gesture towards easing the atmosphere. She telephoned Dolly and made the request.

'*Me* chaperone *you!*' Dolly exclaimed above the strains of her gramophone's 'My Heart Stood Still'. 'But that's too absurd. Anyway, surely there'll be a costume fitter there.'

'I know. It's all so stupid, but . . .'

'Besides, I can't. I'm going shopping – with my new lover.'

'Oh.'

'Yes. Isn't it exciting? His name's Alberto. Terribly handsome, and, my dear, he dances divinely. Italian, of course. Of the House of Montespiore di Cologna. He's here with me now. As soon as he's dressed we're off to join a party at the Opera.'

'How lovely,' Georgina said, unenthusiastically.

Dolly babbled on. 'All my friends are going to be madly jealous. I shall take him everywhere with me. Well, must fly, darling. So sorry about tomorrow. 'Bye.'

'Alberto, darling!' Dolly called, when she had replaced the receiver.

'Yes?' he replied, fastening his white tie.

'That was Miss Worsley on the telephone.'

'Go on!'

'Not "go on", darling. You must say, "Ees not true, uh?" Try it.'

'Ees not true, uh?' Frederick responded, entering the room, an opera cloak over one arm.

'Perfect!' Dolly cried delightedly. 'Bene, bene, mi amore.' She moved into his arms to kiss him. 'Now we must go. We'll need to get a taxi.'

'I'll get one,' Fred said automatically.

'No you won't, *Alberto*. The porter will see to it. Now, come along, you lovely man, and be a credit to me.'

'Hullo, Fred,' Rose said next morning, approaching lunch-time. 'Done the silver?'

'Yep.'

She peered close. 'I'll have to buy you a new razor for Christmas. Good job Mr Hudson isn't here.'

He ran fingers over his chin. There was faint but distinct rasping sound.

'Shows, does it? Got up in a bit of a hurry.'

'Late getting in again, was you?'

'Must have been.'

'I've washed your silk scarf for you.'

'Oh, ta, Rose.'

'Got most of the lipstick off.'

'Lipstick?'

'And perfume. What her ladyship uses.'

'Lots of ladies use that.'

'Wealthy ladies, yes. Here, do you nip in her ladyship's room and pinch a bit to put on your scarf to cut a bit of a dash, eh?'

'Who with?'

'Go on! You're not spending your time off on your own, Frederick Norton, so don't give me that.'

'My private life is private, Rose, like Mr Hudson always says.'
She gave him a conspiratorial smile.

'Only teasing. We've always ribbed each other a bit in this house. You can't be in service in a big house with a staff but what you know a bit about each other's private affairs.'

'I know,' he said, with a seriousness that surprised her. 'That's one good reason for getting out of service.'

'Oh? And what's another?'

'There's better things to do than clean silver all day long.'

'I thought you was quite contented here. Is it because they didn't make you butler?'

'Nope. Mr Hudson'll be coming back, anyway.'

Rose moved closer to him, examining hard his impassive face.

'You're tired out, that's your trouble,' she deduced. 'Can't stay out half the night and be up fresh in the morning to do your work.'

'I know.'

'Look, slip up to your room after lunchtime and have a good sleep until tea. It's your afternoon off.'

'Thanks, Rose, but I can't. Got to slip down to the doctor's about my headaches.'

'You've had a lot of them lately. They getting worse?'

'Just the same. Thought I ought to see him about them, though.'

'Yeh. Fred . . .'

'Mm?'

'Watch how you go.'

'Don't worry about me, Rose.'

In the morning-room at that moment Lady Prudence Fairfax was saying to James, as they sipped sherry, 'I must say, it's frightfully good of you, James, bothering with your ageing Auntie Prue instead of some dizzy young flapper.'

'Quite honestly, Prue,' he said, 'I don't seem to know many dizzy young things these days. They're all either tiresome or married.'

'Well, it'll be very flattering to visit a film studio with a handsome man to escort me. You know, I'm so looking forward to it. I've never seen them making a film.'

'Nor have I.'

'Helen and Archie Croft were taken on to the set in Hollywood last year. Apparently they watched John Gilbert and some heavily painted woman with a Spanish name doing a love scene in a gondola. They met him afterwards. They said he was charming but rather common.'

James gave a grimace of distaste.

'Does Georgina know we're going to be there?' Prue asked. He shook his head. 'Give her a surprise.'

Daisy entered to announce luncheon. James asked her with some surprise, 'Where's Frederick?'

'He's gone to the doctor's about his headaches, sir. He could only get an early appointment, so Edward said it would be all right, as it's his half-day.'

'I see. Edward knows we want the car for half-past two?'

'It's arranged, sir.'

'Thanks. Come along, then, Aunt Prue.'

'Come this way, please, Lady Prudence,' Paul Marvin said, two hours later. 'Please mind your step. There are so many cables to the lamps.'

Followed by James, she picked her way carefully across the narrow space between the brick walls of the converted Islington warehouse and the backs of the plywood and canvas setting, blank on this side, but, as they emerged on to the set, transformed on the other by paint and light into the gaudy semblance of a seedy Parisian nightclub. Instead of the aroma of garlic-laden cooking, there was an equally heady smell of oil paint, size, dust, wood, canvas and perfume, drawing out of the surroundings by the heat of the clustered lamps, brilliant on their tall stands.

A strangely mixed company of men and women moved, stood or sat there. Reading a newspaper at one of the tables was a heavily made-up man of avaricious and untrustworthy aspect whose costume and long apron proclaimed him to be a waiter. Also seated – and discussing, James could hear, the seemingly incongruous subject of the runners at a forthcoming English provincial race meeting — were what looked, from his build and blue trousers and blouse, to be meant to be a French bargee, and a woman of similar proportions, whose blouse and trappings left no mistake that she was portraying a 'madame'. Several of her 'girls' lounged about the place, exaggeratedly made-up for the cameras and displaying alarming lengths of leg through the splits in their skirts. Their male compatriots of the *demi monde*, striped-shirted and capped, chatted with them and again James heard the name of a race meeting mentioned: this time it was Ascot, in connection with certain criticisms of the refreshment arrangements in the Royal Enclosure. Georgina was not in view.

Not even bothering to eye the revealed charms of these shapely girls, there moved about a throng of men of varying ages, sizes and shapes, clad in honest British working overalls. They were doing things to the lights, adjusting furniture, measuring distances with tapes, climbing and descending ladders, and mostly talking simultaneously, though seemingly under some sort of direction from others of their kind. An earnest, plain girl with a clip pad bearing a thick wad of paper hurried backwards and forwards, observing details of the scene and noting them, enabling one scene to move into another with smooth continuity.

Behind a group of bored-looking musicians, equipped with an accordion and other instruments suited to the general conception of a French night club, stood the awe-inspiring camera, being inspected minutely by the man who must certainly be its operator. Nearby stood the tweed-jacketed all-powerful director, a chubby, cheerful man, gesticulating carefully as he made his wishes known to a younger, more anxious looking colleague who was no doubt his assistant.

'My dear!' Prue exclaimed to James, 'Isn't it wonderful? So realistic.'

Paul Marvin, who was attired as neatly as if he had been visiting, explained, 'They are now lighting the set, ready for rehearsal. I will find you a chair, then you can sit here and watch.' He waved to someone and a chair was passed over. Lady Prue sat, while James remained standing behind her.

Marvin continued, 'In a few moments we shall rehearse and then shoot the brawl scene. Some special girls will be at those tables – Miss Worsley among them. At first, people are dancing and making love, as the music plays. Suddenly, down those steps will come Gaston, the lover of one of the girls. But she is in the arms of another man. Gaston draws a knife. A woman screams. They will all stand up, tables will be overturned, and a fight will begin.'

He held up a knife. James said, 'I say, that sounds a bit dangerous. Can't someone get hurt?'

Marvin grinned and shook his head. 'See.' He plunged the knife into his own chest. Lady Prudence's hand flew to her throat as she saw the blade go in, but then she looked sheepish as she heard the artificial rasp and realised that it had retracted into the knife handle and was made only of hard rubber, anyway.

'Everything is unreal,' Paul Marvin said deprecatingly of his industry. 'Even those walls of stone are soft plaster. They can tear like paper if someone is careless. Ah, there is Miss Worsley now. If you wish to speak with her before we start . . .?'

'No, no,' James answered, looking round for Georgina. 'Don't tell her we're here. We'll just keep out of the way.'

'Thank you,' Marvin said. 'It is better she can concentrate on her work. She will not see you, with the bright lights on her face. So, you will please excuse me?'

He bowed and went off towards the camera. The assistant director had begun to call everyone to order. Most of the technicians were retreating into the shadows behind the lights, while the actors and actresses were assuming their allotted positions and attitudes of, respectively, menace and cynical seductiveness.

Both James and Prue, having identified Georgina, were staring at her as if she were a stranger, and not a very wholesome-looking one at that. Her gaudy clothing was similar to that of the other tarts in the scene, though, if anything, a shade more revealing. Her face was thickly powdered and painted and her hair done in a way she would never have worn it in Belgravia.

'Just as well Richard can't see her dressed like that,' Prue said.

Half impressed, half angry at the spectacle, James replied, 'She's got better legs than any of the rest of 'em.'

'Yes, hasn't she? Oh, it's all too fascinating.'

She fell silent and paid attention as the assistant director explained the action to the cast.

'Pay attention, girls. You'll have a tough guy each, seated at your table. The boys are just coming in from make-up. Now, when the director calls for action, you'll start to pet and cuddle with your partners. Make it good and passionate, O.K.? Then I'll clap my hands once and shout "Gaston". On that cue, I want you all to stop what you're doing, look up the steps over there, react to Gaston coming down, get up in a panic and overturn the tables as you do. All understood?'

There was a murmur of assent. The assistant director addressed himself to Georgina.

'Gaston comes down across the dance floor, moving like a panther straight up to your table, dear.'

'Mine?' echoed Georgina, clearly alarmed to be singled out on her first day.

'That's right, honey. He seizes hold of your partner, drags him on to the dance floor. They fight and Gaston gets knifed. O.K.?'

'W. . . what do you want me to do?'

'Just stand and look like you're screaming. Can you scream darling?'

'Actually scream? I suppose so.'

'Then it's better you do. Make it look more realistic. All of you, make like you're real scared. They say some day there'll be a way of recording actual sound on films – I don't think! But the more you scream and jabber, the more scared you'll look. Right, now, here come the boys.'

A group of Apaches entered the set, to be shepherded to

their respective positions by the assistant director. He took one of them by the arm and steered him to Georgina's table. The man was tall and dark, with gummed-on sidechops and a smouldering cigarette in the corner of his mouth.

He was also Frederick.

Georgina's astonishment on recognising him was more than matched by his stare of horror when he saw her. Watching from behind the scenery, at a point from which she had not spotted James Bellamy and Lady Prue, nor had been seen by them, Lady Dorothy Hale nudged the girl-friend she had brought to watch and giggled softly, 'That's it! Do look at their faces. Oh, Freddy'll kill me – or she will.'

Fred and Georgina were still staring at one another, transfixed. The assistant director's whistle blew and he shouted to everyone to stand by for rehearsal. Frederick looked round in panic.

'You two!' the assistant director shouted. 'We haven't got all day. Take the girl on your lap.'

Georgina told Frederick in a low voice, 'Come on. We'll have to.'

'Yes, miss,' he responded miserably, and moved to obey.

No sooner had they adopted the position than another voice rang out which alarmed them twice as much. It was unmistakably James Bellamy's.

'Stop! Just a minute!'

'Oh my God!' Dolly Hale gasped to her companion. 'It's James Bellamy. That's done it.'

James had stepped out on to the set. He was raging.

'What the hell is this man doing here? Who engaged him?'

Prue moved forward to try to restrain him, urging him not to make a scene. He ignored her.

'This man's my servant. He's no right to be here. Who's responsible for this? Where's Marvin?'

Hazarding everything, Dolly Hale ran on to the set to face James.

'James, please,' she begged. 'It was only a joke. I arranged it for a bit of fun. If I'd known you were going to be here . . .'

The stunned silence of actors and technicians had broken now into a confusion of chatter and growls of complaint. From far behind the camera Paul Marvin was hurrying forward as well as the writhing cables and other obstacles would allow.

'I might have known you'd be behind it,' James snarled at Dolly. He seized Georgina by the hand and tried to drag her off the set, shouting at Frederick, 'And you get back to Eaton Place at once, and wait in for me. That's an order, Norton.'

Frederick was bold enough to point out, reasonably, 'But I've been engaged for an afternoon's work, sir. It's my afternoon off, and it's not my fault.'

'I don't care what you've been engaged for. Get out of that ridiculous costume and go home at once, d'you hear?'

Georgina released herself from James's grip.

'You can't do that to him, James,' she protested, as Paul Marvin reached them, clearly bewildered.

'Yes I can. You go and change, too, Georgina.'

'I'll do nothing of the sort.'

'James,' Dolly Hale pleaded, 'you can't upset everything like this. They're making a film.'

'What is going on?' Paul Marvin managed to ask at last. James turned on him.

'It's this woman's fault. I've never heard of anything so infantile and irresponsible in my life.'

Marvin called loudly, 'Clear the set. Save the lights.' The bright colours faded abruptly from the surroundings as the lamps were switched off, making everything suddenly dark and oppressive as the actors straggled away, lighting cigarettes and casting curious glances at the figures at the centre of this unrehearsed drama: the tall, angry gentleman and the well dressed lady anxious beside him; the younger woman looking desperately at the made-up actor, who was glaring daggers at her; the tarted-up actress pouting crossly; and the troubled producer, his habitual suavity lost.

'Georgina,' James said, 'are you coming back with Prudence and me in the car, or not?'

'No, I am not,' she said in a firm voice. 'I am staying here to do my job. Now, go away. You've no business to be here.'

James stared at her, but she stood defiantly. Paul Marvin asked, 'What is all the difficulty, please?'

Frederick answered him. 'I'm sorry, Mr Marvin, but it's all over me. I'm Major Bellamy's servant. I didn't know nothing about Miss Georgina being here. I'd best go home now, if you can get somebody in my place.'

He turned to Georgina. 'Excuse me, miss. Honest, I didn't know.'

'I know it isn't your fault, Frederick.'

'No, it's all mine,' Dolly Hale insisted. 'I'm sorry, Georgina, darling. It was only a joke, though.'

'Well, it wasn't a very amusing one. I don't like to see servants embarrassed, ever.'

'Oh, Freddy wouldn't have minded. It's only because James had to come and spoil everything. We're old friends, Freddy and I.'

'Are you? Well, you're no friend of mine any more, Dolly Hale. Just leave me, please. I've got work to do.'

Sensing an end to the disturbance, the hovering assistant director called out, 'O.K. everyone. Stand by again for rehearsal, please.'

But Paul Marvin said quietly to Georgina, 'I'm sorry, my dear, but since I do not wish to upset Lord Bellamy's family I wish you to get changed. I shall come and speak with you later. Please . . .'

Georgina hesitated for a moment. Then, with a last resentful glare at James, she stalked away.

The assistant director's whistle blew, the lights came up; and the illusion was recreated.

'Hullo, Fred,' Rose greeted him with surprise. 'You back already? Had any tea?'

'Yep.'

'There's some left in the pot if you fancy another cup,' Mrs Bridges said.

'No thanks.'

Daisy asked, 'What did the doctor say?'

'Eh?'

'About your headaches. Rose told us . . .'

'Oh, that. Gave me some medicine. The Major in yet?'

'Yes. Proper mad about something, Eddie said. Him and Lady Prudence came out of them studios nearly as soon as they'd gone in, and him looking like thunder. Told Eddie to drive back here at once.'

'That all?'

'Eddie doesn't listen in, you know that. Why you asking, anyway?'

The morning-room bell interrupted the conversation.

'I'll go, if that's Lady Prudence leaving,' Frederick said. 'I want to see the Major.'

'In your off-duty suit?'

'He won't mind, this once.'

He went up, to find that her ladyship had, after all, been seen out personally by the Major. The latter motioned him into the morning-room. Frederick stood to attention.

'Frederick, I wasn't going to speak to you about this afternoon's performance until tomorrow. Since you're here, I think we'd better discuss it now.'

'Yes, sir.'

'I'm all for an occasional joke, but I don't think, in all fairness, you can expect me to turn a blind eye to this one.'

'Beg pardon, sir, but I didn't know about it.'

'Knowing Lady Dorothy Hale, I'm prepared to believe you. I hope, otherwise, you'd have come and warned me and I'd have put a stop to it. I brought you in and gave you a good job after the war, because you'd been my servant and I trusted you.'

'I'm very grateful to you, sir.'

'Right. Then that's all . . .'

'If I might interrupt, sir.'

'What?'

'Just to explain, sir. You see, sir, I'm very grateful to you, and to his lordship and her ladyship. I have been happy in service here, sir. Only, lately, I've been a bit unsettled.'

'Oh, that business about Edward's promotion. I understand that.'

'Not only on that account, sir.' Frederick swallowed, continuing to stare straight ahead of him. 'You see, since Lady Dorothy called round here when you were away for Ascot, and then asked me to join her and some of her friends for dinner at a café . . .'

'She *what*?'

'. . . I've had the opportunity of seeing how other people live. She's been very good to me, and I've found I can, like, make my own way with people – Lady Dolly's sort of people, sir.'

'Oh, you can, can you?'

'I'm a bit ambitious, as you know, sir. So I've decided to give up service and take my chance in the outside world, if you'd be good enough to accept my notice, sir.'

James moved slightly, compelling Frederick's gaze to meet his.

'Are you telling me that Lady Dolly's been taking you about London with her?'

'Yes, sir. She's been very kind, buying me clothes and nice things . . .'

'Have you no pride, man? Has she been paying you money to go around with her? Actual cash?'

'She gave me some money last week, sir.'

'God! You, Trooper Norton of His Majesty's Life Guards, my old soldier servant and footman – little better than a kept man, a gigolo! Are you mad?'

'I've nothing to be ashamed of, sir.'

'Well, you jolly well should have.'

'Can I take it that you accept my notice, then?' Frederick asked, unshaken.

'What the hell else can I do?'

'Thank you, sir.'

He left the room with dignity and returned to the servants' hall. Mrs Bridges was in her armchair, sewing. Edward, who

61

had just come in from the garage, was leafing through a magazine, with Daisy peering at it over his shoulder. Rose was darning. Fred sat down at the table.

'Well,' he said, looking over them all almost contemptuously. 'Time to say cheerio.'

' "Cheerio"?' Mrs Bridges asked, glancing up without genuine curiosity.

'That's right. I'm leaving.'

All their heads were up now.

'You . . . got the push?' Edward asked.

'Give meself the push. That's what.'

'Got a better job, eh?'

Frederick caught Rose's eye. She was watching him with knowing cynicism.

'I think I can guess, Fred, can't I?' she asked.

'Can you?'

'You've got a wealthy lady friend who wants to marry you.'

Their gazes remained locked, ignoring the others, oblivious of their audible reactions.

'Not getting married, Rose. I've been seeing quite a bit lately of Lady Dolly Hale. Seeing all of her, if you really want to know.'

'So that's who it was! All that expensive perfume on your scarf. Been on intimate social terms, haven't you?'

'The Major knows all about it. I told him.'

Mrs Bridges burst in, 'It's disgusting, Frederick. I've heard of ladies of title amusing themselves being friendly with a footman when it's suited them. But just you remember, that Lady Dolly's a madcap and gets herself into the papers over men.'

'I can get on with people of her sort,' Frederick answered coolly. 'I can make a good living on the films and escorting and dancing with ladies at tea-dance places. I know I can, because they all said I can. Only the other night, at the opera . . .'

'Ho! So we go to the opera now, do we? The royal box, I suppose.'

62

'No, the one next to it. Anyway, Lady Dolly told me I was wasted as a servant. "With your looks and your sex appeal," she said, "you could conquer London." '

'I don't call that conquering London, any more than a tom-cat out on the wall in the moonlight.'

'Mrs Bridges!' Rose protested, more shocked by this than by Frederick's revelations.

'What a thing to say in front of my wife!' Edward agreed, less than seriously.

Mrs Bridges shook her head. 'Time she learnt a thing or two about life – especially if she's going on working in *this* house. All I can say is thank the Lord Mr Hudson isn't here. If he knew his footman was carrying on with a lady what's a friend of the family, I think he'd drop dead.'

Frederick got up, grinning, and went to the door, pausing there to say, 'One day when I'm a famous film star out in Hollywood I'll send you all my photo, autographed, so you can show it to your pals and say "That's Frederick Norton, as used to work here as footman. Done well for himself, hasn't he?" Cheerio.'

He went out, leaving them in varying degrees of devastation. Out from their lives forever went ex-Trooper Frederick Norton. And for all her expression of relief that he hadn't been present to hear such scandal, Mrs Bridges secretly prayed that it might not be long before Angus Hudson might return. Nothing – nothing at all – seemed any longer to be like it had been in the good old days before that horrid war.

CHAPTER FOUR

By nearly the middle of that year, 1927, Mr Hudson was back at his post, fit to resume all his duties. Edward was as pleased as anyone to find him so well, though perhaps he had unconsciously fancied that there might be some small portion of the butler's capacity left for him. It was anti-climatic to step down to mere chauffeur/valet again and, since no replacement had been hired for the errant Frederick, he found himself doing footman's work as well. A modest increase in his wages helped to compensate him for both extra duties and loss of his temporary status.

Parliament had just gone into recess. Virginia was away in Paris with William and Alice, the latter on the verge of coming-out into society and thus being indulged in a visit to the Collections to choose the appropriate clothes. Rose had gone with them.

By a convenient chance, Richard's friend Lord Berkhamstead had recently offered him the use at any time of his fishing lodge in the Scottish Highlands, a place Berkhamstead seldom used himself. Feeling the strain towards the end of a busy session, Richard suddenly decided to take up the offer. James and Georgina were to accompany him, all travelling up in the car, driven by Edward, while Hudson, Mrs Bridges, Daisy and Ruby would go by train.

'I don't think I want to go to Scotland,' Georgina pouted when told of the plan. 'It'll rain all the time.'

'Of course, you don't have to come, my dear,' Richard told her. 'I just think it would be a pity not to. Carnochie's a wonderful place. Plenty of good fresh air will do you a world of good.'

'No traffic, no noise,' James urged her. 'A chance to tramp over the heather, fish for salmon . . .'

'I can't fish.'

64

'I'll teach you.'

'How far will the nearest cinema be?'

Richard smiled. 'Seventy miles – over a rough road.'

'Oh, lord!'

'Take a good book to read, then,' James said. 'Anyway, you've got to come. We're closing this house up.'

'Oh, very well. But don't blame me if I'm sick in the car, travelling all that way.'

None of the servants, except, of course, Mr Hudson, had ever visited Scotland. He smiled indulgently in the train as he listened to excited chatter about kilts and bagpipes and caber-tossing and all the rest of their exaggerated fancies. But as the Highland scenery began to appear outside the windows he felt excitement of his own stirring and didn't hesitate to draw their attention to the privilege they had been granted visiting this 'paradise on earth'.

There proved to be nothing paradisial about the prettily situated lodge once the kitchen door had been opened and the state of the interior witnessed. It was a largish room, full of angles and obstacles, and it needed only one glance from Mr Hudson and the pop-eyed Mrs Bridges at his elbow to tell that it was as dirty as it was disorderly. Acrid smoke hung on the air, emitted by a dingy black coal-fired range, at which a fair-haired woman in a dark blue dress stooped and fretted.

'Good day, Mrs . . . ?' Hudson greeted her tentatively. She turned and regarded him without reply. Her face was thin and somewhat lined, though Hudson doubted that she was beyond her thirties.

He continued, 'You are expecting us, I think? Lord Bellamy's party.'

At last she stood up, unsmiling and without any expression of greeting, let alone deference.

'The landlord's letter arrived by mail-boat only this morning,' she said, in the lilting Highland accent. 'McKay and myself had no warning of you.'

Mrs Bridges had pushed forward and was staring at the

65

range in disbelief and disgust. Smoke oozed from every one of its crevices.

'I hope I'm not expected to cook their dinner on that!' she exclaimed.

'This is Mrs Bridges, our cook,' Hudson explained. 'It's Mrs McKay, I believe?' In the continued absence of any welcoming response he said hastily, 'Well, I'll leave you ladies to the kitchen arrangements. Excuse me.' He withdrew thankfully, only to run into a frowning Daisy, emerging from what was evidently the parlour.

'Mr Hudson, it ain't half damp in here. And the grate's full of soot.' He sighed, and explained the position. A shriek from the kitchen sent them both hurrying there. Ruby, still wearing her hat and coat, stood with her hands over her mouth at the larder door she had opened.

'A dead bird!' she was repeating.

Hudson looked in and grimaced. 'A wee grouse. Last year's, by the smell of it.'

Mrs McKay said tonelessly, 'The larder has not been touched since last season's shooting party left. Give it to me and I will burn it.'

Hudson obliged, then turned to his staff.

'There, now, we must all get our coats off, roll up our sleeves, and set to work. His lordship, the Major and Miss Georgina will be here shortly. The place must be made as clean and comfortable as possible before they arrive. Really, all this smoke! Daisy, switch the light on, if you please.'

Daisy obediently went to the switch. Nothing happened when she pressed it. Hudson turned to Mrs McKay.

'Is the electricity not connected, Mrs McKay?'

'The generator is broken down. You'll have to be using oil lamps for the time being.'

Hudson and Mrs Bridges exchanged glances. Then a shout from the now-recovered Ruby told them that the luggage brake had arrived, and all became preoccupying bustle.

'Well!' declared Mrs Bridges later, as she surveyed the left-over remains of the tinned tomato soup, tinned ham and tinned peaches which Hudson had served in the dank sitting-room, the dining-room having proved utterly impossible to use. 'Well! I hope I never have to serve up a luncheon like that again as long as I live. I hope you explained that I'd ordered ahead for the groceries but they haven't arrived.'

'Of course, Mrs Bridges,' Hudson reassured her for the third time. 'His lordship quite understood. It was lucky there was that bottle of champagne left over from their picnic basket. There was only whisky to offer them before luncheon, and Miss Georgina dislikes it. The poor girl looks thoroughly miserable, huddled by that fire. I explained that the wood box is empty and that it takes peat a long time to burn up.'

'Get those scraps out of my sight, Ruby,' Mrs Bridges ordered. 'Then we'll all get on cleaning up this pigsty. If I'm to work in here for ten days I'm not having it in this state.'

Hudson tried to placate her. 'Never mind, Mrs Bridges. From tomorrow we shall be serving them, and ourselves, with some good fresh trout from the sea loch and salmon from the river.'

'Not out of these pots, we won't. Come along, Daisy. You lend a hand, too.'

The door suddenly opened, without a knock, and a man entered. He closed the door behind him and stood surveying them disdainfully. He was tall and straight-backed, with craggy features, permanently tanned by sun, wind and rain; the features of a man of the outdoors.

'You will be Lord Bellamy's household, no doubt,' he said, as though it were an accusation.

Mr Hudson stepped forward to confront him.

'That is correct. And who might you be?'

'I am Roderick McKay, head ghillie to Lord Berkhamstead.'

'Good evening to you.'

'We were not informed of your visit in time. Nothing is ready. You'll be wise to pack your trunks and return to London.'

'I'm sorry, but I don't think Lord Bellamy is considering any such thing.'

'It will not be comfortable here. You can go and tell his lordship that from me.'

'I certainly will not.'

As the edge of Mr Hudson's voice sharpened, Mrs Bridges quickly said to Ruby, 'Ruby, go and get your room ready.'

'Oh, Mrs Bridges,' the girl replied, 'not by myself. This house gives me the creeps.'

McKay looked at her, then said. 'The lass is right. This old lodge has seen some history, I can tell you. The first Laird of Carnochie fought at the Battle of Culloden, in the last stand of the Highlanders against the Hanoverian King George. That was a tragic day for Scotland. The Laird himself was greviously wounded. They say his servant and his piper lifted him, bleeding from a severed arm, onto a crofter's handcart and wheeled him over the mountain yonder to this very house, to escape from the men of Butcher Cumberland. They hid him in a loft, but he died of his wounds and they took him and buried him secretly at dead of night, to a piper's lament at some spot nearby on the hill, deep in the heather. But to this very day no one knows where.'

McKay's gaze shifted directly to Ruby's eyes.

'The only thing certain is that the Laird of Carnochie returns here from time to time of a dark night, for those who can hear him, groaning with the pain of his terrible wounds as he lies pale and bleeding on the handcart that carried him here from the field of Culloden. God rest his soul.'

A silence hung for long moments as McKay continued to stare implacably at the petrified Ruby, while the others looked on registering varying degrees of trepidation and concern. A sudden rumble of what might have been thunder or gunfire brought little shrieks from both Ruby and Daisy. Edward had to swallow hard before he could ask, 'What's that?', thoroughly expecting to be told that it was the Battle of Culloden still spiritually raging.

McKay answered, 'Did you not pump up the water?'

'Water?'

The ghillie indicated an old-fashioned hand-pump under the kitchen sink. 'It needs to be pumped up night and morning, and in between if anyone takes a bath. Has Mrs McKay not told you? That rumbling is the tank running nearly empty. If it does, with the stove lit, you will be having a real explosion.'

'Edward!' Mr Hudson ordered urgently. 'The pump will be your responsibility. Look lively, now, before the tank runs dry.'

Edward leaped willingly to obey, as the women moved instinctively further away from the range. Mr Hudson said to the ghillie. 'If you will kindly wait a moment, Mr McKay, I will ascertain whether his lordship wishes to see you.'

The man stood there, impassive and rock-like. He had not shifted his position by the time Hudson returned.

'His lordship is up resting in his bedroom, but his son, Major James Bellamy, wishes to have a word with you in the sitting-room.'

He led the still silent McKay away. Over the clank of the pump and Edward's gasps of effort, the three women heard a wind rising, quickly followed by sharp flurries of rain against the window-panes.

'Fat lot we're going to see of the blinking Highlands of Scotland at this rate,' Daisy grumbled. 'Might just as well have stopped in London, if you ask me.'

'I wish we had,' Ruby wailed. 'I don't like it here. I don't like it at all.'

Mrs Bridges gave her usual snort of impatience at Ruby's helplessness; but she had to admit to herself that she wasn't enamoured of Carnochie, either.

'It's McKay, isn't it?' James asked pleasantly, when Hudson had shown in the ghillie and retired.

'It is.'

'This weather going to pick up?'

'It might – and then it might not. There is little telling in these parts.'

'Mmm. Well, never mind the weather. I wanted a word with you about the fishing.'

'The fishing?'

'Yes. I'd like to go out and try for a salmon as soon as I can.'

'You'll be wasting your time, sir. Did not Lord Berkhamstead warn you that ours is a late river?'

'He certainly didn't. He told my father there'd be plenty of fishing.'

The ghillie gave a slight, pitying sigh. 'His lordship is so seldom here. I am afraid Lord Bellamy has been misinformed It will not be worth your while to unpack a rod.'

'But that's absurd . . .!'

The ghillie shook his head. 'There will be no fish in the river now.'

James struck the arm of his chair. 'Dammit, we've come all the way from London to fish for salmon, and you say there are no fish! We can't shoot yet and we don't stalk. So what the hell is there to do in this place?'

'There are good walks and fine scenery.'

James's answer to that was to glance towards the window against which the wind-whipped rain was now positively lashing. McKay's face, angular-shadowed in the gloom, showed neither sympathy nor concern.

When James got rid of the visitor he went looking for his father. Meeting Hudson on the way, he paused to tell him the unwelcome news. The butler's eyebrows rose high when he heard it and he seemed about to say something, but merely came out with, 'Very disappointing, sir. We must hope for the weather to clear up, at least.'

Then Georgina came down, and James told her, with more petulance than he had used in speaking to Hudson. To his annoyance, she had no sympathy to give him. In fact, after a display of 'I told you so!' on first viewing the place in which they were to spend the next ten days, Georgina suddenly seemed to relax and become absorbed in a book she picked out from amongst the few the lodge could offer. Irritably, James asked what it was that seemed to have made her oblivious to discomfort within and vile weather without. She showed him the title on the volume's spine: *Clearances in the Scottish Highlands*.

'It's about the aftermath of the '45,' she told him. 'Jumbo we treated them abominably. The English landlords drove thousands of simple Highland crofters off their land, just because they wanted room to graze their sheep. I suppose that's how Berkhamstead's family got this place; and look at it — being left to rot away, almost.'

James scowled. 'Your book's probably prejudiced. I bet it was written by a Scot. They're always going on about the wicked English. No wonder they're so dour and rude and gloomy, like that man McKay.'

'Well, I don't wonder he's put out. All this time with the place empty, then suddenly a crowd of people arrive with only a few hours' warning.'

Hudson came in at that moment with tea things.

'You see,' James said to Georgina. 'Tea bang on time. Some people can manage well enough under difficulties.'

Hudson permitted himself a little self-satisfied smirk on behalf of the staff. He asked Georgina, 'Shall I serve it now, miss, and not wait for his lordship?'

'Better leave him, if he's still asleep,' James answered, overlooking the fact that only a few minutes earlier he had been about to go up and pour out upon his father his own grievance.

Hudson poured tea and milk. James asked him, 'Hudson, what d'you make of that fellow, McKay? Curious chap, eh?'

'McKay is the head ghillie here, sir. Born and bred in these parts I imagine.' He paused before answering the unasked part of the question. 'I would not seek to question his knowledge of the local river, sir.' He handed them their cups and saucers.

'Mmm. Thanks, Hudson, that'll be all.'

'Thank you, sir, miss.' The butler withdrew.

The fire had begun to perk up a little and the tangy smell of the smouldering peat was permeating the air. The light in the room was fading quickly under the shadow of the lowering clouds. It would soon be quite dark.

James sipped his tea and sat back, cradling the saucer on his lap.

'This place is quite romantic, don't you think?' he asked uncharacteristically. Georgina was surprised, but she nodded warm agreement.

71

'Oh, yes. I feel very . . . different here, already. So quiet and dreamy and . . . and the air's so fresh and cool.'

'It's the sort of place where people . . . fall in love.'

'Oh, yes. Definitely.'

'Or suddenly realise how much in love they are – having not had time to think about these things.'

She was staring into the fire, not really listening to his words any more; simply entranced by the atmosphere of the surroundings.

'Yes,' she said almost dreamily. 'I could easily fall in love in the Highlands.'

The reverie lasted for long seconds before James spoke again.

'Georgina . . .'

'Mm?'

'Is it . . . really too late? For us? We . . . neither of us . . . seem to have anyone special in view, do we? So . . .'

She turned the big, luminous eyes towards his anxious face.

'Please don't, James. You'll spoil everything.'

'But you do love me. I *know* you do.'

'Of course I love you, darling. Only . . .'

The door opened and Richard came bustling in. His eyes lit up when he saw the tea tray.

'Oh, capital! I wondered whether we'd get any. I say, I must have been more tired than I thought I was. I slept like a child.'

Georgina poured for him.

'You need a good rest, Uncle Richard. No politics, no speeches . . .'

'No fish,' James would have put in, in his normal mood; but at the moment there was no acid in him. He said nothing. He was watching Georgina as he listened to his father saying to her, 'It's so relaxing here, I wonder anything ever gets done – if it does. I daresay nobody plots or shouts or schemes. They just get on with their honest, simple lives. We Londoners could learn from these people. How not to be in a hurry, and how to enjoy life while we can.'

Richard sat down with them. The little clatter of their cups on their saucers, the hiss of the fire and the buffeting of the wind and rain were the only sounds as they sat there, two of them in reverie, the other's suddenly-aroused thoughts awhirl.

The whole household slept well that night, apart for its humblest member – Ruby. Lying in the iron bed, beneath the disquieting shape of an antlered head affixed to the wall, she woke suddenly from what had been a good sleep into alarmed awareness. What she heard as she lay there sent her thinking of flying out of bed and out of her room, to burst in frantically on Mrs Bridges. It was more the fear of what might happen to her if she were to leave the comparative security of her bed than the scolding she knew she would get from Mrs Bridges that made her stay where she was; but she pulled up the sheet to cover her whole head.

She had heard the crunching of the wheels of the handcart on which the mortally wounded Laird was being brought home from Culloden.

Next morning she braved wrath by telling her tale.

'Couldn't Daisy sleep in my room tonight, Mrs Bridges?' she pleaded.

'No she could not,' was the indignant reply. 'Whatever next!'

But while Mrs Bridges had reacted to Ruby's story with scorn, and Edward with mockery, Mr Hudson, who had listened seriously, said nothing, but went about his duties with a thoughtful air.

The weather had let up, outbreaks of quite warm sun alternating with cooling cloud. The air almost effervesced and everyone's spirits – excepting again Ruby's – were correspondingly higher. Mrs McKay, who lived with her husband in a cottage nearby, was as dour as ever, but not hostile and she worked as hard as any of them to improve the kitchen. Questioned again about the electricity generator, she replied vaguely that she believed some spare part was needed and had been ordered. There was no knowing when it might turn up.

Mr Hudson made a note to get Edward to have a look at the generator. He might just be able to make a temporary repair. But Edward was away for the day, driving his lordship over to

73

the home of a political friend who lived forty miles away. They would not be back until evening.

Richard had invited James and Georgina to drive over with him. Both had declined. Georgina was enjoying the lassitude of simply sitting about and reading her absorbing book, with the occasional short stroll along the heather-banked pathways which criss-crossed Lord Berkhamstead's estate. James took every opportunity to accompany her, slipping his arm through hers and wondering at the new radiance of her skin and eyes. His mind raced ahead as he tried to decide what next to say to her, but daytime and the fresh air seemed inappropriate to his feelings, and they talked only commonplaces.

After lunch, Mr Hudson announced that he, too, would be taking a stroll. He was going down into the little port of Camochie itself to have a look around. He invited Mrs Bridges to go with him, but she was yawning post-prandially and replied that with 'such air' she would just have to get down for forty winks.

Wearing his coat and bowler hat, Hudson made an incongrously formal figure amongst the villagers and the fisherfolk. The irony did not occur to him that he, of all the Bellamy household, should have been the one to have blended most easily into what was almost his native heath. But he had been long away, and, for all the remnants of his accent and beliefs, he was a Londoner by habit and appearance, if not completely at heart. He found himself observing the locals as if he were in a foreign land.

Perhaps this objectivity was responsible for his chancing to notice something which he might otherwise have missed. He was leaning on a rail close to the small jetty, enjoying the strong sea smell, the dance of the sunlight on the water, the soaring and swooping of the gulls. A dinghy bobbed at the foot of some sea-lapped stone steps near him. Two burly, blue-jerseyed men in it were receiving heavy fish-boxes, being passed down to them by another man, who was taking them from a handcart.

When the last box was aboard, the men in the dinghy cast

off and rowed laboriously the short distance out to a fishing-boat at moorings. Lingering on idly, enjoying this agreeable break from duty, Mr Hudson watched the boxes being passed up out of the dinghy to men on the fishing-boat. As soon as the operation had been completed and the dinghy had turned back towards the jetty, the fishing-boat cast off and turned her prow towards the distant shape of Skye.

A clock chimed, causing Mr Hudson to look at his watch. He began to walk hurriedly away. A sudden thought halted him in his tracks, and he turned to look first at the receding boat, then at the returned dinghy, and finally at the empty handcart.

His mind was ablaze with inspiration as he strode back to the lodge.

Edward arrived back in time for late supper. He sniffed eagerly at the delicious smell of kippers frying in the lamplit kitchen. He kissed Daisy, then rubbed his hands together appreciatively.

'Nothing like a nice kipper, Mrs Bridges.'

'Huh! I don't know whether I'm frying kippers or old boots in this light. I just hope they get done right, that's all.'

'They look lovely,' said Daisy, peering into the sizzling pan. 'You know, I'm beginning to like it here, now we've got the hang of things.'

'It's all right for you, Daisy. You've got young eyes. Mr Hudson, can't we do nothing about that electric light?'

'Yes,' he agreed. 'Edward, as soon as we've finished supper I'd like you to take a lamp and come with me to the generator house. There might be something you can fix up.'

'Sure, Mr Hudson,' Edward agreed willingly. 'Hullo, Ruby. The old Laird of Carnochie been at you yet?'

'That will do, Edward,' Mr Hudson said sharply. 'We'll have none of your feeble jokes at Ruby's expense.'

'No, Mr Hudson. Sorry.'

Light or no light, Mrs Bridges' expert instinct had enabled her to cook the kippers to perfection. 'More luck than good judgment,' was all she would concede in answer to unanimous praise. 'I really can't go on managing with just lamps.'

'Come along, Edward,' Mr Hudson ordered, rolling his napkin. 'And Ruby – off away to your bed. You looked washed out, girl.'

'Stick some cotton wool in your ears,' Edward couldn't restrain himself from adding. A look from Mr Hudson made him take up one of the oil lamps and lead the way out into the black night.

The stone hut which housed the generator was some thirty yards apart from the lodge. The interior smelt of oil and metal. They circled the machine, looking for the clasps that would enable the engine cover to be raised, and as they did so Mr Hudson raised his head and sniffed another smell.

'Just a moment, Edward. Bring the lamp through here, into this other room.'

It was at once cooler, and damp. 'Cor!' Edward exclaimed disgustedly. 'Fish!'

The aroma of wet fish, so less attractive than that of frying kippers, was undoubtedly of recent origin. Mr Hudson looked round with knowing eyes, taking in the marble slab with the single water-tap about it and buckets beneath. In a shadowy corner stood a stack of fish-boxes.

'Fishy is the word, Edward,' he said, and motioned his companion back to the generator room, where it soon became apparent that nothing Edward could contrive would get the machine going. They returned to the lodge and not long afterwards went to their bedrooms.

As she had expected and feared, Ruby heard the handcart again that night. Again, she buried her head under her sheets and muttered the only scraps of prayer she knew.

Mr Hudson, too, heard the cart, but did not pray. He had been waiting for the sound and had not undressed in anticipation of it. Swinging himself off the top of his bed and slipping on his shoes, he lit his lamp cautiously, keeping his body between it and the window so as to show no light, then took it up and went quietly downstairs. Slipping out by the kitchen door, he crept quietly towards the generator house. He could see light there, and movement, and hear the low mutter and grunt of men going about some task requiring physical effort. An empty handcart stood outside.

There was no point in concealing his presence any longer. He turned the lamp up and strode forward, through the door, and straight past the generator into the salmon-house. Three faces turned to him in surprise. One of the belonged to Roderick McKay.

Hudson said nothing, only stood noting the scene: one man at the bench, a fine, glistening salmon before him and a knife poised in his hand; another bending over a fish-box, packing it; and Roderick McKay, straightening up from placing empty boxes in readiness.

After the initial surprise, the other two men looked at McKay, as if for an order that might bring them moving menacingly towards the intruder. But McKay gave a slight shake of his head and came forward himself.

'Carry on,' he said over his shoulder. Then, 'I think, Mr Hudson, a word between us in the lodge kitchen would be as well.'

Hudson nodded and lit their way back. Once inside, they stood facing one another across the table, the lamp between them. Keeping his voice low, Hudson commenced.

'So, the Laird of Carnochie comes home by night to die. On a slab, reserved for your employer's fish, taken from his river and shipped away for sale in the market. And a simple wee kitchenmaid half scared out of her wits as a result.'

The bigger man shrugged. ''Tis a pity you chose to poke your nose into the private affairs of this village – a butler from London.'

'I may be a butler, Mr McKay, but I, too, have been a gamekeeper and ghillie in my day; and my father, I'll have you know, was head ghillie to Lord Invermore in Argyllshire for thirty years. My knowledge told me the river here is not a late river.'

'It is a late river – but it has an early spate at this time.'

Hudson nodded. 'I also know that boxes of fish are usually brought ashore from fishing-boats, not loaded on to them and carried away.'

For the first time a flicker of a smile touched McKay's strong mouth. He was a handsome man in his ruggedness, and, momentarily unmasked, seemed a pleasant one.

'Och aye. You're an observant man, Mr Hudson. I'll give you that.'

'Just as well,' Hudson said, 'before the salmon pools were quite emptied by you and your poaching, thieving friends.'

'There's more in the river than a landlord from England needs, coming here only one or two months in a year. It is a waste of good salmon.'

'That's no excuse for theft.'

'Ach, I'm not proud of it, but it's the way we have to make a wee bit extra to live, and the landlord gets his fish a-plenty, just the same. I suppose you will now be sending a telegram to his lordship on his yacht at Monte Carlo – or maybe just fetching the constable?'

Hudson shook his head. 'I'll do neither. To hand you over to the police or your employer at this time will solve nothing. I'll confess I am not over-fond of absentee landlords myself, but nobody has the right to accept a man's money and poach his game. As I see it, Mr McKay, this can be a matter between you, as ghillie to Lord Berkhamstead, and myself, as butler to Lord Bellamy, to be settled in a civilised manner.'

'Aye. It's better that way.'

'Then, sit down, my friend.'

McKay obeyed. Hudson went to a cupboard and returned with a whisky bottle and two glasses. He made no move to open the bottle, though. He leaned forward, completely master of the situation.

'I will pass no judgment on a matter which is none of my business. But I'll tell you this, Mr McKay: when my family, the folk I've served for forty years, come to visit my own country of Scotland, and get cheated, then it is my business. I'll make a gentleman's bargain with you. The fish you have out there now are dead already so they're yours to do with as usual. But tomorrow Major Bellamy will go out and cast a fly on the river, and I very much hope he will catch a salmon. And you will see to it in future that there is dry wood enough for the fires and hot water in the lodge, and that, as I now believe you know would be perfectly possible, the electric generator is in working order. Is that understood?'

'It is as one Scot to another, Mr Hudson. You can depend on it.'

At last Hudson unstoppered the bottle and poised it.

'Then you'll take a wee dram with me, to seal our bargain?'

'Aye, that I will.'

'Good.'

Hudson poured for them both, smiling at last as he did so. When he glanced up to hand McKay his glass, he saw that the ghillie was smiling, too. They drank together.

Next morning was fine, and Mr Hudson contrived to make James accept unsuspiciously that he had been down early to the river and formed the strong opinion that since the heavy rain there might well be salmon in the Carnochie Estate's stretch. James and Georgina went down together with the equipment, and by lunchtime James had landed a fine fish which he let Georgina help him play.

Roderick McKay had come unseen down to the bank to watch them as they brought it in. He nodded approval.

'Well, McKay,' James said triumphantly, 'the fishing's improved rather suddenly, hasn't it?'

Another nod. 'I knew you'd not catch a fish while the rain and the mist were down the hills, sir. It's the climate that's improved – not the fishing.'

James was too preoccupied with success to square up this remark with the ghillie's earlier prophecy.

'I was wondering, sir,' McKay went on, 'whether the young lady and yourself would care to climb up Shielas Tor with me tomorrow morning? There's an eagle's nest, way up on the top there. Maybe you'd care to take a peep at the young ones?'

'Oh, I'd love to!' Georgina said. 'Could I take my camera and photograph them?'

'You could try, miss. It's a fair scramble up the last part of

79

the crag; and we'd need to leave a wee bit early.'

'Early as you like,' James replied happily. 'Breakfast at seven, and boots, eh?'

'That would be as well, sir. I'll bid ye both good-day, then.' With a twitch of a smile, the ghillie went away.

When he was shown the fish, Mr Hudson smiled secretly. He had already noticed that the wood-box in the sitting-room and that in the kitchen had become miraculously full, and that a plentiful pile of kindling and logs lay near the kitchen door. Mrs McKay, too, seemed to have unbent suddenly from a dry, resentful creature to a real help about the house whose first unprompted gesture was to provide a batch of shortbread of her own cooking which evoked cries of pleasure from the servants at teatime. She willingly lent her old book containing the recipe to Mrs Bridges, who sat at the kitchen table that evening copying it in her laborious hand.

As she was doing so, a surge of light swept into the kitchen so suddenly that Mrs Bridges uttered an involuntary cry.

'The light! Electric light at last.'

'Aye,' Mrs McKay said, moving to extinguish the oil lamps. 'McKay has been repairing the generator for you. You'll be doing without the lamps now.'

'Oh my goodness, what a relief. Now, where was I? "Bake in a moderate oven for about half an hour . . .".'

'It might be a wee bit less,' Mrs McKay said.

'Well, if I can make shortbread as good as yours, I'll have learnt something in Scotland.'

'I'll give you a hand with their dinner tonight, Mrs Bridges,' the housekeeper offered for the first time. 'I'll help the lass prepare the vegetables.'

Both Mrs Bridges and Ruby looked quite stunned. If Mrs McKay noticed, she didn't show it.

In the sitting-room, now warm and cheerful under the influence of a lively wood fire and electric light, James, in evening clothes, stood up eagerly as Georgina came in. She was wearing a sleeveless dress of rose-pink chiffon over a silk under-dress, with a flower on the shoulder.

James embraced her, then held her admiringly at arms' length.

'My, you look stunning. I haven't seen that dress before, have I?'

'No. It's new.'

'Are you going to be warm enough?'

'Oh, I'm very hardy now, after a week in the Highlands.'

'Better put on warm clothes in the morning for our climb, though,' he cautioned, releasing her. 'It's bound to be a bit draughty up on the top.'

She nodded and sat on the settee. He hovered near. He had determined to speak out this evening.

'Well, back to London next week, eh? Start making plans.'

Georgina looked up. 'Plans?'

'Our plans. Shall we . . . tell Father tonight?'

She understood suddenly. Her expression showed her alarm and pity.

'Georgina?' he asked, seeing it. 'What's the matter?'

She answered carefully, 'James, I didn't mean . . . when I said the other night . . .'

'You said you loved me.'

'Of course I love you . . .'

'Then . . .'

'. . . in a silly sort of way. I always have loved you. But not like you mean. Not to marry.'

He protested, 'When I said that neither of us seemed to have anyone special in view, you didn't say that wasn't true, and . . . and I thought . . . perhaps . . . at last . . .'

'I should have been more honest, James. Perhaps it was the feeling of this place, being here alone together, miles from anywhere. Coming up here was like going back in time – peat fires and nursery tea and Bonnie Prince Charlie. It's all been a kind of make-believe. But make-believe is for children. We did love each other . . .'

'*Do*.'

'No, did. During the war. But that's all in the past, darling. Can't you see?'

Her heart swelled as she saw his expression crumple and heard him whisper pleadingly, 'Georgina – don't take this away from me. I haven't anything else left.'

Like their last intimate encounter, this, too, was broken abruptly by the entry of Richard, fresh and happy from his break from work and the extra rest, and totally oblivious of the atmosphere into which he had marched. James turned and hid his face in shadow as his father breezed, 'I say, Hudson's been telling me a tradition he got from McKay that Charles Edward Stuart slept here during his wanderings before he sailed for Skye. There's a lock of his hair in a little glass case, somewhere in the house. Mind you, if that unfortunate young man had given every lock of hair that's kept in his memory in Scotland, he'd have been totally bald!'

He noticed that Georgina was clutching her hands about her arms.

'Georgina, my dear, are you cold? That's a rather flimsy dress for this climate, isn't it?'

The muffled voice of James replied, his back still towards them.

'Perhaps a ghost walked over her grave.'

Very contrastingly clad in tweeds and woollen jumper, Georgina came gaily downstairs to the sitting-room early next morning, to find Hudson adjusting the curtains.

'Good morning, Miss Georgina.'

'Good morning, Hudson. Is the Major down yet?'

'I believe he has gone out, miss. Edward went to call him at seven o'clock and found that he had already dressed and left his room.'

'Oh?'

'He left this letter for you in his room, miss.'

Hudson picked up the long white envelope from the small table. She had barely time to rip it open and start unfolding the note when Richard came bustling in. She whipped the letter behind her back.

'Good morning,' Richard said, and kissed her. 'I thought I'd

82

better come and see you safely off, if you're still going with McKay. I'm sorry James won't be with you. He's gone to London.'

'London?'

'He put a note under my door. Apparently he suddenly remembered he'd promised to play in a polo match. Since we're leaving in a few days, anyway, it seemed a pity to miss it.'

'But how did he go?'

'He says he hoped to get a lift on the fishing-boat to Oban and catch the train from there. Sorry if it's spoilt your day, Georgina. You know how impulsive James can be.'

'Yes,' she answered bleakly. 'I know.'

As soon as she was alone she read the note through once, then destroyed it and its envelope. It did not mention polo. It was the old phrases; the old, unwanted sentiments and re-criminations of a man who seemed destined never to grow up or to allow himself to settle into any sort of happiness.

She went up the tor with McKay, delighted in the sight of the eaglets, got some photographs which in due course turned out well, and so exhausted herself by the day's efforts that she went to bed early and slept like a log, with never another thought of silly old Jumbo.

A few days later the party took its leave, gravely and cour-teously seen off by Mr and Mrs McKay.

'I've put the hamper of fish in the taxi,' said the latter to Hudson, aside. 'I would keep it in the carriage with you. I have known salmon taken from the guard's van before now.'

Hudson grinned.

'These poachers get everywhere it seems, Mr McKay.'

'They do indeed, Mr Hudson.'

They shook hands warmly.

CHAPTER FIVE

James Bellamy sailed away not only from Scotland; he sailed from Great Britain altogether. That is not to say that he crossed the Atlantic in that same fishing-boat, nor even that he took a further summary departure without giving any more reason than a fictitious game of polo.

He was on the threshold of middle age, and, in his own eyes and those of the more honest of his limited circle of friends, a failure. He had failed at business, at marriage, at love, and at life. One of his drawers held a medal and ribbon signifying success in war; but only he knew that its real significance was as compensation for gallant effort, rather than success; for injury, rather than triumph.

The decade of the 'Thirties was almost dawning. England, following the unrest of the General Strike and its aftermath, was a place of contrasting bewilderment and escapism, promising nothing, offering little to a drifting, aimless gentleman of comfortable enough financial means but few intellectual or practical ones. It was a time for uncomplicated souls, those who could accept with thankfulness their possession of a job, a home, a family circle; or for those equally uncomplicated, well-off ones, who could find peace of mind in the artificial pleasures of which there were no lack at this time.

So James went to America, to get Georgina and a lot of other things out of his system and to search for the magic elixir which even his disillusionment allowed him to think must eventually come his way. And Georgina, to purge herself of James and of serious emotions of any kind, plunged back into her old social whirl. It meant taking up again with some of the old set whom she had never wished to see again – Dolly Hale, of the film studio debacle, was one of them – but under the influence of jazz music, cigarettes, champagne and childish pranks, personal animosities faded. One took one's companions in their various permutations, and that was all.

'Oh, blast and botheration!' an already slightly squiffy Georgina exclaimed as she unlocked the front door of a darkened No. 165 Eaton Place in the early hours of a summer morning. 'The servants must all be in bed.'

'Don't put the lights on,' hissed Peter Dinmont, close to her elbow. 'Let's play "Murder".' He seized his own female companion in a mock-ferocious grasp. 'Ethel – you are my vict-i-i-im!'

She gave an uncultured cry of genuine fright.

Georgina did put on the hall lights and led the way to the morning-room. Those who followed her were Peter Dinmont and Ethel Kent: he a young gentleman of no other occupation than drawing his allowance from his father and spending it, she a counter assistant at Selfridge's; Dolly Hale and Darrow Morton, an American drifter with literary pretensions; and Robert, Marquis of Stockbridge, a beefy, amiable young man with no positive attributes except his inheritance, and the negative one of being, in the eyes of Georgina, whom he had been escorting during the evening, a wet fish.

For the past few hours they had all been employing their intellects, breeding and education in the noble pursuit known to their time as a 'scavenger hunt'. It required them to acquire between them a number of unrelated objects, ranging from a policeman's helmet and a housemaid's cap to a programme for the Wembley Exhibition and a used tram ticket, and to convey these by dawn or soon after to a certain house in Sussex, where other similarly occupied teams would, they would hope, arrive after them, thus giving them winning status. Then they would all sit down to an enormous, uproarious and still-tipsy breakfast, to fortify themselves for another day of arduous idleness and waste.

'Darrow,' Dolly Hale instructed the American, 'bring the loot in here.'

It was duly poured on to the morning-room carpet.

Darrow Morton asked, 'Where the hell's the helmet?'

'I have it,' said Lord Stockbridge, sheepishly producing it.

When no one else had been able to think of a way of acquiring a policeman's helmet, short of some resort to violence, he had approached a constable with the suggestion that a kitten had got stuck up a tree and had offered to hold the helmet while its owner had climbed up. The ruse had worked, but Stockbridge was not feeling especially proud of himself for it.

'Isn't he sweet?' said Dolly Hale sarcastically.

'I think he was rather clever,' Georgina defended him, making him blush with pleasure.

'I feel a bit guilty,' he admitted. 'That poor devil of a constable might get into trouble.'

'Rot!' exclaimed Darrow, and turned to examine the rest of the booty. 'Say, we don't have a goddam tram ticket!'

'Ow!' said Peter's shop-girl. 'I prob'ly got one in my bag.'

'Such a lucky thing,' Dolly remarked, 'that Ethel happens to travel by tram.'

The ticket was found and Ethel condescendingly congratulated. 'Right,' Darrow said. 'One parlourmaid's cap is all we need.'

'Where do the dear girls sleep?' asked Peter, with an exaggerated leer.

Georgina answered, 'Our parlourmaid's married to the chauffeur, and they live across in the mews. She may have left one of her caps lying around the kitchen, though.'

'Then, we'll all go down and see.'

'Shan't we wake the house?' Robert Stockbridge ventured. Georgina assured him that there was no one presently in residence above stairs, and they pranced off in melodramatic file, Ethel uttering little cries of fear for the beetles they might encounter and Peter squeezing her waist comfortingly.

'Hey!' Darrow cried, almost as soon as the kitchen search had begun. 'I found some aprons. We must be getting warm.'

'They haven't got strings,' Ethel said. 'They're tea-towels.'

'How clever of you to know,' Dolly Hale murmured.

A strange voice froze them all where they stood: 'What is going on here?'

Clad in dressing-gown and pyjamas, Mr Hudson emerged from the servants' hall and stood blinking in astonishment.

'Miss Georgina!'

She smiled guiltily. 'Hello, Hudson. We're on a scavenger hunt, you see. Just looking for something that had to be down here.'

'And which we have now found,' Dolly Hale cried, holding up one of Daisy's white caps. 'Let us repair aloft and celebrate our success with music, dancing and champagne, before we repair hence.'

'Could you bring us a bottle of champagne, please, Hudson?' Georgina requested.

'Make it two,' said the American, Darrow Morton, drily.

'Very good, sir,' Hudson replied, and they trooped away upstairs, only Robert, Marquis of Stockbridge, lingering to murmur to the butler, with whom he was acquainted, 'Sorry to have got you out of bed.'

'That is quite all right, my lord. Thank you.'

The champagne having been served and Hudson ordered back to his bed, the impromptu party swung merrily. Robert, a trifle hesitantly, went up to Ethel Kent and invited her to dance with him to the gramophone music.

'Oh, Lord Stockbridge, thanks ever so!'

'You know who Robert reminds me of?' Darrow confided to Georgina, as they danced past. 'Little Lord Fauntleroy. All lace collars and democracy, being polite to butlers and dancing with shop girls. I'll bet he calls his mother "Dearest".'

'As a matter of fact, he does.'

'Where on earth did you dig her up?' Dolly demanded of Peter.

'Selfridge's, actually.'

'Bargain basement, I suppose.'

When they came together in a dance, Robert said anxiously to Georgina, 'I wouldn't see too much of Darrow Morton, if I were you.'

'Why not?'

'You know . . . drugs. You must have seen how quickly Dolly got lit up earlier this evening, after she'd gone outside with him.'

'What rubbish. Dolly's always changing moods. And I think

87

it's very bad form to criticise people you're going around with. I can't think why you come, if you disapprove of everything we do.'

'Georgina, that's not fair. I don't mind a bit of fun, but when it comes to risking ruining your life . . .'

'Oh, you're so stuffy. One ought to try everything.'

'Not drugs. Promise me you won't.'

'Promise you? I scarcely even know you, except that you're always hanging round and being a bore. Anyway, we'd better get off to Adele's.'

Georgina swung herself from his hold and cried to them all, 'Come on! Off to Sussex, or we'll lose first prize.'

There was a chorus of assent. The last of the champagne was poured and tossed back, and they meandered out into the night.

'Oh, damn disaster!' Dolly Hale moaned theatrically at first sight of her car. 'Another bloody puncture!'

'We'll have to change the wheel.'

'It's no use. I had a puncture this morning. The spare's still flat.'

'My car's only a two-seater,' Robert said apologetically.

The American suggested, 'Did Lord Bellamy take his car to Wiltshire today?'

'No,' Georgina said. 'They went by train.'

'But how gorgeous, then!' Dolly exclaimed. 'We can borrow it. Clever darling Darrow!'

Robert protested, 'Georgina couldn't take the car without Lord Bellamy's permission.' But Georgina turned on him angrily. 'Why don't you mind your own business? You don't have to do anything daring like coming with us. Come on, the rest of you.'

Discarding all discretion, she led the way across to the mews and up the steps to Edward's and Daisy's flat, and hammered on the door.

'Come on, Edward!' she yelled.

'Open the door – Edward!' Dolly joined in.

Just managing to register that the time was three am, Edward came blearily to the door, startled to see Georgina and seemingly a mob of others there.

'Edward, Lady Dolly's car's got a puncture. We'll have to take ours.'

'Oh . . . Yes, miss. I'll just get dressed.'

'No, it's all right. We'll drive ourselves. If you could just give me the garage key.'

Edward said, as firmly as politeness would permit, 'Excuse me, Miss Georgina, but I don't think his lordship would like anyone but me to drive the car.'

Georgina was as good as prepared to accept this, but Darrow Morton intervened, 'Then there wouldn't be room for all of us.'

'No,' said Dolly from behind. 'I detest crushes, and I absolutely refuse to be squeezed into the back seat with Peter and his shop-girl.'

'Georgina,' Darrow persisted, 'does this car actually belong to your uncle?'

'My guardian? Yes, of course it does.'

'Then what are we all standing around for?' He addressed Edward. 'Would you please fetch the key to the garage?'

'Excuse me, sir, but his lordship is very particular about the car. He doesn't even like her ladyship to drive it without me sitting beside her. I don't think he'd like a stranger to drive it.'

'Oh, don't fuss, Edward,' Georgina said, feeling herself losing face in front of her friends. 'I'll drive it myself.'

'You, Miss Georgina?'

'Look, I promise faithfully that your sacred car shall be touched by no one but myself. That's all right, isn't it?'

Edward had no option but to answer dubiously, 'Yes, Miss Georgina. I'll just get the car out of the garage.'

'Don't worry. We'll see to that,' Darrow insisted. 'Just bring the key.'

'Yes, sir.'

Edward went away. 'Isn't he sweet?' said Dolly, nearly falling backwards down the steps as she wavered and staggered.

The key was fetched and the merry party went excitedly off to claim their prize.

'You shouldn't of let them have it, Eddie,' said Daisy sleepily from the bed.

'What else could I do?' he protested, getting back in, to endure a troubled remainder of the night.

Georgina was not accustomed to driving the Rolls Royce. Getting it out of the garage and through London was tricky. Then Dolly Hale insisted on sitting next to her and shrieking endearments through the open window to the few people about in the pre-dawn streets, waving the policeman's helmet. In the back, Ethel squeaked and giggled as Peter fumbled with her, and Darrow wisecracked with typical American spontaneity.

By the time they had reached Epsom, Georgina was handling the big car with confidence and unconsciously increasing speed. They passed swiftly and gaily through that part of Surrey and then eastward into Sussex, encountering little other traffic moving in either direction. They left the main roads at East Grinstead and meandered along minor ones as they came within ten miles or so of their destination.

It was clear daylight by now and a few more people were stirring. One of them, a village police constable, in shirtsleeves and braces, was pumping up his bicycle tyres against the fence of his cottage. He heard the car, unusually early and fast for that part, and looked up. It swept by, Dolly flourishing the helmet triumphantly at him and calling 'Goodmorning, dahling!'

The policeman didn't smile or wave back. He watched the car out of sight, frowning; and his mind registered its number.

Another early mover was Alf Smith, a cowman whose cottage lay about a mile beyond this village and whose place of employment was another half-mile further still. Day in, day out, Alf Smith's early morning routine was the same: to respond to his alarm clock, dress while the kettle was boiling, make himself a cup of tea and take one to his wife, still abed. Then he would get on his old bicycle and trundle off to get in the cows for milking. A man in his thirties, he had been doing this for eleven years and would likely go on doing it until he was too old to get about.

Or would have done, had not his slightly wobbly emergence from the short lane leading from his cottage coincided with the swoop of the Rolls-Royce over a hump in the narrow lane into which he was riding.

Georgina, horrified, had just quick enough reactions to brake at the moment of impact. But that was too late for Alf Smith. The Rolls screeched to a juddering halt with his bicycle under its front wheels. He himself was flung ahead, to fall spread-eagled face downward in the road. He did not stir.

Robert Stockbridge, following at a safe distance behind the Rolls, drew up near and leaped from his car as soon as it had halted. He ran to the prone figure and made a quick examination. Then he walked back to the Rolls, from which no one had emerged. He looked in at Georgina's side, noting the sprawl of evidently sleeping figures in the back seat.

Georgina and Dolly sat motionless, side by side, their faces frozen with horror. Incongruously, the policeman's helmet still lay in Dolly's lap.

'Where is the car now?' Richard Bellamy, grim-faced, asked Edward later that day. He and Virginia had just returned home, having received a telephone message at their overnight hosts'. An unusually pale Hudson had opened the door to them.

'In Sussex, m'lord,' Edward said, dry-mouthed. 'The . . . the police want it there for the time being.'

'And you didn't drive it there?'

'No, m'lord.'

'Have you any explanation for what happened last night, then?'

'Well, Miss Georgina said she'd be driving, and . . .'

'That is exactly my point. Why was Miss Georgina driving the car, and not you?' Richard was striding up and down in agitation.

'M'lord, she . . . Miss Georgina . . . and some of her friends came along to the mews . . . and it was three o'clock of the morning . . .'

'It makes not the slightest difference what time it was. You

91

are the chauffeur and that car was left in your care. I am ver
disappointed in you, Edward. I'm afraid I shall have to conside
very seriously your position in this household. If Major Bellam
were here . . .'

He broke off as the morning-room doors opened and M
Hudson ushered in Sir Geoffrey Dillon. Georgina, who had bee
tidying herself up, after her return by train, came in at the sam
time. Hudson gestured the resentful Edward out of the roon
with him.

'I'm afraid I have some bad news,' the lawyer said withou
preamble. 'The man died two hours ago.'

'Oh, no!'

'There will be an inquest, of course.'

'I won't have to go, will I?' Georgina asked.

'I'm afraid you will. I gather you went to the police statio:
after the accident, and that you all made statements.'

'Yes.'

'What exactly did you yourself say?'

'I . . . I'm not quite sure.'

'But you were driving the car?'

'Yes. I said that. But Darrow said there was absolutel
nothing I could have done.'

'Darrow?'

'Darrow Morton. An American friend of Dolly . . . Lad
Dolly Hale.'

'Did he say in a statement that there was nothing you coul
have done?'

'Oh, yes.'

'Then his evidence will clearly be vital. What about th
others?'

'Well, they were asleep – apart from Dolly, who didn't seer
to remember much. We . . . we'd had quite a lot of champagne
and been up all night. Oh, Robert Stockbridge was there –
following in his own car. He was awake – if you call it that.'

'Georgina!' Richard rapped sharply. 'This is no laughin,
matter. A man has been killed – by a car driven by you.'

But Sir Geoffrey Dillon's look had turned thoughtful, and h

made no effort to press the questioning. 'Robert Stockbridge,' he mused. 'The Marquis of Stockbridge? Mm! Now that is more promising, I think.' But he would not say why, and took his departure soon afterward.

In the servants' hall, Edward walked past his wife without a word or a look and tore open the newspaper lying on the long table.

'Oh, no!' she groaned, in pretended exasperation. 'Not another winner that can't lose – only it does!'

For once he didn't joke back. *Situations Vacant*, he answered bitterly. She went to him, but he made no response to her touch on his shoulder.

'Eddie! His lordship hasn't ... !'

'He's thinking about it. I get the blame for everything in this house, didn't you know? Well, p'raps I'll beat him to it.'

He leaned earnestly forward towards the vacancies columns, but Mr Hudson interrupted him.

'Edward, here is your third class fare to East Grinstead and your bus fare from there. You will collect the car at the police station and then you may have some bread and cheese and a half-pint of light ale before driving back. One-and-ninepence should cover that.'

'Yes, Mr Hudson,' Edward said wearily, folding the paper and putting it down.

'Edward, from all I hear, it would appear that you were entirely blameless in this matter of Miss Georgina and her friends taking the motor car.'

'Huh! Try telling that to his lordship.'

'Don't be impertinent to me, my boy. His lordship is naturally upset. You have to realise that being in service is not unlike being in the army. Our masters, like your officers, are not always right, and they sometimes blame us for things which are not our fault. But we are not expected to answer back, nor to bear grudges, because those are the terms we accept when we enter service.'

Edward's scowl showed his lack of conviction.

'Maybe that's why I didn't like the army, then. A man has

his self-respect, Mr Hudson. I don't reckon he's anything without that.'

But there were those who did not think the same. When Georgina tried to telephone Darrow Morton at his hotel she was told that he had left there at very short notice, presumably upon some urgent summons back to the United States, for his baggage had been forwarded to Southampton.

Dolly Hale's telephone rang and rang for days, but was never answered. Georgina was trying her yet again when Peter Dinmont was shown into the morning-room.

'Thank goodness for someone!' she exclaimed. 'What'll you have to drink?'

'Er, well, nothing, thanks. I can't stay, Georgina. I just called in to wish you good luck for the inquest. It's tomorrow, isn't it?'

'Of course. But you'll be there, won't you? And Ethel?'

'Well, no, they . . . they haven't called me. They have my statement. I . . . Ethel and I . . . we didn't see anything, so . . .'

'But at least you were in the car. You could say I wasn't driving recklessly. I wasn't drunk.'

'Oh, well, actually, I don't really remember much . . . We were a bit squiffy, you know – and then we went to sleep. Look, Georgina, I'm awfully sorry, but you see, though Ethel's a decent sort and all that, if it came out that I was out with a girl like that . . . I mean, my father does get pretty ratty about what he calls unsuitable girls. And being on an allowance does make it dashed awkward. I hope you see.'

'I see,' Georgina said. 'Thanks, Peter.'

'Awfully sorry,' he mumbled, getting up and going.

So, she was to be on her own. The thought of Robert Stockbridge never so much as entered her mind. If it had, she would probably have dismissed it. But it had not escaped Sir Geoffrey Dillon's mind. He came bustling round to Eaton Place on the morning of the inquest. Richard and Virginia were in the morning-room, waiting for Georgina to come down and join them for the drive to Sussex, where the hearing would be held as close to the scene of the accident as was feasible.

'I thought we arranged to meet down there,' Richard said, surprised.

'We did. But I wanted a word with your first, Richard, Lady Bellamy. I thought you ought to know that Lord Stockbridge will not be giving evidence.'

'But he must!' exclaimed Virginia, who had heard of the defections of all the others.

The lawyer shook his head in his enigmatic way.

'I have just heard from the Buckminster solicitor. The Duke is very anxious that his son should not appear, and Lord Stockbridge is down in the country.'

Richard objected. 'But surely you could have insisted. He'd have given evidence for us.'

'I understand that the Duke has had a word with the Chief Constable, pointing out that Lord Stockbridge was not actually involved in the accident. In the circumstances, I didn't feel it would be advisable to intervene. The hearing will, ah, receive much less publicity without the unwelcome notoriety of a duke's eldest son giving evidence.'

He gave Richard his unemotional stare.

'I see,' Richard said. 'Well, then, are you coming in our car?'

'No, thank you. I have my own. I'll see you there.'

He went out. Virginia asked anxiously, 'But why? Why on earth . . . ?'

Richard smiled. 'My dear, I'm sure it's for the best. I've lived long enough to recognise a deal when I see it – or perhaps I should say, when I smell it. In this case, between two solicitors, who've reached a compromise. One might as well try to break an agreement between a couple of horse-dealers. In any case, there'd be nothing to gain. Ah, Georgina, my dear. All ready?'

And, more sedately, on this occasion, with the still unhappy Edward at the wheel, the Rolls-Royce repeated its journey down into Sussex, to a village hall where a coroner, a jury, lawyers, witnesses and public awaited with emotions of varying intensity, or no emotion at all, the coming of the beautiful, unnaturally pale young woman who was to be the centre of their attention.

The widow of Alfred Henry Smith was the first to stand up before the coroner, the local doctor. He had known her for years, and poor Alf Smith; but the formalities had to be observed.

'Mrs Smith, you have identified your husband?'

She nodded through tears.

'I don't want to upset you, Mrs Smith, but there are one or two questions I must ask. Your husband worked as cowman at Penfold Farm?'

A mumbled, 'Yes, sir.'

'Please speak up a little. Now, when did you last see him – alive?'

'Last Tuesday marning, sir. As usual, he'd set the alarm clock and put it on the biscuit-tin – to make more sound, you see, sir, being a heavy sleeper – and when it went off he says, "It's larmentable cold," he says, "but I reckon it'll be a purty day later." Then he brought me my tea and then he says, "Cheerio," and that was the . . . the last . . .'

Tears welled up more strongly. The coroner looked enquiringly across at Sir Geoffrey Dillon, clearly hoping to spare the witness any further questioning, but Dillon was rising to his feet, with an air of regret.

'Mrs Smith,' he said gently, 'you say your husband was a heavy sleeper. Did he oversleep on this particular morning.'

'Well . . . not exactly oversleep, sir.'

'How do you mean, please?'

'Well, after the alarm had run down I had to call him once or twice.'

'So he did oversleep.'

'Only by a minute or two, sir. He wasn't never late to work, not in all the days we was married. Mr Penfold'll bear me out in that.'

The farmer nodded vigorously. The coroner addressed Sir Geoffrey. 'I really don't see what . . .'

'I was merely trying to establish whether perhaps Mr Smith

was conscious of being later than usual, and was endeavouring to, er, hurry, consequently not riding with quite his usual attention.'

'Mrs Smith,' the coroner asked, 'did your husband ride a modern, high-speed bicycle?'

'No, sir. It was an old iron one what had belonged to my father. "Quite an old friend," he used to say.'

Sir Geoffrey looked interested at this.

'Do you know when Mr Smith last had the brakes attended to on this old bicycle?' he asked.

'Well, I don't know as he ever . . . I mean, he used to tinker with it himself, now and then.'

'Did the brakes actually work at all?'

'He . . . he did used to say they wasn't all that good, but they was all right for round here.'

Sir Geoffrey was nodding his thanks and sitting down, to the coroner's relief. Mrs Smith was released with the Court's expression of sympathy and Police Constable Burridge took her place. He deposed that he had been called to an accident at the foot of the hill known at Carter's Rise, where he had found the Rolls-Royce, the mangled bicycle and the unconscious Alfred Smith. He had recognised the car as one he had seen some minutes earlier.

'Why was that?' the coroner wanted to know.

'It went through the village at high speed, sir. There was a woman leaning out of the window, waving a policeman's helmet.'

'Did you recognise this person?'

'Not at the time, sir, but I later discovered it was that lady over there – Lady Dorothy Hale. I reckoned they'd all been drinking quite a bit.'

'And it was undoubtedly this same car which shortly afterwards was involved in the accident which killed Mr Smith?'

'Yes, sir.'

'Sir Geoffrey?'

'Constable, we have heard from Mrs Smith that her husband was bicycling to work at Penfold's Farm. Now, to reach the farm he would have had to travel directly across the highway from the point at which he emerged.'

'Yes, sir.'

'Is there a great deal of traffic on that road?'

'Very little at all, 'specially at that time of the morning.'

'So Mr Smith would be unlikely to be expecting a car to come along?'

'No, sir.'

'Someone driving a car cannot, in fact, see the foot of Carter's Rise until they are over it.'

'That's correct, sir.'

'Exactly. So we can imagine Mr Smith, on his old and not altogether reliable bicycle, on which it would perhaps be difficult to brake, or turn, or increase speed suddenly in any emergency – we can picture him riding out on to the highway in the path of this oncoming car, whose driver would have had no warning of his presence on the road.'

'That is pure supposition, Sir Geoffrey,' the coroner intervened.

'But it is a supposition which it is very reasonable to make,' the lawyer answered blandly. He turned again to the witness. 'Now, you say you "reckoned" that the occupants of the car had been drinking. Would you not agree that what in fact you observed could have been simply a party of high-spirited young people enjoying themselves in the exhilaration of a country outing?'

A murmur of objection rose from the public seats and the coroner frowned as he reflected it officially. 'Come, come, Sir Geoffrey. I think the constable is as capable as the rest of us of judging whether or not people have been drinking.'

Sir Geoffrey's imperturbable answer was to sit down, leaving the point undisputed.

'Laughing and shouting?' the coroner asked Georgina, after she in turn had described their progress that fatal morning. Sir Geoffrey Dillon protested, but was ignored in his turn. 'You were in high spirits,' the coroner pressed.

'We'd been to a party,' Georgina admitted with a matter-offactness which did nothing to please the locals.

'At what speed do you say you were travelling, Miss Worsley?'

'I really couldn't say. But then, suddenly, this man on a bicycle came out of a side turning, right in front of the car. I put the brakes on, but . . .' She broke off and shrugged in a gesture of helplessness.

The coroner looked at Sir Geoffrey Dillon, who merely stared back as if the other were invisible. The foreman of the jury took his chance to speak up for his restless colleagues.

'Sir, we'd like to ask the young lady if she thinks it's right that an honest working man can't go about his business without getting knocked down and killed by a lot of titled people driving about the countryside because they've got nothing better to do.'

Before Sir Geoffrey could object the coroner had ruled the question out of order. Then Darrow Morton was called and found to have left the country; and Dolly Hale made what could only be termed an appearance, irritating the coroner and riling the locals by her flippant and patronising answers to the questions. Richard Bellamy gripped his wife's hand tightly as both realised what sort of an impression of herself and her set Dolly was conveying to the jury and the few members of the Press; an impression that could only tarnish Georgina, too.

Dillon shrewdly cut short his examination of this unsatisfactory witness and the coroner prepared to give his summary of what had been heard in his court. But he had to pause as a constable hurried in with a note for Sir Geoffrey Dillon. Sir Geoffrey rose and begged for a moment's indulgence. Granted it, he went to the back of the room where a beefy young man stood. They argued briefly, after which Sir Geoffrey, with clear reluctance, returned to his place and the young man came forward towards the witness stand.

'May I ask what is happening?' said the coroner. 'Who is this?'

P.C. Burridge, sitting close by, enlightened him: 'It's the

99

gentleman who fetched me to the scene of the accident, sir. The Marquis of Stockbridge.'

'Yes,' Robert Stockbridge acknowledged. 'I'd like to give evidence, please.'

The coroner shook his head. 'No, no, you can't, I'm afraid. We've finished the hearing.'

'But I was driving just behind. I saw the accident.'

'Even so . . . Oh, very well, Lord Stockbridge. You had better tell us what you know of this affair. Wait a moment, though. You'll have to take the oath first.'

Robert Stockbridge did, and then explained: 'I was driving close behind Miss Worsley's car. I reached the top of the hill and saw her travelling down at about thirty miles an hour. I know that was the speed, because I'd just glanced at my speedometer and I continued to travel at the same distance behind her. I saw a man on a bicycle ride straight out in front of the car from a side lane. There was nothing anyone could have done.'

A silence fell on the room. The coroner looked at the jury, who looked at one another. Richard looked at Virginia, who looked at him. Georgina looked with astonishment at Robert Stockbridge, standing soldierly to attention and staring in front of him. Sir Geoffrey Dillon's eyes never left the papers on the school desk at which he sat.

The first sound before the murmur of general reaction came was the sobbing of the dead man's widow. Whatever mattered to anyone else, only one thing concerned her; and that thing was beyond all practical concern, anyway.

She scarely heard the verdict of accidental death and the coroner's endorsement of the jury's rider to the effect that the irresponsible behaviour of Miss Georgina Worsley and her friends had been a contributory factor in the fatal occurrence. No alarm clocks on any biscuit tins would ever wake her Alf again.

'Oh, that is a relief!' Mrs Bridges declared, when Mr Hudson had read out the verdict from the evening newspaper.

'Fancy the paper getting it in so soon, though,' Daisy said.

'I imagine they had a journalist in court, and he telephoned an account of it to London,' Hudson replied, still reading to himself.

'What is it, Mr Hudson?' Mrs Bridges asked, seeing him frown suddenly.

' "Coroner Rebukes Bright Young People",' he quoted the sub-heading. They looked at one another.

At that moment Eddie came in, jerking open the top button of his uniform jacket and tossing his peaked hat on to the table. He barely acknowledged his wife, let alone the rest of them.

'What was it like in court, Edward?' Mrs Bridges asked. He answered rudely, 'How should I know? I was left outside, minding their precious car.'

'Edward!' Mr Hudson rebuked him, but Edward's thoughts had festered beyond the limits of discipline.

'No,' he said. 'I been thinking about what happened the other day. I've always been second-best in this household, and now this talk of giving me the sack, without a chance to defend myself . . .'

'Edward, I myself explained to you the position . . .'

'Yeah, but you're not his lordship, are you? You're just the butler, and I'm just the chauffeur. Well, I've had enough.'

'What about me?' Daisy asked.

He had thought about that. 'You can stay on here if you want. Go back into your old room. I'll go to Mum's, till I find another place for us both.'

'Oh, Eddie, I know he's hurt your feelings, but . . .'

'Yes, he has.'

'Oh, well . . . You must do what you think right, love.'

'I'm going to, Dais.'

But not many minutes passed before Edward was summoned to the morning-room.

'Might as well get it over with,' he remarked, doing up his buttons again as he went up the stairs from the servants' hall. But he was put off his stride by his lordship's expression as he

101

greeted him in the morning-room.

'Edward, Miss Georgina asked me to speak to you. I was going to in any event. I understand now that you did everything you could to prevent the car from being taken without you that night. From all I hear, you were placed in a very difficult position, and I'm only sorry that when I spoke to you about it I gave you no chance to explain. I hope you will accept my apology, here and now.'

He thrust out his hand with a smile. Edward could do no more than accept it, stammering thanks, and take his leave.

'His lordship apologised!' Daisy exclaimed when he told her. 'Then it's all right, isn't it?'

'Yeh, I suppose so. It's not like the old days, though, is it?'

'How d'you mean?'

'Lady Marjorie wouldn't never have apologised. She'd never have needed to in the first place.'

'Oh, come on and eat your tea. It's haddock.'

'I don't like haddock.'

In the background, Mrs Bridges and Mr Hudson exchanged glances. It was becoming less and less like the old days, it seemed.

CHAPTER SIX

'There they are, then,' said Mrs Bridges, sprinkling cress decoratively around the sandwiches of smoked salmon and thin brown bread. 'Daisy, just moisten that cover and lay it over them in case of flies. Then you can take them up, with the wine chilled just right, as soon as Miss Georgina gets in. I must say, she's taken a real passion for smoked salmon lately.'

Daisy smirked. 'Or Lord Stockbridge has.'

'What's that? What are you insinuating now, Daisy?'

'Nothing, 'cept that it's him has taken her out for the third time in a fortnight.'

'One swallow doesn't make a summer.'

'Mebbe not, but three might. If you ask me, they're walking out proper.'

'Well, it's high time that girl did settle down after one thing and another. Oh, this heat! My ankles is swollen up like bolsters. I think I shall just sit down for a few minutes. You keep a sharp ear for Miss Georgina, in case I just happen to drop off for a second or two.'

'All right, Mrs B.'

Georgina Worsley was not a young lady of many sensibilities. Pleasure and idleness made up her everyday routine, and she felt no urge to change her ways. No ambition nagged at her. Unlike her cousin James Bellamy, still away in America, she knew nothing of frustration and thwarted endeavours. She changed her male escorts almost as often as she changed frocks; or had done until the aftermath of the motoring tragedy.

Her generally impervious emotional skin had been pierced by Robert Stockbridge's gallant defence of her. At a time when all the people she had called her friends had left her to face the ordeal of the inquest alone, the man she had scorned to his face for his insipidity had voluntarily spoken up for her, in defiance of his parents' orders. The act had both touched and impressed Georgina. Robert, now, appeared to her not wet, but gentle. He no longer seemed beefy, but well-made. His attentions were no longer a bore, but a pleasure. For once, Georgina allowed herself to be monopolised by one man; and that man was only too delighted and eager to see her as often as possible.

On this day he had taken her down to his old school, Eton, for the Fourth of June celebrations. The year was 1929, a year of worry and unrest. While Etonians celebrated, more than a million other males queued for jobs or dole, or lounged aimlessly at street corners. The Prime Minister, Stanley Baldwin, puffed phlegmatically at his pipe, smiled his kindly smile, and did nothing, as a result of which the desperate electorate turned out in the greatest numbers ever known to vote his government out of office and give the Labour Party its first real chance to show what it could do, under the leadership of Ramsay Macdonald and a policy of nationalisation and heavy taxation of riches.

Richard Bellamy would no longer be a minister. It did not trouble him unduly. He had served his country faithfully for many years, and would go on serving it in the House of Lords. Although he remained healthy and upright, his looks belying his age by many years, he knew nowadays much more about the meaning of tiredness and strain than in bygone years.

He and Georgina were the only upstairs occupants of No. 165 Eaton Place at present. Virginia was away in Scotland. Mr Hudson's and Rose's holidays had been fixed to coincide with her absence, leaving only Mrs Bridges, Edward and Daisy, and, like a kitchen fixture or implement, Ruby.

Mrs Bridges did doze off for a few minutes. She woke with a start as the morning-room bell rang.

'There they are, Daisy. Take them their wine and sandwiches, and ask if there's anything else they'd like.'

Daisy obeyed. She found Georgina looking at her most radiant, the almost transparent skin glowing from the sun and fresh air. Lord Stockbridge was pink and boyishly beaming. Daisy served the snack, was told there was nothing else required, and departed.

'Tuck in,' Georgina told Robert, 'or you might not get any. I'm famished.'

They ate and drank enthusiastically.

'And thank you for a marvellous day,' she said sincerely. 'I shall always bless old Henry the Sixth for founding Eton on the fourth of June.'

'Dear old Henry,' Robert grinned. 'He'd get a shock now if he could see the result of his labours. All those little scruffs in top hats.'

'I wish I'd been a boy and gone to Eton. Rowing on the Thames on a lovely summer's day. Not like being at school at all.'

'I didn't do much rowing, actually. I was a "dry bob". I played cricket.'

'Were you good at it?'

'Not too bad. I actually got into the Eleven.'

'Do you still play?'

He didn't answer. She looked up, to find him regarding her with an unaccustomed intensity. She smiled affectionately. 'I asked if you still play?'

'Eh? Oh, yes. Yes, I do. For the village team. They've made me captain, though Frank Bowman, our postman, does all the work really. He runs the team, does the fixtures, mows the pitch . . . He's also our demon bowler, and his brother Joe, the blacksmith, keeps wicket. When Joe hits a six it's like a great firework going up. My father still plays sometimes. He creaks a bit fielding, but the Duke's donkey drops are always treated with becoming respect.'

'What's a donkey drop?'

'When you bowl a ball very high, and it comes down almost on the stumps. Quite tricky when the sun's in the right place . . . Georgina . . . Darling Georgina . . . I do love you, you know.'

This switch from boyish gabble to seriousness surprised her by its suddenness. She could make no reply before he went on.

'I love you. I absolutely adore you. I started to fall in love with you ages ago and now I think about you all the time.'

'Could . . . could I have some more wine, please?' she

105

managed to ask, in something of a daze. He poured for her. 'Why didn't you tell me before?'

'I think it was because I was so terrified you'd say no. You . . . aren't going to, are you?'

The frank immediacy of her reply staggered him.

'No.'

'You mean, "yes"? You mean . . . you actually love me, too!'

'Yes.'

'It's . . . it's marvellous. Incredible! If you'd turned me down I don't know what I'd have done. I couldn't live without you, Georgina.'

'Please don't say that, Robert.'

'But it's true. I . . .'

'But please don't say it. Someone said it to me once before. Someone very nice – but I didn't love him, and he shot himself. I suppose I'm just superstitious, really. He'd been in the war and wasn't quite . . . James has never got over the war, you know. He has rages and terrible miseries still. I'm glad you weren't touched by the war, Robert.'

'Only by the lousy food we had at school.'

'It was just after that I decided I didn't want to get mixed up with anyone again. Just going to endless parties, and acting in that film, and behaving like a lunatic. I suppose I was trying to keep real life at bay. It was quite fun, though, being one of the Bright Young Things.'

'Didn't you ever suspect that I would ask you to marry me?'

She looked at him wryly. 'You haven't, actually.'

He flung himself down into the Victorian suitor's pose, one knee bent, hand on heart.

'Miss Worsley, will you do me the great honour of consenting to be my wife?'

'I shall have to think about it, Lord Stockbridge,' she replied primly, but smiled her reassurance when she saw the little shadow of anxiety which passed over his features. It was quickly gone. He sat beside her again.

'Do you think your guardian will approve?' he asked.

'Yes. What about your parents?'

He hesitated, ever so slightly, before answering, 'They'll adore you. Of course they will.'

She didn't notice the hesitation. Neither did it occur to her that the expression of reassurance might have been more for Robert's own benefit than for hers.

He drew her to him and, for the first time in many years, she joined in a kiss with sincerity and genuine love.

'My people are away in Austria at the moment,' he said at length. 'They'll be back next week. It's nearly Ascot and we've got a house party at Shalford. I hope you'll come and stay as soon as possible and meet my parents.'

'I'd love to, Robert.'

'The old place is far too big nowadays, but I hope we'll always hang on to it. Just think . . . in about a hundred years' time you and I will be having tea by the lake, surrounded by hundreds of grandchildren. The old Duke and the old Duchess.'

'What a thought!'

'I must show you a painting I did of Shalford. Give you some impression.'

'I didn't know you painted. Do you do it a lot?'

'Hardly at all, actually. Father isn't too keen on it. He seems to think it's rather . . . well, not quite the thing for a gentleman. One of our neighbours has four sons and one of them paints professionally. Father always refers to them as "three good boys and an artist".'

'Well, when we're married we'll have a studio for you in our London house.'

He gave his boyish smile again. 'That's what I've always wanted. And to go and paint in Paris and Florence and Venice.'

'You shall, darling. Precious few people have any talent at all. You must use yours.'

'I suppose so. I'm rather an idle sort of person, really. It's terribly easy just to mooch around and do nothing in particular, rather like my father and grandfather did when they were young – except they had wars and things to keep them occupied.'

'Thank goodness you're not going to have a war to keep you occupied.'

He nodded seriously, then smiled again. 'I'll have to rely on you to kick me around. Keep me busy. Anyway, I suddenly feel life's worth living, now I've got you. I mean, there's some point in it which there never was before. We have a party, we'll have it because we want to see our friends, not because we're bored and there's nothing else to do. Let's care immensely for the things we mind about and chuck the rest out of the window.'

'Yes, please!'

Richard responded to the news exactly as Georgina had confidently predicted. Robert delivered it in the formal manner, requesting permission to marry Georgina and receiving a warm handshake and a slap on the shoulder in response. But Robert's slight hesitation in assuring Georgina that his own parents would be equally delighted had not been without significance. He telegraphed them in Vienna but received no reply. They returned to London two days later and Robert found himself duly summoned to his mother's presence.

The Duchess of Buckminster was in her early fifties but had had at least a decade of her life restored by expensive grooming and dressing. She was trim of figure, elegant of carriage and gesture, memorable of features, exact down to the last hair and touch of make-up – and as conscious of her authority as any woman who ever combined beauty, position and wealth.

Robert, standing before her expensively furnished desk in her own sitting-room, felt like a schoolboy being called to account by a smiling yet severe headmistress.

'It did come as rather a shock to us, darling . . . just getting your telegram out of the blue.'

'Yes, I . . . I see that. But I thought I'd better let you know . . . well, as soon as I knew.'

'I quite see that. What surprised us, though, was that you hadn't introduced Miss Worsley to us before.'

'Well, you haven't met a lot of my friends. I mean, why should you?'

The headmistress's tolerant smile diminished somewhat.

'This is rather more than a friend, I gather.'

Robert clenched and unclenched his hands. 'I'm sorry, Mother. I didn't really think of it before. I mean, I didn't really know I was going to marry her.'

'You mean you had no idea?'

'Of course I had. But I didn't know what she would say. I could hardly tell you before I'd asked her, could I?'

'*Tell* us? I just wish you hadn't taken us quite so much by surprise, Robert.' She saw his gesture of exasperation. 'You know exactly what I mean.'

'I think so,' he said, the irritation sounding. 'Do I take it from all this that you and Father are against my getting married?'

'Of course not, darling. Only, it is a tremendously important step in your life, and after all the unfortunate publicity over that inquest last year . . .'

'So that's it!'

'. . . after all that, you can hardly expect us to be greatly enthusiastic that you've chosen Miss Worsley. Your father was extremely cross when you deliberately went against his express wishes, you know.'

'Mother, I had to give evidence at that inquest. Georgina might have gone to prison if I hadn't.'

'I think that most unlikely.'

'Anyway, don't let's go all over that again. It's over and done with. When you get to know Georgina you'll change your mind, I'm sure.'

'We don't know her yet, of course – but we do know of her.'

'What exactly do you mean by that, Mother?'

'I mean she is . . . quite a well-known young lady. She seems to get her face in the papers quite a lot.'

'Only because she enjoys doing original things, and happens to be very beautiful. I don't think you can blame her for that.'

The immaculate Duchess sighed, and smiled wistfully. 'You must believe me, my darling, that your father and I only want what is best for you. Your future happiness is terribly important to all of us. You will admit it has all been . . . rather sudden.'

'I don't admit anything of the sort.'

'Oh, do be reasonable, Robert!'

'I'm being perfectly reasonable.'

'Darling, we only think you should give it time. Think about it, so that you're quite, quite sure.'

Robert, who had been shuffling to and fro across the carpet in growing irritation, exploded in a manner worthy of his father.

'Don't you think I've thought about it . . . endlessly . . . for hours and hours? And you talk about giving it time! Heavens above, I love the girl and she loves me. We want to get married. Isn't that enough?'

His mother touched her perfectly set hair. There was a little tinkle of bracelets as her hand moved.

'No, darling. I don't think it is.'

Robert wanted to telephone Georgina as soon as this painful interview was over, but he remembered just in time that she was acting as hostess to her uncle at an important function and decided not to disturb her. He called on her next day. She received him in her room, where she and Daisy were sorting through some clothes. She dismissed her maid and turned anxiously to Robert's clouded face.

'You've seen your parents,' she said, more in the manner of a statement than a question.

'Not Father. He went straight down to Shalford. I knew that was a bad sign, for a start. I've had a blinding row with Mother. Oh, damn it, they're being utterly prejudiced and idiotic.'

'You mean, they don't approve,' said Georgina, who had been not unprepared for the news.

'For the most ridiculous reasons. I haven't introduced you. You're "notorious". Good God . . . !'

'Well, I suppose if you look at it from their point of view, you are quite a catch, darling. I mean, they probably think I've been chasing you and once I've got my tiny claws into you I won't let go until you marry me.'

'Damn her! Damn them both, that's all I can say!'

'It's no good saying that,' she said. 'I wish I could just meet them.'

'I know. They're so damned prejudiced. But they don't own me, you know. I'm not going to "think again", Georgina. I shan't let you down.'

He seized her hands and clutched them hard. She asked, with real curiosity. 'Would this be the first time you'd . . . defied them?'

Robert looked surprised. 'I suppose it will,' he said slowly. 'The first important time.'

There was a knock at the door. They stood apart and Daisy entered, carrying a small silver salver. Robert recognised the brand of pink envelope it bore, and the large, sloping handwriting addressing it to Georgina.

When she had read it she handed it to him.

'There you are,' she said happily. 'Your mother's asked me to tea tomorrow.'

Robert read the note. The expression on his face didn't match Georgina's, though.

The Duchess greeted Georgina with the utmost graciousness, thanking her profusely for taking the trouble to call and see her, sending the liveried footmen at once for tea and pouring it herself when the butler had brought it. Georgina could imagine that the tray, the silver, the porcelain were all priceless. She was being given the first-class grade of reception, which seemed to augur very well. The nervousness she had brought with her began to recede.

'I'm sorry we haven't had the chance to meet before,' the Duchess smiled, proffering another of the delicious sandwiches. 'I had lunch with Lady Berkhamstead yesterday. She said you were a nurse in the war.'

'Yes, I was. I tried to do something, like everyone else.'

'She said you were a very good one. And how is Major Bellamy? My brother was with him in the Life Guards, you know. He was killed, sadly.'

'Oh, James is in America. From his letters, he's enjoying himself and doing quite well. Financial dealings, you know. He's hoping to come back to see us this autumn.'

'Really? Have you been to America, Miss Worsley?'

'Yes, once. I enjoyed it.'

'I expect you went to Hollywood, to make films.'

It did not escape Georgina's notice that the Duchess had evidently been doing some thorough research into her background.

'No,' she answered. 'I went to stay with James's sister Elizabeth. I'm afraid my film experience has been rather exaggerated. I've only been in one, and that was just for fun.'

'You young people do have a great deal of fun nowadays. So much freedom compared to my time as a girl. One hears of all sorts of people doing all sorts of things. I suppose it's good really, but they don't seem to stick at any one thing much, do they? I'm afraid that's rather typical of Robert, too . . . He doesn't seem able to stick at anything.'

'He tells me he's very keen to paint.'

'Oh, yes. He really has a talent. I remember how proud I was when he won a prize at school . . . but he hasn't kept up with it really.'

Georgina ventured to ask, 'Has he really been given the chance?'

The Duchess's smile didn't wane. 'Oh Lord, yes. But, as I say, he doesn't stick at things. He was up at Oxford but left after a year or so. Never took his degree – not that he needed one particularly. Robert's a charming, easygoing person and my husband and I love him dearly. But people with that sort of nature can make so many mistakes in life . . .'

She let the sentence die away and poured them both more tea. Then she smiled winningly at Georgina again.

'You're a very pretty girl, my dear. Much prettier than your photographs. I'm sure lots of men must have fallen in love with you.'

'Well, plenty have said they were. Some of them asked me to marry them, but I've never accepted anyone . . . before. I didn't love them, and I do love Robert. I think he's the sort of person who will never let me down.'

'I'm sure he wouldn't let anyone down . . . not deliberately, anyway.'

Georgina shook her head. 'Not in any way. I haven't met anyone quite like him before.'

'It's very nice of you to say so.'

There was a pause. Georgina sensed that the next word must be from the Duchess, and that the critical moment of the interview had been reached. She was not wrong.

'We've decided,' the Duchess said, matter-of-factly, 'that the best thing for Robert would be to go abroad for a few months.'

Georgina's mouth almost dropped open. This was a decision whose possibility had not remotely occurred to her. It was quite a shock. The Duchess was continuing, 'My husband has arranged it all. He'll be going all over the world. During that time we don't want you to see each other. You seem a sensible girl, and I hope you'll help us persuade Robert to do as we wish. If you love each other as you say you do, it will make no difference in the long run.'

'I think that's unfair,' Georgina said boldly. Her effrontery didn't seem to put the Duchess out at all, though. She continued, as if she were wearing her coronet as she spoke: 'Robert is our only son. He is very dear to us indeed. He's also heir to a great inheritance. I don't mean just titles. I mean, land, responsibility to people, thousands of people. We don't think he's quite ready to take on that responsibility . . . not that he will have to, we hope, for some time. And we don't think he's quite ready to get married.'

She got up, timing it perfectly. Georgina rose automatically.

'I don't expect you to agree with me,' the Duchess said, 'or even to understand why I seem to be behaving like a fussy old hen. But at least I thought I owed you an explanation.'

She pressed the bell beside the fireplace.

'Thank you,' was all Georgina could find to say.

'Not at all. I've so much enjoyed meeting you.'

113

The footman was holding open the door. Georgina obediently took her leave.

'I'll write every day, wherever you are,' Georgina assured Robert when they met for the last time. 'And you must promise to have a good time. It'll be a great experience for you. You can find all sorts of exciting places to take me when we're married.'

Her initial disappointment had given way to resignation and then to a sort of contentment. She had consulted her Uncle Richard, who had pointed out that the bargain implied by the Duchess of Buckminster was a pretty fair and satisfactory one, and, looked at objectively, a sensible one, too. If Georgina and Robert's love survived the few months of separation and they had faithfully obeyed the condition imposed on them, then they could not reasonably be refused their reward. If it didn't survive so simple a test, then they could both feel they had had a lucky escape from a great mistake. He advised Georgina to ask herself how she would have spent the next few months anyway, had no such prospect existed. As things stood, she could live as usual, but with the exception of a happy end to the aimless drifting which no longer held any attraction for her.

She kissed him and thanked him, and went off positively glowing with satisfaction.

Robert found it harder to accept the situation philosophically.

'I still think I'm being damned weak, giving in to them like this,' he grumbled. 'If I want to marry you, why shouldn't I?'

'Darling, you will. I'll be here for you.'

'Yes, but the waste of all those months . . .'

She laid a finger to his lips.

'We've been through it all so often. I tell you what. Let's plan a date to get married. Then it'll feel so positive and I can cross off every day in my diary.'

She got her little diary out of her bag and consulted it.

'June next year,' Robert said at a hazard.

Georgina examined the date chart. 'June the twelfth,' she chose. 'A Thursday.'

Robert grinned, happy now. 'Thursday, June the twelfth, 1930. That's going to be a day when history is made.'

'Goodbye, my love,' Georgina said when they had kissed, long and lingeringly.

He left her. She sat down with the open diary still in her hand, staring at the rows of figures which tabulated the future.

It was, of course, her own and Robert's future which concerned her solely at that moment. She did not plague her fancy with anyone else's — which perhaps was just as well.

CHAPTER SEVEN

James returned from New York in October. He was little changed, apart from some becoming graying of his hair and a tendency to use an occasional Americanism in his speech, which had always been so precisely English.

Unfortunately, it was not long in becoming apparent that his manner had not changed, either. He answered Mr Hudson's enquiry as to whether he had had a pleasant voyage by saying that there had been too many people jostling about on the ship for his comfort. He grimaced when informed that Richard and Virginia had been unable to stay in to receive him, having had to attend an official reception at the unlikely venue of Madame Tussaud's waxworks, and that Georgina was out visiting Robert Stockbridge's aunt, Lady Isobel Dawson.

He was offered tea, but rather brusquely ordered a bath instead. An atmosphere of anti-climax seemed to attend his homecoming.

There was even a hint of sarcasm, although it was overlaid with raillery, in his questioning of Georgina that evening about Robert Stockbridge. She had greeted him with a fond kiss and embrace and told him how good it was to have him back.

'You don't need me, by all accounts,' he replied. 'Anyway, congratulations, if they're still in order. Here. This is for you.'

'This' was a fur which must have matched in expense the emerald necklace he had just presented to Virginia and the more masculine gift he had brought his father.

'Oh, James, it's wonderful! Thank you so much.'

'I hope your intended takes it in the right spirit.' He turned to Richard. 'Is this fellow as splendid as she makes out in her letters?'

'Well, I'm very fond of him myself. We all are.'

'Hm. Bit Victorian, isn't it? Sending a fellow half way round the world to get rid of him.'

'Tell that to the Duke,' Georgina said with feeling. 'Persuade him to let him come back to me.'

They went in to dinner. As she had always done on James's first day back from school or any other prolonged absence, Mrs Bridges had cooked Spotted Dick for pudding to follow the pheasant. He appreciated the wine more.

'Chateau Lafite. Excellent. I haven't tasted anything like it in two years. Prohibition must be the maddest law ever passed.'

Georgina said, 'When I was there, rich people broke it all the time.'

'Oh, everyone breaks it now. They fight over it. I was nearly killed in a riot in Phoenix.'

'You never told us that!'

'Well, naturally. Elizabeth and Dana keep their liquor in a dug-out in the garden. I must say, she's in her element. One of the most talked-about hostesses in New York. The house is jam-packed with politicians, writers, the best society. But the brokers are the real lions of the moment. The talk's all money.'

'How boring,' Virginia said.

'No, you don't understand. It's extraordinary. The excitement, uncertainty – like a game. Dana used to take me to Wall Street with him. There's an incredible sort of fellow-feeling there, just like the war.'

'Dana advised you on money matters, did he?' Richard asked.

'Yes. He's become a director of Goldman Sachs, the big trading corporation. Right in the thick of it. I owe all my new-found wealth to his expertise.'

'Golly, James!' Georgina exclaimed. 'Are you really rich?' All three had been rather wondering this, in the light of the presents he had brought them, but delicacy had prevented their raising the subject.

'I'm not a millionaire,' he replied. 'But I'll pay for any scale of wedding you ask for. No, I insist. And Father . . . I've been thinking about this house. I might sell it for something larger. More convenient for you two and the children.'

Virginia touched his hand. 'It's a kind thought, James, but

the children are almost grown up. I don't think we need any-where larger, do we darling?'

'Something smaller, if anything,' Richard agreed.

'All right, then. We'll have a villa in the South of France. Or a yacht.'

'You don't really mean it?' Georgina asked, agog.

'Of course I do. You don't seem to understand. It's open to everyone out there to make a small fortune. Everyone here, too, if they want it. Dana's chauffeur overheard a conversation in the back of the car, put all his life savings into Bethlehem Steel, and was able to retire overnight.'

Virginia was frowning. 'It somehow doesn't seem right to me,' she said.

'Why not? Why should it be regarded as immoral to make money? We work all our lives looking for prosperity, and when it comes it's treated as something vulgar. O.K., then. I stand rebuked, but unrepentant.'

'There's no question of rebuke,' Richard hastened to say, noting the ominous pink flush which had suffused his son's cheeks. 'Just a note of caution. One hears rumours . . .'

James laughed. 'Wall Street thrives on rumour. Anyway, money doesn't have to corrupt. So, will anyone join me in a toast to my investments . . . coupled with Georgina's wedding? May they both bring happiness to us all.'

'I'll join you,' Georgina said enthusiastically; and they all raised their glasses and drank.

Hudson and Daisy had been in attendance during the meal. Afterwards, for once, Daisy couldn't prevent herself alluding to a topic overhead.

'How do you make money on the Stock Exchange, Mr Hudson?'

He frowned his disapproval of her breaching the taboo, but decided that the question, being general and not personal, might be answered.

'You buy shares in companies dealing in certain commodities, Daisy. When the shares rise in value, you sell them and keep the profits. That's the simple principle.'

'Sounds easy. Can anyone do it?'

'Yes. But, you see, the shares can lose their value. Then when you sell them you're out of pocket. It's a matter of great expertise, judging which and when to buy and sell.'

Rose had been listening in. She said, 'But you have people to advise you, don't you? People who know about it.'

'Yes, Rose. You also have people advising you on horse racing, and look where they can land you. Speculation is just another word for gambling.'

'I wouldn't call the Major the gambling type.'

'That's different,' Mrs Bridges contributed her part to the discussion. 'The Major's a gentleman.'

'Quite right, Mrs Bridges,' Hudson said. 'The Stock Exchange is not for the likes of us.'

But a sudden madness had struck Rose. It grew on her overnight, resulting in many wakeful hours and, at length, a decision. Next morning she made a point of looking for something in the morning-room at a time when she knew James to be there.

'Hello, Rose,' he said. 'Where is everybody?'

'His lordship went out early, sir, and her ladyship just after breakfast.'

'Hm. And how have things been with you, Rose?'

'Much the same as usual, sir, thanks.'

'That's fine.'

'You're looking very well, sir.'

'I'm O.K.'

'Er . . . sir . . . could I talk to you for a minute, if you're not too busy?'

'Sure. Go ahead.'

'Well, I don't know if you remember, sir, but I was left some money by Sergeant Wilmot. It's in deposit in the bank, but I was wondering if I ought to invest some of it. You know, on the Stock Exchange.'

'That sounds like a good idea, Rose. Make more for you than lying in a bank.'

'I don't mean a lot of it, sir. Only a small amount.'

'The more you put in, the more you make. It's as simple as that.'

Rose hesitated. 'Hudson was talking about the Stock Exchange as if it was like gambling on horses.'

'Nothing of the sort. There's a world of difference between gambling and speculating. Your investments will help to build new factories, make new jobs for thousands of people. The bigger your company gets, the more profits it makes for you.'

She brightened. 'I hadn't thought of it like that. The trouble is knowing how much I should invest, and what to do?'

'I can see to it for you if you want me to, Rose. As to the amount, it's up to you.'

'I've got twelve hundred and seventy-five pounds altogether, but . . .'

'That's very good. But you must decide. It's your money.'

'I . . . I'd sooner leave it to you, sir.'

'All right, then. We'll put it all through an investment trust. That's like a bank, really, except that there are expert people to decide what to buy on your behalf and then keep selling and buying to your advantage.'

'That'd be fine, sir. I'm ever so grateful.'

'Not a bit. Well, there's no time like the present. What's this bank of yours?'

She told him, and by that afternoon the formalities had been completed. This little flurry of activity over, James found himself at a loose end. Looking round his own room, he suddenly decided that it depressed him with its sameness from so many years. He determined to clear it out and have it redecorated.

'I'll help,' Georgina said, equally glad of the prospect or activity.

'Thanks. It'll keep you out of mischief. I'm sure young Stockbridge would be glad of that. When's he coming back anyway?'

'One hundred and sixty-five days.'

'Right. For one hundred and sixty-five days you're in my charge. We'll start tomorrow. Ride before breakfast. Downstairs in the hall sharp. O.K.?'

'O.K.'

After the ride and breakfast they started work on his room, beginning to clear the wardrobe and drawers. They had not been long at it when Edward came in with a letter on a salver. Seeing foreign stamps, Georgina hoped it was for her from Robert, but Edward proffered it to James.

'You still collect stamps, Edward?' James asked, tearing open the envelope carefully.

'Yes, sir.'

'There's a couple of George Washingtons for you, then.'

He handed over the envelope. Edward thanked him and went. James unfolded the notepaper unhurriedly and glanced at it. Georgina had turned her back to him, so did not see the sudden and dramatic change in his expression.

'I have to go out,' she heard him say, and the strain in his voice made her turn to him curiously. He was distinctly pale.

'What's the matter?'

'It's . . . nothing. But I must go out. I'm sorry.'

And he hurried from the room, leaving her to look helplessly at the disarray and then shrug her shoulders and go on adding to it.

Below stairs, the servants gathered round Mr Hudson who held an early edition of one of the evening newspapers. His ejaculation, 'Terrible news!' had drawn them away from their various tasks.

'What's happened?' Mrs Bridges asked, fearing a royal death or a railway disaster. His reply puzzled her.

'The slide has begun in earnest, I'm afraid.'

'Slide? What slide?'

'The economic slide in America. On Wall Street. The bottom has fallen out of the stock market.'

Rose's head jerked up sharply at this news. No one noticed. She had said nothing to them of her venture. She listened with growing concern to Mr Hudson's précis of the rest of the report.

'There have been signs of it for several days now. Rumours

circulating that shares have lost their value. Investors panicking and trying to sell, causing the shares to drop further in value. They're finally not worth the paper they're written on. Thousands have been ruined.'

'You see what I was telling you the other day,' he addressed Daisy. 'Exactly like placing money on horses.'

Rose risked saying, 'Anyway, it's lucky it's America and not here, isn't it?'

The butler shook his head gravely. 'Not at all, Rose. These affairs of high finance are international. Mark my words, the London Stock Exchange will react very badly to this.'

'You don't mean . . .' said Daisy, who had been thinking over his earlier words; '. . . you don't mean the Major's lost his money?'

Forgetting that only he and she had overheard the conversation in the dining-room actually alluding to the Major's newly won wealth, and that he had ordered her to say nothing to the other servants about it, Hudson answered, 'Short of a miracle I fear that may be so.'

Rose tried desperately to see James. She encountered him in the hall, just coming back into the house.

'Major James, sir . . .'

But he shook his head, hurrying towards the morning-room. 'Not just now, Rose.'

He went in, closing the door on her.

Richard, Virginia and Georgina were there with their copies of all the evening newspapers. James went straight to the drinks tray and poured himself a whisky. He drank it down and poured another.

'Put us out of our misery, James,' Georgina said.

'How badly has it hit you?' Virginia asked.

He banged the glass down hard. 'If Dana had only cabled instead of written I might have had time to do something. As it is, yes, I've been hit pretty hard.'

'Wiped out?'

'I don't know . . . Yes, I think so.'

Richard asked, 'Couldn't your London broker have warned you?'

'It happened too fast. First hint of real trouble was last Thursday, but the bankers stepped in and checked it. Yesterday, when the news was bad again, everyone thought they'd do the same, only they didn't. Goldman Sachs was buying its own stock, swindling itself to get confidence back. It was too late. Out of touch over here, that's the trouble. Lack of proper information. Snowball. Panic.'

He drained his glass and filled it again.

'We can sell my necklace,' Virginia volunteered.

'Yes,' Georgina added. 'And my fur.'

James shook his head numbly. 'No! Drops in the ocean, anyway. I borrowed a fair bit.'

'What about Elizabeth and Dana?'

'I shouldn't worry about them, Father. They'll have salvaged something.' He remembered something. 'There are other people to worry about than them.'

He sent for Rose to his own room. It was a summons she had been hoping for, yet fearing. She sensed the worst from his serious face and the invitation to her to sit on his green, buttoned leather settee.

'I'm not sure how much you know, Rose,' he began. There was no need to say about what.

'Hudson's explained some of it, sir, but I don't quite understand . . .'

'No. You see, certain things have happened on the American stock market which were unfortunately . . . outside our control. I'm afraid that my own investments . . . and the money you put in, too . . . well, they've both been lost.'

'You mean . . . all of it, sir? There's nothing left?'

'Nothing worth talking about. I'm sorry, Rose. I don't know what to say to you. I know how you must be feeling.'

She was feeling nothing. Strangely nothing.

'It wasn't your fault, I'm sure,' she said remotely. 'Never did mean much to me, anyway – money.'

He himself was aware of some relief.

'It's good of you to take it like that, Rose. It helps me feel better. And you must understand that we'll always look after you. You'll never want for anything. I give you my word on that.'

She got to her feet.

'Yes, I know that,' she said. 'Thank you, sir.'

Like an automaton, she left the room and went down to the servants' hall. There was no point in holding back from the others now. Her appearance showed them all that she had suffered some blow, and she was only grateful that Mr Hudson and Mrs Bridges shooed the junior servants away before persuading her to unburden herself.

'I . . . I don't know what to say, Rose,' Hudson stammered, trying not to sound harsh but unable to keep the note of censure out of his tone. 'Didn't I warn you? Did you not listen to what I said?'

'You said the stock market was for gentlemen, Mr Hudson. Well, the Major's a gentleman. He's supposed to know about money.'

'You didn't give him it all?' demanded Mrs Bridges, horrified at the sudden thought.

'Yes. I only wanted to do a little, but he said the more I put in, the more I'd make, and there wasn't any risk.'

'How could he do it?' Mrs Bridges demanded of Hudson. 'Risking a servant's money like that!'

'The Major's always had a rash streak in his nature, but I agree, this takes the biscuit.'

Rose was saying, 'What would Gregory have said, that's what I want to know? It was his money. I was, like, keeping it for him.'

'Now, now, dear . . .'

'Yes, Rose, calm yourself. It's not the end of your life. You still have us to look after you . . .'

She turned on him angrily.

'I don't want you to look after me. I want to look after myself, and I can't now. I'm stuck here for the rest of my rotten days, and Gregory'll never forgive me.'

She ran from the servants' hall. If Mr Hudson had been in her path to the door she would probably have pushed him out of the way.

The news inevitably reached Richard and Virginia. James had said nothing and Hudson, in consultation with Mrs Bridges, decided that no word should be allowed to leak from below stairs. Rose, too, had decided to say nothing, but some chance remark of Virginia's undermined her resolution and she broke down. She was gently persuaded to tell all.

When Virginia told Richard he reacted with shocked astonishment.

'James invested her money! What the devil did he think he was doing?'

'We must do something to make it up to her,' Virginia said.

'I'll stump up, but it can't be much.'

'I want to see him at once,' Richard said. She had never seen him so tense with anger as he rang the bell.

'Not now, Richard,' she requested. 'It's nearly lunch.'

'Damn lunch!'

Hudson was sent to fetch James to the morning-room. His father commenced savaging him as soon as the door was shut.

'I know you've lost a lot of money, but I never thought you'd stoop to borrowing from servants.'

'I did not borrow money. She came and asked me to invest it for her. Of her own free will. What was I supposed to do? Turn her away?'

'Of course you should have. Have you no sense? It's an absolutely unshakable rule that one never meddles with a servant's money.'

'I did not meddle with it. I invested it soundly. Anyway, it's not some private club for gentlemen only to become rich.'

'If she had "become rich", what then? How would a girl like Rose know what to do with wealth? You'd have given her ideas, dreams, responsibilities she couldn't have lived with.'

'What arrogance! She's not some half-wit family retainer. She's an intelligent woman. She knew the risk.'

'How? Did you tell her? Or did you say it was all easy? Did

she trust you as she's always trusted us? Either way, you've ruined her life and now what's to become of her? You can't afford to pay her back.'

James gestured helplessly and Virginia felt deep pity for him. He had acted foolishly, she could agree, but only in an attempt to help someone else. That he had failed had been a cruelly unlucky coincidence of timing. And to suggest that he had 'borrowed' the money, or that he had deluded an innocent with grandiose promises, struck her as downright unfair.

He mumbled, 'I'll do what I can for her. Not just at the moment, but as soon as I can.'

But Richard was unrelenting. 'You're wiped out, boy. What can you do? I just thank God your mother was spared this.'

'Mother?'

'She wouldn't have believed it of you. It would have broken her heart.'

'Mother lived in a different age, Father. We've moved on. There's been a war . . .'

'Oh, don't use the war as an excuse again. Anyway, we fought the war to keep your mother's world, to preserve certain standards of decent behaviour.'

Virginia saw James's control snap as he told his father, 'Now you're talking like an old fool!'

'What? How dare you . . .!'

'If you believe . . . Oh, it's hopeless even trying.'

'Hopeless. Yes, hopeless. That's the word for it exactly.'

'What do you mean?'

'I mean you, boy. Everything you do. Everything you turn to. Why – can you tell me – why, with all your advantages, it always ends the same? So much you could have done with your life, in whatever field you'd chosen. That by-election . . . You had a flair for politics, but no, you didn't stick with it . . .'

'Politics! You discouraged me, Father, right from the start. Now don't deny it. So what else was there? Back to commerce? Or stockbroking? Yes, that was possible – so long, I suppose, as I didn't throw any tips to poor servants and kept them strictly for us.'

'James . . .' Virginia said urgently, but neither man heard her. They were standing face to face, like fighters, swinging verbal blows at one another. Virginia was becoming frightened.

'Go on, what else?' James was demanding. 'The Colonial Service? Endless parties in damnable climates. Yes, that would have kept me out of trouble. Or after Hazel I could have found a nice, rich widow and become a gentleman of means and leisure. Would that have pleased you?'

'Yes, you could have married again. It would have given you responsibility, happiness . . .'

'Made me less selfish, you mean?'

'Frankly, yes. Children . . .'

'Are children so important to a man's happiness? Judging by this conversation, I'd have thought not. Anyway, if you remember, Hazel miscarried.'

Richard relented a little at this.

'Yes, yes, I know,' he said unaggressively. 'That was sad. But there's still time, James. It's up to you. I can't tell you what to do. All I can offer is my support and . . . and love. The love of the whole family. We're all behind you.'

'Love? Or pity?'

'Damn it, not pity!'

'I'm an embarrassment, aren't I? An awkward reminder of failure. Your failure, perhaps. Your disappointment.'

'Don't be absurd.'

'It's there in everything you say. Your friends confirm it every day, I expect. "How's James? Still drifting? Time he settled down and gave you a grandson or two to carry on the Bellamy line." '

'That's *self*-pity. Cynical, defeatist talk, and I can't bear to listen to it.'

'You started it . . .'

'*You* insisted on it. I merely wanted to arouse some pride in you. Some guts. To help you.'

'Help? You accuse me of some kind of immoral act with Rose. You attack my character on all fronts. Help! You haven't begun to understand what I am. I don't need you to tell me.'

Virginia's sympathy sprang to Richard now, as she saw how this had hurt. He almost pleaded, 'James, my dear boy . . .'

James shook his head. 'No. No conciliations now. That's how we always end up – patching the wounds. Let's leave them open this time.'

He strode to the door, wrenched it open, and went out, slamming it behind him. Richard stared after him, half-stunned. Virginia moved to his side.

The door opened again and Georgina came in, looking alarmed.

'What's the matter with James? What's been going on?'

They didn't answer. She ran out again, calling after James. She ran up the stairs and as she neared his door a blast of Wagner came from behind it. Although she knocked and called repeatedly and tried the handle, he would not let her in. The music crashed on, in reflection of his mood.

'Daisy – where's Rose?' Mr Hudson asked after the delayed luncheon had been served and the servants were about to sit down to their own.

'Dunno, Mr Hudson,' she replied. 'I saw her with her hat and coat on. Didn't say where she was going.'

'Gone out!'

'For a little walk, I expect,' Mrs Bridges said, dishing up. 'Settle herself down a bit.'

'She's no right to go for a walk without permission.'

'Oh, Mr Hudson, I think we have to be a bit more understanding, in view of what's happened.'

'I was quite prepared to be understanding, Mrs Bridges. But you heard what she said to me, as if I were to blame for the mess she's in. All that talk of independence . . . I've heard that before and it makes no impression on me. She's been free to leave this house these past ten years if she wanted to. She's always chosen to stay.'

Daisy said, 'She told me it's Gregory she feels she's lost.'

'Gregory? She lost him years ago.'

'Daisy's right,' Mrs Bridges said. 'So long as Rose had the

money she still had her Gregory. Now she's lost it, she's got nobody and nothing.'

He looked baffled. 'It's quite beyond me what the two of you are driving it.'

'That's because you're a man. It's hard for a man to understand these things.'

In the morning-room, Virginia was finding it equally hard to get Richard to understand.

'Why did you tell him he's a failure? It's the oldest thing in the world for a father to attack his son for not living up to expectations. You two are past masters at that sort of fight.'

'You're blaming me for what happened, then?'

'Yes, you must take some of the blame.'

'Damn it, someone's got to drive the boy. He seems totally unable to do it for himself.'

'He's perfectly able, if you'd only leave him alone. He was fine when he got back from America. Masses of energy.'

'But the wrong kind, my dear. Too volatile. Too highly strung. Too obsessed with the glamour of money. And now he's lost it all. I repeat, I meant simply to rap him over the knuckles, and suddenly we were laying his whole life out for examination.'

To his surprise, she was almost crying.

'Richard,' she said, with a kind of desperation, 'I think we must leave this house. Or James must. The two of you are impossible under the same roof. You bicker and fight. You upset everyone, including the servants. I won't stand for it. I can't do with it!'

'Virginia . . .' he began, but broke off as Hudson came in to take away the coffee tray.

Virginia blew her nose and asked, 'Hudson, do you know where Rose is? I was looking for her.'

'I believe she went out, m'lady. Without permission, I'm afraid. She was rather upset after the Major explained to her . . . Mrs Bridges and I did our best to console her, but . . .'

'I'm sure you did. Let me know the moment she comes in, will you?'

'Yes, m'lady. Would the Major like anything to eat? A tray in his room?'

'I expect he'll call if he wants anything.'

'Very good, m'lady.'

Georgina gained access to James's room at last. It was later that afternoon and the storm of music had ceased some time ago. She found him composed again as he added to the piles of objects taken from his various drawers.

'Come back to help?' he greeted her, and she joined in willingly.

One little pile, she noted, was entirely made up of wartime relics – a field compass, a telescope in a short leather case, a bayonet in a scabbard. He saw her looking at it.

'Edward can take that lot out to the rag-and-bone man for a start,' he said.

Georgina had wondered whether to steer clear of what had evidently been a painful scene in the morning-room, but curiosity and a desire to help and comfort James overcame her discretion. She asked, 'James, were you and Uncle Richard having one of your rows? What was it about?'

'Ask Father.'

'I'm asking you. Come on, Jumbo, don't keep it all bottled up.'

He turned to her. 'One thing I won't forgive him for – using Mother against me.'

'Your Mother? How?'

'Didn't he know? Didn't he know that coming back on that damned boat, all the time, I was staring down at that damned ocean, knowing she was down there somewhere?'

'Oh . . . James!'

'And he used her memory as a weapon against me.'

'He didn't mean it. He loved her, too. You mustn't hold it against him. Think of the future now. Don't keep looking back.'

He said wearily, 'Yes, you're right. I'm sorry. Here – photo of you and Hazel. You want it?'

'Don't you?'

'Take it, and all the rest of them. Make a scrapbook out of

them for your children. I don't want them.'

'Please don't be bitter.'

'I'm not.'

'I know you're unhappy. I know things are difficult. You've lost all that money and you're worried about . . .'

'The money's nothing, Georgina, believe me. I've only one regret about it, and that's that I can't give you the wedding I promised.'

'It doesn't matter.'

'It matters to me.'

'You'll still be there. You'll be the most important person, you know that.'

'What are you talking about? Your husband will be the most important person. I'll be of no use whatsoever.'

Another of his wounds had been rent open. He flung a pile of letters on to the rug in front of the burning fire. She recognised them at once.

'Those are my letters to you. From France,' she said.

'I know. I'm going to burn them. Did you keep mine?'

'I . . . They're somewhere, yes.'

'Fetch them. We'll make a pile of them and burn them together.'

'No!'

'Of course we must. You don't want your husband to find them by accident, do you?'

But Georgina had scooped up the pile of envelopes and was holding them protectively. He tried to snatch them from her and they struggled slightly over them.

'I don't want them burnt, James! They're mine. They're memories. They're nothing to be ashamed of, and I want them kept.'

He was too strong for her. With his mouth set cruelly, he gave the letters a vicious twist out of her hands and flung them on to the flames. Almost hysterically he snatched up others from a table top and flung them on, too. One fluttered to the rug. Georgina swiftly retrieved it, glanced at it, then looked at him horrified.

'This is from Hazel!'

'Yes!' he cried, seizing it and flinging it into the grate. 'And these are Mother's. They're all going. The whole bloody lot!'

The scene was too painful for her. She went sadly from the room and to her own. After a few minutes' brooding, she pulled herself together and sat down to write her daily letter to Robert. Within moments, James and his troubles were out of her mind.

An hour later, Virginia, crossing the hall, was surprised to see James coming downstairs in his hat and coat and carrying a valise.

'James . . . ?' she began, but he explained, 'I'm sorry I won't be in to dinner, Virginia. I've decided it's best if I go away for a few days. Give things time to cool off.'

'Where are you going?'

'An old army friend, Charles Stapleton, and his wife, in the country. They've often asked me.'

'James, your father's bitterly regretting what happened. We've been talking about it so much, and he says he didn't mean half of what he said. He's in his bath now, but won't you wait and talk to him before you go?'

'It'd be too soon. Some of the same things would be bound to be said. Just . . . tell him not to blame himself. He didn't say anything I didn't know already. Will you say goodbye for me?'

'Perhaps you're right. Yes.'

'Goodbye, Virginia.'

She looked sadly after him as he went through the front door. She longed to see him reconciled with his father and settled into some satisfying routine of life, but neither thing seemed possible to attain. Virginia sighed and went on into the morning-room.

It was after eleven o'clock that night, and Rose had still not returned. Edward and Daisy had retired to their flat over the garage and Ruby had long since gone up to her room. Mr Hudson and Mrs Bridges kept yawning vigil in the servants' hall. For the umpteenth time he looked at his watch and snapped it shut again.

'I must lock up soon,' he said.

'You can't, Angus. You can't shut the poor girl out. If you like, I'll wait up for her myself.'

'No, no. But if she's not back by midnight I feel I must inform her ladyship.'

'But they've gone to bed.'

'She is very anxious for news. I'm sure she would wish to be told.'

At that moment the front door bell rang. They looked at one another.

'She wouldn't come to the front door. Oh, Mr Hudson, I hope it isn't some bad news about the poor girl!'

Frowning worriedly, he slipped on his jacket and went up. He had no sooner disappeared from sight than the area door opened and Rose came in. She was drooping wearily.

'Rose! Wherever have you been all this time?' Mrs Bridges cried, more relieved than annoyed. 'Oh, we've been so worried, you naughty girl. Thank God nothing's happened to you.'

Rose sank into a chair, not removing her coat or hat.

'I took a bus ride,' she said in a flat tone. 'Number 25, Victoria to Ilford. My old route. I went and sat in the garage canteen. The old woman behind the counter remembered me. Then I got the last bus home.'

'And now you feel better, do you, dear?'

'Yeh. Funny, really, isn't it? None of it seems important any more. I'm just sorry I caused such a nuisance.'

'That's all right, dear,' Mrs Bridges smiled, patting her shoulder. 'I understand and so will Mr Hudson when I explain it to him. You get off to bed now. You must be tired out. Everything'll be all right in the morning, you'll see.'

Rose nodded and forced herself to her feet. They both turned towards the short staircase – and saw Hudson standing at the foot of it, ashen-faced.

The burly, grey-haired man who had introduced himself at

the front door as Chief-Inspector Rodwell and had insisted on Lord Bellamy's being roused, enlarged upon his doom-laden announcement to Richard and Virginia, who had come down together in their dressing-gowns.

'He was found two hours ago in a hotel room in Maidenhead. A chambermaid heard the shot and went to his aid, but he was dead within minutes. I can assure your lordship and your ladyship that he can't have suffered.'

'Shot?' mumbled the stricken Richard, who had been asleep when Hudson had called him and couldn't believe that he wasn't dreaming still. 'James – shot?'

'He appears to have shot himself through the roof of the mouth with a Service revolver, my lord.'

'Oh, God!' Virginia cried, and subsided onto the settee.

The inspector was holding out a white envelope towards Richard.

'He left this letter addressed to you. Also two others – for the coroner and for Sir Geoffrey Dillon, his solicitor.'

He fingered his bowler hat. 'I won't trouble you further tonight, my lord. We'll call back in the morning and see to the formalities, then. My, er, sincere condolences.'

He saw himself out. For a few moments Richard stood motionless. The stranger's absence made the situation feel even more unreal, as though it had never happened. But when he looked down he saw the envelope still in his hand. He crumpled onto the settee beside Virginia, who clutched him and nursed him like a child.

It was many minutes before they could bring themselves to open the envelope and read the letter:

Dear Father,

Do you remember me telling you about that German officer in the shell crater at Passchendaele who should have finished me off but declined to? Well, I'm doing the job for him. It's nothing to do with our talk today. Mother always said to leave when you're winning is not ethical, and we both know my losing streak has been going on far too long

Try and see it as a soldier's way out when he can no longer do justice to himself or the men under his command. I choose this place so as not to make a mess of my room or inconvenience anyone more than is necessary. I've sent my will to Sir Geoffrey (unwitnessed I'm afraid, but I'm sure he will manage). Goodbye, Father. Give my love to Virginia and to Georgina. Don't be sad.

James

CHAPTER EIGHT

James's suicide did more than end his life and plunge his family into grief and their servants into shocked dismay: it precipitated the disintegration of the household enclosed within the walls of No. 165 Eaton Place.

Sir Geoffrey Dillon, spelt out the implications of it to Richard, Virginia and Georgina in their morning-room one early summer morning of 1930. The months which had elapsed since the tragedy had, as the passage of time usually will, served to diminish the pain and sorrow, but had conversely deepened everyone's concern for what the future held in store. Now the calculations had been made and Sir Geoffrey's habitually dour countenance showed no special sign of reassurance for the occasion.

'I'm afraid the final report doesn't make very pleasant reading,' he said, shuffling papers. 'You, Miss Worsley, as the principal legatee of Major Bellamy's estate, are the person most concerned. But, to put it in blunt lay terms, I'm afraid there won't be any estate left to inherit.'

It was Richard who questioned him. 'You mean, there are no ... ?'

'Assets? No. Rather the reverse. Unfortunately, James incurred a great many debts in the last few months of his life. In addition, he was very generous in loans to his friends.'

'He thought he was rich,' Virginia pointed out. 'He was, for a time. How could he guess the crash was coming? I mean, no one else did.'

'I am not trying to allocate blame, Lady Bellamy. I'm just explaining the facts, as is my duty as executor of your stepson's estate.'

Georgina asked anxiously, 'Sir Geoffrey, it won't mean that I'm liable for ... for his debts?'

'No, no. Oh, no, no.'

Richard asked, 'You have taken into account the sale of the remainder of the lease of this house? I mean to say, we've been expecting that it will have to be sold.'

'It will indeed have to be sold. As you know, however, it was James's property and the proceeds must be set against his liabilities. I have already made some enquiries about the best method of selling. The property market isn't exactly buoyant at this moment, but happily there is still some interest in houses in Belgravia such as this one – for redevelopment.'

'You mean . . . they'll pull it down?'

'Oh, no. Convert it into flats. Modernise generally. I mean, nowadays, when nobody can afford servants any more . . .'

He lapsed into a tactful fit of coughing as he saw Hudson and Daisy come through the door with coffee things. Virginia could perceive from Daisy's eyes that she, at least, had overheard the last few words. She told them to leave the tray for her to manage. Hudson put it on a low table beside her and the servants retired.

Sir Geoffrey resumed. 'There's a question of fixing a date for the auction . . .'

'Auction?' Richard echoed. 'I thought an agent would deal with it.'

'Of the contents, I mean.'

Virginia looked up from pouring coffee. 'But won't Georgina even get the furniture?'

'I'm afraid not. Everything will need to be sold to help pay the debts. By the way, I would be glad if you would make a list of those goods and chattels you believe to be your personal possessions.'

Virginia saw the shaking of Georgina's hand as she accepted her coffee cup. She recognised that the girl was struggling to hold back tears. The suicide of the only man she had really loved apart from Robert had hit her harder than any of them. Her pity for James had been profound and she had been tormenting herself with the thought that if she had only accepted his most recent proposal to marry her he would have been alive still and perhaps happy and fulfilled at last. This specula-

137

tion was fuelled by the continued absence of Robert, who had been abroad for some weeks longer than the bargained-for period. She had found it difficult to write to him since James's death. Although he was now en route for home at last, she felt that he and she were drifting apart, rather than coming closer. Depression and a loss of any confidence in the future seemed to be weighing more heavily upon her each day.

Virginia asked, 'Sir Geoffrey, is there anything you want Georgina to sign?'

'No. Not at present.'

'Then may she be excused?'

He raised his eyebrows in uncomprehending surprise at the request.

'Certainly. Of course.'

Georgina went quickly and thankfully, just managing to preserve her self-control as far as her room, where she lay on her bed and cried.

Richard explained to the lawyer, 'The poor girl's rather upset still, I'm afraid.'

'Quite. Now, about a convenient date for the auction? And, indeed, for vacant possession of the premises.'

'This has all come at a difficult time for us, you see, Geoffrey,' said Richard. 'It rather depends if and when Georgina gets married. To Robert Stockbridge, you know.'

'Ah, yes. But I rather thought that had fallen through.'

'There's no reason to presume that. He's due back any day now, and then they have to decide.'

'If I know the Duchess of Buckminster,' Sir Geoffrey said bleakly, 'she'll be the one who decides.'

'It was more or less an unspoken agreement that if they still wish to marry after this separation, they may.'

'Mm.'

Virginia said, 'So if we could have just a little longer before making any decisions? It would be so much more convenient if she could be married from here.'

Sir Geoffrey replaced the papers in his case and snapped it shut as he rose.

'Very well, then. At your earliest convenience.'

Virginia went up to Georgina as soon as the lawyer had gone. She found her dry-eyed but sounding deeply pessimistic.

'I haven't had a letter for seventeen days.'

'But if he's on the ship I don't expect he can write.'

'It calls at different places all the time. Aden and Port Said and Malta . . .'

'I don't imagine the post is too good from those sort of places. If . . . if anything drastic had happened . . . If he'd . . . changed his mind, I'm sure he would have let you know by cable or something.'

Georgina shook her head. 'Knowing Robert, I think he'd want to . . . to tell me to my face.'

Virginia smiled and patted her. 'I'm sure he'll want to tell you to your face that he still loves you. Where does the ship arrive?'

'Plymouth first. Then it comes on to London.'

'Shall you go to meet it?'

Georgina thought for a few moments.

'I think I'd better not,' she said at length.

In yet another contravention of the rules about reporting conversation overheard above stairs, Mr Hudson had had no compunction in confiding in Mrs Bridges; and Daisy had told Eddie, who had agreed with her that, if there was going to be a bust-up, it was only fair and proper that Rose and Ruby should know, too.

'Well, it didn't come exactly as a surprise, did it?' was Rose's reaction. She, more than any of them, had been in the forefront of the preceding events.

Edward looked up from the newspaper. 'Not a thing in *Situations Vacant*. Columns of *Situations Wanted*.'

'No wonder, with over two million unemployed,' Mr Hudson answered. 'What we want is a man like this Mussolini. Anyone out of work in Italy he puts on to making roads and railway stations.'

'I don't want to make roads and railway stations! What I want to know is, where's all the money gone to? I mean, one minute everyone's rich – lots of gold, money in the bank, shares and all that. Next minute they're all skint. I mean, gold doesn't vanish into thin air!'

Mr Hudson was for once on the side of unreason, making none of his usual efforts to rationalise things for his inferiors.

'It's all the government's fault,' he said. 'They never should have got rid of Mr Baldwin. Though I say it myself, Ramsay MacDonald's a disgrace to Scotland. But then, I've heard tell the MacDonalds weren't too steady at Culloden, either.'

'Yeh. But it's all right for you, Mr Hudson,' Daisy said truculently. 'Not all of us have sisters leave us boarding-houses at Hastings.'

It was true. In one of those gestures which Fate seems to extend towards some people of opening a fresh door just as an old one seems about to close, Mr Hudson's sister Fiona had died. Her will had proved to be simplicity itself, as notified to him by her solicitor: she had left him the going concern of the last of her succession of establishments, 'Seaview', Cambridge Road, Hastings. Pausing briefly to consider what his reaction to this would have been had his future at Eaton Place been secure, he had made up his mind and called Mrs Bridges into his pantry for a long discussion, from which they had emerged partners in the new venture of running 'Seaview'; he as proprietor and dining-room manager, she as cook and housekeeper.

'Guest-house, Daisy,' he corrected her use of the term 'boarding-house'. 'Our aim will be to attract the children of the better class . . . and, of course, their nannies and governesses.'

' "Seaview",' Edward mused. 'Be able to watch all the ships then.'

'It, er, doesn't actually overlook the sea. It is considered better not to be on the actual front, on account of the storm . . . and the noise of the traffic.'

'That's right,' said Mrs Bridges, entering. 'But from the top floor there's a lovely view of the cliffs, over the other house tops.'

Edward winked at Daisy. She was too concerned for their own future to be much amused.

'Look!' Ruby exclaimed, waving the old copy of the *Tatler* she was cutting up for her scrapbook. 'There's a picture here of the Marquis of Stockbridge dancing with the Lady Felicity Cairns at a ball. Ooh, she does look happy!'

Rose looked, and said contemptuously, 'At the Viceregal lodge in Delhi. That was weeks ago.'

'Nevertheless,' Mr Hudson reminded her, 'last year, Lady Felicity, who, by the way, is the daughter of the Earl of Leyburn, was considered one of the most eligible debutantes of the season.'

'Yeh,' said Rose. 'I wouldn't wonder if the Duke and Duchess of Buckminster hadn't remembered that.'

Ruby said, 'Poor Miss Georgina. I don't reckon she's got a 'ope.'

'Ruby, is the water boiling for those sprouts?' Mrs Bridges demanded. 'If it isn't, you'd better get it turned up, 'stead of sitting there talking about things that don't concern you.'

'Yes, Mrs Bridges.'

The much-tried cook rolled her eyes ceiling-ward. 'That girl! She wouldn't know Christmas from Easter!'

Next morning, Daisy took Georgina's breakfast up to her room. She found her mistress dressed and made-up, but sitting in front of the dressing-table mirror, staring at her reflection.

'I don't want anything,' she said. 'I look a hundred, don't I?'

'I'm sure everything will be all right, miss. You must try and eat a little . . .'

The sound of a taxi coming to a halt outside caused Georgina to leap up and rush to the window. Daisy heard her gasp, then stepped quickly aside, trying to keep the tray level, as Georgina ran past her out of the room.

Hudson opened the front door to Robert Stockbridge, leaner and fitter-looking, tanned by tropical suns, wearing a rumpled suit which gave evidence of hurried travel.

'Hello, Hudson. Nice to see you again.'

'Yes, indeed, m'lord. I trust you enjoyed . . .'

141

Lord Stockbridge's eyes were no longer on him. They were on the girl who had reached the bend of the stairs and paused there, holding her breath, uncertain whether to come down further.

'Darling!' he cried, running forward. 'My darling Georgina! It's all right!'

Hudson slipped discreetly away through the pass-door. Georgina came slowly down the remaining stairs, letting Robert take her in his arms and almost hanging there.

'It's all right,' she thought she heard him say again. 'I saw my parents yesterday, in Nice. They've given us their blessing.'

'Nice . . . ?' she murmured, overwhelmed.

'Yes. They're staying on the Riviera, so I nipped off the boat at Marseilles and came back on the train. They were really very decent. Father was pleased as Punch, but he didn't dare admit it, and Mother said it was never anything to do with you, but it was me who was the hopeless, catty, unreliable one.'

He steered her firmly into the morning-room, which was empty.

'It was all terribly silly, the whole thing. Mother deliberately throwing every suitable girl in my way from Gibraltar to San Francisco, but I didn't turn a hair. I passed my test with flying colours. And, darling, darling, I love you so much . . . Have you heard a word I've said?'

'Not . . . really,' she murmured dazedly. 'I've . . . spent so long telling myself it wouldn't happen . . . and now it has, I just . . .'

She swayed in his arms. He hastily guided her on to the settee.

'I'm sorry, darling,' she said. 'I hope I'm not going to be sick. I feel all giddy.'

'Are you ill? Have you seen a doctor?'

She shook her head. 'It's not that. It's just that . . . everything's been so awful.'

Robert sat beside her, holding her hands.

'Yes, I know it has. I nearly came back when . . . when it

happened; but then I thought it might ruin everything if I did. Mother could say I'd cheated. You poor things! What a ghastly time you've had.'

Georgina said, almost to herself, 'I didn't realise how much James meant to me. I thought I'd managed to get him out of myself long ago. I suppose our lives had been mixed up together for so long . . . just burning letters and throwing things away wasn't any good. When it happened, I knew just how much I loved him. Oh, darling, it's not how I love you – not a bit like that. It's something I can't actually explain. I just feel as if a whole bit of me was numb . . . not working. I . . . I really don't think I ought to marry you.'

Robert, who had looked increasingly unhappy during this, was now alarmed.

'Darling, that's just silly!' he protested.

She went on: 'What I really mean is that I don't think you should marry me. I'm the scatty, unreliable one. That's what your mother really thinks, and she's right. I oughtn't to marry anyone, let alone try to be a marchioness. I don't want to see anyone. I don't want to do anything . . . Anyway, I can't get married. I haven't any money. I can't even pay for my own wedding dress.'

'But that's absurd,' he argued anxiously, sensing approaching hysteria in her tone. 'We'll be married in a Registry Office. I don't care two hoots what people will think . . . We'll find a way. All that matters to me is that I love you and adore you, and want you for my wife.'

But again she seemed not to have been listening. She murmured, through welling tears, 'You see, James was going to give me my wedding – the best wedding there's ever been, he said. And he left me everything he had in his will . . . only, the awful thing is that he didn't have anything. He had nothing. Poor James! He had nothing at all!'

Before he could clutch her she had run from the room, weeping.

Robert, who had had very little sleep on the train and, besides, had burned up much energy in sheer nervous tension, sought out Virginia and had a brief and friendly, though anxious, interview with her. He reported what Georgina had told him of her doubts and fears, and especially of her seeming insistence that since James's wish to pay for her wedding could not now be fulfilled, and she could not afford it herself, no wedding could take place.

'I see now I should have sent a cable or something from France,' he said miserably. 'I wanted to give her a surprise. I suppose it was the wrong thing.'

'Don't blame yourself, Robert,' Virginia said. 'She's been in a turmoil ever since James killed himself. She absolutely refuses to see a doctor, though. She won't even take a holiday. It's like some sort of obsession. Oh, I'm so sorry you've come back to find it like this.'

Absence and enduring love had done much for Robert Stockbridge's spirit, however.

'I'm not going to give up now,' he assured Virginia. 'Not after waiting so long.'

That evening she was working out lists and estimates when Richard came into the morning-room, shaking his head. His first action was to pour himself a large whisky and soda.

'I am absolutely bamboozled by the whole thing,' he declared. He had just come from Georgina's room.

'How is she now?'

'Oh, perfectly calm. She says she's sorry to have caused us so much trouble – that she isn't sure she ever wanted to get married in the first place – that we're to go ahead with our plans for leaving this house as if she didn't exist . . . I really believe there may be something in that old wives' tale about a streak of madness in the Worsley family.'

'Nonsense. I understand exactly how she feels.'

'*You* understand?'

'Yes. Being a woman, too, I'm also a bit mad and illogical.'

'Well, if you'll kindly explain . . .'

'Oh, I couldn't possibly explain.'

Instead, she got up and kissed him, then drew him over to her desk.

'Darling, I want you to look at these estimates I've been making of the cost of the wedding. See if you agree.'

'But . . . but there isn't going to be . . .'

'As the Boy Scouts say, "Be prepared!" If she does decide to get married, we must pay for it.'

'That goes without saying. I'm her guardian. Somehow or other I must pay for it. But since she absolutely refuses . . .'

'I want to pay half. I've got some War Loans that should just about do it. No, don't look like that. If I want to stump up, I shall. Now, do have a look please.'

He did, and was astounded.

'Seven hundred and fifty guests! St Margaret's, Westminster! My dear Virginia, surely everyone will understand if it's a quiet wedding . . . the little church as Southwold, perhaps?'

'If it's to be done at all, it's to be done properly.'

'Ah, well, since it's only pure speculation anyway . . . "Choir and organist, seven pounds" . . . That's a bit steep, isn't it?'

'No. I've checked.'

' "Tip to verger, flowers in church, hired cars, printing and engraving . . . reception, thirty shillings a head"!'

'That's with a good champagne.'

He smiled, feeling now that he was entering into a joke with her.

'Quite right. Bad champagne at the reception is the worst start a marriage can have. Good Lord! "Trousseau and wedding dress, three hundred pounds". What on earth does it all add up to?'

'About seventeen hundred and fifty pounds.'

'Phew! I'm beginning to be quite glad it may never happen.'

'Just leave that to me, darling.'

He looked at her with deepest suspicion. She was smiling an enigmatic smile whose significance he had learned to respect.

A few days later, Mr Hudson showed Sir Geoffrey Dillon into the morning-room. Virginia received him. He refused sherry but accepted gin and bitters, of which, with her back to him, Virginia made a strong mixture.

'I have the lists of goods and chattels from your husband,' he said. 'Rather more comprehensive than I had expected, but I've no doubt I'll be able to get them past the creditors.'

'Good.'

'Now, as to the date of the sale . . .' he was getting out his diary. 'I presume that is what you wished to discuss with me, Lady Bellamy?'

'No. At least, not entirely. Sir Geoffrey, I know what a tower of strength to this family you've been over the years . . .'

He simpered a little. The strength of the gin was to his liking.

'. . . and I wanted to ask for your advice and help. It's about Georgina and her marriage.'

A request for help was always enough to put Sir Geoffrey Dillon on to his guard. He waited cautiously. Virginia went on, smiling winningly, leaning a little towards him in a con-spiratorial way.

'It's a little delicate and highly confidential. I want you to write to Georgina, officially, saying you have discovered that when all was paid up there was still two thousand pounds left from James's estate.'

'But . . . but that's not true!'

'I know. Here is a cheque for two thousand pounds, made out to your firm.'

He looked at it in her hand as if to touch it would give him an electric shock.

'Are you asking me to . . . to enter into a conspiracy with you . . . To . . . to utter a lie in writing?'

'A little white lie isn't a crime, is it?'

'It's most unprofessional. If the Law Society were to hear . . .'

'They won't. Only you, and I and Richard will ever know.'

'And if the creditors heard of it they'd quite rightly want to know . . .'

'But they won't hear of it either.'

'Can you tell me the reason for this – this escapade?'

Virginia shook her head. 'I'm sorry, I can't. But I can assure you that we shall always be very grateful to you for your . . .'

(she had the right word ready) '. . . your courage. I am sure Georgina will remain your client, and of course, she will one day be a duchess.'

They looked at one another, long and hard. Then he sighed, reached out his hand, and without a word took the cheque. He locked it away in his case as swiftly as if it had been some creature likely to escape through his fingers.

Two mornings later Daisy brought in Georgina's breakfast on a tray. Georgina, still in bed, glanced at it with her usual distaste.

'Good morning, Daisy,' she said listlessly. 'How did you get on yesterday?'

Daisy's glumness matched her own.

'We went to two more agencies. They wouldn't even put us on their books when they heard we was married. It was like having leprosy.'

Georgina's gloom deepened even further. She languidly picked up the envelope lying on her tray and slit it open with her butter-knife. Daisy went on, 'They just said they was full up. Then we went to the Town Hall, and they said Edward would get seventeen bob a week on the dole, and I'd get nine. So we had a cup of tea and a bun and came home, miss. Edward's started talking about emigrating.'

Georgina said, 'I think I'll have to join you . . .' But she had by now unfolded the letter and taken in its brief, typewritten message.

'Daisy!' she cried.

Daisy, who had turned away to tidy Georgina's clothes, looked round, to see her face aglow and eyes wide.

'Daisy!' she repeated. 'Dressing-gown. Quick!'

The astonished maid provided the silk gown. Georgina was already out of bed and into her slippers. Flinging on the robe, she ran from the room.

'Uncle Richard!' she cried, bursting into the morning-room, where he and Virginia were examining some catalogues. 'Virginia! The most fabulously extraordinary thing's happened!'

She thrust the letter into Richard's hand. As soon as he

147

recognised the letter-heading of Dillon's firm he found it necessary to restrain himself from glancing up at Virginia.

'Two thousand pounds?' he managed to exclaim with convincing surprise. 'Darling, wonderful news. Georgina's going to inherit two thousand pounds from James's estate after all!'

Virginia was not to be outdone in acting. She made it easier for herself, though, by seizing Georginia in a great hug, so that it was over her shoulder, under the quizzical gaze of her husband, that she exclaimed in turn, 'Oh darling, how wonderful!'

Both Richard and Virginia knew inward relief when Georgina said what they had been almost praying she would: 'Do you think it would be terribly wickedly selfish and extravagant to spend it on getting married?'

'Of course not, darling,' Virginia told her.

Richard was able to say in all sincerity, 'That's what James would have wanted you to spend it on.'

From that moment Georgina was a changed person, to everyone's delight, not least Robert Stockbridge's. Her banished gloom and eager participation in the wedding preparations served to expunge the last of the grieving over James and restored optimism for what the future would have to offer each one of them.

Virginia remained in charge of the preparations, though. As the great day approached she sent for Mrs Bridges. The cook came into the morning-room with a wary air, as if expecting trouble.

'You wished to see me, m'lady?'

'Yes, Mrs Bridges. Sit down. It's about the wedding reception.'

Mrs Bridges sat with relief.

'As you know, it will be at Seaford House. Lord and Lady Howard de Walden have always been family friends.'

'Oh, I've often had the pleasure of cooking dinner for his lordship and her ladyship as guests.'

'Of course. It's sad we can't have it here, though, but there simply wouldn't be room. There will be caterers looking after the drinks and refreshments, but I was wondering . . . well, it was Miss Georgina's suggestion, really . . . I was wondering if you could undertake to make the cake?'

It was as well that Mrs Bridges was seated. Standing, she would perhaps have reeled, so great was the astonishment she showed.

'The wedding cake? Oh, lor' . . . Beg pardon, my lady. I mean, I should be delighted . . . and honoured. Of course, it would have to be some size, wouldn't it?'

'The bigger the better.'

'I've never done more than two tiers before, but I have seen four tiers. There was an illustration of one in the *News* when the Princess Royal married Lord Harewood.'

'Do you think you could manage four tiers, Mrs Bridges?'

'Well, I'll have a try. If I had to stop at three, I hope that would be acceptable?'

'Of course.'

'But I'll do my best for four, m'lady. It will be rather costly, though – all that marzipan.'

'Don't worry about that.'

'We'll have to hire a silver base, and I'll need a turntable for doing the decorating. But I can borrow one from my friend at Gunter's.'

'Splendid. No other problems?'

'No thank you, my lady.'

Mrs Bridges got stiffly to her feet.

'May I say again, m'lady, it's an honour and a pleasure.'

'Good luck, Mrs Bridges.'

Mrs Bridges was past the stage of being able to move quickly, but she made her way down to the kitchen with surprising energy. Ruby watched with open mouth as she selected a book which had remained unmoved from its place on the shelf for as long as Ruby could remember. Taking it to the table, Mrs Bridges began leafing through. Ruby moved closer and saw illustrations of wedding cakes of all sizes and designs.

'I haven't had this book out since Miss Elizabeth's wedding,'

Mrs Bridges said. She stopped turning the pages and pointed.

'There! That's the one I'll try – The Imperial.'

'We'll never manage that, Mrs Bridges!'

'Won't we, indeed? Listen to the ingredients: four pounds orange and lemon peel, eight pounds citron, sixteen pounds currants . . . Just think of that – *sixteen* pounds of currants. Ruby, just you get out all the baking pans we have in the house and start cleaning them. This instant!'

'Yes, Mrs Bridges.'

Through in the servants' hall, Rose and Mr Hudson looked up with – respectively – surprise and disapproval as Edward and Daisy came clattering down the short staircase together.

'Edward! Daisy . . . !' Mr Hudson began, but they ignored the reproof.

'They've asked us to work for them!'

'Who's "them"?' Rose asked.

'Lord Stockbridge and Miss Georgina. They just had us in and said they're going to move into a house on the estate at Shalford. If we wouldn't mind the country there's a nice little cottage for us.'

'Mind! We wouldn't mind an old tin shack, would we, Eddie?'

'He said he didn't want a chauffeur, as he likes driving himself. But they was looking for a sort of general manservant . . .'

'A butler, you mean?' Mr Hudson asked.

'He didn't say that exactly . . .'

'Then I think you should get it made very clear, Edward.'

'Well, beggars can't be choosers.'

'There is such a thing as dignity and respect.'

But they were in no mood for the niceties. Daisy bubbled, 'And Miss Georgina said she'd like me to be her personal maid, but that if I was . . . if we was to start a baby again, or anything, it would be quite all right. They'd always look after us.'

She burst into tears.

'Here, – Dais – what you crying for?' Edward asked, putting his arm round her.

'Oh, you wouldn't understand,' Rose told him. 'Honestly – men!'

Mrs Bridges set about the cake like an architect building a cathedral – except that no hands were allowed to touch the edifice besides her own. Ruby's function was strictly that of preparer and supplier, though with strict instructions not to come near the table more than was necessary.

'I've sieved the rest of the icing sugar, Mrs Bridges,' she ventured to say from a distance.

'Bring it here, then – *carefully*!'

Ruby laid down the basin on a corner of the table, amongst the litter of nozzles, syringe-like instruments and pieces of decoration.

'Now you can break four eggs and separate the whites.'

'Yes, Mrs Bridges.'

Mrs Bridges looked up at the cringing girl and softened a little.

'What are you going to do, Ruby?'

'Break four eggs and . . .'

'No, no! I mean with yourself? In the future?'

'I haven't really thought, Mrs Bridges.'

'Well, it's high time you did, then.'

'I might be an usherette in the cinema. You can see all the films free, twelve times a week.'

'Still got that Rudolph Valentino on the brain, have you?'

'Oh, no, he's gone a long time. It's talkies now.' Her eyes glazed. 'Ramon Novarro, Ronald Colman, John Barrymore . . . Oh, he's lovely, is John Barrymore.'

In her trance she had wandered dangerously close to the part of the table where the cake stood. Mrs Bridges shooed her away and resumed her concentration.

'May I suggest this tie, m'lord?'

Mr Hudson was valeting Richard as he dressed to go down to the House of Lords. Richard approved the choice.

'Yes – suitably sombre for my last speech from the front bench.'

'If I may say so, m'lord, it is a sad day for the Conservative Party, and for the nation.'

'Oh, nonsense. High time I made way for someone younger. Anyway, I'm looking forward to a quiet life in the country, writing my memoirs and just sitting back.'

'Your lordship will have a good deal to write about, I fancy. We have lived through some stirring times.'

'Yes. We've lived through a lot of history together, haven't we, Hudson?'

He put his arms into the morning coat Hudson was holding for him.

'I shall miss you very much, Hudson. You and Mrs Bridges. No one has been luckier with servants than we have. I only wish there was some more material way in which we could show our appreciation.'

'Oh, don't worry about that, m'lord, thank you. Mrs Bridges and I are well placed between us in that respect.'

Richard turned for Hudson to adjust his buttonhole and his eye fell on the open wardrobe with its long row of suits.

'Look at all those suits,' he said. 'You've never let me get rid of a suit, have you, Hudson? Some of them hardly worn and I'll never need a quarter of them. If . . . if there are one or two that would be any use to you, you have only to say so.'

'Why, thank you, my lord. That is exceedingly kind of your lordship.'

Richard took his leave. When he had gone, Hudson went to the wardrobe and examined the suits with interest. One in particular took his eye. He took it out on its hanger and held it in front of himself before a mirror. The jacket was black and the trousers pepper-and-salt. The reflection in the glass was much to his liking.

When Virginia had kissed Richard and seen him driven off by Edward she went back into the morning-room where piles of correspondence – mostly acceptances to the wedding – awaited her. Rose came in and stood expectantly.

'Oh, Rose, I won't be able to go through those drawers with

you today, after all. Look – I'm completely snowed under with all this.'

Rose laughed. 'I can see that, m'lady.'

Virginia came to her. 'Rose, my dear,' she said, 'in all the huffle of Miss Georgina's wedding I haven't really found time to talk to you about your future, have I? I'm afraid his lordship and I have just rather taken it for granted that you'd be coming down to Dorset with us.'

She wasn't aware how relieved Rose was to hear this. She had been wondering why nothing had been said, and what that might portend.

Virginia went on, 'Of course, we'll be living a much more quiet and modest sort of life. We'll have to manage with fewer servants . . . just a cook and a girl from the village. So it's only fair to say that if you feel you would be happier elsewhere – staying in London, perhaps – then you're quite free . . .'

'Oh no, m'lady,' Rose interrupted hurriedly. 'Don't you worry. I'm quite a jack of all trades. I can turn my hand to most things about the house. All except cooking – I don't think I could boil an egg, even. But I'm country born and bred. I used to be a dab hand in the garden. When we was all in the village school at Southwold we each of us had a little garden of our own by the playground, and one year I won the prize, a new sixpence. I think I've still got it among . . .'

She broke off, suddenly realising how she had gabbled on in her relief. She added more slowly, 'I really am looking forward to going on looking after you and his lordship, and Miss Alice and Master William, my lady. Thank you . . . for letting me.'

Virginia smiled. 'You're one of the family anyway, Rose.'

The door opened. Georgina came in and held it ajar to enable Mr Hudson to pass in with a tray piled high with more letters.

'Oh, no!' Virginia groaned. 'Do you know, so far we've had three hundred and seventy-two acceptances and only thirty-one refusals?'

'Lor'!' Georgina exclaimed. 'We'll never fit them all into the church.'

Hudson and Rose left, each smiling for a different reason.

That evening, Richard and Virginia paid a state visit to the kitchen. Mr Hudson received them, smirking anticipatorily Rose, Edward and Daisy were shuffling into line. Ruby was holding a chair, on the seat of which stood Mrs Bridges putting the final touches to the most magnificent cake any of them had ever seen. It was four tiers tall.

'Oh, it's marvellous!' Virginia said.

'Superb!' Richard agreed. 'I really think someone should fetch Georgina down to see it.'

'Oh, no, m'lord,' Mrs Bridges said, as she was helped down 'It would never do for a bride to see her cake before The Day.

'I see. Well, congratulations, Mrs Bridges. I'm sure this is your masterpiece.'

'That, my lord, is what we have all been saying,' said Mr Hudson. He was positively beaming.

And so the wedding day came, and London society rejoiced Georgina, wearing the Buckminster tiara – so precious that i had had to be brought to her by a policeman – was radiant Robert was handsome and happy. The Duke and Duchess of Buckminster went out of their way to be friendly with Richard and Virginia and finished up being genuinely so. A chimney sweep, just chancing to be passing as Georgina was about to enter the car, kissed her for luck, to loud cheers, and received a golden guinea which just chanced to be ready in one of Richard's waistcoat pockets. And when it was all over, photographs were taken, and champagne drunk, and speeches made and more champagne drunk, and the great cake cut (loudest cheering of the day) . . . and the happy couple were driven of to the station, while the rest of the Eaton Place household returned – none of them entirely steady on their legs – to house which had been visited in their absence by the estate agent's men and an auction notice hung on its railings.

This did little to depress their spirits, though, for there was a further celebration to come within less than twenty-fou hours. Late the next morning, an incredulous Richard an Virginia turned towards the morning-room doors, to see Mr Hudson – who had asked for an appointment – usher Mr

154

Bridges in and stand by her side. Richard noted that Hudson was wearing a dark jacket with pepper-and-salt trousers which he seemed to recognise.

'My lord, m'lady — if I might introduce Mrs *Hudson* to you?'

They gasped audibly. Then Richard stepped swiftly forward to shake his butler's hand, while Virginia gave her cook a great kiss.

'It has taken a wee while to get her to the altar, m'lady, but I've managed it at last,' Hudson explained, while Richard poured drinks for them all. 'However, we're just back from the Registry Office' — he produced the certificate — 'so she can't get away now.'

'The man was ever so nice, m'lady,' Mrs Bridges said, colouring up. 'He said in the eyes of the Lord it was better late than never.'

Richard insisted on their both sitting down to take their drink, then gave a toast to their happiness.

Hudson explained, 'We thought it best, m'lord, seeing that we are about to enter a new social circle in which our relationship might be misinterpreted.'

His wife nodded vigorously. 'They've got evil minds, some of them with nothing better to do at them small places by the sea. I remember in the war when I went down to visit my sister and brother-in-law at Yarmouth after that terrible bombing. There was a woman in the next street who'd been killed and found stone dead in bed with . . .'

Her husband placed his hand under her elbow and helped her to her feet.

'Yes, my dear, but that's rather a long story, isn't it? Now, if you'll excuse us, m'lord, m'lady, it is half-past twelve, and luncheon is at one.'

'Of course,' Virginia said. 'Congratulations again, both of you. And, by the way, if you would like some of the pots and pans and kitchen things to help stock your guest house, please be sure to let me know before the auctioneers come to make their inventory for the sale.'

'That is most kind of your ladyship.'

'And I hope you'll have an appropriate celebration tonight in the servants' hall – at my expense, of course,' Richard added.

'Thank *you*, m'lord.'

When they had gone, Richard poured Virginia and himself another glass.

'Well, well,' he said. 'Made an honest woman of her after all these years, and only because of what other people will think. What a funny people we are. Goodness, that would have made . . .'

He stopped. Virginia said, 'You were going to say "Marjorie laugh", weren't you?'

'Yes . . . I was.'

'I don't mind, darling. I've never minded. If they're as happy as you and I've been, they'll be very lucky.'

He went and kissed her tenderly and gratefully.

The servants' hall resounded as it had never done since the days of Sarah as Mr and Mrs Hudson's nuptials were celebrated that evening in whisky, gin, beer, stout and quantities of food-stuffs. Then, at one stage of the evening, Daisy managed to announce: 'Here, Mr Hudson! Eddie's got a surprise for you.'

They all looked at Edward, who protested that it was too late but was pushed by his wife through the door into the butler's pantry. He emerged some minutes later looking sheepish but smart in a brand new tailcoat.

Mr Hudson went to him. 'Edward! You mean to say . . . ?'

'I spoke to Lord Stockbridge about what you said, Mr Hudson, and he said, "Well, if that's Hudson's advice, we'll take it". So I'm to be butler, and there'll be another chap for the general duties.'

A general cheer went up and glasses were replenished.

'It suits you well, Edward,' Mr Hudson said. 'Mind that you always wear a high collar with it, though. None of those modern slipshod flat things.'

'I will, Mr Hudson.'

'That coat – your uniform – it is your badge of office. You are *the butler*. You are the one in charge of the house. A grea responsibility will rest on your shoulders . . . a great deal of worry. If anything goes wrong, it is your fault, no one else's. If standards fall, it is your fault alone. You have tasted some of that responsibility already, Edward, but now you inherit the great tradition, centuries old, and I hope the training I have done my best to give you will always stand you in good stead.'

'Yes, Mr Hudson,' Edward said, a trifle huskily.

'Unhappily, there are not many households that can still afford proper servants. The world we have known seems to be falling about our ears. You are one of the lucky ones, my boy. One day you may be butler in a ducal household . . . a great honour and a great responsibility, so make sure you are always worthy of it. I would like to think that when you find yourself in any trouble or doubt, as you certainly must do from time to time, you will try to think what my action would have been in the circumstances, and that that will pull you through.'

Edward could only nod. Mrs Hudson was dabbing at her eyes.

Mr Hudson turned away to the sideboard, opened a drawer and drew out a book which Edward recognised at once. It had been temporarily in his care during Mr Hudson's illness.

'Here is a little gift for you. A legacy, you might almost call it.'

'Your . . . your pantry book . . . !'

'Take it, with my blessing – with the blessing of us all. I fancy you'll find a few wee wrinkles in it that the modern generation don't know much about.'

Edward took the book and returned his mentor's handshake, almost in tears. Daisy ran forward and kissed Mr Hudson on the cheek. Then Ruby, who had already drunk more than she could take, hiccuped, and everybody laughed, and the party went on again.

When the time had come for an end to be called, Edward and Daisy prepared to clear away the mess.

'No you don't,' Mrs Hudson said. 'Not on your last night here. Go on off to your flat.'

'I'll do it,' Rose volunteered.

157

'No you don't, neither. Off to bed you go, and leave Mr Hudson and me for a few minutes to ourselves.'

Edward and Daisy went. Rose gestured towards Ruby, fast asleep now, with her head on the table. Mrs Hudson waved her out. Her husband came to her side and together they looked down at the crumpled form, with the hair hanging untidily loose and the frock as creased as if she had been rolling on the floor in it.

'What are we going to do about her?' Mrs Hudson asked. 'We can't let her run loose on the streets like a stray dog. She could no more fend for herself in this town than an ostrich could.'

'I'm sure I don't know, Kate.' But he did. It was she who put it into words, though.

'We shall have to take her with us, Angus.'

He nodded.

'Why not? She can do some of the washing and the heavy work, the same as she does here.'

His wife looked at him censoriously. 'That wasn't my reason at all, Mr Hudson. My reason was Christian Charity.'

'Of course, my dear.'

He drew her to him and they kissed as decorously as befitted a newly-wed old butler and cook, about to become proprietor and proprietress of a respectable seaside establishment.

Ruby slept on as they cleared up around her. She was dreaming of John Barrymore. He was the Marquis of Something-or-other too foreign for her to pronounce. She had passed him on the stairs often and noticed how he had made a point of catching her eye.

And now, suddenly, there he was, coming down the steps into the servants' hall, his dress shirt gleaming in the half light, the diamond studs in it twinkling.

He strode across to her, wordlessly, and placed one arm around her waist. With the other hand he smoothed the hair from her brow. He leant forward, bending her backward, and his eager lips sought hers . . .

A clatter awoke her. Her dazed vision took in Mr Hudson

and Mrs B . . . – no, it was Mrs Hudson now – carrying glasses and bottles.

'What . . . what's happening?' she asked.

'Oh, nothing – 'cept we're doing your work for you,' Mrs Hudson replied. But she said it without any sarcasm; and Ruby wondered what she'd done for them both to be smiling at her so nice?

MICHAEL HARDWICK is an author, playwright and broadcaster whose many writing credits include novelizations of major films and television series. Among his best-selling books are novelizations of Billy Wilder's THE PRIVATE LIFE OF SHERLOCK HOLMES, Richard Lester's THE FOUR MUSKETEERS and John Huston's THE MAN WHO WOULD BE KING, as well as many unforgettable episodes of UPSTAIRS, DOWNSTAIRS.

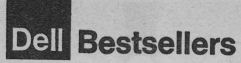
Dell Bestsellers

Second Generation

Howard Fast

**THE SECOND TRIUMPHANT
NOVEL IN THE TOWERING
EPIC LAUNCHED BY**

THE IMMIGRANTS

Barbara Lavette, the beautiful daughter of rugged Dan Lavette
and his aristocratic first wife, stands at the center of *Second
Generation.* Determined to build a life of her own, Barbara
finds danger, unforgettable romance, and shattering tragedy.
Sweeping from the depths of the Depression, through the dark-
est hours of World War II, to the exultant certainty of victory,
Second Generation continues the unbelievable saga of the
Lavettes.   A Dell Book $2.75   (17892-4)

8 MONTHS A NATIONAL BESTSELLER!

EVERGREEN

by

BELVA PLAIN

From shtetl to mansion—Evergreen is the wonderfully rich epic of Anna Friedman, who emigrates from Poland to New York, in search of a better life. Swirling from New York sweatshops to Viennese ballrooms, from suburban mansions to Nazi death camps, from riot-torn campuses to Israeli Kibbutzim, Evergreen evokes the dramatic life of one woman, a family's fortune and a century's hopes and tragedies.

A Dell Book $2.75   (13294-0)

Danielle Steel
SUMMER'S END

author of *The Promise*
and *Season of Passion*

As the wife of handsome, successful, international lawyer Marc Edouard Duras, Deanna
had a beautiful home, diamonds and elegant
dinners. But her husband was traveling between the glamorous capitals of the business
world, and all summer Deanna would be alone.
Until Ben Thomas found her—and laughter
and love took them both by surprise.

A Dell Book $2.50